CAPTURE

ROGER SMITH

First published in 2012 by Serpent's Tail,
an imprint of Profile Books Ltd
3A Exmouth House
Pine Street
London EC1R 0JH
website: www.serpentstail.com

ISBN 978 1 78125 002 0
eISBN 978 1 84765 839 5

Designed and typeset by sue@lambledesign.demon.co.uk
Printed by Clays, Bungay, Suffolk

10 9 8 7 6 5 4 3 2 1

Reality is merely an illusion, albeit a very persistent one.

Albert Einstein

L ATER VERNON SAUL WILL WONDER WHAT WOULD'VE HAPPENED IF HIS LEFT leg – the one crippled by the two bullets that ended his days as a cop – hadn't chosen that exact moment to give him grief, if he hadn't sat his ass down on that rock overlooking the private beach and seen what he'd seen. Fate, is what it was. Lady Luck reaching down and planting a big, fat kiss on him.

He'd hauled himself over the boulders, sweating, skin itching beneath the Kevlar vest all Sniper Security patrolmen had to wear on duty, when he felt a sudden spasm of pain behind the knee, like he'd been tasered, and he nearly fell. Cursing, he'd lowered himself to the rock, waiting for the pain to pass, lost in the long black shadows thrown by the dying sun.

Still sitting there five minutes later, massaging his wasted limb, invisible to the two white men standing on the beach that fronted the big house, windows kicking back the burst fruit colors of the sky. They were smoking weed – Vernon caught a whiff – the remains of a kid's birthday party on a table behind them.

The pain was easing and he was about to lever himself to his feet and get moving when he saw the child, maybe four or five years old, come running out of the house, blonde hair catching the failing light. She jogged up to the two men and tugged at her father's swimming shorts but he ignored her, deep in his dope-head conversation.

The girl gave up on him and went across to the toy sailboat floating in the water, the riptide pulling at it, choppy waves tumbling and churning on the shore, sucking back along the shelf that fell sharply from the beach.

The kid reached for the boat but it bobbed away, getting drawn toward the boulders on the opposite side of the little cove from where

Vernon sat. The girl turned to the men, shouting 'Daddy!', but they had their backs to her.

She ran over to the boulders and clambered up onto them, following the sailboat. Slippery as hell, those rocks, strands of kelp lying across them like a bald man's comb-over. The kid nearly grabbed the boat, then it swirled away from her and she reached out even farther. She stretched, her fingertips almost touching the mast. And then she slipped and she was in the water. Fucken cold, nut-shriveling water. Got her panicking and fighting and splashing.

She went under.

Vernon watched as the kid surfaced, her mouth wide open, then a wave smacked her head against the rocks and she disappeared and didn't come up for a few seconds, her one hand grabbing at the air. The water dragged her under again.

Vernon rose, ready to shout to the men – who were still unaware of what was going on behind them – about to hurry down there and make like a hero. Then he stopped himself, crouched again, like a lizard in the shadows.

Let this play out a while, brother.

Let it play out.

chapter 2

NICK EXLEY WOKE EARLY ON THE MORNING OF HIS DAUGHTER'S BIRTHDAY, eager to get her into his studio, but first he had to escape his wife, who lay sprawled face down beside him as if she'd plunged from a height. He edged out of bed, desperate not to rouse Caroline. He needn't have worried. She snored on, poleaxed by the meds that kept her, in the optimistic jargon of her psychiatrist, high-functioning.

Exley stepped into a pair of board shorts and pulled on a T-shirt. He lifted his glasses off the dresser and slid them onto his nose, bringing the bedroom of the rented house into focus: a study in browns and beiges, as impersonal as a hotel suite. Caroline, face creased by sleep, moaned but she didn't wake, a bubble of saliva fat as a tick at the corner of her mouth.

Exley left the room and clicked the door shut, only the distant whisper of the ocean intruding on the silence of the morning. He took a large box, gaily gift wrapped, that leaned against the wall of the carpeted corridor and went to Sunny's room. The door stood ajar and she lay on her stomach, surrounded by a tumble of toys. He kissed her forehead and she smiled up at him, eyes still closed.

'Happy birthday, Sunny,' Exley said, the wrapping paper rustling as he sat down on the bed.

'What's that?' she asked, opening her sleep-smeared eyes, stretching for the package.

He held it just beyond her reach. 'You'll see. First there's something we have to do.'

'What, Daddy?'

'What we always do, baby. What we always do.'

Exley scooped Sunny up out of the bed, her body warm and sweet-smelling beneath her pajamas, and carried her and the gift downstairs to the latest incarnation of the studio he'd kept in all their homes over the years – too obsessed with his work to be separated from it.

He slid the tinted glass door closed and the hiss of the surf was replaced by the white noise of the air-conditioner. Screens stared at him blindly and the sleek dermis of a workstation gleamed in the wash of hidden spotlights. He booted up the computer, hearing the bushfire crackle of static as the monitors awoke.

Exley undressed his daughter, then squeezed her wriggling body into a skin-tight black outfit – the first motion capture suit he'd had especially tailored for her. He'd taken delivery of it only yesterday.

When Sunny turned one, in Paris, it had been a Babygro that housed the constellation of sensors, forever capturing her clumsy, lurching attempts at walking. A pair of Donald Duck pajamas did the job on her second birthday, celebrated in a townhouse in Santa Monica, and a tight T-shirt and leggings on her third, as she imitated Fiona from *Shrek* in their London apartment.

What remained constant was the latticework of tiny, weightless digital trackers dotted across her body, the nervous system of the motion-capture device that had made him a wealthy man (sold in scores to animators, special effects houses and developers of computer games) and brought him out here to Cape Town for three months.

These sensors, alive to the slightest movement – even the birdlike flutter of her heart – translated the essence of Sunny into thousands of digital impulses, fed into the computer that hummed gently in the background. The monitors, giving a real-time display, showed a skeletal wireframe figure, moving as Exley's daughter moved. Later he'd replace the wireframe with the 3D model he was building of her, realistic and complete down to every hair follicle and pore of skin on her body.

Exley sat at the computer, the digitized image of Sunny reflected in his glasses, his hands moving across the keyboard with easy familiarity, the soft mouse clicks rising above the murmur of the hardware.

'Dance for me, baby,' he said, aligning the streams of optical input, finessing the quality of the capture, as his daughter – with heartbreaking solemnity – became a clumsy ballerina, twirling, arms held aloft, toes on point.

Sunny enjoyed the process, which was as familiar as Exley reading her a story at bedtime. These capture sessions weren't restricted to her birthdays, although Caroline's recent objections (inspired, Exley believed, by paranoid jealousy, a by-product of her condition) had limited his access, but there was more of a sense of ceremony on these occasions, a marking of time that had passed. In the way that another father stood his child against a wall or door-frame and fixed its height with a pencil, calibrating its growth since the previous year, Exley had evidence of the increased bodily coordination, fluidity and strength in his daughter.

He'd done this a thousand times before, with countless subjects, and even though he was an avowed heathen Exley couldn't shake the sense that there was something almost metaphysical at work here, that he was capturing the thing that his mother – battling dementia on the New Mexico ashram where he'd ended his childhood – would call Sunny's *atman*.

Her soul.

Sunny's enthusiasm for the dance was flagging, her eyes drawn to the gift-wrapped box sitting near the door. 'What did you get me, Daddy?'

'You'll see in a minute. Just lay a few more of those moves on me.'

She completed a listless pirouette and stood knock-kneed, wriggling, squirming inside the suit, tugging at the fabric, her patience exhausted, the digital skeleton a mirror of her frustration. 'Daddy, I want to open my box. Now!'

Laughing, Exley saved the data and crossed to Sunny, peeling her free of the clinging Lycra and dressing her again in her pajamas. He slid open the door, revealing the absurd beauty of a Cape Town summer's day, and the sun, flaring off the ocean beyond the living-room windows, flooded the studio.

Sunny grabbed the gift and flopped down onto her backside, tongue peeping through her lips as she tore at the wrapping paper, the sunlight turning her hair to flame. She fought the box open, exposing a model sailing ship complete with masts and rigging.

Her eyes widened. 'Daddy bought me my boat!'

'It's from Mommy, too.'

She stared at the sailboat, transfixed. An unlikely gift for a small girl but she'd desired the ship with a single-minded passion since she saw it at a toy store at the Waterfront.

'Can we sail it, Daddy? Please?'

'Sure. Go and fetch your swimsuit.'

Sunny ran back upstairs and Exley carried the boat out onto the deck that overlooked their small beach, where Caroline, straw-hatted and swathed in layers of cloth to keep her pale, freckled skin safe from the African sun, was laying a table for the birthday party.

Arranging plates and napkins, she didn't look up. 'You do realize that creepy thing you do to her is a kind of identity theft?'

Keeping things light, Exley said, 'Caro, even you know that identity theft is something different.'

'Christ, don't be so bloody literal, Nicholas. I'm trying to make a fucking point here.' Looking at him now, shaking her head. 'I think we spoke about this?'

'No, you spoke about it.'

'True. You stayed mute and aloof in your emotional igloo, didn't you?'

Caroline used her plummy English voice as a weapon. A voice that had once enchanted Exley, so different from his own with its unplace-able accent. Brits thought he was American, Americans assumed he was Canadian and a TV commercial director from Toronto recently mistook him for an Irishman.

Caroline shook her mid-brown curls. 'I'm wasting my bloody breath, aren't I, trying to get through to you?'

Exley walked past her out into the sun, trying to stay calm, but tension knotted his shoulders as he felt Caroline's eyes on him. He was retreating – again – from his wife's rage, a rage so massive that it seemed to exist as a separate entity from her.

What was the reason for this rage? There was no reason. It was not reasonable. When chemicals in her brain produced a toxic soup of paranoia, Exley and Sunny were there to pay the tab for all the world's slights (real and imagined), made apocalyptic by some misfire in Caroline's synapses.

Of course, there were the few good days when she woke up happy and the skin seemed looser and plumper on her skull and her eyes shone rather than sucked in light and she was girlish and flirtatious and patient with their child, indulgent of her interrogations about flowers and animals and clouds, manufacturing answers to unanswerable questions.

But today was not one of the good days.

Waiting for Caroline's shadow to fall on the sand beside him, Exley crossed the small inlet that was enclosed by high boulders on each side, forming a channel, the Atlantic lying still as a mirror, so placid and unthreatening this morning, reflecting the bowl of golden mountains and the seamlessly blue sky.

The water was icy on his toes as he set the sailboat down in the water. No matter how hot the day, the ocean stayed frigid. He risked a look behind him, relieved to see that Caroline had disappeared into the house and it was Sunny skipping toward him in her swimsuit, laughing and splashing, singing a little song in her high, sweet voice – '*Sun*-ny *Ex*-ley is having her *birth*-day' – repeated over and over like a nursery rhyme as she sent the model ship skimming across the shallows.

The day hadn't started so good. Vernon Saul had been plagued by bad dreams the night before – his mind churning up images of pain and torment from his childhood – and woke up covered in sweat, the stink of his long-dead father like a live thing in the airless bedroom.

He felt tired and edgy the whole day and by late in the brutally hot afternoon, jammed behind the wheel of the cramped Ford pick-up, his head pounded with a familiar headache and he was in no mood to deal with the new dispatcher giving him grief about his tardy overtime records.

'Your mother's cunt,' Vernon said into the microphone that spiraled from the radio mounted on the dash, hoping the dispatcher, a fat white bitch with zits and hair dyed the color of pus, caught this before she signed off.

She did. 'What you say?' Her voice shrill through the static.

'You fucken heard me,' Vernon said, holstering the mike, laughing as he imagined her froth of consternation back in the Sniper HQ down in Hout Bay.

He took a couple of painkillers from the glove box and dry-swallowed them, tasting acid on his tongue, like he'd licked a battery terminal. He needed a break, to stretch his legs, take a piss and have a smoke. Check in on one of his projects.

Vernon smacked the red Ford into gear and rocketed off from where he was parked on the shoulder of the road switchbacking down to Llandudno, this suburb of palatial houses that clung to the slope of the mountain and danced a conga line along the shore. A place nobody could spell and half the people in the Cape Flats ghettoes – where he came from – couldn't even pronounce. And who could bloody blame them?

As he passed the wooden Sniper sentry box that guarded the road Vernon leaned on his horn, startling awake the fat darky who dozed inside, wagging a thick finger in warning as the uniformed man leaped off his stool and came to attention in the doorway, like Idi Amin inspecting his troops.

Vernon drove to the ocean below, passing glittering confections of stone and glass hunkered down behind high walls and electric fences, most of the houses wearing the red signage of Sniper Security.

It was Saturday, which meant that hundreds of cars clogged the streets; people from all over the Cape Peninsula come to swim at Llandudno beach, popular with picnicking families and surfers and body-boarders. Parking bays down near the beach were limited and the day-trippers ended up blocking the driveways of the rich bastards, who phoned Sniper to sort things out.

Vernon had just about got used to the plummet in status from being a police detective to a rent-a-cop, but he couldn't handle being a glorified traffic warden, hassling these sunburned whities to move their cars, and he had no intention of sticking around here. He waved at a couple of Sniper patrolmen who manned the boom that stemmed the flood of cars and drove along the shore until the road narrowed and the houses dribbled away, and there was just one glass box out there on its own. With the ocean and the sky reflected in the windows, the house looked like it was floating, ready to drift out on the tide.

A clutch of Benzes, Beemers and chunky SUVs cluttered the road outside the house and, as he eased the truck between them, Vernon saw a little parade of white families – well-fed men in their thirties, their gym-crazy wives and pale kids – exiting the Sniper-branded front gate, getting into their cars and driving away into their perfect lives.

The house disappeared in his mirror and the road ran dead, rocks and scrub blocking the view of the ocean. Vernon parked the Ford behind the granite boulders that flanked the house, forming one side of the small bay that opened from the private beach.

Easing his bulk out of the Ford, his withered leg stiff from the hours behind the wheel, Vernon felt the sweat on his chest and around his balls. He ran a hand through his dark, wavy hair, leaving his palm and fingers wet. With his mid-brown skin and straight nose he was almost handsome until he removed his fake Ray-Bans and revealed his khaki eyes, too small and set too close to his nose, like they were retreating into his skull. Pitbull eyes. He wiped the sunglasses clean and slid them back on.

Vernon took a warm can of Coke and an uneaten Big Mac, still in its Styrofoam container, and left the truck, the radio muttering as he walked away. He adjusted the hang of the Glock at his hip and limped up onto the rocks, in shadow now that the sun was low, his dun-colored uniform blending with the boulders. The rocks were slick with kelp and he stepped carefully, finding purchase for his boots.

Walking along the ridge until the ocean came into view, he looked down at the private beach and saw a small group of whities gathered around a table, all festive with balloons and empty bottles.

Slowly, Vernon descended to the water, the rocks blocking the house from sight. There was no beach here, not like on the other side, just a shelf of rock, where a black man, bare-ass naked, was on his hands and knees, matted dreadlocks dangling into the ocean. The Rastaman shouted and moaned like a wild beast.

'Hey! Hey, Bob Marley!' Vernon yelled.

Vernon had no idea of the lunatic's name but the darky answered to this one now and looked up and smiled a gap-toothed smile.

'Cover up your stinking ass. Quick, quick.'

The darky stood and pulled on a torn pair of khakis over his dangling balls. His naked torso so thin that his ribs pushed out at his flesh like xylophone keys.

'Here,' Vernon said, setting down the Coke and the Big Mac on a rock.

The Rasta clasped his hands, bowing. Vernon had never heard an intelligible sound come from his mouth. Reckoned the fuckhead couldn't speak. Suited him. Heard enough bullshit from the world, day in and day out. The darky went at the food like an animal, stuffing it into his mouth.

Vernon turned his back, unzipped and drilled a stream of piss onto the rocks, releasing a long sigh of relief, working his shoulders to loosen some of the tension. He zipped and sat down, stretched his bad leg out in front of him, shook a Lucky Strike from the pack in his pocket and fired it up, letting the smoke do its magic as he stared out toward the horizon. The tide was ebbing, and the hot breeze whipping off the mountain drove waves into the shore.

The darky had inhaled the food and was washing it down with the Coke, his pitiful belongings spread out around him. A torn blanket. A few shopping bags full of fuck-knew-what. A pile of old newspapers, pages waving in the breeze. A row of plastic Coke bottles filled with sea water. They drank it, these darkies, as a purgative.

When Vernon had first seen the Rastaman sneaking down here a few weeks back, he'd been of a mind to kick the shit out of him and run him off. But something held him back. Some intuition. And Vernon was a man who trusted his intuition, knew all too well that not everything was plain and simple, that life didn't run in nice straight lines: it zigzagged like a bastard, took off in unexpected directions. A successful man understood that. Stored up things that could be of use to him.

So he let the darky be. Turned him into one of his projects. Brought him food now and then, made sure he didn't stray from this desolate spot and stayed well hidden from the houses of the rich. The man had come to think of Vernon as his benefactor.

Vernon stood, his leg bitching at him. 'Okay, my friend, I'm going now. I see you soon, okay?' He flicked his unfinished smoke at the Rastaman, who caught it, juggling it in his outstretched palms, bobbing his wild head as he sucked on the end.

Vernon hobbled back toward the truck and as he crested the rocks the house rose into view. Now there were only five people on the little beach: the skinny white guy standing with his wife, who looked like the sun had faded her to nothing, their girl kid, and two other men. One was the Australian dope smoker who lived in the cottage of a house a few streets away, a loudmouth with a red face and a big gut. Vernon heard his laugh, carried on the breeze. The other guy, older, tall with white hair – some kind of European – owned a massive place that backed up against the mountain.

As Vernon saw the woman go off into the kitchen, the kid at her heels, his leg caved on him and he sat down on the rock. He kneaded his hamstring, watching as the white-haired guy said something to the other two, shook their hands, laughed and disappeared into the house, sniffing after the wife.

Caroline Exley stood at the kitchen window watching Nick talk to Vladislav Stankovic, who had been fucking her for the last two months. Vlad threw his head back and laughed at something the hideous Australian ex-cricketer, Shane Porter, said. Then he turned and stared at Caroline and winked.

Her husband and her lover couldn't have been more different. Nick was small and slight, Peter Pannish, looking nowhere near thirty-six, dressed in the baggy clothes favored by people who spent their lives in communion with computers.

Vlad was at least fifty (too vain to disclose his age) and tanned the color of old teak. With his beak of a nose and thick, iron-gray hair swept back from a high forehead, he looked like a Serbian ethnic cleanser. She called him Vlad the Impaler. Of course.

So different between the sheets from her husband, too. Nick had used humor to seduce her. He'd been quite funny back when they met, ten years ago. They flirted, kidded and joshed one another into the sack. Sweet it may have been but Nick was never passionate.

Sex with Vlad was a carnal brawl – he smothered her with his big body, damp flesh stinking of meat and Balkan cigars, his barrel chest covered in a carpet-like gray pelt, his coarse pubic hair abrasive on her clitoris. He fucked her until the voices were stilled and her rage softened and dispersed like smoke. The thought of his fat cock inside her made Caroline wet and she had to grip the kitchen counter to compose herself.

She ran a hand through her hair, looking around the kitchen, overwhelmed by the evidence of the gross excess of her life. Plates of half-eaten food occupied every available surface: marbled gouts of birthday cake torn at by greedy little mouths, then discarded in favor of Belgian chocolates, syrupy Chinese confections and fluffy orange centipedes that stained fingers and tongues tartrazine-yellow.

The toothy adults had eviscerated olive breads and croissants, leaving them to drown in a soggy smear of Chardonnay, balsamic vinegar, Brie, Roquefort and gaudy dips. Even the leaf salads looked stripped and violated.

Sunny, who'd followed her inside, sat perched on a kitchen chair, keeping up an endless, inane patter that Caroline ignored. In some pretence of tidying up, she lifted a plate still coated with caviar, thick as sand on a lava beach, and nearly vomited at the gynecological reek. Dumping the plate, she closed her eyes and massaged her temples, trying to rub away the voices that were stirring within. A reminder to take her medication.

The day had sapped her energy and she was glad it was nearly over; the obscenely cheerful thirty-somethings and their unruly brats left her feeling frayed around the edges. God knows, she had done her best to keep her disdain – and her incessant, nagging rage – in check.

Vlad exchanged handshakes with Nick and Porter, trotted up onto the deck and breezed into the kitchen, dressed in his ridiculous Eurotrash outfit: a pink Lacoste shirt and blue drawstring trousers, tanned legs sockless in white espadrilles.

'Darlink,' he said in that joke accent.

'Careful. Little ears,' she said, nodding at Sunny, who watched them, squinting, as if she sensed something.

'It was lovely day,' he said. 'Thank you.'

'Next time you must bring your wife.' A running gag this, between them. The unnamed, eternally absent wife – away at health farms and spiritual retreats.

'Of course.' Coming closer, laying his broad-fingered hand near hers.

She could smell him, his fleshy odor welling up beneath the noxious designer aftershave. Every time she saw him she told herself that he was absurd, a buffoon. And then she let him fuck her, anyway. He didn't know or care that she had been shortlisted for the Orange Prize for her first, and only, novel. Or that after three years her publishers were demanding back their piddly little advance for the book on the Brontë sisters she had never quite been able to write. All he wanted to do was shag her stupid.

Caroline looked out the window and saw Nick and the Australian hunched over a joint, laughing smoke. Idiots. Then she saw the toy ship bobbing in the shallows, the retreating tide lapping at it, rocking the sails, the backwash threatening to suck it into the waves. This gave her a moment's inspiration.

Pushing her hair out of her face, Caroline turned to Sunny and smiled her most maternal smile. 'You had better go and rescue your boat, darling,' she said, sending her daughter to her death so the Serbian philistine could shove his thick fingers inside her sticky knickers.

N

Exley could relax at last, now the guests had left. He'd had to be vigilant all afternoon, waiting for one of Caroline's episodes. But she'd been on best behavior. Aloof and distant, sure, but that was Caroline. There had been no insults, no tantrums, no broken glass. A pretty good day, then, after all.

Shane Porter handed him a joint, saying, 'Come on, mate, let's get baked.'

Exley seldom smoked weed but he had a little buzz going from drinking wine and maybe a hit or two would keep his good mood afloat. And he sensed that Porter could be persuaded to tell him about that incident in Islamabad three years before when a world of shit had landed on the spin-bowler-turned-commentator's blond head, leaving him living like a remittance man here in Cape Town.

Exley had googled Porter and it seemed that he'd called a Pakistani opening batsman (a bearded character who knelt, faced Mecca and kissed the cricket pitch every time he scored a hundred runs) 'Osama bloody Bin Laden' during a commercial break, not realizing his mike was still live and that he could be heard all across the subcontinent. But the details were vague and contradictory, the Wikipedia entry warning that the allegation was unsubstantiated, and the garrulous Aussie had spoken of everything except his fall from grace in the two months Exley'd known him.

Emboldened by the weed, Exley said, 'Tell me about it, Port.'

'And what would that be, Ex?'

'What really happened in Pakistan?' Floating the question out on a cloud of smoke.

Exley was aware of Sunny at his side, saying something as she tugged at his boardshorts. He absent-mindedly stroked her hair, his attention on the Australian, and she slid away from his hand.

Exley took another hit and passed the joint back to Port, who sucked it down to nothing, exhaled a fragrant cloud and flicked away the butt toward a sky streaked with reds and mauves. He spluttered, wiped his mouth with the back of his hand, shaking his head.

'Nah, you don't want to ruin a beaut of a day.' But Exley knew he had him, the mix of Cape wine and Durban weed acting like truth serum, and Porter asked, 'Sure you want to hear my tale of woe?'

'Yeah, I'm curious.'

'Ah, it was bloody awful mate, I can tell you,' Port said, conjuring another joint from his shirt pocket and firing it up. 'One day I was on top of the world, calling a Pakistan–Australia game in Islamabad, next day I had to jump on the silver budgie and bugger off home, to disgrace and universal condemnation.'

The Australian stopped, the joint halfway to his lips, when Caroline's scream tore the air. At first Exley thought it was just another one of her episodes when she came hurtling from the house, yelling, relieved that only the Aussie reprobate was here to witness this.

Then Porter grabbed Exley by the shoulder and spun him to face the ocean. 'Jesus, Ex!'

It took a moment for Exley to understand that the driftwood he saw tossed on the water – the Atlantic rough now that the tide had retreated and the wind was up – was his daughter's arm breaking the waves in the shadow of the gray rock. Sunny's pale head rose for a moment and then disappeared beneath the tumbling swell.

Exley took off, plunging into the freezing breakers, feeling the shelf fall away from under his feet. No sign of Sunny. He dived, made heavy by his clothes, and saw her sinking toward the wagging fingers of kelp, her hair floating away from her head in Medusa coils, a few bubbles escaping her mouth.

Panic had him swallowing water and Exley surfaced, gasped for air and dived again, flailing his way down to Sunny. He grabbed her and towed her upward, fighting his way out of the surf, dragging his daughter onto the sand, crouching over her, his hair dripping onto her face that was a pale death mask.

Exley opened Sunny's mouth and breathed into her, feeling how cold her lips were. Jesus, he'd never learned CPR. Is this how you did it?

Through his terror he was aware of Caroline kneeling with her knees on Sunny's fan of wet hair, pale hands fluttering uselessly. Shane Porter stood frozen, staring.

Then powerful arms shoved Exley aside and a big brown man in a rent-a-cop uniform appeared from nowhere, straddled Sunny and pumped her chest, water spilling from her. The stranger used both hands to open Sunny's jaws and covered her mouth with his own, forcing air into her lungs, getting into a rasping rhythm, as Exley heard the mad wail of sirens.

chapter 3

MAJESTIC. THE WORD COMES TO VERNON AS HE PILOTS HIS PIMPED HONDA Civic through the curves, headlight beams skewering the coast road into the city. You were fucken majestic, my brother.

Vernon has a monster sound system in the car – tweeters perched above him, six-by-nine speakers bulging beneath the rear window, sub-woofers occupying half the trunk – but tonight he prefers the quiet, just the soothing thrum of rubber on the twisting road and the little crackle of his Lucky as he inhales. He lounges in the bucket seat, face glowing green from the instrument panel, comfortable now in his jeans and T-shirt, the Glock holstered at his hip, and replays the last few hours.

Vernon knew the child was dead the moment he got to her. But he also knew this was a moment he must seize, and he put his mouth over hers and breathed into her like he was blowing up one of the party balloons that still caught the breeze on the table near the house. He felt her little ribcage rising beneath him as her dead lungs swelled with air.

Vernon got a groove going, breathing, sitting up to pump at her chest – seeing the hope and desperation on the three white faces hovering over him – then down again, his mouth over hers. Pointless, but he kept at it. Exhausted by the time the emergency crew came jogging up with their EMT kits.

Vernon stood, his bad leg almost buckling, fighting for breath, looking down at the father. 'I'm sorry, sir. She's gone.'

The medics tried to work their magic, but it was no good. In the midst of all this the Australian faded with the last of the sun and the two parents were left on the beach with the medics and the cops who came up from Hout Bay. The mother sat on a rock, hugging herself so tight she looked like she was in a straitjacket, and the father paced up and down in his teenager's shorts and T-shirt muttering 'Jesus Christ' over and over again, like somebody, somewhere was going to make this all okay.

Vernon stage-managed everything. Getting the ambulance crew out of there, interfacing with the police – led by a darky captain, more politician than cop – who asked polite and sympathetic questions of these rich white people.

The highlight, the masterstroke, was not letting the cops take the body. When he saw the vultures from the police morgue bumping a gurney over the sand, throwing long shadows as they triggered the motion detectors that drove the house's spotlights and surveillance cameras, Vernon cornered the father, whose eyes swam with tears, magnified by his thick glasses.

'Sir, I have to advise you not to let them take your daughter,' Vernon said, speaking soft, right up in the whitey's ear.

'What?'

'These technicians from the police morgue. I wouldn't let them take her.'

The man stared at him. 'Why not?'

'Things happen in the morgue. Sexual interference. Theft of body parts.' The guy gaped, confused. 'I have a personal connection with an undertaker, sir. A man who will treat your daughter with respect. Respect and dignity.'

Dignity. Now, where the fuck had he found that word? Like a bloody infomercial on the TV.

Vernon laughs, tapping his horn as he passes a slower vehicle, bringing the spiral coil of the car lighter up to the tip of another Lucky, getting the cigarette paper burning – that nice, toasty smell in his nostrils. Of course the white guy lapped it up and Vernon phoned a mortician connection of his from the Flats who arrived in his best shiny black suit, a furtive assistant dogging his heels.

After the cops filed out and the undertakers drove away with the dead child laid out in the back of their truck, the father took Vernon's hand in both of his, like he was holding on for dear life.

'Thank you, Mr…?' Staring at him blankly.

'Please, call me Vernon, sir. Just Vernon.' Digging into his uniform pocket and finding a card – had them printed at his own expense – with his name and cell number on. 'You or your wife need anything, anytime, you just call me, hear?'

The whitey nodded and Vernon limped off toward the front door, ready to drive down to Hout Bay and punch out and change into his civvies. The cherry came as he walked through the living room, passing a table full of rich-kid birthday gifts. He boosted a Barbie Doll, staring out at the world through a plastic box, eyes as blue and dead as the drowned girl's.

Vernon also took a piece of colorful paper that was barely torn and wrapped the Barbie up nice down at Sniper HQ, and now it lies on the back seat, rustling as he speeds through the curves at Oudekraal, the lights of Camps Bay glittering ahead like a rich lady's necklace. What the fuck, the kid wouldn't be playing with that dolly, not where she is now.

Dawn Cupido lives in fear that the same sick shit that made her childhood a nightmare will be visited upon her daughter. Which is why she pays more than she can afford for this dump in blue-collar Goodwood, a predominantly white-Afrikaner neighborhood of small houses and blank-faced apartment blocks, wrapped in razor wire to keep out those grasping dark fingers from across the railroad track.

Dawn, dressed in a faded toweling robe, stands in the dingy kitchenette of the studio apartment, making a cup of instant coffee, the locked balcony doors behind her barely muting the night traffic rising up from Voortrekker Road – one of the longest in Africa – that chains this sad suburb to wealthy Cape Town.

Through the bars of the cracked kitchen window she can see the sodium light towers hovering like UFOs over the mean houses and shacks of the sprawling Cape Flats. She grew up out there, in apartheid's dumping ground, with its millions of mixed-race inhabitants, where kids are raped and murdered at a rate that defies belief.

Dawn takes the coffee and a packet of crinkle-cut chips and flops down on an old sofa that hemorrhages stuffing, gazing blankly at a ballroom-dancing competition on the mute TV. Her four-year-old daughter, Brittany, lies on the double bed, sleeping in the embrace of one of her many soft toys. Dawn reaches over and strokes Brittany's copper-colored curls, careful not to wake her. Marveling, as she does each and every day, that this beautiful blonde creature resulted from a desperate ten minutes in the back of a car with some long-forgotten white john.

Dawn blows on the steaming mug, staring at the dancers – all glamorous and graceful – as they twirl and prance across the screen. She crams her mouth with chips and washes them down with coffee, having one of those moments when she sees, really fucken *sees*, the squalor of her life. And to underscore it, the room throbs with the opening bars of a bad cover version of 'Eye of the Tiger,' signaling that the titty bar across the road is open for business. Means that Dawn has less than half an hour to get Brittany to the babysitter and get her ass over to the bar where she'll spend another night flashing her stuff at fat, sweating whities.

Jesus.

Dawn knows she is going to need a little help getting through the night, so she digs under the cushion and finds a zip-lock baggie bulging with weed. She lifts a copy of *People* magazine from the carpet patterned with burn marks and dumps some of the weed onto Angelina Jolie's goldfish lips. The green mound smells like all the rooms from Dawn's childhood and she has to shut her eyes for a moment, as if that will stop the memories.

Dawn busies herself separating the stalks and pips from the weed. Hates the way the pips explode when you smoke a joint. Knows she shouldn't be doing this shit. She lost Brittany once already, two years ago when she was hooking, because of her meth habit. Cleaned up now and got the kid back, but it'll all be over if she gets busted again.

She draws a Rizla paper from the orange pack and rolls a joint, just a one-blader. Normally she is expert –three-bladers are nothing for her

– but getting this little shorty together tonight is tough, shit starting to seep out of the shadows at her, the memory train rolling on down the tracks.

She licks the paper to seal it, twists the end closed, tamps the other with a match and then sets fire to the joint. Sucks in a chesty and holds it until her lungs nearly burst and she coughs out smoke.

Dawn grips the joint in her teeth and loosens the elastic that holds her hair in a ponytail, squinting through smoke at the TV as she shakes her hair loose – long, wild corkscrews that brush her shoulders. Her mother's hair. Except her mother blew hers straight, the way they do out there on the Flats. Her mother was a beauty. Proud of her light brown skin and her curves. Wielded that hairdryer like a weapon, killing any evidence of the African blood way back in the gene pool.

Dawn can still hear the scream of the hairdryer, catches that burned-hair smell when her mother put her to bed, ready to go out on the town, lit up by pills and booze. Leaving Dawn with her uncles and cousins, barely out the door when they were already sliding their drug blurred eyes over her, pushing her little body into the mattress, suffocating her with their manstink.

The joint is nothing but ash burning her fingertips, so Dawn drops it into the cold coffee and hears it die. She goes and sits on the bed, staring at herself in the yellowing mirror propped up against the wall.

'Come on, bitch,' she tells herself. 'Get it together.'

She reaches for the eyeliner on the bedside table and gets busy, not caring that she smudges it. Smears rouge under her high cheekbones (got those from her mother, too) and gets an Angelina pout going, feels the lipstick warm and waxy as she works it into her lips, running her tongue over her teeth to clean off the red that looks like blood.

The knock at the door startles her. And she panics when she hears that familiar *rat-a-tatta-tat-tat*. What the fuck is he doing here?

She jumps to her feet, pulls the robe tight around her. 'I'm coming!'

Dawn grabs an aerosol can of the cheap deodorant she uses and sprays the room like she is trying to exterminate bugs. Hurries across to the balcony doors, unlocks them and throws them open, allowing in the car fumes and the noise. She takes the magazine and shakes it over the balcony, letting the stalks and pips float down to the sidewalk. The knock again, louder.

'Hey, chill, man!' she shouts, battling to keep her voice from shaking.

She rushes to the front door and slides back the bolts and chains, fixing a smile on her face as insincere as a welcome mat as she opens the door to Vernon Saul.

As Vernon limps into the apartment, clutching the gift-wrapped box under his arm, he feels the elation leak out of him like a dribble of piss, leaving behind that feeling of emptiness and anger. The way of the fucken world.

He sniffs the air, catches the sharp tang of the deodorant overlaying the usual brew of stale cooking, woman-flesh and dank underparts, and the sour-sweet child smell. But it is the stench of weed, thick and cloying, that swamps all the others.

The open balcony doors are another giveaway: the little bitch never unlocks them, no matter how hot the weather, terrified that some fucker will go King Kong and clamber up three floors and make a meal of her and her daughter.

Vernon turns to Dawn and holds out his hand. 'Gimme it.'

'What?'

'The shit. Gimme it.'

Vernon sees a lie coming and he is over to the sofa and he sees the joint floating like a dead fly on the scummy surface of the cold coffee. With a wrist-flick he tosses the liquid at Dawn and it catches her full in the face and dribbles down onto her robe, the stub of the joint dangling from the collar.

She blinks, reaching for a towel lying on the floor. 'Jesus, Vernon!' Hissing at him, soft-like, so she don't wake the kid, who squirms and makes little sucky noises.

'Gimme it.' He holds out his hand again and she dabs at her face as she digs the baggie of weed out from under the cushion on the ratty old sofa.

He grabs it from her. 'Is this the lot?'

'Ja.'

'You sure?'

'I fucken said ja, didn't I?'

He looks at her, nods, knows she's telling the truth. He sets the doll down on the sofa and crosses to the bathroom – tiny and grim, no bath, just a toilet and shower, pantyhose dangling like body parts from the shower head. He empties the weed into the shit-pot and flushes, watches the green stuff get sucked away into the vortex, drops the baggie on the floor and goes back into the room, where Dawn is repairing her make-up.

She looks at him in the mirror as he comes up behind her and she flinches. 'Where you get it?' he asks.

'Just some guy.' Lipstick like a dog's cock running round her mouth.

'Boogie?'

'No.' Not looking at him, lying bitch. 'Dunno his name.'

'You fucken stupid in your head, or what? You wanna lose her again?' Dawn shakes her curls, twisting the lipstick closed with a little click. 'What I tell you when I helped you get her back?'

Dawn says nothing, retreating from him now, nervous eyes on the child. He follows her, crowding her between the sofa and the TV. 'You got fucken ears? What I tell you?'

'If I use, you get her taken away again.' She looks across at the kid, who makes a mewling noise like a cat and opens its eyes, blinking at them. 'Please, Vernon, it's just some weed, man,' Dawn says, her voice a whisper.

He eyeballs her for a long time before he speaks. 'You disappoint me, Dawnie. This is your last fucken chance, you hearing me?'

Dawn nods and Vernon sits down on the sofa and lifts the gift-wrapped box, holding it out to the child, who blinks at him stupidly. 'Here.'

The child looks at the parcel, then up at her mother.

'What is it?' Dawn asks.

'Here, take it,' he says to the child, ignoring Dawn.

The child grips the box in its little monkey hands and tears off the wrapping paper, revealing the doll with blonde hair.

The kid's face lights up like it's Christmas. 'It's a Barbie!' The kid might look white, but it speaks like just another colored brat.

'Where you get that?' Dawn asks.

'I bought it.'

'Bullshit.'

He slides a hand under her robe, up her naked thigh, and grabs the skin right up beside her thing, can feel the scrape of her cunt hair as he pinches the flesh between thumb and index finger. Hard.

She stiffens, and he sees tears come into her eyes from the pain, but she doesn't cry out, not wanting to scare the child, who's combing the doll's blonde hair with a brush clogged with Dawn's coarse black curls.

Vernon releases his grip and Dawn sinks down beside him, knees tight together, hands squeezed between her legs, like she is holding back a piss. 'What you say to the uncle, Brittany?' Voice high from pain.

'Thank you, Uncle Vermin.'

'Vernon,' he says, the kid looking at him blankly. He hauls himself to his feet, leaning his weight on the back of the sofa, flexing his bad leg. 'Okay, Dawn, I better get to work. I'll see you down there later.'

Dawn nods and Vernon lets himself out, sees her staring at her white child grooming the white doll as he closes the door. He humps his way down the stairwell – no fucken elevator – out the lobby and through the stream of traffic across to where the bleeding red neon of the strip club flashes promises of pussy into the night.

chapter 4

NICK EXLEY ROAMS THE HOUSE LIKE A SLEEPWALKER. HE STARES BLANKLY AT the mess in the kitchen, the room leached of life by the fluorescents. A clatter like distant bird wings draws him across the living room toward the deck. A white linen cloth, rising from the table on the beach like a Halloween ghost, flaps in the wind that has grown in force since sunset. He doesn't have the courage to go out there – out to where Sunny died – and fold the fabric and bring it inside.

He hears the muffled pad of Caroline's feet upstairs, moving between bedroom and bathroom. They've avoided one another since the police and the emergency crew left. Since the undertakers slid Sunny into a child-sized body bag – the zipper ripping through Exley's head like a bone saw – and took her away with them.

Exley feels a rush of hot puke and makes it back to the kitchen just in time to spew an acid brew of wine, cheese and bread onto the plates stacked in the sink. He runs the cold water over the dishes until his vomit is gone, rinses his mouth and splashes his face. For a moment he doesn't recognize the man reflected in the kitchen window.

Exley turns and goes upstairs. He stops in the doorway of Sunny's room, blue moonlight washing the walls and the bed. He can't bring himself to hit the light switch and reveal the room's emptiness, and the realization that he will never read his daughter another bedtime story leaves him strangled by grief. A door creaks and he sees Caroline standing in their bedroom, watching him.

He walks toward her. 'Caro, tell me this isn't happening. Please.'

'Sorry, darling,' she says in a voice that could cut crystal, 'but it is happening. Why don't you have another joint and maybe it'll all go away in a little puff of smoke?'

Exley looks into his wife's eyes and sees her mania has congealed around the notion that he is to blame for what happened.

'Jesus, you're not saying it was my fault?'

'Oh, I am, Nicholas. I am.'

They stare at one another and he thinks for a moment that this will escalate into one of her episodes, ending with rage and tears. He'd almost welcome that, now. At least it would be a connection, no matter how screwed up. Anything to distract him from the memory of Sunny tugging his boardshorts, and him ignoring her. Sending her to the water.

But Caroline shrugs and he hears her consciously slow her breathing as she runs a hand through her hair.

'I'm going to bed,' she says. 'I suggest you do the same, there'll be a lot to do tomorrow.'

Caroline turns and before Exley can stop himself he reaches out, embracing her. She stands with her back to him, body rigid, all bones and hard angles, and when he drops his arms, releasing her, she closes the door in his face.

chapter 5

DAWN STEPS THROUGH A CURTAIN ONTO THE NARROW RUNWAY THAT RAMS A path into the crowd of drunk white men. When a spotlight cuts through the haze of cigarette smoke, fingering her, she stands dead still, like she's lost. Looks it too, in her thrift-store jeans and plain white shirt, her hair hanging loose, like a civilian who has wandered in here by accident. She plays it up, all wide-eyed and innocent. Her hook.

The regulars hoot and the newcomers stop their shouted conversations, drinks halfway to their mouths. Used-car dealers and motor mechanics and copier salesmen, escaping their pale wives for a stolen night of dark meat.

Then, as the opening bars of 'I Bruise Easily' ooze out of the sound system, Dawn gets her ass moving, the ass that fills the jeans out too nicely. Her mother's ass. Yet another reason to hate the bitch. If Dawn angles her butt just right you could balance a champagne glass on it, and it's a magnet for the scores of booze-blurred eyes.

Dawn stays deep inside herself, letting the music take her, those words of vulnerability and pain deafening her to the surge of drunken yearning that comes at her like a wave, avoiding eye contact with the men, spinning away from the hands that grab at her.

At the start of the first chorus she unbuttons the shirt – just a plain white bra underneath – shrugs it off and lets it float to the ramp. Unclips the bra and drops it, freeing her small breasts, her dark nipples prominent as thimbles, making the trash out there believe she's turned on.

Dawn unzips her jeans and works them loose, revealing her white panties, like a virgin girl would wear. When she steps out of the denims, letting them fold into a heap in time to the last swell of music, the lust in the room could ignite a mountain fire.

The guitar intro of the old Police ballad 'Every Breath You Take' fades up and as she slides the panties down her thighs – the spotlight almost surgical as it exposes her trimmed pubes and the folds of her vulva – there are gasps and throttled oaths. This is the closest most of these men have come to beauty. It still sometimes astonishes Dawn, when she sees her naked body in a mirror, that the years of hell have somehow left no mark on her. No tattoos, no knife scars, no needle tracks, no Aids melanoma – just her smooth caramel skin that makes every vicious bastard out there want to violate her.

Get in line.

Still dancing, Dawn arches herself back until her hands touch the tacky ramp, singing along inside her head to Sting's words of obsessive love, not letting herself feel the hundreds of eyes that rip at her flesh. She pushes up on her hands and comes back to standing, as lithe as a yogini, just as a fat pink man heaves himself up onto the runway, cheered on by his buddies, moving his beer gut in time to the music, writing a love letter in the air with his dick.

He reaches for her and she steps back and he stumbles and falls to his knees, still trying to paw her. She dances around him, never once lets him touch her. Never allows any of them to touch her. Not like the other girls, who encourage the men to grope them and eat them out on the ramp, getting the pathetic losers all worked up so they can take them into the filthy cubicles in the rear and fuck them for money.

The man stares up at her, a look of confusion and longing on his drunken face. Vernon smashes a path through the men with his shoulders and elbows, shoving them out of the way, ignoring spilled drinks and curses. He grabs the drunk by the shirtfront and lifts him into a right hook that snaps the man's head back and brings a smear of blood to his cut lip.

Vernon drags him from the ramp, has him sprawling across a table, scattering bottles and glasses. He lifts the dazed man, punches him again and then propels him toward the door, powering forward with his good leg, the injured one visibly punier, dragging after him like a reluctant dance partner.

To the crowd this low-level violence is a moment of light relief in a city numbed by car-jackings and home invasions. Dawn doesn't miss a beat as she watches Vernon hurl the man through the doors, out onto Voortrekker, the very road where Vernon busted her just over a year before.

She'd been in a downward spiral for years. Escort agencies and massage parlors and then the street. She'd been smoking meth heavily for six months and life was a blur of backseats and blowjobs.

When a car pulled up beside her one night, she was so wasted that her cop radar was missing in action, and it wasn't until she slid into the passenger seat and mumbled her price for a BJ and a screw, and the driver had badged her, that she realized what was going down.

As the car slid into the stream of cars, taillights red as lipstick, she said, 'Fuck you,' waiting for this cop to backhand her.

But he didn't, and he didn't take her to the cop shop either, just turned off Voortrekker into a quiet side street, stopped outside an Afrikaans church, empty, silent and godless. Dawn reached over to his lap, fumbled for his zipper, knowing he'd want her to suck him without a condom. He grabbed her by the hair and smacked her head against the side window, and she tried to focus through the *tik* on his blurred face.

'I don't want your filthy mouth on me.'

'Then what you want?'

He looked at her before he spoke. 'I seen you for a while, on the street.'

'And so?'

'How you end up there?'

'What you fucken care?'

He fired up a smoke and offered her one, even lit it for her. 'What's your name?'

'Angel.'

He exhaled a laugh. 'Your real name.'

'Dawn.'

'Okay, Dawn, tell me your story.'

'Why?'

''Cause I like stories is why. Talk to me, or I throw your ass into a cell.'

So she let the meth do the talking about the years of rape and abuse, about how she started hooking and how her kid had been taken away by the social services.

'You want her back? Your kid?'

'Of course, yes.'

'If I get her back for you, you stop this shit?'

She looked at him, trying to make some sense of this through the haze of meth. 'You can get her back?'

'I know people. But you stop the *tik* and you stop selling your ass. Understood?'

'Why you give a fuck?'

'Let's just say it's your lucky night and leave it at that.'

'And what must I do, to earn money?'

'Can you dance?'

'Ja.'

'Then I'll get you a job.'

'You mean it? You not fucking with me?'

'I give you my word,' he said, starting the car and heading back toward Voortrekker, merging with the traffic.

For a moment Dawn thought it was raining the way the taillights blurred through the windscreen, then she realized she was honest-to-God crying. She didn't know that she still could, thought all the tears had been wrung from her years ago.

Vernon was good as his word. Got her this gig at Lips, and – after she'd been clean for three months – got her Brittany back.

Dawn kept on waiting for the sexual favors. But he never wanted that and she knew without him telling her that he'd had done to him what was done to her. One survivor recognizes another. Vernon just kind of moved in on them, watching her all the time at the bar, coming round to her apartment like he was her father or something. Giving Brittany gifts. Brittany didn't like him, battled with his name, called him 'Vermin,' which pissed him off no end.

Dawn looked the word up in a dictionary at the bookshop in Voortrekker Mall, and she nearly hosed herself when she saw what it meant. But he creeped her out, acting like she was a puppet, the threat always there that if she put one fucken foot out of line, Brittany would disappear.

When Dawn heard he'd been shot she prayed for him to die, but he was back at Lips in two weeks, limping and not a cop no more. But still in her face. Still in her life.

The song is ending and she brings herself back into the room, the little runt, Boogie, eyeballing her from the bar, miming smoking a joint. She looks away quickly, right at Vernon, who stands near the door, staring at her before he shifts his gaze across to Boogie, those little eyes of his missing nothing. She picks up her clothes and lets the yells and applause drive her from the ramp.

chapter 6

CAROLINE LIES ON THE BED, FEELING DWARFED BY THE ARCTIC EXPANSE OF duvet. They rented the house furnished and the bedroom is everything she hates – hidden soft lights and beiges and browns, the oatmeal shag carpet like a living organism beneath her bare feet. A room that could suffocate you with its malevolent blandness.

She tucks her feet under her, closes her eyes and leans back against the headboard. How does she feel? Numb, maybe. Anesthetized. Grief, she knows, will come later, riding in on the back of the black-dog guilt. She reaches for the pill container beside the bed and pops the cap, goes as far as dumping two pink and green bombs on the palm of her hand before she stops herself.

No, fuck it, she isn't ready to find some pill-induced rationality and the anguish that will bring. But if she lets her mania kick in, with all of its attendant rage, she can dodge some of the pain and guilt. Cowardly, of course. And there'll be no closure. But closure is such a TV word, anyway.

She drops the pills back into the container and snaps the lid shut.

How many times has she wished Sunny dead? Or rather, wished that Sunny had never existed? Had never come into being? Well, her wishes have been granted. Her child is gone.

Unbidden a memory clobbers her from the left field and her abdomen and thigh muscles contract at the echo of the eviscerating pain when the pink, bloody thing was torn from her, the twisted umbilical reaching deep into her and detonating something, like the pin of a grenade being pulled. It was as if the arrival of Sunny had triggered the birth of a part of Caroline that had lain slumbering, a manic Rip Van Winkle, who awoke enraged and out of control.

She can remember the exact moment when she emerged from the

agony and saw the world as she had never seen it before, saw that florid-faced, furious infant, like a hideous old man, its mouth wide opening, howling. Announcing it was here.

Forever.

She looked into that face, eyes like slits, mouth wet and wide, bawling demands, little fists clenched, and saw no beauty, only rage. And felt its reciprocal inside her, flowing out hot, thick, into her blood, feeling her body expanding with it, as if her cells were stretching their matrix to accommodate this other Caroline, her muscles sinewy and strong, her skin stretched vellum-tight across her skull. There was no post-natal glow. No bliss.

Her nipples were dry and retracted, denying the hungry infant, and when the thing screamed she pushed it away into the hands of the nurses, who looked at her with loathing. Her mouth tasted of metal and her sight and hearing were acute: she swore she could see the atoms around her shift and resolve as the doctors and nursing staff paraded through her room, and they seemed to form a shroud of confusion and self-pity around her husband, who tried smiles and hand pats, the feel of his fingertips repulsive to her.

Then came the psychiatrists, the pill-happy shamans, with their diagnosis of post-partum depression. Men with cold, calculating little mouths and eyes like scanners, the scratch of the pens on their prescription pads like blades tearing at her skin. They wrote up a list of medication as she sat staring at nothing, tits dry, her rejected child outside in the waiting room with a stranger wearing a wedding ring.

This was the start of her journey into some drugged netherworld, where color faded to monochrome and the soundtrack was mall muzak and her thoughts were blunted and fuzzy, and she knew she'd never write again.

Ever.

She remembers the exhaustion, the resentment that she felt when her career – Jesus, her life – was put on hold as she was enslaved to this tiny human, while her boy-genius husband tinkered with his clever gadget and sold it for millions. Her writing disappeared under a torrent of diapers and food allergies as she followed Nick Exley around the globe while he hawked his invention in Sydney, Los Angeles, São Paulo, Paris, Copenhagen, and now here on the godforsaken tip of bloody Africa.

Her agent, a bull dyke who still spoke in the clanging tones of her native Auckland, waited patiently for her next novel, and when it wasn't forthcoming sent her an email containing only Cyril Connolly's famous warning: 'There is no more somber enemy of good art than the pram in the hall.'

Caroline feels a shortness of breath. She opens her eyes and jumps up, pacing the carpet, hugging herself as she's done since she saw Sunny lying dead, the thuggish rent-a-cop crouched over her, forcing his breath into her in a way that was at once obscene and – his gammy leg spasming like a frog's in a lab experiment – horribly comical.

Before she can stop herself, Caroline has her mobile phone in her hand, speed-dialing the only person who can ground her right now. The phone goes straight to voicemail, Vlad urging her to 'leave message.' She doesn't. What is she meant to say? While you were fingering me, my daughter drowned?

And she is back in the kitchen, her jeans and knickers bunched at her knees, Vlad walking away, kissing those very fingers in salute, whistling his way out the front door. Caroline turning, fixing her clothes, looking out the window, past the two stoned men, as Sunny goes under for the last time.

The bedroom seems to close in around her, suffocating her, and Caroline knows she needs to talk to somebody. Not her parents – they are long dead in a car accident in Provence. Not her brother, the aging roué who lives in Singapore or Kuala Lumpur, and definitely not her shovel-faced, menopausal sister, as bovine as the cows she farms in Herefordshire.

Desperate to connect to somebody, even her husband, Caroline rushes out into the corridor. She finds Nick in Sunny's room, asleep on her bed, curled up in a fetal position, the nightlight burning, his thick glasses lying in the jumble of toys on the bedside table.

In a rare moment of tenderness Caroline decides not to wake him, and clicks off the lamp and goes back to their bedroom, where exhaustion hits her like a freight train. She pulls off her jeans, too tired to brush her teeth and wash her face. But not too tired, suddenly, to kneel down, in her knickers and T-shirt, feeling like a primitive with her praying hands held in front of her, as she surrenders to some absurd impulse, trying to find some long-forgotten Church of England platitudes from her childhood.

She mutters a few words, a pathetic plea for Sunny and for herself and the boy-man asleep in their dead daughter's bed. But kneeling there, her bare knees itching from the carpet, Caroline feels a sudden, cold certainty that there is nobody out there listening. Nobody at all.

chapter 7

DAWN HAS NO IDEA HOW LONG SHE'S BEEN SITTING IN THE ONLY CUBICLE IN the women's toilet, door shut, lid down, just chilling, wrapped in a towel, her clothes bundled in her lap. The music and the shouts and the lust-yells still penetrate the plywood walls, but at least she is alone for a while.

Then the girl who works the door, a thickset misery with cross-eyes and a mustache, bangs on the wall and Dawn drags herself back from wherever and leaves the bathroom, walks past the fuck-rooms, hears grunts and moans like pigs feeding. Sylvia the cleaner, skinny, black, invisible in her housecoat, comes out of one of the rooms with a mop and a bundle of soiled towels. Unglues a used condom from one of the towels and drops it into a garbage bag.

Dawn goes down a narrow corridor toward the dressing room, the music muted now, the voices of a couple of dancers coming to her loud and raucous from inside, the smell of *tik* thick in the air, and all at once she sees herself heating a glass pipe over a lighter flame until the contents bubble like fat. Gripping the pipe in her fist and taking it to her mouth, her cheeks falling hollow as she sucks, eyes closed. Feeling that complete release as the smoke fills her and blows the top of her head off, and every care in the world flies away and leaves her blissed out, like God himself has anointed her.

Fuck, Dawn, get yourself together. She stands, calming herself, letting the drug-lagged talk wash over her.

'And she say—' A cough.

'What she say?'

'She say no!'

'No?'

'Ja. No.'

'So what you say?'

'I look at her and I say, I kick you back deep in your mother's cunt.'

'Of course, yes.'

'Of course.'

Dawn sees Brittany, sleeping with the soft toys, and that gives her the strength to go into the room. Two long-time veterans of the skin trade are lazing naked in their chairs in front of the mirrors, bouncing a Styrofoam cup of tequila and a *tik* pipe, their dark brown bodies patterned with varicose veins, bruises, burn marks and Cesarean scars, breasts heavy from suckling unwanted and unloved babies, coarse pubic hair waxed away to narrow landing strips to allow fast access to their plumbing.

Dawn looks at them and sees herself in ten years, if she doesn't do something – any fucken thing – to get herself away from this.

They check Dawn out and the fat one says, 'Excuse us, Lady Di.'

Lady Diana, a name that came from God knew where and has stuck. The way it works on the Flats with these bitches who want to pull you down. Dawn calls them the Ugly Sisters, because she is the fairest skinned of them all. One of those stupid private jokes that gets her through the night.

Dawn ignores them and drops her towel, knowing her beauty hurts them more than her words could. She sits in front of the chipped mirror, wipes her sweaty face, repairing her make-up.

The club owner, Costa, comes into the dressing room, as immune as a butcher to the spread of naked flesh. He's a sallow-skinned man in his fifties, with hair the color of cigarette ash and a soft paunch that swells above the stone-washed jeans that his colored trophy wife insists he wears.

'I tell you not to smoke that shit in here,' he says. The pair laugh like hyenas, blowing their *tik* smoke in Costa's face.

'The cops give you hassles, send them to us and we suck their cocks like always,' the fat one says, making kissy sounds, pink gums visible through her missing front teeth.

Costa sits down beside Dawn and says, 'Out,' to the other two, waving his unlit cigarette toward the door.

'It's our fucken break time.'

He waves at the door again. 'Take it in the shithouse, then.'

They don't argue, wrap dirty, make-up-smeared towels around their bodies and exit, mumbling. Dawn hears 'little cunt' as they go.

Costa offers her a cigarette and when she shakes her head he inserts a smoke beneath his sad mustache and fires up. 'You think about what I tell you?'

'Ja. And the answer is still no.'

'Dawn, you nice girl, but I can't keep carrying you like this.'

'The customers like me, Costa.'

'Sure, they like you. Sure. And they want to fuck you. For good money. And you? You say, no. No, no, no.'

'Costa, I hooked. I done it. Then I pulled myself straight.'

He waves a tired hand at her nakedness. 'You calling this straight?'

'They can eyeball me all they like, but no man's touched me in a year.'

'And that makes you, what? Better?'

'No. Fuck knows I'm not proud of what I do, but I can still look my daughter in the eye.'

'Thing is, Dawn, you taking up the space of a girl who will go with the customer into the rooms. You costing me big money.'

'You firing me?'

'No, not yet. I want you to think. Think nicely.'

'I thought.'

'You can earn maybe a thousand a night. Do it for a year, you can take your daughter and go somewhere.'

'And what, Costa, start on the *tik* again, like those two, so I can fuck my brain up enough to allow those fat Boers to shove their filthy things into me?'

He stands, sighing, drops his cigarette on the floor and grinds it dead with a thick-soled Nike. 'You think, Dawn.' Tapping his temple. 'You think nice.'

He leaves and Dawn dresses herself again as one of the girls finishes her set, ending, like always, with a pedophile double whammy: R. Kelly's 'I Believe I can Fly' and Michael Jackson's 'Billy Jean,' to fractured applause. Dawn waits by the curtain, in the gloom, as the girl, naked and sweating chemicals, slinks her skinny ass out, dragging her costume, sequins winking in the red light.

Dawn cracks the curtain and goes back out there, into the haze of smoke and booze and overheated men's bodies, finding that place inside herself that keeps her safe and distant.

Vernon leans against the bar, drinking a Coke. He doesn't touch alcohol when he is on duty. Isn't much of a drinker anyway, the stuff has a way of screwing with his nerves.

It is close to 3 a.m. and the crowd has thinned, but a scrum of horny white men clog the ramp, staring up into Dawn's thing like it's the answer to their prayers. And the little *tik*-head, Boogie, still wanders around like a mongrel dog from the squatter camps. The kind that nips at your heels and when you kick out at it you see it's rabid, froth like shaving foam hanging from its jaws.

Boogie is dark and skinny, in the universal banger uniform: outsize T-shirt, his cargo pants hanging low and loose enough to reveal the elastic of his boxers when he lifts his arms above his head and does a little dance step. Even with the racket of the music Vernon can hear the fuckhead's cartoon-sized sneakers squealing like baby mice on the tiles as he does his MTV thing.

Boogie finishes his dance like he expects applause then he leans down to talk to one of the whores, his voice high pitched, spitting words from his bucktoothed mouth as he shouts over the music.

Costa figures that since a place like Lips is going to attract the meth merchants, better to know who the supplier is, keep tabs on him, regulate things. So Costa tolerates Boogie, with his gang-talk and prison ink staining his pipecleaner arms, and a permanent brand on his lower lip from the hot *tik* pipes. Vernon lets him be, long as he don't sell his shit to Dawn. But the little fuck-head is taking a liberty.

Dawn finishes her set and walks her bare ass back out through the curtain, not even gracing the audience with a look. They'll have to take their hard-ons out onto Voortrekker, now the bar is closing. The music ends and Vernon hits the overhead lights, industrial-strength fluorescents that hammer down hard and cold, revealing just how tacky and soulless the bar is. The punters blink, suddenly back in the real world, ashamed to look at one another. They grab their jackets and car keys and shuffle toward the door like condemned men.

A drunken john and a girl are still falling in love at the bar, oblivious to the light. She is so *tikked* out that if the john didn't have his hand up her skirt, anchoring her, she'd fall from the barstool. Vernon grabs the john by the back of his shirt and shoves him in the direction of the door. The man stumbles, manages to stay upright, then just carries on straight out onto Voortrekker, not even looking back. The girl follows, falling off her high heels.

Costa is by the door, keys in his hand, ready to lock up. Vernon waits until Dawn comes out of the dressing room, wearing sweatpants and a T-shirt, hair pulled back into a ponytail, a bag slung over her shoulder like she is going to the gym.

Boogie, still looking hopeful, tries to catch her eye but she ignores him and walks out. Vernon follows, stands on the sidewalk under the dead neon, watching her cross the deserted street, lighting up a smoke as she walks, disappearing into the dark lobby of her apartment block.

The barman, the cleaner – almost unrecognizable in jeans and a beret – and the last of the girls fade into the night. Boogie comes out last and Costa locks up from inside. The *tik*-head flaps up his hoodie and takes off down the sidewalk, toward where his nasty little Ford Escort rusts under a streetlight.

'Boogie,' Vernon says.

The runt stops and turns. 'Ja?'

'Slow down, my brother. You and me gotta have a talk.'

Vernon sees Boogie tense, and knows he'd be no match for him in a footrace. Fixes a smile on his face and holds up a hand. 'Relax, man. I wanna talk business.'

'Ja?'

'Ja, ja.' Vernon catches up with him, outside a construction site, an apartment block that has been gutted and is being transformed into low-rent offices and stores. 'I hear you the man to talk to if I want some good shit?'

'For sure, Vernon. You know me.'

'Ja, ja, I know you.' Vernon puts an arm around the skinny man's shoulders and eases him off the sidewalk, behind a wall of corrugated sheeting. He catches the burnt plastic stink of *tik* on Boogie's body as he grabs him by the throat, lifting him onto tiptoe with his left hand. 'I know you been selling weed to Dawn.'

The *tik*-head tries to speak, can't find his voice, so he shakes his head. Vernon winds up a right hook, brings it from low down, all his weight behind it, and he feels face bones cracking under the blow.

Boogie sprawls on his back on the cement floor, like some rags thrown in the trash. Vernon goes straight in with a boot to the guts. Air comes out Boogie's nostrils, and he holds himself, curling like a worm, too winded to cry out.

It had been Vernon's plan to scare him, hurt him just enough to get him honest again, but then he sees his father when he looks down at Boogie, caught in a spill of streetlight: the glazed eyes, the filthy teeth, the prison artwork. Feels that old pain. And righteous fucken anger.

Channels that anger, as he grabs the hoodie and pulls it up, stretching it tight over Boogie's head. He smashes the piece of shit's skull against the graffiti-scarred wall. It makes a muffled thud and he hears the fucker groan. Feeble hands grab at his wrists. Next time he batters the head against the bricks he feels something give way under the cloth, like a rotten melon in a string bag, and the hands sag to the floor.

Vernon gets a groove going, battering away like he is trying to knock a hole through the wall, till the skull is all spongy beneath his fingers. He releases the pulped head and lets it fall to the floor with a moist slap. Puts two fingers to the *tik*-head's throat. Nothing.

Vernon sits a moment, slowing his breathing. Feels something wet and sticky on his hands and his face, realizes the hoodie slipped down while he was doing his percussion thing, and Boogie's blood has sprayed like a power shower.

Vernon drags Boogie's body farther into the construction site, leaves it behind a pile of builder's sand. He wipes his hands on the dead man's jeans and stands in the shadows, waiting until a taxi rattles by, then he limps to his car.

chapter 8

SUNNY TUGS AT EXLEY'S BOARDSHORTS, SAYING SOMETHING ABOUT HER BOAT in the water. Her milky child-smell comes to him before he opens his eyes to the darkness, before his brain allows him to recall what happened the evening before. Instinctively he reaches for her, the feel of her skin already on his fingertips before reality sucker-punches him and he sits up, fighting through panic to find air.

The room filled with Sunny's toys and clothes, her scent rising from the pillow, is too much for him to bear and he flees out into the corridor. The door to the main bedroom is still closed and he knows that facing his wife now is impossible.

Exley goes down the stairs and walks toward his studio, the insulated box shrouded in welcoming gloom, sliding open the door, the chill of the A/C on his face. He closes the door and without switching on the lights sits down in his Aeron ergonomic chair, feeling it mold its shape to him like a lover. Reaching beneath his workstation, his hand red in the muted glow of a pilot lamp, Exley boots up his computer.

He closes his eyes, listening to the whine of the hard drive rising to a low scream, like a distant jet taking off, hears the static crackle and low burp as the monitors come to life, followed by the cluck as the motherboard engages the CPU, catches that familiar hot-wire smell of the innards of his computer waking from their slumber, information coursing through the suddenly alert banks of memory.

As he sits in the dark, his eyes closed, a flashback hits Exley that almost overwhelms him with its intensity. He's lying with Caroline on the bed in their tiny London flat, his hand on her swollen belly, staring into her eyes as he feels their child kicking in her womb. Caroline, orphaned at twelve, raised by her much older sister – an aloof, distant woman – reaches up and touches his face and says, 'This is all I ever wanted, Nick. A family.'

Exley's eyes open, and he grips the arms of the chair, staring into a cold and barren future. Even when Caroline's madness exiled her, he'd had Sunny and the simple, undiluted love that flowed between them.

Gone now.

The computer grunts and Sunny, or rather the digital familiar of his daughter, appears on the monitors. He stares at the loop of dancing pixels and hears her singing just the day before, '*Sun*-ny *Ex*-ley is having her *birth*-day', and he finds himself mouthing the words endlessly, giving them her childlike cadence, until they make as little sense to him as her death.

chapter 9

THE CAR ENGINE WAKES YVONNE SAUL, THE GLASS IN HER BEDROOM WINDOW buzzing as it vibrates from the low rumble. She looks at the clock next to her bed – just gone 4 a.m. The engine cuts, and the car door smacks shut, then the front door of the house opens and slams. She lies still, listening to his footsteps getting closer to the door that she can't lock since he kicked it in.

The door hits the wardrobe as he pushes it open. 'Hey!'

Yvonne keeps her eyes closed, pretending to be asleep. As if that will stop him. Suddenly cold as he pulls the blankets from the bed, leaving her lying in her nightdress, her knees lifted to her chin. 'Move your fat fucken ass. I'm hungry.'

She opens her eyes. He stands over her, switching on the bedside lamp. As the light floods the room, she sees the blood on his shirt and jeans. Dried dark red on his arms and hands. So much blood.

Yvonne can't stop her mother's reflex. 'Boy, you hurt?' Sitting up, reaching a hand to her son.

He slaps it away. 'You gonna be fucken hurt if you don't get up. I'm not talking again.' He slams out of the room.

She lifts herself from the bed, a tall, thickset woman in her mid-fifties. The wild young beauty she once was lost in the flab and the wrinkles that have left her looking ten years older than her age. She draws a robe around herself, slides her feet into slippers and goes to the cramped kitchen.

He is by the table, stripping off his bloody shirt, dropping his jeans and kicking them across to her. Standing there in his underpants. Yvonne can smell sweat on his body and the metal stink of the blood.

'Wash these clothes,' he says.

She bends to pick up the bloody jeans. 'What you done now, Vernon?'

His bare foot catches her in the abdomen and sends her flying against the stove. The back of her head smacks the oven door. 'Who the fuck are you to question me?' Staring up at him as he looms over her, making a fist, waiting for him to beat her, as he's done too many times before. But he holds back, leaning in until his face is close to hers. 'Now you cook me eggs and steak and you wash my clothes. And there was never no blood. Nothing. You hear me?'

'Ja. I hear you.'

He smiles but she can't see no softness in that face. Handsome like his dead father, and just as sick in the head. He disappears into the bathroom and she hears him splashing water, then he goes to his room, slamming the door after him.

Yvonne closes her eyes, praying for God knows what. When she's done she stands and carries the clothes to the bathroom and soaks them in the tub, the water stained red by the blood.

Vernon feels it coming as he lies on the bed in the gloom, chilling, listening to Motown. The panic rising in him, making him restless, afraid.

Before he was shot everything he did was about power, about imposing his will on people weaker than him. But since he came back from that terrifying blackness things have changed. There is a fear in him now. A fear that he could just evaporate, that the darkness could claim him.

He sits up and clicks on the lamp. His room is neat, the way he likes it, nothing out of place. Just a bed and a table and a wardrobe. No pictures on the wall. Nothing. Doesn't need that shit. Fucks with his head, which is already crammed too full of pictures. Takes a deep breath. He sits for a bit, just breathing, telling his nerves to stop shouting at him.

After a few minutes he is feeling a little better. Loose. His hands not shaking no more. So he stretches out on the bed and then makes the mistake of allowing his eyes to close.

And there they come, the images of his father, right here in this bedroom, with his tattoos and his missing teeth and his rancid smell, like a backed-up drain. Coming at him with the broken bottles and the lit cigarettes.

Vernon's little-boy skin smoking black as his father holds the cigarette to his stomach, hand over his mouth and nose, shutting out any screams. Not that his mother hears. Deaf she is, to all this. Blind, also, to the marks on his body and the blood between his legs when his father is done getting his jollies.

Vernon has to fight hard not to scream. He sits up, telling himself it is all in the past, man. His rancid fuck-up of a father long dead. But his heart is like a boot trying to kick open his breastbone and the sweat is heavy and rank on his body.

He hears his breath coming in gasps as terror drives him from the room. He opens the front door of the house and stands battling to breathe. Catching dust and diesel fumes from the buses and taxis, the roads busy even this early on a Sunday morning.

The streetlamps – the few that work here in Paradise Park – still burn, dropping green light down on the weekend workers hurrying to the buses and taxis. He ducks back inside and flops down on the sofa and channel-surfs the TV, not seeing the succession of darky politicians and those frosty bitches on CNN.

He can't sit still and he's up again and goes back outside, where it's lighter now, the streetlamps dead, and grabs the garden hose and starts washing his car. Wipes a smear of Boogie's blood from the driver's seat and hoses the exterior, trying to calm himself with work. But his throat is still tight, like his father's hand is on it, throttling him.

chapter 10

EXLEY WAKES AT HIS WORKSTATION, KEYBOARD DENTING HIS CHEEK, THE strobing monitor agitating his eyes through their closed lids. As he sits up and squints at the wireframe that still dances, he can't stop himself from sliding back along the timeline to the moment when Sunny came to him on the beach, desperate for his attention.

But now, in his fantasy, he hands the joint to Shane Porter and he turns to Sunny and sees her pointing to the little sailboat, bobbing in the waves like some cheesy Hollywood model shot from pre-digital days, and he hauls the boat to safety and gives it to his daughter who, as a result, is safely asleep upstairs, her golden hair covering her pillow like fleece.

Exley's bulging bladder brings him back to reality and he hits the pause bar on the keyboard and stands, his legs uncertain as he leaves the studio and crosses the living room, opens the sliding door onto the deck and walks down to the sand, cool and powdery beneath his bare feet, a Turner landscape of soft blues, reds and yellows lying before him. The ocean is flat and motionless, with barely a lick of a wave.

Avoiding the spot where Sunny's body lay, he crosses to the humpbacked boulders, fissured and veined, indigenous bush growing like scraggly beard in the folds of the granite, digging his penis – uncomfortably stiff from the weight of his bladder – free of the boardshorts. Exley pisses away his hard-on and stows himself, wondering what to do next.

The enormity of his grief takes his legs from under him and he sinks down onto the sand and dry-heaves, producing nothing but the taste of bitter bile in his mouth. He sits again, his back to the small wooden rowboat that lies against the rocks, oars neatly shipped, watching the gulls squabble on the huge, flat rock near the mouth of the inlet, its slopes alpine with bird shit.

On calm days like these, before the sun got too high and too hot, he rowed Sunny out past the bird rock, laughing as she pinched her nose at the stink of the guano.

The memory of her, dwarfed by the orange life jacket, her curls electric in the sunlight, burns his retinas when he closes his eyes, and he finds himself nostril-breathing, inflating and releasing his diaphragm as he was taught to years ago in the yoga classes on the ashram. It helps to calm him a little and the sun on his face is soothing and maybe if he just sits here and doesn't move, the sorrow will drain from him, drop by drop.

Exley feels the chill of the waves on his feet, then something more solid nudges his toes and he opens his eyes to see Sunny's toy sailing ship bobbing in the shallows, returned on the tide.

He grabs the thing and stands, lifts it over his head and smashes it down on the rocks and doesn't stop until the boat is string and matchsticks. Tears blur his eyes and his face is a macramé of snot.

He drops the splintered toy and looks up to see big, black Gladys, the cleaning woman, standing on the deck, watching him. She doesn't usually work on a Sunday, but last week Caroline asked her to come up from her shack in Mandela Park, to help clean up the mess after the party, and nobody thought to phone her.

As Gladys approaches him, her shiny, low-heeled shoes sinking into the sand, Exley sees that she is crying. Caroline must have told her what happened, when she buzzed her in.

'Mr Nick,' Gladys says, 'Sunny, she is…?'

Exley wipes a gout of snot from his face with the back of his hand, nodding, and this woman to whom he has said maybe ten words in the months she has cleaned their house enfolds him to her massive bosom, the scent of cheap soap and talcum powder rising from her warm flesh. It is comforting, being held like this, and he wishes he could stay here forever.

She releases him and walks to the water's edge, staring down at the sand, scuffed by the feet of the paramedics, a single latex glove – muddied and obscene – lying just beyond the reach of the surf. Gladys points out at the water in the cove.

'Is it there that she died?'

Exley sees Sunny floating down near the kelp, her hair trailing, the last few bubbles of air escaping her mouth, and he's sure now that she died underwater, and that the rent-a-cop – despite his heroic efforts – did nothing but fill her dead lungs with his breath.

'Yes,' Exley says. 'Did Caroline tell you what happened?'

The big woman shakes her head. 'No, I don't see Miss Caroline. She is only buzzing me in. Sunny tell me, in a dream.' Gladys steps close to Exley, who says nothing, staring at her. 'Last night, I dream about water. About Sunny. This morning when I am coming in the taxi my heart it is very cold. And when I see you here, I already know.'

'You saw Sunny in a dream? Last night?'

'Yes, Mr Nick.'

Exley feels as if he is looking down on himself from on high. Part of him realizes how absurd this conversation is, how dumb he is to be grasping at this simple woman's superstition. The other part speaks before he can stop it. 'What did you dream?'

'She is coming to me. Crying. And the way she is looking I know she has passed.'

Madness, of course. Primitive hocus-pocus. But he feels dizzy with loss.

'In our culture the death of a child is a very bad thing,' Gladys says, 'and the child must be protected from the bad spirits, must be guided to the ancestors on the other side. You understand?'

He nods. Crazy as it may seem he does understand. There is a whacked-out symmetry between what this Xhosa woman is saying and the teachings of the self-styled guru on the ashram he fled as a teenager, where his mother still lives. These teachings – tales of souls wandering lost in an endless maze of hellish afterlives – terrified the living shit out of him.

'What can I do?' asks a man who is not quite Nicholas Exley.

'We believe that the spirit of the person stays where it dies for a few days, before it crosses over. Only the love of a parent, Mr Nick, is getting Sunny to the other side.'

Then she sets off, heavy and slow across the sand, and into the house. Later he will see her sitting on Sunny's bed, singing in Xhosa, weeping without shame.

A movement in the house draws Exley's eye. Caroline watches him from an upstairs window, smoking. Then she turns away and disappears.

Exley goes inside, tramping water and sand across the tiles. He considers climbing up to the bedroom, but is too raw to deal with Caroline's anger, so he ducks into the studio and slumps down in his chair, triggering the mo-cap loop of Sunny. He feels a disturbance in the air and swivels as Caroline steps into the room, dressed in dark tights, an old sweater baggy on her slight frame. The sweater is her security blanket, the wool mottled from years of use and scarred by cigarette burns.

'What are you doing?' she asks.

'Nothing,' he says, pausing the loop, his fingertips stroking the smooth rectangular spacebar.

'Is this how you're going to handle it?' she asks. 'Locked away in your bloody hobbit hole?'

'I'm just watching her.'

'That's not her. That's not Sunny. That's nothing but a collection of zeros and ones.'

He doesn't rise to this. 'What did you say to Gladys?'

'Not a word. I just buzzed her in. Then I saw the two of you having your little pity party on the beach. Why, what did she say to you?'

He shrugs, eyes on the frozen wireframe figure on the monitor. 'She knew Sunny was dead. Said that she had a dream about her last night. Something about water.'

'Jesus, what a load of voodoo bollocks.'

'How did she know, then, if you didn't tell her?'

'The bloody bush telegraph, how do you think? The taxi would have been full of it this morning when she came up.'

'She doesn't strike me as a liar.'

'Oh, come on, Nicholas, you don't seriously believe this nonsense, do you?' He stays mute. 'You know these bloody primitives and their conceit that they are born with a connection to some greater power. A connection that we have somehow lost. It's just a form of spiritual one-upmanship.'

Caroline sees his face and laughs. 'Shit, how pathetic,' she says. 'You want to believe it, don't you, to lessen your guilt? To believe that Sunny is out there in some cozy afterlife, instead of lying dead in the mortuary? My God, despite your protestations of rationality, you're your mother's son, after all.' Exley does what he always does when she gets like this: retreats into silence. 'Well, sorry to piss on your parade, darling, but Sunny's dead. Gone. Shuffled off the mortal bloody coil. *Muerto*. Fucking get used to it.'

When he doesn't look at her and stays closemouthed he hears her breath – a hiss of frustration – and waits for the torrent of rage, his shoulder muscles tensing, his hand gripping the mouse. But the door slides open and shuts with a muffled kiss and he's alone.

Exley nudges the spacebar again, setting free all that is left of Sunny, her little proxy dancing and twirling on the twin screens of his glasses.

chapter 11

A GALE ATTACKS THE CAPE FLATS AS VERNON DRIVES DEEP INTO PARADISE Park, steering the Civic through the mustard-colored dust. He's really fucken freaking out now, gripping the wheel of the car. The past overwhelms him and voices scream in his head and his nerves are stretched tight as garrottes, ripping into him from the inside. The way he lost it with Boogie was a signal that bad shit was coming down. Vernon doesn't regret killing the little fucker, but he doesn't like to lose control. Ever.

The wind smashes the cramped houses and ghetto blocks, getting the roofs of the shacks banging like a steel band. Pedestrians stagger, leaning into the blast, clothes billowing as they battle their way to buses and taxis.

A bottle of brandy lies wrapped in plastic on the seat at Vernon's side. Not for him. He needs stronger medicine.

He catches the stink of the landfill as he parks outside a box house that backs onto the dump. The house stands alone, beside a mound of rubble that's all that remains of its Siamese twin. The landfill looms behind, the wind sending trash into the air in a toxic rain.

Vernon grabs the bottle and fights the car door open, takes sand in both eyes, blinded like he's been maced. Blinking away tears, he walks over a scrap of dead grass to a scuffed door and bangs, hearing the inevitable mutter of cricket on TV from inside.

The door cracks an inch and an eye wet as an egg peers out. Opens wider, revealing a small, flabby man in his sixties, with a bald head and skin the color of piss. He sighs out brandy breath and steps back.

'Detective,' the once-upon-a-time doctor says.

'Doc,' the ex-cop replies.

Vernon closes the door, nostrils already rebelling at the stench. He's used to squalor, but this place is something else. Looks as if the dump behind has flowed in through the back door and flooded the house. An unswept floor covered by a filthy carpet. A couch and two chairs, smeared with dirt. Empty bottles, junk-food wrappers, newspapers and unwashed dishes litter every surface. Where other people have three flying ducks on the wall, Doc has a stitching of high-caliber bullet holes. One window is taped up, wind whistling through the cracks in the glass. Evidence of the gang war Doc found himself in the middle of a while back.

Rising over the filth is a TV the size of a billboard. Doc's eyes are glued to the screen: men in cricket whites against a lush green outfield, Table Mountain in the background.

Vernon holds out the bag, plastic shaping itself to the bottle inside. 'Here. Brought you something.'

Doc grabs at it with a hand so palsied it looks like he's busy with an invisible cocktail shaker. He doesn't worry with taking the bottle out of the bag, just unscrews the cap and hits the brandy hard. The old abortionist lowers the bottle, closes his eyes and wipes his mouth with the back of his hand.

A doctor once, a broken alkie now, locked away for years in Pollsmoor Prison after too many of his patients died. Earns his living dealing in guns, sewing up gangbangers, and chopping body parts supplied to him by cops from the police morgue, selling the bits off to the darkies for witchcraft. Selling bits of information, also, to cops and gangsters alike.

When the booze has worked its magic, Doc coughs, wipes slime from his lips and stares up at Vernon. 'What you want, Detective?'

'Can't sleep, Doc. Going up the flipping wall. I need a shot.'

'It's that wind. It unhinges a man.'

'Ja, must be the wind.'

'You wait here.' Doc leaves, taking the brandy with him.

Vernon hasn't crashed in two days and exhaustion sucks his bones deep into one of Doc's greasy armchairs, making him oblivious to the stink of the dump incoming on the draft through the bullet-starred window.

Vernon tries to keep his eyes on the cricket, but they find the filthy carpet and the bloodstain like the shape of Africa. His blood. And he's spinning back to that day, a year ago, when bystanders looked on while he was shot, nobody doing nothing to stop his life pumping out into the gutter while the gunmen disappeared onto Flats.

Vernon, still chewing his lunch of KFC and fries, was ambushed as he walked to his cop car parked outside a Paradise Park strip mall, gunmen firing at him from the rear of a Benz that was later found abandoned near the airport. Vernon didn't see the hitmen, but he knew who they worked for: a gang that was pissed off buying protection from him. Said he was getting greedy. Fucken pay up, he said.

Then the ambush.

Vernon felt the bullets like body blows, taking two more in the left leg that dropped him to the gutter behind his car and probably saved his life. He looked up at the people around him: a mother dragging her big-eyed kid away, three old ladies clucking like hens, a couple of street sluts laughing *tik* laughs. Knew none of them would lift a finger to help this plainclothes cop who wasn't exactly Mr Popularity.

He dragged himself along the gutter, reached up and grabbed the handle of the car door, locking his fingers on the metal, pulling himself to his knees, felt blood running hot and sticky under his clothes. He opened the door and hauled himself into the driver's seat.

He cranked the car. Fucker coughed like a dog. Cranked it again and this time the engine took. His left leg was useless, shoe filled with blood, so he didn't worry with the clutch, just jammed the lever into first, gearbox stripping cogs, and hit the accelerator, taking the rear bumper off a Toyota as he lurched out of the parking bay and drove foot-flat here to Doc's, hand on the horn to scatter the taxis and the street trash, the world fading and curling up at the edges like an old photograph.

When Vernon reached Doc's house he hit the curb and passed out, slumped over the steering wheel, his bloody chest sounding the horn. That got the old boozer away from his TV, and somehow Doc dragged Vernon – in seizure by then – into the house.

Vernon drifted back to consciousness lying on the carpet, as Doc ripped away his shirt, entry wounds like ripe raspberries on his barrel chest, the drunk lurching off to fetch his bag on the kitchen table – an old leather satchel filled with the tools of Doc's one-time trade. Doc stilled his fingers long enough to find a bandage, brown with age, and hold it against the most severe wound, Vernon's life leaking out round the edges.

Vernon heard the scream of the ambulance and the medics came in and set up an IV line and worked at stabilizing him. Blood loss smacked Vernon back into blackness as white men in cricket togs celebrated the loss of a wicket on the big screen in the background.

He woke in hospital two days later, on a respirator, tubes draining fluid from his one collapsed lung and a catheter draining piss from his dick. He'd survived. His leg was fucked, though, and his superiors used it as an opportunity to offer him a disability pension. Made it clear that if he resisted there would be an investigation that wouldn't go well for him. So Vernon took the golden handshake and limped off into his future as a rent-a-cop.

Doc's back in the room now, carrying a hypodermic and a little bottle of thick, clear liquid. The anesthetic he used on the women he aborted. He draws the liquid into the syringe, his eyes back on the TV, watches a red ball sail out of the ground, into the crowd, the commentator yelling like he's shot a load in his pants.

Then he gets Vernon to pump his arm and make a fist, and a nice vein rises blue and knotted from his forearm. Doc's hand is suddenly still, like he's received some miracle cure, and he eases the needle into the vein, and Vernon feels that beautiful nothingness and goes deep under, way too deep for even his father's ghost to find him.

Sunny watches Exley from the monitor. He took the photograph only last week, a full-face portrait, and remembers how hard it was to get her to stay still.

He is modeling his daughter's face in 3D software and has constructed an intricate mesh, a latticework that follows the contours of her bones. Exley could have made a career as a computer artist – he has the chops – but his motion-capture device, developed when he was a young animator too poor to buy one of the extortionately expensive systems sold by the people who would become his pissed-off competitors, set him on another course.

But he has never lost his love of 3D modeling, creating life from a digital wire mesh, finding nodal points with cursor arrows and using the subtlest of wrist and finger movements on his mouse (a tool that is an extension of his hand) to drag and warp the mesh until it takes human form and seems to transcend the two-dimensional plane of his monitor. Not for nothing is this animation software called Maya, Sanskrit for illusion.

Or delusion.

When he renders, skins and textures this face, it will be the focal point of a photo-realistic representation of his child. He'll graft the head onto a model of her body and give it life by marrying the figure to the motion-capture data he has stored.

Almost like bringing her back.

Exley rejects this notion. Blocks out the voice of Gladys on the beach earlier, telling him that his daughter is still out there, reachable, in some limbo between life and afterlife.

There is no fucking afterlife.

What he is doing here is a father's expression of love for his dead child. Nothing more. If he were a painter, he'd paint her. If he were a musician, he'd record something like Eric Clapton did after his four-year-old son plunged to his death from that apartment building in New York City. He is using his talent to create a memorial to his dead daughter and he'll screen it on the day of her funeral.

When an imaginary Caroline – at her schoolmarmish best – appears in his head to tell Exley that this digital evocation of Sunny is merely his way of sublimating his guilt, an act of penance disguised as obsessive love, he rolls his chair away from the workstation, closes his eyes and slides his fingers under his glasses, massaging his sinuses. He needs food and sleep and comfort.

With a couple of mouse-clicks he saves the information on the computer and leaves the studio, stepping out of the air-conditioned room into the heat. Somehow it has become afternoon and the wind is roaring in, turning the sea choppy, white heads of spume blowing up onto the beach.

Exley goes into the kitchen, spotless now that Gladys has done her magic. He opens the fridge and contemplates the leftovers. He's been a vegetarian since his days on the ashram, so he looks past the cold cuts and caviar, opens the foil on a wheel of Brie, but the ripe stink rises in his nostrils and he is overtaken by nausea. He crosses to the sink and drinks forever from the faucet, wiping his face.

When he opens his eyes he sees Caroline through the beads of water, soundless in her bare feet, still dressed in the tights and sweater, smoking, thin lines radiating out from her lips as she inhales.

'That horrible little undertaker left a message on the answerphone. He wants you to call him.'

'Sure, okay.'

She turns to go.

'Caro?'

'Yes?'

'I was thinking that we should hold the service here, on the beach, not in some God-awful crematorium.'

She laughs. 'What are we going to do? Bury her at sea?'

Exley doesn't react, just watches his wife, her skin whiter than he's ever seen it, her eyes wild in her head. Is she taking her meds?

Then, battling to keep his voice level, he says, 'We need to make a decision about that.' He clears his throat. 'I mean, do we bury her or cremate her?'

Caroline's eyes squeeze closed and when she opens them, just for a moment, he sees the woman he fell in love with. 'Oh, Jesus, Nick, is this really happening? To our baby?'

He goes to her and she lets him hold her, her voice muffled by his shoulder. 'I can't imagine Sunny in the ground. It's just too hideously Edgar Allan Poe. Worms and claustrophobia.'

'I feel the same. So we agree on cremation?'

She breaks free of him and Exley sees blankness settle on her face like a mask. 'Burn her. Burn her, for God's sake. Just get it over and done with.'

EXLEY SITS ON SUNNY'S BED LISTENING TO THE MUFFLED RATTLE OF CAROLINE touch-typing from behind the closed bedroom door. A sound he hasn't heard in a long while. He has his phone in one hand and Vernon Saul's card in the other, trying to find the courage to call him and ask for his help.

A low rumble drowns out Caroline's keyboard as a car with a powerful engine surges to a halt outside the house, exhausts burping when the engine is cut. Walking toward the window, Exley catches a few bars of 'I Heard It Through The Grapevine,' before Marvin Gaye is silenced.

A brown man in jeans and a T-shirt emerges from the car – some kind of customized Honda – and it takes Exley a moment to recognize Vernon Saul out of uniform. The rent-a-cop limps toward the gate, as if he is responding to some telepathic summons. Exley waits for the buzzer but the big man disappears from view.

Exley leaves the room and walks down the stairs, through the front door and goes down the pathway and out the gate. Vernon stands before a small metal door that opens onto a space recessed into the wall.

'Mr Exley,' Vernon says, looking his way.

'Call me Nick, please.'

'Nick. I'm just replacing the hard drive that stores the images from the surveillance cameras. The last one was full.' Vernon holds up a small black metal rectangle. 'Sorry if I disturbed you.'

'No, you haven't disturbed me at all, Vernon. In fact I was about to call you.'

The big man checks that the new hard drive is seated correctly and connects its terminals. Then he closes the door and locks it before replying. 'Is there something I can do for you?'

Exley stares at the hard drive in the man's hand. 'The cameras would have captured what happened last night, wouldn't they?'

Vernon shrugs. 'Some of it, yes.'

Exley feels sick as he understands those lenses caught him smoking weed while his child drowned. Witnessed his culpability.

'Vernon, what happens to that drive?'

The big man steps up to him. 'Look, Nick, I haven't been completely honest with you. The drive's not full.' Exley battles with Vernon's accent, trying to follow this. 'I'm taking it because, well, because I know the data on here is sensitive. Tragic. And I also know that there are people out there who are... let's just say they're *sick*. They get their hands on this type of material and next thing it's up on YouTube.' He shakes his head. 'I'm sorry if I'm upsetting you, but this is just the way the world is.'

Exley can only nod.

'So, I'm taking this down to Sniper headquarters and I'm personally going to erase it. You can rely on me.'

Exley exhales his relief. 'Vernon, you're off duty now, aren't you?'

'Ja, I'm not working today.'

'So you came all the way here, to do this?'

Vernon shrugs. 'Nick, I was there last night. I understand the depth of your pain. I can't let nobody add to it.'

Exley steps out of his own internal chaos for long enough to register that Vernon Saul stinks of sweat, that his clothes are creased and look slept in, and that his dark hair dangles in wet bangs over his forehead. Exley finds himself imagining how this man – a working man, a poor man – lives. Imagining the mean and narrow life he leads. And yet he has still found the time for this act of kindness.

Exley places his hand on the rent-a-cop's arm, feeling the knotted muscle. 'Vernon, my God, I don't know how to thank you.' Some privileged white man's reflex sending his fingers into his pocket for cash. 'At least let me give you some gas money.'

Vernon holds up a broad hand. 'No ways. This is the least I can do in your time of grief.'

How can Exley impose further? But he finds his voice. 'Vernon, I hate to do this, but I wonder if I could ask you a favor?'

'I told you already, Nick, there's anything you and the wife need, you just have to ask.'

'We want to bury Sunny, our daughter, as soon as possible. Tomorrow if we can. And we want to have the service here, on the beach.'

'Okay,' Vernon says.

'Thing is, I spoke to your undertaker guy, and he tells me that to get a person to officiate at the service is going to be a problem if it's not held in a church. He says there are procedures.'

'Leave it to me, Nick.'

'Really? I'm sorry to lay this on you.'

'Nick, you just relax. I'll sort this. I'll call you in a while, okay?'

The big man extends his hand and takes Exley's in a surprisingly soft grip, then he limps away to his car, leaving Exley overwhelmed by the compassion of this stranger.

All day long Yvonne Saul's nerves have been playing up something terrible, since she seen that blood on her boy's clothes, and him gone out all day, God knows where. As she stands by the open front door, the fierce wind flinging in heat from the south, she feels the water running between her breasts and down her thighs. She has been peeing non-stop, and no matter how much water she drinks, she can't satisfy this thirst of hers.

Yvonne feels lightheaded for a moment and puts a hand against the doorjamb to steady herself. She closes the front door and walks through to the kitchen, catching sight of herself in the wall mirror. She can't, honest to God, remember looking worse. Her skin is the color of dirty dishwater and the pouches under her eyes are dark with exhaustion.

She tried to sleep in the afternoon, but the incessant, nagging cries of the child in the wooden shack crammed into her neighbor's backyard kept her awake. A skinny little rubbish with gang tattoos and no teeth lives in there with a teenager and her little child. Mrs Flanagan, Yvonne's neighbor on the other side, says the girl sells her ass on Voortrekker, the milk in her breasts not even dried up yet. Don't need no newspaper with Mrs Flanagan around, leaning her big chest on the Vibracrete wall outside her house, her laser eyes missing nothing.

Mrs Flanagan says the jailbird is sexually abusing the child, a girlie no older than eighteen months. Yvonne walked away from her neighbor when this came up, her mind spinning back to what used to go on under her own roof, when her Vernon was little. God knows, she blames herself every livelong day for what he has become. She should have taken a carving knife to her sick bastard of a husband. Instead she'd closed her bedroom door and watched the TV or mumbled useless prayers and looked away from the blood and the bruises and the pain in her baby's eyes.

The cries are louder here in the kitchen, cutting into Yvonne's head, so she clicks on the old portable radio that stands on the counter top and church music rises up thinly through the static, and she almost can't hear those pathetic sounds no more. She opens the small freezer door on the top of her fridge, the cool air like a kiss on her face.

Yvonne removes a pack of frozen vegetables and rubs it against her cheeks and forehead, then she gapes her dress collar and rests the pack against her chest. Takes a few deep breaths before she stows the vegetables and opens the fridge, sees the last bottle of insulin sitting in the door, next to two brown eggs.

She told Vernon last week she's running low, and he said, 'Don't fucken nag me. I'll get it for you.' But he hasn't and she's scared to ask him.

He gives her no money, keeps her a virtual prisoner here in the house. Takes her shopping for provisions once a week. Drives her to church and back on a Sunday evening. Otherwise she spends her life sitting in this house, staring at the TV, or gossiping with Mrs Flanagan over the fence.

She's been holding off using the insulin but the room swims again and she knows she has no choice. She takes the cool little bottle through to the windowless bathroom, airless and stinking of mildew and urine that no disinfectant can erase.

Yvonne places the insulin on the lip of the discolored basin, the enamel stained black and red beneath the faucets, pitted as old skin round the plug hole. Vernon's toothbrush, dental floss and Aquafresh toothpaste lie beside the soap. He has always been proud of his white teeth.

Yvonne prepares the syringe and, holding it in her right hand, lifts up her dress with her left, the wet flab of her abdomen sagging over her panties. She uses an alcohol wipe to clean an area beside her navel, the heat drying the alcohol even as she rubs. She pushes the needle into her flesh, sinking the plunger all the way in to inject the insulin into the fatty tissue, not even feeling the pain after all these years.

Removing the needle, Yvonne mops up a few beads of blood with the alcohol wipe. She leaves the bathroom and puts the insulin back in the fridge, knowing she has enough left for maybe two shots.

Yvonne walks through to the living room and sinks down onto the sofa, the sticky fake leather grabbing at the fat on her legs. She feels a little better now the insulin is working and thinks about what she'll wear to church this evening. There is an old man, a very decent widower, Mr Tobias, who has been showing some interest in her the last few weeks. He is new to the congregation, moved down from Paarl to live with his daughter when his wife passed away. Yvonne's little fantasy of a life without Vernon ends with the rumble of the Civic, coming on fast, and the squeal of dusty disc brakes as his car stops outside, idling engine setting a teacup rattling on top of the TV.

Even over the wind Yvonne hears the front gate screaming like a wounded animal and feels sick to her stomach, wondering what mood he'll be in now, hearing the scrape of his key in the lock.

Vernon bursts in, his clothes rumpled and dirty, his thick hair dangling over his forehead. 'Get your ass up, we leaving.'

She stares at him. 'But church isn't for an hour.' She flaps a hand at her sweat-stained dress. 'I can't go like this.'

'Then fucken stay.' He's gone, slamming the door, and she has to grab her purse and rush to catch up with him, barely in the car before he guns the engine and takes them off into the maze of cramped houses, sun sagging like a blood orange into the thick dust.

⚡

Vernon hurries out of the pastor's house into the hot wind that attacks the arriving worshipers, women tugging down ballooning dresses and older men holding onto their Sunday hats.

The house, a two-level affair with barred windows, is joined at the hip to a squat pink happy-clappy church, the Tabernacle of Christ Our Lord, occupying a street corner in the middle-class part of Paradise Park, two blocks of nice houses with smart cars parked in the driveways, hidden behind high walls and fences. The houses of school headmasters and accountants and drug dealers, gazing hopefully toward distant Table Mountain but near enough to the landfill to catch the stink and see the useless people from Tin Town, the maze of shacks that grows out the side of Paradise Park like a disease, foraging for anything of value on the dump. The Tin Town Mall, the locals call it.

As he fights his way to the Civic, Vernon sees his mother walking toward the church, hunched against the wind, yakking to an old fucker whose tie rears up and smacks him in the face. His bitch mother's hair – naturally a stew of tight curls that has been straightened and gelled hard as a helmet – doesn't even move in the gale.

Vernon fires up the Honda and speeds away, tailgating taxis, using his horn to scatter pedestrians, many of them drunk this Sunday evening. His mother's stink still hangs in the car and he jabs a finger at the A/C button and the refrigerant hisses out of the vents, visible for a few seconds like a meat locker's been opened, coming in so cold it burns his sinuses. He wonders who that old man is. Wonders if this situation needs watching.

Then he breathes deep, lets the cold air calm him as he releases all the tension in his body. He's in the zone now. Fucken invincible. That shot Doc gave him put him under for nearly eight hours of dreamless sleep and he awoke with a renewed sense of purpose, not questioning the impulse that told him to drive over to Llandudno, to recapture the feeling of power that came to him last night on that private little beach.

Things are starting to line up again, fall into place, so it didn't surprise him when Nick Exley appeared and put himself deeper in Vernon's debt by asking for that favor.

Organizing the preacher man for the funeral had been no problem. A year ago Vernon busted a petty thief, a repeat offender who was looking at a long stretch inside. In a backyard plea bargain the dipso told Vernon he'd boosted a laptop from a pastor's car and found filth on it.

So Vernon got the thief to boot up the laptop, the hard drive toxic with downloaded child porn. Vernon, gagging back his memories, was tempted to bust his mother's preacher, send him to Pollsmoor where his fat ass would be torn open by the prison gangs – give him a taste of what was done to those kids. But sanity prevailed. This sick fuck was worth more to him out here.

Vernon visited the pastor, showed him the computer, watched him sweat as he saw his life dissolving away in the puddles that pooled beneath his arms. Vernon told him it was okay. He would keep it quiet. But if he ever needed something…

'Anything,' the sick bastard had said. 'Anything for you, Brother Vernon.'

So when Vernon bulled his way into the pastor's house and told him to meet him outside the church in the morning with his Bible in his stinky paw, the fake man of God didn't even try to argue.

Nick Exley's kid would have her little send-off.

Vernon arrives home, grabs himself a Coke from the fridge and settles his ass in front of the TV, setting fire to a Lucky. He's got an hour before he has to fetch his mother. Downtime. Time to chill.

He takes a shiny silver disc from his shirt pocket and feeds it into the DVD player, muting the hiss of audio that erupts from the TV speaker. The screen is black for a few seconds before a time code window pops up, frantically counting away the frames. Then Vernon's watching split-screen footage from the cameras mounted on the deck of Exley's house: the group of whities standing on the beach, the three men, the woman and the child.

The cameras record at six frames a second, so the movement is hectic, super-fast, like a speed-cut music video: black shadows racing across the sand, the clothes of the people flapping like crazy scarecrows in the breeze.

Vernon's connection, Don, the technician at Sniper (a pill-head all hot to add the kid's drowning to his highlights reel of home invasions and car-jackings caught on the Sniper cams), could have slowed the transfer from the hard drive down to real time, but that would have taken too long, so Vernon let him dump it as was.

There's a jump-cut: getting darker now, just Exley and the Australian on the beach, smoking weed. Vernon sits forward when the kid comes zooming off the deck, grabs at her father's shorts, him ignoring her, sucking on his spliff. The kid runs out of frame. But Vernon knows where she's going. Going to get herself dead, is where.

The images stop. Flashes of noise and drop-out. Then they kick in again when the woman triggers the motion detector as she belts out the house, waving her arms. Exley sprints toward the water, leaving the wife and the dope smoker looking on, the woman falling to the ground like something in an old-school comedy. Vernon glugs his Coke, chuckling.

The skinny fucker, dripping, carries the dead kid out of the ocean. She's almost too heavy for him, the little weakling. He dumps her on the sand and gets on top of her, not knowing where the fuck to begin, his panic made all the more hilarious by the fast motion.

Then it comes, the moment Vernon's been waiting for, when he appears in frame and pushes the white man aside and starts breathing into the dead kid. Vernon finds the slo-mo button on the remote, and the DVD advances frame by juddering frame as he breathes and breathes into the dead child, the whities orbiting him like this is some weird religious thing from the Discovery Channel. Suddenly the medics and the cops are there and it is dark and the spotlights kick in, and the whole thing is a fucken Hollywood movie with Vernon Saul as the leading man.

The screen fragments into a rash of static and Vernon rewinds and watches it all again. And again. And it just keeps getting better and better.

He shuttles back and finds the moment when the kid comes up to Nick Exley, to ask him to get her boat from the ocean, and the pathetic white fucker just sucks on his joint and ignores her. Vernon hits pause, the frozen frame rocking on the screen, grainy and blurred, but clear enough to see the child heading toward the water as a stream of white smoke leaves Exley's mouth like a speech bubble.

Vernon reaches for his phone, hits speed dial, and after a few rings he hears Exley's voice.

'Nick, Vernon here.'

'Yes, Vernon?' The man all tense and breathless.

'Just wanted to tell you it's sorted for the morning. I have a pastor lined up.'

'Hell, Vernon, I can never thank you enough.'

'My pleasure, Nick. My pleasure.'

'You'll be there tomorrow? At the funeral?'

'Well, I wouldn't want to intrude.'

'Please, I really would like you to be there.' Pleading. Pathetic.

'Then, of course, Nick. Of course.'

Vernon ends the call.

Oh, I'll be there tomorrow, fucker. Wouldn't miss it for the world.

Vernon drops the phone and drives the remote, finds Exley staggering from the water, dumping the dead kid on the beach. Vernon thumbs the rewind and the kid flies back up into Exley's arms and the whitey reverses his ass into the water. Jabs the play button and here comes Exley again, stumbling out of the sea, and the kid splats wet and dead to the sand.

As he sits watching this demented little loop Vernon cackles like he used to when he watched cartoons as a kid, right here on this sofa, trying to block out his father's voice calling him to the bedroom.

chapter 13

EXLEY SITS IN THE PERMANENT MIDNIGHT OF HIS STUDIO, COMFORTED BY THE familiar hums and clucks of his computer. Cape Town is far away, his mad wife a vapor trail of cigarette smoke upstairs in their bedroom, and his dead daughter is slowly returning to life on the monitor before him, in time for her funeral in the morning.

And it is honest-to-god Sunny staring back at him. A bald Sunny but he'll soon fix that. He accepts that it will be a work-in-progress that he'll present to the mourners tomorrow, but this is the best he can do in the time that he has. He'd like to put her in a party dress, a lacy, frilly thing, the fabric billowing and wafting as she moves, but that is beyond him now, and instead he models a tight-fitting T-shirt and shorts, typical of Sunny and easier to create convincingly.

Now for the hair. He accesses a plug-in that generates hair follicles and a slider allows him to choose the exact length and amount of curl. As he applies dynamics and gets a real-time preview, rotating the model in 3D space, Sunny's hair bounces and flows.

It is so convincing that he finds himself reaching out to touch a curling lock, knowing that he's being an idiot, but laying his hand on the monitor anyway, feeling the hairs on his arm lifting, as if from the force field of Sunny's aura.

It's fucking static, asshole.

And just like that his daughter is dead again and he's staring at nothing but her effigy. Exley, suddenly sick with grief and guilt – in actual, physical pain – pushes himself free of the chair and walks through the silent house, out onto the deck, standing in the gathering gloom, listening to the ocean that took Sunny's life.

The irony that this happened in Cape Town doesn't escape Exley. When he was offered the opportunity to flee the northern winter, come out to Africa and market his mo-cap gadget, he seized it. As a business opportunity, it was a smart move (South Africa has something of a film and TV industry and pulls in foreign movie makers with its climate, beauty and its currency's weakness against the dollar and euro) but it was also a chance for him to bring his family to the closest thing he ever had to a hometown.

Exley's father was an American, a foreign correspondent for the *New York Times*, and his mother is an Anglicized Australian whose womb closed up shop after Exley was born. They had lived in five countries by the time they arrived in Cape Town in the early eighties, his father landing the post to cover South Africa and its neighbors. Apartheid was at its most repressive and international condemnation of the white regime was becoming more vocal.

The Exleys lived for three years in a rambling colonial house in drizzly Newlands, far from the ocean, tucked up against the mountain, near enough to the cricket stadium to hear genteel whoops on game days.

It was the time of the Reagan administration (one of the reasons that Exley's father accepted what many thought of as a hardship post rather than return home) and Tom Exley hated the Gipper with a passion, referring to him exclusively as 'Ronald fucking Reagan.' When seven-year-old Exley, hair shorn, wearing the dumb uniform of his all-white school, was asked by a thin-lipped teacher who the president of the USA was, he blinked at her and blurted out – of course – 'Ronald fucking Reagan.'

Which led to censure and consultations with his parents. His father made all the appropriate noises, but he winked at Exley as they left the school and Exley knew he dined out on the anecdote for months at the Cape Town Press Club.

Two years later his father stepped on a landmine while covering the Angolan civil war and Exley and his mother lived for a while in Australia, with grudging relatives, and then the UK, before his mother found the ashram in New Mexico and Exley was trapped there until he was old enough to bolt. And now his mother doesn't remember him. Wouldn't remember that she'd once had a grandchild.

It's only when the spotlight hits Exley that he realizes he has wandered down onto the beach and triggered the motion detector. The hard light washes the sand where Sunny lay, and when he flashes on Vernon Saul trying to resuscitate her, Exley has to turn away.

As he climbs the steps up onto the deck, he sees the two surveillance cameras roosting like doves in the eaves of the roof and finds himself silently thanking the big rent-a-cop for erasing all evidence of his guilt.

Exley wanders back into the studio, sits and stares blankly at Sunny's face on the monitor, seeing only the artifice and the imperfections.

Rousing himself, he minimizes the animation program and calls up his Facebook page, desperate for some connection with the outside world. He has no notifications or messages, the blank letter-box slit of his status asking him 'what's on your mind?' So he types 'My daughter drowned yesterday. We're burying her tomorrow,' and before he knows what's he's done he's hit the share button and let it go out there to his three thousand and sixty friends, mostly absolute strangers.

He takes off his glasses and massages his eyes, thinking of Vernon Saul, another stranger. But a man who has been more of a friend to him than anybody else in the last day. He wonders how he can thank him.

Exley, suddenly embarrassed by what he has released into the ether, returns his glasses to the bridge of his nose and takes up the mouse, ready to click on the remove button on Facebook, but it is too late: he already has twenty-two notifications. Beth from Lexington says: *My prayers are with you and your family.* Bob from Paris says: *She walks now with the angels.* Kara from Kuala Lumpur says: *I so sorry for you.*

Exley can read no more and kills Facebook. But his BlackBerry, loaded with Facebook and Twitter and all the other social networking apps, blinks endlessly beside the keyboard, taking the toll of the outpouring of meaningless expressions of sympathy.

For Caroline it is as if being off her medication for two days has freed a constriction. She sits cross-legged on the bed, chain-smoking, computer on her lap, a torrent of words spewing from her fingers onto the keyboard. A surge, an expiation, and even if she's not sure precisely what she's writing, she knows that it's better than anything she has written in years.

It is not exactly autobiographical (there are no dead daughters) but there's a frustrated woman writer and a bloodless husband who smells of motherboards and solder and there's a European lover with a past. And it's good and caustic and sexy and funny and bloody clever, actually. Zadie Smith meets Martin Amis, she dares to venture.

When Caroline surfaces from her interior world she has lost all sense of time and realizes that the room is dark, the only light coming from her laptop monitor. She sets fire to another fag and lifts the computer from her lap, her groin warm from its overheated battery. She still works on an ancient Mac, sluggish and probably festering with viruses. Nick keeps offering her the latest thing with all the bells and whistles but she refuses, some silly superstition forcing her to keep the laptop on which she wrote her only notable work. Stupid, she knows, to invest magical properties in a piece of machinery, that kind of hocus-pocus is best left to her geeky husband.

She stretches and walks across to the window, watching the last light fade over the Atlantic down near Sandy Bay, the nudist beach where Vlad likes to take her, striding along with his beak thrust forward and his uncircumcised dick slapping his thighs like a fat kielbasa while she follows in his wake, self-conscious in her naked, freckled skin.

Caroline clicks on the bedside lamp, digs her phone out of the folds of the duvet, sees the flickering message light. The phone has binged all afternoon, like an arcade game. She checks her missed-call list. All from acquaintances, no doubt with clumsy attempts at solace. Nothing from Vlad. She speed-dials his number. Voicemail again.

This time she leaves a message: 'Sunny drowned just after you left yesterday. We are having a service for her on the beach here at home at ten tomorrow morning and I would very much like you to be there.' Sounding like a prissy Home Counties housewife inviting the vicar to tea.

Caroline dumps the phone, clicks off the lamp and lies back on the bed, dropping the cigarette into the cup on the bedside table. She finds that she has pulled down her tights and knickers and her fingers are at play on her inner thighs. She tries, with little success, to pretend they are Vlad's chunky but skilful digits.

She runs the fingertips of her right hand over her thin pubic fuzz, no bikini waxes for her. Her fingers travel south, over her bony mons, and find the lips of her vagina. Ungenerous, was how a very ex lover described her twat. But it is wet and she slides in a finger, trying to take herself toward some kind of pleasure. She has never been a good masturbator, usually becomes distracted and loses interest before she can come. Tonight is no different.

Unbidden, her fingers slide out and creep up her belly until they reach the fault-line of her Cesarean scar, the tissue still a thicker texture than the surrounding skin, and all at once she is overwhelmed again by the reality of Sunny's death, feeling as fragile as when she briefly allowed Nick to embrace her in the kitchen earlier.

This will not do, Caroline. This will not fucking do.

She sits up, switches on the lamp, the walls of the room starting to recede from her, and she knows she's about to tip into a void from which there will be no return. She grabs her computer and massages the touchpad, opening Skype, and almost sobs with relief when she sees that her oldest, dearest friend Julia is online.

Caroline presses the green phone – *doo-dee-doo-dee-doo-dee* – and there is Jules, blinking at her, a cigarette dangling from her lips as she gets herself seated.

'Jesus, Caro! How are you, darling?'

It is a relief to hear somebody who speaks as she does, in a slightly downplayed version of Received Pronunciation, with well-rounded vowels. Out here in South Africa, English is wielded like a blunt weapon.

Jules gushes on. 'Can't talk for long,' she says, 'I've got some Bangladeshis or Afghanistanis downstairs for dinner. Associates of Ollie's. Bloody horrible, misogynistic little jihadists. I just sneaked up here for a fag.' Caroline can see the bookshelves in the background of the room on the top floor of the Georgian mansion in Fitzroy Square. Oliver is something in the City and has made many fortunes. Julia squints at her monitor, frown lines furrowing her brow. 'What's going on, Caro? You look absolutely knackered.'

'Jules,' Caroline says, 'Sunny's dead.'

This catches Julia in mid-inhale and she chokes and coughs. 'Bloody hell, Caroline, what are you saying?'

Caroline tells her, outlining the events of the last day, while Julia stares, the ash on her forgotten cigarette lengthening and dropping into her lap, a moment of frantic swiping, and muttered 'fucks' and 'sorrys.' 'My God, oh my God.' Julia stubs out the cigarette and shakes her head. 'Caro, I'm so sorry…'

'I know.'

'Come home, darling. Promise me that you'll come home.'

Before Caroline can reply, Jules, Julie, Jule-*yah* – dead these last two years of ovarian cancer – disappears from the screen. Biting back a scream, Caroline flings the computer onto the bed and jumps to her feet, wrapping herself in her arms, as if she's trying to contain her racing heart.

This is a bad one, the thing that has her in its grip. Worse than its predecessors.

Frantic, Caroline roots through the mess on the beside table, finds her pills, and is busy popping one of them out of the blister pack when she is gifted with a flashback of her husband last evening on the beach, standing with that Australian fool, pot smoke seeping from his head and, just like that, her terror morphs into a rage that rises in her and cauterizes the pain. Burns away her grief. Burns away any residue of guilt.

Targets the man holed up in his cave below.

Exley, beyond exhausted, slumps at the workstation, unable to shake the fear that what he has built is as crude as a blow-up doll. His face is itchy with stubble and sourness comes in waves from his dirty T-shirt.

Some primitive notion has him in its grip, telling him that if he showers and changes he will erase all that remains of his daughter, as if he holds the last of her on his unwashed skin and soiled clothes.

He shrinks the modeling interface and takes himself back to the source: brings the motion-capture data onto the monitor, looking for a sequence to extract and loop.

His device caught every tiny movement of Sunny's body as she danced, and Exley sits entranced, watching the pure, unmediated essence of his child. The way she moves from a clumsy pirouette to stamping her feet like a squaw – copied from a *Pocahontas* DVD – her pigeon-toed, slightly knock-kneed stance, the Bollywoodesque arm and hand movements, how her chin thrusts forward and her backside juts out to balance her.

He is so transported that he doesn't hear the door slide open, knows only that his wife is in the room when her fist strikes him behind his right ear. She says nothing, her breath coming in rasps, her eyes wild and unfocused.

'Jesus, Caroline, stop!' he says, lifting his arms to protect himself from her flailing limbs.

But his words are useless in the face of her violence. She grabs the computer monitor, trying to hurl it at him, sending a glass flying to the ground where it smashes. Exley stands and gets his arms around her waist, pulling her away from his workstation, dragging her from the room.

Caroline shakes loose from his grip, raking his jaw and neck with her fingernails. She slaps him. He takes her by the shoulders and pushes her backward. Their limbs tangle and they fall to the tiles outside the studio, Caroline thrashing beneath him.

Her knee catches him in the balls and his arms fall open and she is on him, swinging her fists, a blow to his nose bringing tears to his eyes. He grabs her wrists and feels her manic strength as she rips an arm free and punches him in the chest. He gets to his knees and envelops her again, falling on her, somehow pinning her to the tiles.

It is a silent brawl, she's biting and kicking and scratching, but neither of them says a word, the only sound their broken breath. An eavesdropper would swear they were fucking.

Caroline arches her spine and drives her legs upward and it is all Exley can do to stop himself being thrown off her. Then suddenly it is as if a plug has been pulled and all the manic energy drains from her and she lies still, her breath coming in rasps.

'Let go of me,' she says, her voice flat with exhaustion.

He waits a moment to check that this isn't a ruse, but Caroline is spent and he rolls off her, sitting with his hands wrapped around his legs, staring at her as she lifts herself to her knees, brushing her hair away from her face.

'Are you taking your medication?' he asks, breathless, his heart hammering.

'What do you think?'

'I think you're not,' he says. 'And you know you should. Especially now. You're taking a lot of strain.'

She stands. 'Oh, drop the euphemisms, Nicholas. Go ahead and say it. Say the word you've so carefully avoided all these bloody years.'

He gets to his feet, still wary. 'Caroline…'

'Fine, then I'll say it: mad. I'm totally out of my fucking mind, aren't I, Nick?'

'Please, go upstairs and take you medication.'

She ignores him. 'Okay, maybe I am mad. But, by God, who is sitting in a darkened room trying to breathe life into our dead daughter?'

DAWN SEES A COP VAN AND AN UNMARKED WHITE TOYOTA REFLECTING THE titty bar neon in their windshields as she crosses Voortrekker, the wind like a hot hand pushing against her. She stands on the center line waiting for a gap in the traffic, hair blowing into her eyes, still half upstairs with Brittany in the old Portuguese lady's apartment (ugly wooden furniture and stained doilies and dusty crucifixes and the stink of soup brewed from offal), Mrs de Pontes bitching that she wants more money to babysit and Dawn peeling notes she can't afford from the skinny roll in her purse.

But Brittany, God alone knows why, likes the Porra woman and the old bitch keeps her place locked up tight against the tide of brown and black people who've muddied up this once white area. She and the other whities scuttling like roaches once a day for supplies, muttering their way along in little groups, clutching their purses, lost in a sea of dark faces shouting and bartering and arguing in Cape Flats Afrikaans and African tongues from here and up north.

A taxi rattles by, the driver half out his window to see Dawn's ass, and she gives him the finger and takes a gap and makes it to the other side serenaded by car horns. Passes the police vehicles and heads for the doorway of Lips, reckons they're here to shake Costa down again, these cops. But a uniform – pimply thing with a smear of mustache – blocks her at the door and asks her if she knows Glenville Faro.

'Who the fuck's Glenville Faro?' Dawn says, dodging him and getting inside the near-empty club, out of the wind.

'Boogie. He means Boogie.' This from one of the Ugly Sisters, the fat one, leaning against the bar, her tits making a break for freedom from the top of her dress, the young cop all eyes and yo-yoing Adam's apple.

Dawn sees Costa and a plainclothes – chunky brown guy – near the ramp and knows this is some other shit going down.

'What's Boogie done now?' Dawn asks, putting her bag on the bar top, nodding to Cliffie the barman.

'Gone and got his stupid brains beat out,' Cliffie says, sliding a can of Coke across to her, like he does every night.

'Dead?'

'Ja.'

Dawn cracks the tab and hears a mutter of fizz, catches a few cool little bubbles on her fingers. Drinks from the can, that metal taste on her tongue, the syrup only making her more thirsty as it goes down her throat, but the caffeine giving her a little kick.

'Where this happen?' Hiding a burp behind her hand, all ladylike.

Cliffie jerks his head toward the street. 'Construction site.'

The plainclothes cop comes over, an ugly fucker with nostrils like shotgun barrels. He adjusts the hang of his balls while he window-shops her rack. 'You work here?'

'Ja.'

'What's your name?'

'Angel.'

'And I'm Winnie fucken Mandela.' He gives her a smirk. 'When last you seen Glenville Faro?'

'You mean Boogie?'

'Ja, whatever. When you seen him?'

'Last night. Early hours.'

'Where?'

'The street.'

'Who's he with?'

'He come out with us, me and Cliffie and Sylvia and them.' Flicks a finger in the direction of the Ugly Sisters; the skinny one's come in the door now, standing with her friend, voices shrill as parakeets as they talk up the drama.

'And then?' the cop says, weighing his nuts again.

'Then nothing. I walk across the road to where I live.'

'Anybody else there?'

'Ja, him,' she says, nodding toward Vernon, who appears in the doorway, checking out the scene. Vernon's looking at her now and suddenly Dawn knows just what went down with Boogie and why, and she feels sick as she asks, 'Can I go get ready?'

'Ja, go,' the cop says. 'Maybe I get me a front-row seat for the show, so make sure your thing don't stink.'

'Like your mother's, you mean?' Dawn says, and he looks like he's going to smack her, but he just flushes and clenches his fists and she empties the can down her neck and takes her bag and heads for the dressing room, feeling Vernon's eyes on her, an icy little chill in her gut that's got nothing to do with the cold Coke.

The cop, name of Dino Erasmus – Vernon remembers him from Bellwood South headquarters – goes red under his muddy skin, Dawn giving him lip. Good at that, the little bitch, walking away now, swinging her ass.

Vernon gets himself up to the bar, slides in beside the plainclothes. 'So, Dino, what's the fucken story?'

The detective lights a smoke to give himself a moment, shaking the match dead and flicking it onto the floor, exhaling twin vapor trails through that snout of his. 'Vernon Saul. Thought you were a security guard but here you are babysitting pussy.'

Vernon knows he mustn't get on the wrong side of this bastard, even finds something resembling a smile, showing off his nice white teeth. 'I'm in armed response, Llandudno side. Work here some nights. What else can a man do with our excuse for a pension?'

'The shit you made, you lucky you even get a pension.'

Vernon fixes his smile in place. 'Come on, Dino, nobody got nothing on me.'

Erasmus sniffs through his double-barrels, scanning the almost deserted club. The cop van outside scaring away the early punters, who are timid anyway – desperate and furtive and not yet filled with booze and come-lust.

'What you know about this little piece of shit Faro?'

Vernon shrugs. 'He used to deal to some of the girls. Small-time.'

'He ever hassle you?'

Vernon laughs. 'Me? He wouldn't try.'

'So when last you see him?'

'When we closed, round three. He was walking down to his car. I went the other way, to where I park back of the club.'

'That's it?'

'That's it.' Vernon leans in closer to Erasmus. 'Dino, why you on this anyway? Who cares about that useless little fuck?'

Erasmus shakes his head. 'Man, whoever sorted out Faro did the world a flipping favor but I wish to Christ he done it across the railway line. This side we got some whitey local politician making a noise about community policing and all that bloody bullshit, so now SI gotta do window dressing.'

This knocks the gleam off Vernon's smile. Special Investigations is a new outfit, supposedly incorruptible, formed to clean up the image of the cops. 'Since when you with SI?'

Erasmus shrugs. 'Few weeks.'

Means he's still on probation. Way it works at SI. Means this dumb cocksucker is gonna be all hot and sticky to prove he's worth the bump in pay if he goes permanent. Vernon doesn't like this. Not one fucken bit.

Costa, looking harassed, dims the lights and cues the DJ. Loud bass pumps out, distorting through the crap sound system, Costa too cheap to upgrade, and Dawn's coming through the curtains, in her jeans and white shirt, not even looking at the handful of men who sit around the ramp. In her own little world, that one. Same to her if it's ten losers or ten thousand. She stares into space, moving her ass, shedding her shirt and bra.

Erasmus is all eyes. 'What's her name, that thing?' Leaning in close, shouting into Vernon's ear, breath heavy with KFC and cigarettes.

'Dawn.'

'You fix me up with her in one of the rooms?'

Vernon shakes his head. 'She don't do that.'

'Why not? She think she something special, her with that bushman hair?'

Vernon shrugs. 'She just don't do it.'

Dawn loses the jeans and has her thumbs hooked into the waist of her panties, sliding them down far enough to show some pussy fur. Even with the racket of the music, Vernon can hear the wheeze of Erasmus's breath. Then the plainclothes clears his throat and reaches into his pocket and hauls out his flashing cell phone, covers one ear, and shouts something into it.

'Got to go,' he says, and grabs the uniformed cop by the collar of his shirt and walks him to the door, the pimply kid almost breaking his neck to look back as Dawn steps out of her panties.

Vernon limps up to the ramp and sits in the front row, massaging his bad leg that's paining like a fucker, watching Dawn dance, her eyes closed, unaware of his presence, moving her bare naked body in time to some sticky R&B. She kneels and bends backward, her thick corkscrew curls brushing the ramp.

Her box is level with Vernon's face, and if he leaned forward he could bite the clit peeping at him like a little pink tongue through the concertina folds of cunt meat. Means nothing to him. Zero. But when Dawn lifts her head up from the floor and her eyelids flicker open and she stares straight at him and he sees the terror in her eyes, now that's when he's turned on.

chapter 15

IT IS VERY LATE — CLOSER TO DAYBREAK THAN TO MIDNIGHT — AND EXLEY, RIDING the wave of adrenaline the battle with Caroline pumped into him, has completed the model of his daughter. He takes Sunny out of the modeling environment and is ready to animate her, ready to marry her body to a sixty-second segment he extracted from the data stream of her dancing.

This is what Caroline calls his Victor Frankenstein moment: when he breathes life into his monstrosities. Or she called it that back before Sunny was born, when she was interested enough to stand at the computer, staring over his shoulder, her cigarette smoke irritating his nostrils.

Exley presses the render button and watches the progress bar at the bottom of his monitor creep from empty to full. But he pauses before he hits the spacebar to trigger playback.

He can't bring himself to watch what he has brought into being. Not yet. Terrified that he's created a travesty of Sunny, which would be like a double death.

He pushes his chair away from the console and stands, taking a few seconds to come upright. His lower back aches, his shoulders are locked and he feels a twinge of carpal tunnel in the joint of his right thumb. When he takes off his glasses and massages his eyes it's as if he's rubbing broken glass into his corneas.

Exley slides his glasses back on and steps out of his studio, standing for a moment in the darkness of the living room. The house is silent. Caroline must be asleep.

He opens the door to the deck and crosses to the railing, looking out at the moon hanging low and heavy over the ocean, feeling a gauzy vapor of sea air on his face, the stink of rotting kelp thick in his nostrils.

The water hisses and sucks, small waves slapping the sand where Sunny lay dead. He walks through to the dark kitchen and opens the refrigerator. There is only one bottle of Evian left and he reminds himself to call the liquor store in the morning, get them to deliver water and beer and wine. For whoever shows up for the funeral.

Exley released a flock of text messages earlier, to all of his acquaintances in the city and the parents of Sunny's playmates. The replies are lost in the barrage he encouraged with his dumb Facebook post.

He stands in the kitchen and drinks, pours Evian into the palm of his hand and wipes his face and rubs some of the water into his hair, drops falling onto his glasses like rain on a windshield. He uses a washcloth to clean his glasses and then he knows he can delay no more, so he heads back to the studio, sits down, his hand hovering over the smeared spacebar. He closes his eyes, mumbles something that may be a prayer.

Then he hits playback.

And there she is, Sunny, dancing, lifting her arms, twirling, her hair floating away from her smiling face. She is perfect and he allows himself to cry for the first time since he saw her lying dead on the beach.

chapter 16

D AWN BRUSHES BRITTANY'S HAIR. IT'S EARLY MORNING AND AS ALWAYS SHE HASN'T
had enough sleep. Still got to get the kid to play school, little group
of mainly white kids, Brittany looking like them but speaking different –
although Dawn has noticed this is changing as she spends more time with
the whities. A good thing? Shit, maybe. Why should Dawn feel anything
for the Cape Flats? Never gave her nothing but heartache and grief.

'Mommy?'

'Ja?'

'Is Mommy going to marry Uncle Vermin?'

'Jesus, what makes you say a thing like that?' Dawn snags a knot in
the kid's pale hair and her daughter yelps. 'Sorry, man. No, my baby, I'm
not going to marry Uncle Vernon.'

'Then why he come on here all the time?'

'He looks after us.' The lie sticks in her throat.

'Why then Mommy don't marry him?'

'God, what's with all the bloody questions?' Dawn finishes brushing
and stands. 'Go pee now so I can get you down to the taxi.'

Brittany rushes off to the bathroom and Dawn takes jeans and a
spaghetti-strap top from the closet, but before she can dress there's a
knock at the door. Too loud for Mrs de Pontes. Not loud enough for
Vernon. Must be the bloody landlord hassling her for the rent money.
Landlord's an old Greek guy – buddy of Costa's – and he always gives
Dawn the eye, so she runs a hand through her matted hair and pulls
down the T-shirt she wears over her nakedness, making herself look a
bit more decent.

But when she opens the door it's not the old Greek, it's the cop from last
night. The one with the nostrils and the balls that need constant adjusting.

'Ja?'

'Let me in,' Erasmus says.

'Why for?'

'I need to ask you a few questions.'

'So ask.'

'You want your neighbors to hear?'

'I got no secrets.'

But she steps back and the cop comes in, looking around with a sour expression.

'Nice,' he says. Meaning *shit.*

'And where the fuck you live? Beverly Hills?'

'Quite a mouth you got on you.' Cups that package. 'Maybe I fill it with something.'

Dawn stares at his groin. 'I take that in and I still got space for my breakfast.' She smiles as she sees him color and grabs a smoke from the top of the TV and lights it. 'So talk.'

His eyes flick away from her tits as Brittany comes in from the bathroom, looking up at the cop, saying nothing, just staring the way she does.

'And where you get that?' Erasmus asks. Dawn doesn't answer. 'Social services know you sell your ass?'

'I don't sell my ass.'

'What? You give it away for free?'

He laughs, but this is uncomfortable for her. She doesn't need no cop digging into her life. Brittany is watching them, understanding too much.

'Britt, go brush your teeth.'

'I already brush them.'

'Then brush them again. Go!'

Grumbling, the child returns to the bathroom and Dawn closes the door.

'So, what you want, Detective?' Putting some nice into her voice.

'The Boogie story. Something I got to ask you.'

'What?'

'Vernon Saul. Him and Boogie have any issues?'

'Like what?'

Uninvited he sits down on the sofa, and Dawn sits opposite him, making sure her T-shirt covers her snatch. Doesn't stop Erasmus taking in the view like a tourist.

The cop shrugs. 'You know Vernon. I hear Boogie was selling shit at the club?'

'I wouldn't know.'

'Maybe Vernon wanted some of the action?'

'Told you, I don't know fuck-all about that.'

But she's sensing something here. Some messy cop business. Boogie was a nothing, wouldn't warrant this kind of attention from the law. This cop doesn't like Vernon. She guesses that it's an old grudge, that he would like to take Vernon Saul down if he could.

And Dawn's back on the street the night Boogie got himself dead, crossing Voortrekker, about to let the lobby of her building swallow her up, when something makes her look behind her and she sees Vernon catch up with Boogie, putting a heavy arm around his shoulders. Then she's in the building and she sees no more.

'What?' the cop asks, smelling something, his nostrils flaring so wide she swears she can see his brains.

For a moment she almost tells him, thinking how fucken good her life would be with no Vernon Saul in it. But she knows the risk is just too great and she shakes her head.

'Nothing. I got nothing more to tell you.'

'What's your relationship with Vernon?'

'We don't got a *relationship*.'

He nods. Looks around, then back at her. 'Gonna offer me some coffee?'

'Can't. Gotta get my kid to play school.'

The cop stands, grunts, adjusts the hang of those balls. He takes a card from his jacket and drops it on the table next to the dirty mugs and the overflowing ashtray.

'You remember anything, don't care what, you call me, understand?'

'Sure.'

'Okay, then.' He takes a last look at her ass and then he walks to the door. 'Be good now.'

'You too.'

He laughs and he's gone, leaving a whiff of armpits and cheap aftershave.

Yvonne Saul hardly slept. The pathetic wailing of the child in the shack next to her – so close she could reach out her bedroom window, across the low Vibracrete wall, and touch the peeling wood of the hut – kept her awake again most of the night. She can still hear it, softer, though, here in the kitchen, as she stirs scrambled eggs, bacon already spitting in the pan. Preparing Vernon's favorite breakfast. She hears him thumping around in his room and wonders what sort of mood he'll be in today.

He limps in, dressed only in his underpants, his hair standing up in spikes. He doesn't greet her, just sits down at the plastic kitchen table, that thin, scarred leg thrown out to the side. It's withering away, the muscles going slack. He's meant to do exercises to build it up but she knows he can't be bothered and doesn't dare to speak to him about it.

Yvonne dumps half a can of baked beans onto the plate and serves him. He holds his fork in his right hand, hunched over the table, feeding his face without so much as a word of thanks. She takes her place opposite him. No breakfast for her, a cup of black tea is all she can keep down in the morning.

The crying continues, she can count each sob as the poor little creature fights for breath. 'You hear that?' she says before she can stop herself.

'Little brat needs a hiding.'

'Vernon, people saying things about them in that shack.'

He doesn't look at her, shoveling egg into his mouth. 'What things?'

'Mrs Flanagan—'

'That fucken big-mouth bitch?'

'She say the man is abusing the child.'

He laughs a yellow spray of egg. 'True's God?'

'Ja.'

Now he's staring at her, his fork clattering onto his plate. 'And suddenly you give a shit? When it's happening to somebody else's kid?'

'Vernon, God only knows how sorry I am—'

'Sorry? Sorry means fuck-all.'

His dark little eyes – spitting image of his father's – burn with hatred and she is afraid that he's going to reach across and hit her. She stands and hurries across to the sink, busies herself washing the pot and pan, the bacon fat floating on top of the muddy water.

She sneaks a glance at Vernon. He has pushed his plate away, his breakfast unfinished, and he sits with his elbows on the table, his huge shoulders slumped, his hair falling across his face, and she feels a sudden terrible pity for him, this wounded thing that is her son.

Yvonne dries her hands on a washcloth and edges past the table, wanting to slip away from the tiny kitchen. She was going to ask him about her insulin but she can't bring herself to mention it now. Vernon grabs a handful of her pink chenille nightgown.

'That old fucker I seen you with at church last night, who's he?'

'Nobody.'

He yanks at the nightgown and the fabric rips and the front falls open and half of a sagging breast is exposed. Shamed, she tries to close the nightgown but he tugs all the harder, and she has to fold her arms across her breasts.

'Tell me his name.'

'Mr Tobias.'

'You not getting fucken ideas in your head, are you?'

'No, boy. Never.'

He pulls her down so her face is near his and shoves his fork at her, the tines denting her cheek. 'I'm fucken watching you.'

He drops the fork and pushes his chair back and bumps past her, going into his bedroom and slamming the door.

Yvonne, feeling like she is going to faint, sags down into a chair, resting her head in her hands, fighting back tears. And she hears that crying again, sawing through her head, enough to drive her mental.

chapter 17

THE AUBERGINE-COLORED PREACHER SOUNDS LIKE HE'S COMMENTATING ON A horse race with his mouth full of marbles, and it takes Caroline a while to realize he's speaking English, or what passes for English out here. She catches a few words: *young life cut short, in the arms of Jesus, merciful God*, and then tunes out. Her eyes lift from the man's sweaty face – rivulets of water running down his flat cheekbones, tracing the bulges of his many chins and pooling around his shirt collar – and she stares out over the channel of blue ocean at the bird shit on the rocks beyond, like icing on a stale cake.

She wears a sunhat and dark glasses, a simple white cotton dress and Indian sandals. Her feet sink into the molten beach sand and she has to keep shifting them to stop her exposed toes from burning.

Caroline looks back, as she has done every few minutes since this absurd charade began, looks over her right shoulder – even though this means passing her eyes over her husband, to whom she hasn't said a word since their set-to last night. If she looked to her left she would avoid him, but then she'd see the little white coffin that lies on a flower-strewn bier under a striped shade-tent, the type of thing found at a tacky sidewalk flea market.

The upper panel of the coffin is open. Caroline allowed herself one glance, earlier, before hurriedly looking away. Just long enough to see that Sunny's hair has been blow-dried almost straight and her face painted like that of a Mexican child whore.

Caroline knows that if she looks at the coffin again she will come undone. So her eyes skid across Exley – he stares down at the sand, his face pale beneath his tan, a small square of toilet paper, hard with dried blood, glued to his left mandible – and travel over the sad little group that has assembled: Gladys the maid, rock-like in the blazing sun, dressed in black from head to toe. A blonde woman, the mother of one of Sunny's playgroup friends, trying vainly to find shade near the deck, sneaking a look at her watch. The sallow undertaker, his worn suit so shiny he could be in a glitter band, standing with his hands clasped before him in the manner of a professional mourner. The rent-a-cop brings up the rear, bullish shoulders barely contained by a fake leather jacket, sunlight dancing on the frames of his sunglasses, shifting his weight from the leg that is visibly skinnier than the other.

A movement catches Caroline's eye and for a moment she feels a rush of hope but it is only Shane Porter slinking in, wearing a jacket over jeans and a T-shirt, like some aging rock star, his cowboy boots sinking low into the sand.

Nobody else from Saturday's soirée has pitched up: funerals are obviously way less popular than boozy parties.

And no Vlad.

I'm not fun, now, Caroline thinks. I'm trouble. Too much trouble for him.

She looks forward again, in time to see the buffoonish cleric – just where the fuck did Nick find him? – close his eyes and lift his arms heavenward, beseeching 'Jay-sus' in an ever more incomprehensible gabble. Maybe he's speaking in tongues? Then she catches the name Jane, repeated over and over, bobbing to the surface of the sea of clogged vowels, and this very nearly shatters her composure.

Their child's name was Jane Exley. But Nick, from the day the infant came home from the hospital, started calling her Sunshine, and then Sunny, cooing at her in the crib, wiggling his fingers at her. Making her smile and giggle.

Caroline feels her throat tighten and fixes her gaze again on the rocks, watching the birds hovering and lifting off and jostling one another, trying to dodge the tendrils of emotion that reach their suckers out toward her.

Caroline's sense of smell, acute as always when she is off her medication, catches something foul drifting in from under the shade-tent to her left. Just the flowers in the hideous wreath, she tells herself, but she is unable to stop imagining that it is Sunny's body rotting.

But of course they must have done something to her, some barbaric embalming. All at once her mind is alive with images of her child lying naked on a steel table, being eviscerated, her innards lifted from her and thrown into a bucket, her blood sluiced away by a savage in gumboots.

Caroline must have reacted to the horror of this image, allowed a groan to escape her lips, because Nicholas tries to take her hand, his fingers cold and clammy on her skin. She pulls her hand free and folds her arms and goes so very, very far away that she barely registers when her husband stands beside the dark charlatan and fumbles and stumbles his way through what he imagines is a eulogy.

'Sunny, I love you with all my heart and I always will. The thought of you gone is more than I can comprehend. I keep wanting to say, come back. Come back to me.'

Nicholas sheds the only tears and then it is over. The undertaker is joined by two flunkies and they screw the faceplate of the coffin in place and wheel Sunny away and collapse the shade-tent into lengths of pipe and rolls of cloth. Caroline watches the little white coffin disappear around the corner of the house, on its way to being burned. Sunny will turn to smoke and float up into the sky in some mean, industrial part of the city.

Nick shakes hands with the preacher (she glimpses the palming of banknotes) and the fat man labors off after the undertakers. A shadow falls onto Caroline and she smells last night's booze as Shane Porter mumbles some Antipodean platitude in her ear.

'Shane?' she says.

'Yes, love?'

'Eat shit and die.'

He stares at her, mouth gaping open on capped white teeth, and she turns and heads toward the house.

As she gets closer she hears the twang of an acoustic guitar and a frayed American voice whines out at her about his daughter in the water. The old Loudon Wainwright song that Exley used to sing – wildly off-key – to Sunny, splashing with her in the sea, while Caroline watched from the cool sanctuary of the house.

She crosses the deck and sees that her husband is having his moment. That he has unveiled to the uncomfortable group of would-be mourners what he has been slaving away on since Sunny died, locked away in his studio.

A giant plasma TV is suspended above the table of drinks and crisps and nuts, and Sunny dances on the screen, radiant against an infinity curve graded from white to blue. A more alive Sunny than the thing she glimpsed in the coffin, Caroline has to concede.

Then she gets closer and understands just what grotesqueness her husband has wrought. It is realistic, of course. He is skilled, her boy-man. But it is not real. She sees in the face of this computer-generated effigy something unhealthy and unappealing that disturbs her on a primal level. A knowingness in the eyes of this faux-Sunny, something wanton, almost lascivious in the curl of the lips. Caroline's instinct is to recoil.

If she feels a rush of revulsion she is not alone. The soccer mom mutters some blandishment and bolts for the door, her absurd heels drumming her off the Good Ship Exley. Gladys quickly busies herself ferrying in cups of tea from the kitchen. Shane Porter takes refuge in a glass of wine. Only the rent-a-cop stares at the screen, transfixed.

'Sir?' he says to Exley.

'Nick,' Exley says.

'Nick. This,' pointing a blunt brown finger at the screen, 'this isn't no video, right?'

'No. It's computer animation.'

'Like *Avatar*, kinda?'

'Something like that.'

'And you done it?'

'Yes, Vernon, I did.'

'It's beautiful. Beautiful.' Coming out as *bewdie-fool* in his strangled accent.

Caroline can take no more of this and she heads for the stairs, rushes into the bedroom and slams the door, suddenly needing to pee so badly that she can feel drops escaping into her knickers. She grabs her phone on her way into the lavatory, lifts her dress and squats, speed-dialing as she drills a noisy stream into the toilet bowl.

Vlad's voicemail again. The vitality drains from her body and it is all she can do to wipe herself dry and drag herself to the bed where she falls face down and allows sleep to take her.

chapter 18

EXLEY FEELS BARELY TETHERED, LIKE A HELIUM BALLOON THAT THE SLIGHTEST gust could lift and set on a course for the sun that pummels the house. He stands with Vernon Saul and Shane Porter. The dark man sips noisily from a teacup, his eyes on the monitor.

Port inhales a glass of white wine. 'Jesus, Ex, I can't imagine how you feel, mate. I've hardly got any shut-eye since the night when... Since that night.'

'It's been hell, Port. The reality still hasn't hit home yet,' Exley says, longing for a Scotch but reaching for a safer option, a beer.

'I wish there was something I could've done, you know, to help. But I'm an Outback boy, always been a crap swimmer.'

'There was nothing anybody could have done. Not even Vernon.' Exley points his beer bottle at Vernon Saul, who can't drag his eyes from the dancing Sunny.

'Yeah, he was a Trojan.' Porter empties the wineglass and Exley takes it from him.

'Can I fill you up?'

'Against my religion to refuse a drink, mate, but I've got to get moving. Some business in the city.' He shakes Exley's hand. 'If there's anything I can do, Ex, all you have to do is shout.'

'Thanks, Port. I appreciate it.'

Porter slaps him on the shoulder, nods to Vernon, and heads off into the brightness of the day. Gladys is in the kitchen, washing up. Caroline is in hiding upstairs and Exley is alone with Vernon. This big man in his cheap jacket, check shirt and tie looks like a plainclothes cop but Exley is pleased that he's there. Something about Vernon Saul reassures him.

The brown man speaks without taking his eyes from the screen. 'Could you do me, like this? In the computer?'

'I guess. It's a lot of work, of course.'

'I understand. I understand.'

Exley lifts another Grolsch from the table and pops the cap. 'Would you like a drink, Vernon?'

'No, thank you.'

'You're not on duty?'

'No, I'm pulling the nightshift.'

'Then have a drink with me. Keep me company.'

'Okay. I'll take a beer.'

Exley hands him the bottle and leads the way out onto the deck, sitting down at the table in the shade. Vernon takes the chair opposite him and lifts the beer in salute. 'Better days.' He chugs from the bottle, then inspects the label. 'This is imported, right?'

'Yes.'

'Nice.'

Exley drinks and feels the alcohol go straight to his head. He has to concentrate not to spin off into some interior monologue and focuses on Vernon's broad face, watching him drink.

They sit in awkward silence for a moment. Then Exley's cell phone rings inside and he stands. 'Excuse me.' He walks into the house.

Vernon swigs from the bottle. Too sweet for him. He's not much of a beer man and he's used to South African brew with its bitter, chemical taste. Still, it's good to park here on this deck, watching the ocean, drinking expensive booze.

Not a life he desires. No, not for him this fancy shit, but he'd like to develop his relationship with Nick Exley – finesse it – so that he can drop in like a friend, have a drink and a chat. That would be nice.

He's used to controlling people out on the Flats. People made vulnerable by poverty. Or people desperate to avoid punishment for their crimes. Too easy. But this is something he's always dreamed of: exerting power over a rich man. A man who wears his wealth like a suit of armor. And Vernon has broken through that armor.

Exley returns, looking pale, his eyes red behind his glasses. As the sun catches the whitey's face, Vernon sees livid tracks down one side of his neck. Scratch marks. Wonders what hell this pathetic bastard has been living through these last days. Almost feels sorry for him.

'You okay, Nick?'

'Yes, sure. People from overseas. Condolences, you know?'

'Of course. A trying time.' Vernon nods, sips. 'So, what are your plans?'

'I expect we'll pack up and leave, as soon as possible.'

'But you don't want to?'

Exley looks at him in surprise. 'No, I don't suppose I do. I'm not really sure why.'

Vernon uses the neck of his beer bottle to describe an arc, taking in the house and the beach. 'This place, of course, is full of bad memories. But it's also the last place you saw your little girl alive. Maybe you want to hang on to that?'

Exley nods, his hair flopping down over his forehead like a kid's. He pushes it away with a skinny hand. 'Yeah, yeah. That's it exactly. Is that weird?'

'No, no. Not to me.' Vernon settles back, finding a groove here. 'Nick, there are two schools of thought.' Where did he get this smooth bullshit? 'One is to get away and forget. The other is to feel your pain and work through it, travel a journey, sort of. In my experience, the second is better.'

'And what's your experience?'

'I was a cop for twelve years. I seen a helluva lot of grief.'

Exley drinks, nods. 'Your leg? That end your career?'

'Ja.'

'I don't mean to pry—'

'No, no. It's cool.'

'What happened?'

Vernon wipes his mouth with the back of his hand, stifling a burp. 'I was a detective, out on the Cape Flats. You know about the Flats?'

'Not much. But I hear it's a dangerous place.'

'More dangerous than a bloody war zone, I'm telling you, Nick. Gangs. People crazy on *tik* – what you call meth. Not just the young-sters, neither. Grandmas vacuuming their houses half out of their minds. A place where you gotta watch your back. Serious.'

'I've seen the crime stats on TV.'

'Under-reported, believe me. And I dunno if you heard, but there's this child abuse epidemic out there on the Flats? Bad shit you won't believe, excuse my French. Anyways, about a year ago I get a call that a piece of rubbish is raping his toddler daughter.'

The white man flinches and Vernon struggles not to laugh. Shit, he should be a bloody writer.

'I go over to the house and the bastard's locked in the bedroom with the kid, so I kick in the door and the fucker's got a gun and he plugs me four times, leg and chest. Before I go down, I take him out. Permanent.'

Exley stares, wide eyed.

'Next thing I'm lying on stomach and I'm looking at my blood soaking into the carpet and everything goes all quiet and dark. And then...' Vernon pauses to drink, milking the moment. 'Then, honest to God, Nick, I go into this light. A big, bright, shining light. And it's beautiful. Beautiful. And I know if I just keep on going into the light, I'll be in a better place than anywhere I ever been before. But, Nick, you know what?'

'What?' Exley asks, sitting forward in his chair.

'I say to myself: Vernon, it's not your time, my brother. So I turn my back on that light and head into the darkness, and I wake up in hospital next day full of bullet holes and me not a cop no more.' He shrugs. 'That's it.'

Exley shakes his head.

'You don't believe me?' Vernon asks.

'No, no, I do. I believe you.'

Vernon shrugs, manufactures a bashful look. 'Ja, that experience changed me. I used to be a pretty hard bugger, you know? But now, I dunno, I'm just a bloody softie.' Laughing quietly, like he's embarrassed.

Exley checks him out. 'Vernon, I really appreciate all you did the other evening.'

'I wish I could have done more.'

'You've been a true friend. I mean it.'

The whitey chokes up and there's an awkward moment and then he stands and in a sobby little voice says he'll get them more beer and ducks into the house.

Vernon sits, relaxed as all hell, well satisfied with his performance. He's got Exley now, reeled him in. But exactly what he's going to do with him, Vernon isn't sure. He drinks and stares out over the ocean. Let it play out, my brother. Just let it play out.

When Exley gets to the living room he finds that Gladys has cleared away the drinks, so he walks through to the kitchen. The bulky woman stands at the sink with her back to him, hands lost in soapy water.

'Mr Nick?' she says.

'Yes?' Exley replies, lifting two green bottles from the fridge.

'That thing you are making of Sunny...' She stops, setting a glass in the drying rack.

Exley crosses to her, staring at her profile. She doesn't look at him. 'What's wrong, Gladys?'

'That thing you are making, it is very bad luck.' She stops again, scrubbing at a plate, and Exley feels a stab of irritation.

'Bad luck how, Gladys?'

'It is like you are trying to bring her back.'

Exley colors. 'Come on, that's crazy.'

She looks at him now, clasping her hands, soapy water dripping from her fingers. 'Some of my people are doing such things. They are using photos or clothes of the dead who have just passed. Taking them to the sangoma, the witchdoctor, to use for muti. Witchcraft. Very bad, Mr Nick. Very bad. It is keeping her here, Sunny, not letting her go.'

Exley can find nothing to say. She's right. That's what he's doing. Behaving like a primitive. Trying to bring his daughter back.

Exley turns away from Gladys and retreats out onto the deck to where Vernon Saul sits staring over the ocean, his awkward bulk barely contained by the chair, his wounded leg thrown out to the side. The big man sneaks a look at his wristwatch. Suddenly Exley doesn't want him to go, doesn't want to be left in the house with these two disapproving women.

Exley dredges up a smile. 'Hey, Vernon, were you serious about me animating you?'

The dark guy nods. 'Ja, man. It would give me one hell of a kick.'

'Okay, come on, then.'

'What? Now?'

'Yeah. We can do the first part. The motion-capture. Bring your beer.'

Exley leads the way into the chill of the studio and fires up the workstation.

Vernon looks around, taking in the computer gear and the monitors, and lets out a low whistle. 'So, Nick,' he says, 'this is where you make your magic?'

'Yep. This is the place.'

'State of the art, hey?'

Exley shrugs, opening the steel cabinet where a few mo-cap suits hang, and selects the largest one. He holds it out to Vernon. 'Here. Strip down to your underwear and put this on.'

Exley sits at the computer, booting up the motion-capture software, his back to Vernon, hearing zippers and grunts, smelling overheated flesh.

At last Vernon says, 'Done,' and Exley turns, seeing for the first time how big this man is. The tight material stretched across his barrel chest, his shoulders square and wide, his good leg thick and muscled. The runt at its side has withered away to half its size.

Exley opens the studio's sliding door and beckons. Vernon lumbers through onto the tiles, moving awkwardly in the tight suit, his limp even more pronounced.

'So, how's this work?' he asks.

'Those sensors on the suit translate your movements into digital impulses and send them to the computer.'

'Okay,' Vernon says, blank. 'And what do I do?'

'Anything you want,' Exley says. 'I'm capturing you right now.'

Vernon walks, looking awkward, dragging his weak leg. Then he loosens up and pretends to draw a gun, bending his knees, doing a James Bond thing. He beats his chest like an ape. Sails into a waltz with an invisible partner.

Exley is amazed to hear himself laughing. The big man joins in. 'So, how's that?'

Exley says, 'I think we've got it, Vernon,' and he stops the capture.

He wheels another chair to the computer and gestures for Vernon to sit. He selects the segment of Vernon drawing the weapon and marries it to a 3D skeleton, the wireframe's movements a perfect replica of the rent-a-cop's.

Vernon sits, entranced, his breath coming in snorts. 'Fucken amazing, Nick. Awesome. How did you learn to work all this stuff?'

'Well, I designed the system.'

'You telling me you made this machine yourself?'

'Yes,' Exley says.

'Jesus, you're a fucken genius.'

'Nah, just a little gimmick.' He crosses to the steel cabinet and removes a plain brown cardboard box, one foot square in size. No fancy branding, no adornment, just the words LIFE IN A BOX stenciled on the top. He opens the box and tilts it so Vernon can look inside, showing him the small metal-cased driver unit that jacks into a computer and the mesh of low-cost sensors that transmit the data.

'I built this thing so anybody can do motion-capture. There's no magic to it, believe me.'

Vernon waves this away. 'No, no. Don't come with that.' Watching the figure on the monitor. 'So, what's it like, sitting here playing God?'

Exley shakes his head. 'If only.'

Vernon looks embarrassed, hesitates. 'Nick?'

'Yeah?'

'You gonna make some kinda model of me, have me walking and stuff?'

'Yes, over the next while.'

'Can you fix my leg? Make me, like, normal again?'

Exley stares into Vernon's eyes and reaches out a hand and puts it on his shoulder. 'Sure, I can do that for you. No sweat, my friend.'

Caroline's mobile startles her awake. She battles to open her eyes and when she tries to move her limbs she feels as if she's swimming through treacle. As her fingers fumble for the phone, doing its little dervish dance on the dresser beside the bed, it falls mute. Caroline checks her missed-call list and when she sees *Butcher* – her code name for Vlad – her body is jump-started by panic. Sudden terror that she has missed her last chance to connect with him.

She sits up, her sweaty hair dangling in damp tendrils across her face. The room is suffocating, the sun flooding through the open curtains, advancing on the bed. Caroline squints against the glare and turns her back to the window, hitting the speed dial, knowing that she'll get his voicemail again.

But the phone purrs in her ear. 'Come on,' she whispers.

'Yes?' It's him.

'Vlad? Caroline here.'

'Yes. Yes. I try you.'

'I know. I was asleep.'

'This thing with your child. I am sorry.'

'Yes. Thank you.'

'I can't come this morning. Business, you know?'

'I understand.'

'What happen? With the child?'

'I'll tell you when I see you. When are you free?'

Vlad hesitates and she hears his breath echoing, remembers it hot against her ear as he came. He says something that she can't catch.

'What? I lost you?' she says.

'I am in car, by mountain. Maybe now you need some time. With your husband.'

Exactly what she doesn't need. 'Vlad, let's meet. Please.'

'You think?'

'Yes. Absolutely.'

A wash of static and she thinks she's lost him again, visualizing the signal bouncing off that gray anvil-shaped heap of rock and out into space. Then his voice is in her ear, clear enough for her to hear his lack of enthusiasm. 'Okay, tomorrow. Lunch. I phone in morning, okay?'

'Okay. Yes.'

The mobile is dead in her hand and she drops it on the rumpled duvet and goes into the bathroom, splashes her face. She feels better, knowing that she will be with him tomorrow. Refuses to let a few tentacles of negativity – nasty little voices whispering that he'll make an excuse or, worse, stand her up – take hold. She leaves the bathroom and sits cross-legged on the bed and boots up her computer. It grunts and moans and she knows it'll take forever to grind itself awake.

She decides to go down and brew some filter coffee, to jolt the last of the sleep from her body. She pads downstairs, barefoot, hoping that Nick is locked in his studio. But he lies on the sofa in the living room and looks up at her and stands. As she heads toward the kitchen she feels an unwelcome flash of sympathy for him.

'How are you doing?' he asks, following her.

'How do you think I'm doing?'

He stands with his back to the fridge and she can't quite suppress a twinge of pain when she sees one of Sunny's crayon drawings beside his head, held in place by little magnets in the shape of cartoony suns.

'Caro, talk to me, please. I can't do this alone.'

Caroline looks at her husband and unbidden an old memory surfaces, like something captured on glass, of how he was when she first met him. His shy smile. His goofy sweetness. Caroline realizes she's in danger of succumbing to her emotions, feeling an urge to confess, to tell him what happened in this very kitchen with Vlad. How she sent their child to her death.

But Dark Caroline shuts that down pretty damn smartly, and she turns pain to fury and seals all grief and compassion behind her barrier of implacable rage.

'There is nobody to talk to, Nicholas. You're like one of those bloody wireframe things of yours, an empty, soulless little man.' The coffee maker is still half full from this morning and she clicks it on. It'll be bitter, but she's not in the mood to grind fresh beans with her needy husband lurking. She dodges him and makes for the sink, where her favorite mug stands upended on the drying rack. 'Oh, you dress yourself up with fake emotions, like how much you loved Sunny, but you're fooling nobody.'

'Caroline, stop. Not now.'

He approaches her and tries to put an arm around her waist but she shrugs him off and pours a cup of black coffee into the mug. Adds two heaped spoons of sugar.

'And you're all caught up in this pathetic act of penance. Building that monstrosity, that has everything to do with your ego – your God complex – and nothing whatsoever to do with our dead child.'

He wilts before her eyes, which only spurs her on. 'She's dead, Nick, and no amount of wanking on your computer is going to change that.'

She grabs her mug and heads for the door.

'Caro,' he says.

She ignores him, walking away.

'Caro, we need to speak. About tomorrow.'

She stops in the doorway and turns. 'What about tomorrow?'

'There's that thing in Jo'burg.'

'What thing?' Then she remembers: some gathering of the nerds, with Nicholas showing off his toy. 'Okay, yes. Right. What time do you fly?'

'I'm supposed to leave early in the morning.'

'Okay.'

'But I don't think I can go. Not now.'

'Why not?'

He runs a hand through his greasy hair. 'Jesus, Caroline, I'm a mess.'

'I think it'll be good for you. Go and demonstrate your gadget and have them tell you how brilliant you are. Better than moping around here.'

'You're serious?'

'Perfectly.' She knows he wants to go. To escape from her.

'So you don't mind me leaving you?'

She laughs. 'Jesus, Nicholas, grow a pair of balls. Can't you see that's exactly what I need? For you to get your wretched carcass out of my sight?'

Then he does that thing she hates: morphs his face into a martyr from a Byzantine painting, pain dripping like stigmata from his eyes. 'Are you sure you'll be okay?'

'Believe me, I'll be fine.'

'I'll catch an evening flight back. Be home by nine tomorrow night.'

'Lovely,' she says, turning.

'And I'll ask Vernon Saul to keep an eye on you.'

'Oh no you fucking won't!' She spins back to him, spilling her coffee, cursing as it burns her hand. 'You'll keep that degenerate very far away from me,' she says, sucking on her index finger.

'He's a friend.'

She spits a laugh around the scalded digit. 'Friend? He's a bloody pervert.' Nick's staring at her. 'When he was busy with Sunny, it was almost as if he knew she was dead, but still he didn't stop doing that thing to her. Like it turned him on.'

'Jesus Christ, Caroline, he tried to save our daughter's life,' he says, shaking his head. 'Why the hell would he pretend?'

'To impress you. And he succeeded.' He's still shaking his head. 'Nicholas, just keep him away from me, okay?'

'Okay. Fine. Have it your way.'

She turns for the stairs, carrying her coffee, shutting him out. Again.

chapter 19

VERNON SAUL PILOTS THE CIVIC ACROSS PARADISE PARK, SQUINTING AT THE early morning sun through his Ray-Bans, already dressed in his rent-a-cop gear even though his shift doesn't start until midday. As usual the wind gusts between the cramped houses, lifting trash high in the air, plastic bags and paper scraps chasing each other like fighting birds.

Vernon's got a little R&B going on the sound system, that old Ashford and Simpson thing from way back, 'Solid As A Rock.' He's feeling good – on top of the fucken world, in fact – and he chimes in during the chorus, in a decent tenor, reason he always got chosen for the school choir when he was a kid. He nudges the Civic through the traffic, using his horn against the minibus taxis that clog the streets like arterial fat.

He's felt on top of his game since his time with Nick Exley the day before. Feels even better after the call he got early this morning – woke him up, but what the hell? Exley phoning him from his car, on the way to the airport, saying he's flying to Jo'burg for the day and would Vernon keep an eye on his wife? He's worried about leaving her alone.

Vernon saying, 'Hey, no problem, Nick.'

The white guy hesitating. 'Listen, Vernon, could I ask you to keep a low profile?'

'Sure, I know your wife don't like me.'

'Caroline's just freaked out.'

'Ja, but I can tell she don't want me around. Relax, buddy, I'll be discreet.'

Exley getting all kiss-ass, thanking him. Vernon laughing now as he drives, booming out the chorus, arm resting on the open side window. The traffic slows to a stop on a narrow road, outside two shipping containers squatting side by side on the sand, fronts open to the street: a hair salon and a phone shop.

The hair stylist, an acne-ridden cross-dresser in his forties with a peroxide bob, teases a teenage girl's hair into a froth. He looks across at Vernon and whistles through his missing front teeth. Passion-gap, they call it here on the Flats.

'Hey, nice voice, handsome!' the drag queen yells.

Another day Vernon would pulp the thing's head under his boot but he blows a kiss and the queer howls a raucous laugh and tap-dances his wedge heels in delight as Vernon hits the gas and flings the Civic around a taxi.

Life is good.

He's not even letting the Boogie thing stress him out. He's put in a few calls to old cop connections and found out that Dino Erasmus is still sniffing around. Vernon knows that Erasmus doesn't like him. Dino is that most dangerous of things: a dumb, honest cop, with ambitions. Always trying to get something on Vernon, back when he was on the force. Never smart enough to get it right, Vernon laughing in his dog-kennel face. Ja, if Erasmus can get even he'll go for it.

But Vernon knows the detective's caseload won't allow him to waste much more time on a nothing like Boogie. Only warning flag is when one of the cops tells him Erasmus has been nosing around Dawn. Now Dawn knows fuck-all about what went down that night, but she's smart, that one. Could put a few things together. Float an idea Dino Erasmus's way. But no problem, Vernon has his ways to manage the Dawn situation.

He stops the Civic outside a nasty cluster of dust-brown brick buildings that back up against the railroad line. A library, a clinic for mothers and kids and the offices of the district social workers. Vernon kills the music and closes the car window, levering himself out of the Civic, his bad leg giving him grief.

He presses the button on his keychain and the car chirps as the doors lock and the alarm kicks in. Vernon shakes the blood back into his leg and walks along the pathway toward the social workers. An old guy in the overalls of a city employee prunes a skinny tree, bent out of shape by years of being hammered by the southeaster.

'Morning, my brother,' the man says.

'Morning,' Vernon says, already reaching into his pocket for his Luckies. He offers the pack to the guy, who draws one out, cupping his hand around it as Vernon flicks his lighter. Prison ink spills out of the sleeves of the jumpsuit. The guy was an American, back in the day.

Vernon lights a Lucky for himself, knowing he can't smoke inside the offices, and he stands with the ex-con for a few minutes, talking rugby and the weather, then he offers the half-smoked cigarette to the old guy, who pinches it dead and stows it behind his ear for later.

'Bless you, my brother.'

'Keep an eye on my car, okay?'

Vernon walks into the dingy little reception room, past the line of miserable-looking creatures that snakes out onto the pathway. He goes to the head of the queue and the receptionist gives him a look.

'I'm here to see Merinda Appolis.'

'You'll have to wait.' Wagging a painted nail at the line of losers.

'Just tell her Vernon Saul is here.'

The receptionist shrugs and mutters something into the telephone. Looks up at him, 'She'll be out now,' then buries her nose in *You* magazine.

After a minute a door opens and a girl of maybe fourteen emerges with a baby on her hip. Both mother and child are crying, noses gluepots of snot. Merinda Appolis stands in the doorway. 'Mr Saul.'

Vernon steps into the room and she closes the door after him. The office is cramped and cell-like. Barred windows, cement floor, a functional steel desk and two plastic folding chairs. A calendar with a color photo of kittens is the only personal touch.

'Vernon, you're a stranger,' suddenly all informal now nobody's listening.

He shrugs and sits. Merinda stands a while giving him the eye, then takes the chair opposite him, allowing him a good look at her legs before she tugs at the hem of her dress. She's maybe thirty, yellow-brown, just a little chubby, all trace of natural curl blown out of her hair. She smiles at him, lips wet with gloss.

'How are you?'

'Can't complain, Merinda.' Flashing her his best grin. She's always had the hots for him, this one. That's how he got her to recommend that Dawn's girlie be returned to her.

'That uniform suits you. Kind of macho.'

'Thanks, but I won't be wearing it much longer.'

'Ja? And why not?'

'They kicking me up to head office, making me a regional supervisor. Reckon they can better use my skills there.' The lies flowing like honey from his tongue.

'Nice, Vernon. Congrats.'

'Thanks.'

'So, what do you want from me this time?'

'Can't I visit, even?'

'Come on, Vernon, you saw outside. I'm a busy girl.' But she smiles.

'You remember last year, the Dawn Cupido thing?'

Her smile evaporates. 'Ja. Of course, yes. I did that against my better judgment, you know?'

'I know. I owe you.'

'You do. Big time. Don't tell me I made a mistake?'

'No, no. I thought you could just look in on them. Maybe scare her a little.'

'Scare her?'

'Ja, you know?'

'Why, is there a problem?'

'No way. Just to keep her in line, like.'

Merinda Appolis's eyes – like dark fish swimming in a sea of blue eye make-up – flick over him. 'You want to use me again, don't you, Vernon? I'll scare her, and you'll tell her that you handled me. To impress her.'

'Hey, slow down—'

'What? Are you screwing her?' All ladylike pretence has gone now. She's just another little Cape Flats tramp acting all sour and scorned.

Vernon feels himself redden, has to keep a lid on his fury, fighting to control himself. He doesn't screw women. Never had nothing to do with their filth. Glad he is useless down there, since his father did what he did.

'Get a life, Vernon,' she says.

He pulls himself to his feet, his dead leg dragging, and he almost knocks the chair over. 'Forget it,' he says. 'Just fucken forget it.'

'No, I won't forget it. I'll visit them.' She gets a pinched, prissy look on her face and makes a note in the book on the desk. 'Purely out of concern for the child. And if I find anything wrong – *anything* – I'm taking that kid away. For keeps. You hear me, Vernon?'

He nods, not trusting his voice, and thuds his way out, shouldering through the straggle of pathetic humanity that waits docile as sheep. For once he is pleased to feel the wind on him, blowing away her cloying stink.

chapter 20

CAROLINE'S SHORT-WHEELBASE LAND ROVER RATTLES ALONG THE SERPENTINE coast road, the mountains rearing skyward to her right, the Atlantic foaming on the rocks far below to her left. A road of such spectacular beauty that it took her breath away the first few times she drove it but, like so many things in this narcissistic little city, it quickly became a major pain in the backside.

The old Land Rover – her Landy, her Caroline of Africa fantasy car – is sluggish and hard to drive, each gearshift taking an effort of will. It has no air conditioning to combat the oppressive midday heat and she finds herself envying the soccer moms whizzing by, blonde and aloof in their climate-controlled SUVs.

Last night she lay awake, fretting, worried that Vlad would stand her up. To add to her discomfort, Nick came to their bed and tried to embrace her and she had to control the impulse to lash out with her foot and catch him in the balls. Instead she kept her back to him, pretending to be asleep, the two of them like continents, separated by a sea of sorrow and anger. After Exley left for the airport, around dawn, she fell into a fitful sleep.

Mercifully, Vlad called her just after eight. He sounded hurried and cool but told her to meet him for lunch in the city. This will be the first time they meet in town, perhaps his idea of delicacy: lunch and then a fuck in a hotel room far from the tragedy.

She showered and dressed with more care than she had in days, even found a bottle of scent – amazingly not stale – and dabbed some on her pulses and behind her ears. No make-up. Once, early on, in an effort to please Vlad, she'd arrived for one of their assignations wearing lipstick and hint of blusher. He forced her to wash her face before he fucked her.

Vlad likes her plain. And that is what I am, she tells herself, catching a glimpse of her face in the rear-view mirror, her reflection multiplying as the Land Rover judders along. Plain. She's given up trying to understand why he is attracted to her.

She met Vlad on the beach, a week after she, Nick and Sunny arrived in Cape Town. Caroline isn't a beach person but they'd come out of a grim European winter and the sea and the sunshine were difficult to ignore. So, leaving her husband and daughter to prepare breakfast, she wrapped herself in layers of cloth, put on her biggest sunhat and darkest glasses and coated the few bits of exposed skin with SPF sixty before venturing onto the long Llandudno beach.

It was a weekday, so the beach wasn't full. The inevitable surfers in their wetsuits, hair bleached blond by the sun. A few mothers and kids. And a man walking a wolf. The wolf, white with blue eyes, bounded across to her and Caroline swatted at it with her hat, cursing, telling it to bugger off. She had her period and the wolf shoved its snout into her crotch like some proxy of its master, the ridiculous man who came jogging after it, with his deep tan and his chest fur and his gold neck-chain, dressed in a tiny blue Speedo heavy with cock and balls, long gray hair pushed back from a beaky face.

'Please, I apologize,' he said, hauling the wolf away, dazzling Caroline with the best smile money could buy.

'That bloody thing should be in a zoo, not on the beach.'

'No, no, no, he is quite tame.' Kneeling, embracing the animal, who was still interested in truffling in her twat, calling it what sounded like Sneg, which she later learned was Serbian for snow.

She was to learn a lot more about Vladislav Stankovic. He pursued her. Ambushed her again on the beach. Ran into her in the 7-Eleven and the booze store down in Hout Bay. Then came his masterstroke: he befriended her husband. He contrived to meet Nick and Sunny on the beach one day, Sunny falling immediately for Sneg, and Exley – unaware of Vlad's motives – invited him back for a drink. He became a regular visitor. Vlad feigned interest in Nick and his work but his attention was always on Caroline.

Despite herself she was amused by his absurd attempts at seduction, so unselfconsciously pre-feminist that they were almost refreshing, and it wasn't as if her marital bed was all fun and games. Sex with Nick had never been exactly torrid and after Sunny was born it became an afterthought, brief, cursory. Duty more than pleasure.

So one day she let Vlad take her to his house, a laughably ostentatious folly that clung precariously to the slopes of the mountain. He told her that he and his wife (her name was never spoken) had an 'arrangement' and lived in separate wings in the sprawling monstrosity. The wife was away, in Switzerland, taking a cure.

They ended up in Vlad's bedroom, on his massive bed with its ornate carved headboard, the air thick with Balkan cigarettes and old leather and carnivorous man. She climaxed repeatedly, while he breathed Cape red wine and Slavic curses into her ear. His sweat, rising from beneath his cologne, reminded her of the butchers of her childhood in the Home Counties: blood mingled with sawdust. So different from Nick's scentless, vegetarian body. Christ, it was good to be well and truly fucked. Afterward, chafed and satiated, if she felt guilt it was never enough to stop her coming back for more.

Caroline feels no affection for Vlad – God knows she doesn't even like the man – but when he is inside her, thick and insistent, the terrors that haunt her are banished, and she needs him more than ever now, to earth her.

She rounds a curve and there it is before her, the view that launched a million postcards: Lion's Head perched like a Basuto hat over Camps Bay, flanking the bulk of Table Mountain with its smudge of white cloud, swanky Cape Town huddled at its feet.

The place has charm, she has to concede. Like New York isn't America, Cape Town isn't South Africa. It has European pretensions and its downtown is home to art dealers and precious little coffee shops, not Zimbabwean refugees and Nigerian drug lords like other South African cities.

Cape Town believes it has taste. Style. De Waterkant, where she is to meet Vlad, is the gay quarter. Chintzy slave houses painted bright colors wink at each other across narrow cobbled streets jammed with cars. Nowhere to park the Landy, so she leaves it in the lot at the Junction Hotel and walks a block to the new mini-mall, where she finds Vlad sitting in a bistro. He is dressed in a suit. Another first. It is a good suit, bespoke, she guesses, but it reduces him somehow, neuters him. He looks uncomfortable, tugging at the collar of his shirt as if he is being throttled.

Vlad rises and kisses her on the cheek, like she's his aunt. Follows it up on the other cheek, to make it seem more continental. But he avoids her lips.

'I haven't seen you,' she says.

'I don't want to intrude.'

'I could have done with an intrusion.'

He doesn't respond with one of his clumsy double entendres, and – after they have ordered – he asks her about Sunny. The last thing she wants to talk about, so she gives him a shorthand version and he emits low grunts of sympathy.

Their meal arrives, fussy and nouvelle, with awful little doodles of food coloring around the edges of the plates. Caroline ignores her line fish and Vlad manages a few mouthfuls of fillet before pushing it aside and demanding Turkish coffee.

He leans toward her, his big, hairy hands on the table. 'I go away for a while. Tomorrow.'

'Where?'

'Belgrade. Paris. Business thing.'

He's lying, she's sure. He's dropping her. She moves in close enough to see the blackheads on his nose and grips his hand. 'Oh, come on, cut the new-man crap, Vlad. Take me across to the Junction and fuck the living daylights out of me.'

He frees his hand. 'Caroline, it is better maybe if we don't see each other for a bit.'

'Are you dumping me?'

'I think is best. Because of your situation.'

'What the fuck do you know about my *situation*?'

Her voice is too loud, people are staring, and his eyes drift away from her, drawn to the bright sunlight outside like he is thinking of escape. He's embarrassed. Another first.

But when he looks back toward her, she can swear his eyes are moist. 'We too had child. Me and Martina.'

Who the fuck is Martina? The question is already forming on her lips when she realizes this is the unnamed, unseen wife.

'A boy,' he says. 'Jannic. He live to just second birthday.' He taps his chest. 'Heart. That is why we come here, to Cape Town. Twenty years ago Chris Barnard was best in world for the heart surgery. But even he can do nothing.' He wipes his eyes, and sniffs, and she finds herself repulsed by this side of him. 'We try to move away but somehow we cannot. Cannot leave his memory.'

Caroline imagines a room in an unseen wing of the house. The dead child's room. Intact, untouched. A shrine. She sees the truth about Vlad: his marriage is inviolate. A sealed unit. She has outlived her usefulness.

He's waving his credit card, the waiter swishing over with the portable terminal, fussing. Vlad goes through the business of punching in his PIN and the machine pukes out his credit card slip. He stuffs it into his pocket, stands and leans down to peck her on the cheek and then he's gone, big shoulders slumped, de Bergerac nose thrust forward.

Caroline sits a while and sips her water, feeling herself slipping farther from her mooring. A metallic taste on her tongue, her sweat acrid beneath her scent.

The breakdown is close, now. All the telltale signs.

She reaches for the pills in her bag but she doesn't take any. Instead she stands and rushes out, the pillbox still clutched in her fist. She opens the box, grabs the foil blister packs and dumps them into a trashcan in the courtyard, but returns the empty box, with her name on the printed pharmacist's label, to her bag – some paranoid impulse telling her to not leave any sign of her presence.

As she hurries on she senses she's being followed, spins around and confronts a mime in white pancake make-up, some Marcel Marceau clone in black tights and silly pumps, who has been tailing her, mimicking her agitated walk to the amusement of the strollers.

'Oh, just fuck off,' she says, and the mime holds up his hands and clutches at his heart as if he has been shot, staggering, then he finds his feet and tucks in behind a queer carrying a bouquet of roses.

Caroline flees out into the street, the hard afternoon sunlight blinding her.

chapter 21

THE MINIBUS TAXI IS THERE OUT OF FUCKEN NOWHERE AND VERNON JAMS HIS boot flat to the floor and somehow gets the little red Sniper truck out of its way, his nostrils full of burning rubber as the taxi skids past, horn blaring like a train hurtling into a tunnel, ass wagging crazily across the road. The face of the darkie taxi driver flashes by, mouth gaping on white tombstone teeth and pink tongue, and Vernon's sure that the taxi will roll but it doesn't, just comes to a sliding stop, broadside to the traffic, smoke boiling from its tires.

Vernon puts his foot down away from Hout Bay, the taxi shrinking to nothing in his rearview. He didn't even see it he was so caught up in his fury. Furious with Merinda Appolis for dissing him like she did. Furious with himself for miscalculating so badly. It was this kind of overconfidence that nearly got him dead last year, so sure that the American's gang – their leader locked away – wouldn't have the balls to come after him. But they came.

And now, because he underestimated that fat little bitch with her cellulite-dimpled thighs and her mouth like a weeping wound, he's opened a door that he should have left tightly closed. Vernon knows it was no empty promise: Merinda will make it her mission to take Dawn's brat away, just to spite him. Leaving him with no handle on the little whore.

For a moment he is tempted to phone Dawn and warn her, he even has his phone in his hand, sliding it open as he drives. Then he calms himself and clicks the phone shut. No. No more miscalculations. No more fuck-ups.

Vernon slows his breath as he crests the rise and sees the ocean, hangs a left into the road that leads down to Llandudno. One road in and out of this place, making it so easy to police. Vernon slows to a stop, pulling onto the shoulder in front of the wooden sentry box.

He leaves the car, waves at the Sniper man inside the box, walks across to the silver barrier rail on the ocean side and lights himself a smoke, letting the nicotine chill him out. A different universe this, from the Cape Flats. The mountains enfold it and protect it from the wind. The sun seems more golden, friendlier. The ocean, far below him, rippling with slow waves, is an intense shade of blue that he can't even begin to name. The land of bloody milk and honey.

He fishes a fresh pack of Luckies from his pocket and walks over to the sentry box. The fat darkie sitting inside in the thick heat, a couple of droning flies to keep him company, tries to pretend that he's alert but his drooping eyelids tell another story.

Vernon kicks him in the leg just below the knee and the darkie yelps. 'Wake up, Banzi. Next thing the supervisor catches you sleeping and your wife and piccaninnies go hungry.'

'Yes, sir.' The 'sir' is because Vernon's got lighter skin and is a patrolman, and because he's just plain fucken scary.

'The woman? She back yet?'

'No, sir. I phone you if she is.'

Vernon grunts, leans against the door jamb, the little box heavy with the sweat of this black man. 'And when she leave this morning, you sure she's alone?'

'Like I tell you, sir.'

Vernon tosses the pack of Luckies into the guard's lap. 'Here, don't burn the bloody box down.' He steps back down onto the gravel. 'Minute you see her, you call me, okay?'

'Yessir.'

Vernon cruises down the streets, empty of pedestrians, just white women in fancy SUVs chauffeuring their spoiled little brats. Vernon bought a half-chicken at the KFC down in Hout Bay but there's no way he's going to eat it with his gut knotted tight like a fist, and the reek of the rendered fat and the spices is getting too much for him, so he cruises past Nick Exley's house and stops the truck in the dead end.

He finds the path through the undergrowth and goes down to where the Rastaman lives in his own crazy world. At least the bugger's got his pants on today, sitting in the shade of the overhanging bush, smoking some brand of weed that stinks like garden rubbish.

The Rasta shows his rotten teeth and bobs his head so his dreads fly around like kettle cords, clapping his hands, saying not a word.

Vernon tosses him the red and white striped KFC box and the Rasta opens it and gets busy, the joint stubbed out on the rock beside him, tearing at the chicken and shoving it into his mouth, juice gathering in his fuzzy beard.

Not something Vernon wants to watch. So he waves, which gets the darkie jiggling like a wind-up toy, and hauls himself up onto the rocks overlooking the house, finds some shade, a nice breeze coming in salty off the ocean, cooling him down.

He stretches out his bad leg, massaging the muscle above the knee, taking himself inward, to where all the fury lives. Finding it. Containing it, like it's nuclear waste. Storing it where it can't hurt him no more, but where he can draw on it when he needs it.

A trick he learned when he was a youngster, eleven years old.

His father had been abusing him since before he could remember, dragging him into the bedroom and doing things to him that tore his body and did worse to his soul. His mother at church, or sitting in front of the TV, hearing and doing nothing.

The only time it stopped was when his father went to prison. But because his father was small-time – a bit of housebreaking, selling stolen goods, dealing in a little weed – he was never gone for long. Vernon had just had his eleventh birthday when his father came back from three months in Pollsmoor and it all began again.

But something had changed inside Vernon. Instead of being frightened and hurt he was just plain fucken angry. One Sunday afternoon his mother went to go to church, to bullshit to some nonexistent God, leaving Vernon alone with his father.

Vernon, sitting in front of the TV watching cartoons, knew what was coming and it wasn't long before he heard his father calling him from the bedroom.

'Hey, you little rabbit. Come here.'

It was a hot day and Vernon was wearing only a pair of boardshorts. They were his favorites – Adidas – so he took them off and left them folded neatly on the sofa, not wanting them dirtied. He walked naked into his parents' room, where his father lay on the bed, also butt-naked, a bottle of brandy in one hand and his dick in the other.

'Well, look at the little rabbit, already stripped for action. You like it, don't you?' The stink of his unwashed body filling the room, his eyes yellow from Mandrax and liquor.

Vernon climbed onto the bed, straddling his father, grabbing his cock. It was thick and hard, and for some reason it was how Vernon imagined it would feel if he took a goose by the throat. His father's eyes dipped closed and Vernon could feel the pulse drumming in the stiff thing in his hand. He reached under the bed and came out with the hammer he had hidden there earlier in the day.

'Daddy,' he said. He wanted the bastard to see this. Those glazed eyes opened slowly, pus-filled smears in the map of wrinkles that etched his skin, prematurely old from the drugs. The sick fuck saw the hammer, even managed a wet laugh, before Vernon brought it down and struck him on the left temple.

His father lifted a skinny, tattooed arm, but it was useless. Vernon was already big for his years, showing signs of the broad shoulders and powerful biceps of his mother's side of the family. He brought the hammer down again and again and again. Until his father's head was mush, flesh and brain and bone sprayed out across the wall and the pillows and the comforter.

Vernon, when he stopped hammering away like a blacksmith, was astonished at the amount of blood that had come from the thing on the bed. Felt it dripping from his face and his body.

He wiped hair and brain and gore from the hammer and slid off the bed, carrying the tool with him into the bathroom. He showered, washing himself until there was no trace of his father on him. Washed the hammer down, too.

As he walked to his bedroom, Vernon looked into his parents' room and saw his father's dead arm dangling off the bed, already seething with flies. He found himself a T-shirt and pulled it over his head and grabbed his tennis ball. Padded through to the kitchen and wrapped the hammer in a yellow Checkers bag, then retrieved his boardshorts from the sofa, pulled them on, and went out, leaving the front door of the house standing open, way it always was during the day. Nobody in the area was going to mess with Vernon's mean snake of a father.

Vernon dumped the Checkers bag in a drain and walked down to the store, bouncing the ball on the hard sand of the sidewalk. He made a bit of a production of buying a Double O orange drink. Pretended he couldn't find his money, the old Muslim behind the barred counter getting all pissed off. Then he paid and left, knowing if anybody asked, the old man would remember him.

He went to the open lot near his house – car wrecks and rubble and weeds and gang tags – and drank his Double O and played keepy-uppy with the tennis ball the way he always did. Spending hours moving the ball from head to toe, to chest, to head, this loner of a boy.

Vernon saw his mother coming home through the dust, walking up from the taxis. She called to him but he ignored her. Head, to toe, to knee, to head. Watched her out the corner of his eye as she went into the house and when the screams came he didn't even lose the tennis ball, controlled it nicely and let it drift to the ground, trapping it under his bare foot and slowly walking toward home, bouncing the ball, to where his mother came flying out the front door like something shot from a cannon, falling to her knees, dress riding up her fat thighs so he could see her pants, the neighbors running over and his mother gabbling, spit dangling from her mouth and one of the neighbors going in and then coming out again in a hurry and parking his lunch in a flower bed.

Eventually the cops arrived and Vernon's mother told them she came home from church and found the thing in the bedroom. Vernon said he left his father sleeping and went and bought a drink and played with his ball. Didn't see nothing or no one.

The cops took the body away and said it was 'gang-related.' And that was that. Vernon's mother was left to clean up the mess. Vernon sat watching TV as night fell and his mother was in and out of the bedroom, gray under her copper skin, carrying buckets of bloody water, her hands crammed with matted rags and newspaper. Vernon laughed, somewhere deep inside.

At 10 p.m. she was finished. By this time Vernon was in his room, reading his comics. His mother sat down on the bed and when he looked at her it was as if she'd seen some kind of hell she couldn't describe.

'I'm sleeping in here with you tonight, okay, boy?'

She drooped toward him, putting an arm around his shoulder, wanting some sympathy from him. He slapped her face. She jumped away, hand to her cheek, staring at him.

'You take your stinking fucken ass out of my room,' he said. 'And from now on, you listen to me, and you do what I say, otherwise I do to you what I done to him.' The bitch backed away from him, another kind of hell in her eyes now. 'Understand?'

She understood.

Sitting on the rock, more than twenty years later, Vernon can feel the satisfaction, the sense of power, like it was yesterday. The turning point in his life. Made him what he is today.

His phone purrs in his pocket and he slides it out. 'Ja?'

It's the darkie in the sentry box. Caroline Exley is on her way home. Vernon, perfectly camouflaged in the shade, hears the high whine of the Land Rover, sees it bumping and rattling up to the house. The motorized gate rumbles open and the Land Rover rolls in. He hears the echo of the engine in the garage before it cuts. After a few minutes the door onto the deck of the house slides open and the woman stands there, staring out at the ocean, then she disappears inside.

Vernon sits. Waiting.

chapter 22

THE VOICES ARE BACK. A CHORUS OF BANSHEES, ALL SCREAMING AT ONCE OF murder and plague and death and hell and damnation. The energy that her rage at Nick gave Caroline – the protection that it afforded, the way it insulated her from her emotions – is gone.

All she feels now is the inevitable slide toward a major breakdown, and she is alone, without her medication and without her husband. Driving down to the pharmacy in Hout Bay and refilling her prescription is a bridge too far and Nick's return is in a future too distant to imagine.

She's terrified.

Caroline has had two breakdowns. One after Sunny was born and another, three years later, while they were living in Paris. Her psychiatrist, a bland asexual man with rooms in an anonymous medical center in leafy Constantia, assures her repeatedly that by dutifully swallowing her pills each day and managing her stress – as if he were talking about balancing her checkbook – she will prevent another breakdown. Where, she wonders, as the voices scream and roil inside her head, did a dead child and a now ex-lover fit into the notion of stress management?

Somehow Caroline finds herself in the kitchen and, though she knows better, she opens the fridge and grabs a half-empty bottle of Riesling lying beside the leftovers, her fingers chilled by the sweating glass. She frees the cork and tips the bottle, glugging like one of the bloated fetal-alcohol mutants who shamble along the Cape Town sidewalks. The wine is sour and she drops the bottle and it shatters on the ceramic floor tiles. Rushing to the sink, her sandals crunching over broken glass, she spits out the vinegary liquid.

She heads for the sitting room but the windows are too big and she's left the door open onto the deck and the sunlight blares in at her and she has to turn and flee, kicking off her sandals and taking the carpeted stairs two at a time, until she comes to the cool dimness of the upper level.

She passes Sunny's room, the door standing ajar (left open by Nick making his morning pilgrimage of pain before leaving for the airport) and the voices channel her daughter, mimicking her laugh and her off-key rendering of a nursery rhyme: 'Ring a ring of roses...' Caroline slams the door and hurries away into her bedroom.

She grabs her Nokia from beside the bed and dials her husband and gets his voicemail, delivered in that bizarre mid-Atlantic mélange he calls an accent, and the only message she can think of leaving is a scream of terror, so she ends the call and throws the phone onto the duvet.

Caroline walks through to the bathroom – a marble mausoleum with a terrifyingly large mirror – and stares at her reflection. Horrified by what stares back at her, she tears herself away, the light in the bathroom streaking and lagging like bad video, the molecules in the air thick and heavy, pressing down on her, resisting her as she goes back into the bedroom and sees her computer, a folded clam lying on the bed.

Her own voice, almost lost now in the psycho-billy chorus, tells her to leave it unopened. But she doesn't hear or she doesn't listen and she sits down on the bed, the comforter an alive thing, slick and fleshy, ready to suck her down and suffocate her. She escapes its clutches and sits cross-legged on the carpet and lifts the computer onto her lap.

Her hands shake, palsied tremors that make opening the Mac almost impossible, her thumb finding the little slider that releases the lid – the serrations painful to her skin – but losing purchase and skidding off onto the cool plastic. She has to use both her thumbs, one on top of the other, to release the catch. She lifts the lid and her index finger taps wild Morse code on the power button before she stills it long enough to apply enough pressure to boot up the Mac.

The computer hums to life, the whine of its electrics at a pitch too high for Caroline to tolerate, and she dumps it onto the carpet and stands, hugging herself, as the machine grunts and moans its way to alertness.

When it trills its frantic little greeting she returns to it and opens the document file that contains her work-in-progress, the only thing that has sustained her, given her hope these last days.

Miraculously, the voices recede as her eyes fix on the familiar black Times New Roman script against the blue-whiteness of the monitor. She hears a backwash of churning and sucking, and then nothing. Quiet. Allowing her to concentrate fully, to weigh each word for meaning.

To face the truth.

Christ knows it is puerile crap. The most God-awful, adolescent shite she has ever written. The lowest form of chick lit. She is stunned almost to sanity and then the voices are back, delighted, whooping and laughing and jeering at her.

She grabs the indigo and crème computer and stands and swings it in a wide arc, repeatedly smashing it against the wall, gouging chunks of white plaster, brick red as flesh beneath, until at last the case of the iBook splinters and its innards are revealed: stippled little boards festooned with silver solder and M&M-sized doodads, colored wires like braided hair held in check by cable ties.

The battery flies loose and lands on the instep of her bare left foot and the pain only spurs her on to greater efforts as she swings and smashes, not even noticing when the torn plastic cuts into the palm of her left hand. At last Caroline stands with blood dripping from her, surrounded by a graveyard of computer body parts.

Leaving a trail of blood, she goes back into the bathroom and kills the light. Then she finds the basin in the gloom and opens the cold faucet, letting the water sluice the blood away. She is not sure how long she stands there but when she lifts her hand it stings as the lacerations make contact with the air.

But the bleeding has stopped and the voices tell her what she must do next. And who she must see.

The whole dog and pony show, billed as 'a motion-capture master class with the creator of Life in a Box,' is the brainchild of Billy Chalmers, the tanned South African hustler who grins at Exley from the front row of the audience. Exley, placed before a display of artfully stacked brown boxes, the open laptop his only shield, stands at a podium facing two hundred people seated on folding chairs in the vast, windowless, climate-controlled space.

Exley, on autopilot, pedals his digital snake oil, convinced that if he stops talking and allows reality in, he'll fall apart.

In the morning a car driven by a silent black man met him at O.R. Tambo airport. As the Beemer carved a path through the rush hour on the freeway, Exley, brain fogged by anguish, watched without seeing the rash of condo developments en route to Sandton, Johannesburg's money belt, far from the post-apocalyptic inner city and the endless sprawl of ghetto townships he'd glimpsed from the air.

When the ugliness softened and blurred through tears, he was sure he'd have to be poured from the car, a messy puddle of snot. The driver's eyes, skewering him in the rearview before sliding back to the road, shamed him into pulling himself together.

Once inside the movie studio that hosted the presentation, Exley could have been anywhere from Sydney to Stockholm. The usual mix of accents and ethnicities, members of the digital diaspora, united like Freemasons by geek-speak unintelligible to a civilian.

Exley fell back on the safety of his rituals: fussing with the laptop, trotting out his mantras. Digging into his usual bag of tricks, sending mo-cap sequences through to the big-brother bank of flat screens that floated in the gloom.

Now there is a break for a late lunch and Exley dodges Chalmers and the money men who want him to eat with them, and finds a room to hide in. He sets his phone alarm for an hour hence and crawls under a plastic table, ignoring the foot-rot stink of the curling carpet tiles. Drawing his knees into a fetal position, he falls asleep and tumbles down some rabbit hole and emerges on the beach, getting baked with Shane Porter, feeling Sunny tugging at his boardshorts, ignoring her, fobbing her off, seeing her floating underwater, a chain of bubbles escaping her open mouth.

Exley battles his way out of the nightmare, banging his head on the underside of the table, awake now. Reality is worse. His daughter is dead.

His phone's red eye winks and he sees he has a missed call and a voicemail message from Caroline. But when he plays it he hears only the hiss of her breath and a muttered curse. He considers calling her but he's feeling too fragile for the inevitable confrontation.

Exley gathers his belongings and finds a bathroom and washes his face and straightens his clothes. Then he stands in the darkness at the side of the studio, like a performer waiting in the wings, as the audience of strangers drifts back to its seats.

Driving is almost beyond Caroline. The Landy's absurd gearstick, rearing up out of the floor between the front seats, is a difficult beast at the best of times but with Caroline's tremors hitting the upper limits of the Richter scale controlling this wobbling, spindly-thing is impossible and metal grates and tears as Caroline forces the car into gear. She is still barefoot, the soles of her feet protesting at the painful contact with the rubber-sheathed pedals.

The heat is suffocating and the smell of gasoline fills the car, burning her eyes and nose. The side windows are open but there is no breeze to stir the air. Her brain feels swollen, pressing up against the backs of her eyes, and even though she drives slowly the passing houses are a pointillist blur of swirling color.

The voices continue, one minute screaming obscenities at her, the next falling to hissy sibilance. These whispers are the most dangerous, inviting her to stop fighting, to surrender to her madness. But she fights on. Holds onto some last shred of herself as she battles the Land Rover up the hill to Vlad's house.

If she sees him, she tells herself, then she'll be okay. He'll fix her. He'll still the voices. All he has to do is hold her, envelop her, and the madness will recede.

She bangs the Land Rover into the curb outside his house and falls from the high car, leaving the door hanging open as she rushes toward the front gate. Like all the other houses in this suburb of riches, Vlad's is a castle keep surrounded by looming brick walls, strands of electric fencing singing at the top. The barred gate towers above her, topped by a cross-hatching of ornate spikes. A burnished metal plate is recessed into the masonry beside the gate, with a white button and a compound-eye oval of speaker holes.

She presses the button, the plastic sticky to the touch, knowing that somewhere in the house she has triggered a buzzer. Peering through the bars, she sees slices of the nouveau riche monstrosity: blank windows firing the sun at her, patio furniture, palm trees, the huge oak door like a closed mouth at the top of a flight of wide stairs. No movement.

The voices kick in at a pitch so loud she feels something has clobbered her behind her knees and her legs almost give in and she has to grab the bars of the gate for support, her face pressed up against the hot metal. She breathes. Curses. Begs. Gets hold of that bloody button again.

Static crackles beside her ear, dispersing the chorus. A sexless voice comes through the speaker, a tinny echo. 'Yes, yes? What is it?'

Caroline surrenders the button and moves her mouth close to the metal plate. 'Vlad?'

'Who is this?'

'I must see Vlad.'

'Mr Stankovic is not home.'

'I must see him.'

'Go away.'

A dismissive clunk and silence.

Caroline gathers all of her concentration to send her skittish finger to the buzzer and once she finds it, she knows she won't release it until somebody comes.

Eventually the door yawns open and a pale figure stands revealed. There is a blur and the scratch of nails on cement and a whining enquiry and she realizes that Sneg has run down the stairs to the gate, trying to force his snout and tongue through the bars. Oh God, he knows me, she thinks. He knows me.

She slides two fingers between the bars and feels the animal's hot, sandpapery tongue on her skin.

'Sneg!' At the curt command the wolf's tail curls around his balls and he retreats and slinks back up the stairs, watching Caroline from behind a woman's long legs.

The woman is halfway down the stairs now. She stops. 'What do you want with my husband?'

Caroline's sight clears enough to see that this is not the dumpy babushka of her imagination. The wife is tall, elegant – chic is the only word – with straight blonde hair streaked with gray, coiled into a loose chignon. She is dressed in a beige and white pantsuit, her manicured toes emerging from a pair of designer sandals, nails painted a muted pearl.

When she speaks it is in plummy tones not unlike Caroline's, with just a hint of eastern Europe in the vowels. 'I ask again: what do you want?'

'I must see him.'

'Who are you?'

'Caroline Exley.'

There is a bark, but it is too polite for Sneg and Caroline realizes the woman has laughed. 'Ah, yes, the latest bit of crumpet.' An eyebrow arches. 'A little frumpy even for my husband.'

'Where is he? Please.'

'Oh, for pity's sake, go away. Can't you see he is finished with you, you little idiot? Do you think you are the first? Or will be the last?'

The woman is turning away, hissing at Sneg.

Caroline grabs the bars of the gate and shakes it but it is too sturdy to rattle. She hears a wild scream and it takes a moment to realize it is hers. The woman retreats toward the front door.

A hand grabs Caroline's upper arm. Vlad. Thank Christ.

She spins, ready to embrace him, but it is the rent-a-cop, khaki-faced in his absurd action figure outfit.

'Mrs Exley,' he says. 'Let me take you home.'

Caroline is momentarily shocked into silence and so are the voices.

The security man half-bows to the wife, who hovers on the stairs. 'Mrs Stankovic.'

'Officer.' Like a baroness greeting a serf.

Sneg bares his teeth and growls at Vernon, the first time Caroline has seen him behave this way.

I'm right, she screams inside her head, drowning the voices for just a moment. I'm right about this fucker. But she's given voice to the thoughts – bellowed them – and he tightens his grip on her arm and she can feel her pale flesh bruising beneath his fingertips.

'Mrs Exley, please.'

She fights loose. 'Take your hands off me, you fucking brown bastard!'

'Mrs Exley.'

'You fucking savage. You knew she was dead, didn't you? You knew she was dead, knew my child was dead, yet you lay on her and filled her with your breath like she was a blow-up doll?'

He tries to take her arm again and she slaps him, screaming, hits out, her fists bouncing off his body armor. A car pulls up at the house next door and a pale woman mother-hens her gawking kids into the garage as the roller door closes.

The rent-a-cop has got behind Caroline, trying to wrap his arms around her, her skirt riding high on her thighs, her pale, freckled legs pedaling the air. 'What? Did you want to fuck her?'

Two sturdy black maids, dressed in pinafores and caps, walking fluffy lapdogs, stop and stare and Caroline can feel their Xhosa clicks like slaps to her face.

Somehow she breaks free of Vernon Saul's grip, still screaming, landing on all fours. She is drooling and weeping and snot dangles from her nose. She finds her feet and rushes for the Land Rover, dragging herself aboard, fighting the wheel and the pedals and the gears, and sets off lurching and veering down the hill.

Down toward the suck of the sea and that vapid soulless house. Down toward total fucking toys-in-the-attic madness.

chapter 23

O N THE TWO-HOUR FLIGHT BACK TO CAPE TOWN, AS EXLEY SITS WITH HIS laptop open, tweaking his model of Sunny, a sense of dislocation nags at him, screwing with his concentration. He closes his eyes and reaches for a memory of his daughter on the morning of her birthday, desperate to have her close. But he can't find Sunny's face – her real face. He can only conjure up the digital version that he's built.

A stewardess brings him a Scotch, his second – or maybe third – and he shuts down the laptop and puts it aside, feeling the pleasant burn of the booze on his tongue, trying to reassemble the timeline of his afternoon. The best he can do is a series of frame grabs. He must have spoken with enough conviction and dazzled the faithful with enough wizardry because he stepped down from the podium to loud applause, and young bum-fluffy geeks mobbed him, firing questions.

Exley, limp with fatigue, disappeared into the darkness, leaving Chalmers to run interference, shepherding the punters and their credit cards toward a cocktail bar that somehow manifested at the side of the studio, complete with lounge music and a barman in a bowtie.

On impulse Exley, before he slipped out to the waiting car, triggered a loop of Sunny dancing and sent it through to the bank of monitors. The loop started with a wireframe model, stark white lattice-work against black, then transitioned through to his child fully rendered and textured.

A few people, drinks and snacks in their hands, paused in mid-conversation and turned to the screens. More followed their cue. A reverential silence fell as conversations fragmented and stopped.

This should have pleased Exley, flying into a sunset mauve with pollution, this proof that his reclaiming of his daughter is transcending the gap between the imaginary and the real, pixel by pixel. But he is unsettled by the understanding that Sunny has been replaced forever in his memory by what he has conjured from zeros and ones, and when he thinks of returning home and facing his wife he feels nothing but despair. Sunny was the glue that kept them together and now that she's gone, he and Caroline stand revealed for what they are: antagonistic strangers. Not even united by grief. Driven farther apart, if anything.

The drinks trolley, pushed by a black stewardess with cruelly straightened hair, appears at his side again and Exley asks for another double Scotch straight up. The woman hands him the drink in a small plastic container, like a urine sample.

He throws it back in two swallows, desperate to escape this place where every thought and memory cuts like a blade.

chapter 24

THIS IS DAWN'S WORST FUCKEN NIGHTMARE. OKAY, NOT THE WORST – THAT'S all about some sick filth doing to Brittany what was done to her way back – but, still, this is bad. Really bad.

Dawn, already late for work, took Brittany down the cabbage-stinking corridor to the old Porra woman's apartment. Banging loud and long enough to get another neighbor – fat Boer loser, dressed only in his underpants – out his door, moaning. Dawn flipping him the finger with her left hand, right hand still banging away.

He muttered something like 'bushman bitch' and then he was gone back to his beaver books and his Kleenexes. Finally, after the sound of many locks and bolts being worked free, the door opened to reveal Mrs de Pontes, small as a child, dressed like always in her widow's black.

'I sick,' the old woman said.

'What you mean?'

'I sick.' To prove it she let rip with a cough that sounded like a power saw attacking metal, Brittany staring up in awe.

'Jesus, Mrs de Pontes, you can't drop me like this. I gotta work.'

The coughing spasm ended with the old woman hacking up something into a tissue and slamming the door in Dawn's face. Locks were locked and bolts were thrown.

Dawn, with her kid down on Voortrekker – the familiar perfume of exhaust fumes and KFC and dust and poverty – takes a gap in the evening traffic to get them across safely, the neon of Lips blowing them kisses.

The wall-eyed doorwoman with the mustache checks Brittany out like she's trash. 'Ja? And what is this?'

Dawn bites back a curse, taking Brittany inside. Fortunately the stage is empty, nothing that Dawn has to shield the kid's eyes from. She gives Cliffie a wave and he nods, setting out bottles on the bar top. Dawn heads into the back, leading Britt up a short flight of stairs covered by a gum-tacky carpet. A steel door painted the color of flesh blocks the top of the stairs and Dawn knocks. Soft and polite.

'Ja?' The muffled voice of Costa, locked inside with his money.

'It's Dawn.'

Just one lock is turned – a serious one, Dawn knows – and there's Costa with a cigarette married to his lip, squinting at her through the smoke.

'Yes, Dawn?' His gaze travels south and he finds Brittany, who clutches Dawn's hand, disappearing halfway behind her ass at the sight of this white man.

'Costa, I got me a babysitter problem.' The Greek sighs. 'Please can I leave my kid here with you? I'll sit here with her between my sets.'

'Jesus, Dawn. You come to me with this?'

'Costa, man, please?'

He's shaking his head, already closing the door, cigarette smoke tracing patterns in the air.

'I been thinking about what you want,' she says, desperate. 'The rooms. With the men.'

The door stops and he looks at her. 'Ja? And?'

'Okay. Just give me a couple of days and I'll do it.'

'You not bullshit me?'

'No,' she says, shaking her head to hide the lie in her voice.

He nods, shrugs, opens the door. 'She can sit by me. But tonight only, you understand?'

'Yes. Thanks, man. Thanks.'

He walks back inside and sits down at his desk, fingers flying like a piano player's across an old adding machine. Dawn settles Brittany down on the floor, opens the bag that the kid always takes to Mrs de Pontes. A coloring book. Comics.

'Okay, now listen to me, you sit here and you draw and you read, hear me?' Brittany nods. 'You don't hassle Uncle Costa, okay?' Another nod.

A loud exhalation comes from the Greek at the desk, rising over the whir of the adding machine.

Dawn is out of there, with one final glance at Britt sitting on the floor staring up at the strange man. Don't fucken cry, she pleads silently, quickly closing the door and getting her ass through to the changing room, where the Ugly Sisters drink and smoke and scratch at her like barbed wire.

She ignores them and gets into her stage outfit and makes it just in time to catch up with the opening bars of 'I Bruise Easily.' The place has filled: the usual white faces, the usual stink of booze and cigarettes and that man-smell. Dawn leaves her routine to muscle memory, willing the minutes to pass, her mind on her child.

She exits, naked and covered in sweat, carrying her clothes. Dennis, the other bouncer, lurks backstage. He's family of Costa's and works the nights Vernon does his rent-a-cop thing. Dennis always hangs around Dawn, his eyes like slime on her.

She brushes past him and hits the dressing room, ready to get into her clothes and go through to Costa's office and be with her kid. Now not much stops Dawn in her tracks, but this sight does: Brittany sits on the make-up counter in the dressing room, the two Ugly Sisters, naked flesh dangling like meat in an abattoir, bookending her, the fat one teasing the child's hair into a blonde halo, the skinny one painting her face in garish smears. The room is smoggy with *tik*-smoke and the two bitches laugh like backed-up drains at their handiwork.

'What the fuck?' Dawn says. Brittany stares up at her, dazed.

The fat thing turns and says, 'Oh, here's Mommy!'

'Where's Costa?' Dawn asks.

'Had him an emergency by the house, so he left your little blondie with her aunties!' A shrieking laugh.

Dawn is ready to haul off and hit and kick and cause serious damage when she hears Dennis behind her.

'Dawn,' he says.

'Not fucken now, Dennis!' Spinning around to face him, but instead finds herself looking at a pinched-faced brown woman in a skirt and jacket and court shoes.

'Ms Cupido,' Merinda Appolis says, 'I was at your apartment for a routine inspection. Since you weren't home, I thought I'd try your place of employment. I'm very glad I did.' The bitch social worker enjoying every moment of this. 'You will appear before a magistrate within the next two days. I will be petitioning the court for this child to be removed from you and taken to a place of safety.'

'You can't do that,' Dawn says, sounding like a stranger.

'Oh, I can, Ms Cupido. And I shall.'

Appolis does a smart about-turn on her little heels and clicks herself out of there. Dawn grabs her phone from her bag and lifts Brittany off the counter and carries her toward the bathroom, speed-dialing, wanting nothing more now than to hear the voice of the man she hates more than anybody else on God's earth.

chapter 25

As Vernon draws his cell phone from one of the pouches in his Kevlar vest – the 'Private Dancer' ringtone telling him it's Dawn calling – he sees the lights of Exley's Audi convertible strobing through the bush, the car taking the last curve toward the house. Vernon sends Dawn to voicemail and stands up out of the Sniper truck, walking to the middle of the narrow road, holding up his right arm to halt Exley, shielding his eyes from the halogen beams with his left.

Exley stops, the tires crunching on gravel, and Vernon walks past the hot grille of the car with its distinctive four rings interlocking like some magic trick. The top of the Audi is down, Exley's hair yellow in the spill of the street light.

'Vernon,' Exley says.

'Nick.' Vernon leans on the door of the Audi, taking the weight off his bad leg, which throbs after the couple of hours he's sat vigil outside the house.

'Is there a problem?' Vernon can smell booze on Exley's breath. Scotch, he reckons.

'Ja, look Nick, Mrs E went a bit random this afternoon.' He gives an edited version of the events at the Stankovic house.

Exley shakes his head and massages his eyes beneath his glasses. 'Jesus, Vernon. Thanks for handling it.'

'It was nothing, buddy. But I think you've got a bit of a situation on your hands.'

'Caroline gets like this when she's off her meds. This thing with Sunny has derailed her, but Vlad's a friend and this is fucking embarrassing.'

Here's the gap Vernon's been waiting for. He baits his hook. 'Nick, him and your wife are more than friends, if you get what I'm saying.'

The whitey gazes up at him, gullible as a bunny. 'Not sure I do, Vernon.'

'Listen, I know this is one helluva time but I think there's something you should know.' Vernon pauses like a TV actor, milking the moment, making his voice all low and serious. 'For the last few months they been spending a lot of time together, your woman and him. Up at his house. While his wife's away.'

'You've seen them?'

Vernon shrugs. 'When I patrolled I couldn't help noticing Mrs E's car in his driveway.'

'That right?'

'Ja, and he takes her to Sandy Bay.'

Exley shakes his head. 'Caroline? On a nude beach? No way.'

'I seen them, Nick.'

'You must be mistaken.'

'Do you want me to go into detail, Nick, about what I seen?'

The whitey stares at him before he speaks. 'Jesus. You're sure?'

Vernon nods. 'Yes, Nick, I am. Sorry it has to be me telling you this.' He reaches out a hand and touches Exley on his bony shoulder, feels the tension in the man. 'Hell, my friend, I know you don't need no more shit right now.'

'Thank you, Vernon,' Exley says, all whispery. He clicks the Audi into drive and Vernon steps back and watches as Exley triggers the gate, which rattles open, lets the convertible through, then swallows it.

Happy fucken families.

Vernon lights a smoke, allowing himself a smile now as he pictures the shit that's going to go down inside that glass and wood box. He slides into the truck, smoking, facing the house, ready to eavesdrop on any action, when the radio hisses and squawks.

He reaches for the mike. 'Car Two.'

The dispatcher. No love in her voice. Probably a dyke. 'Alarm activation at forty-four Sunset.'

'Copy that. On my way.' Fuck it, probably a false alarm, but what can he do?

Vernon starts the truck, light bars making like Christmas, throws a U-turn and takes off at speed.

'So, what, were you sucking Vlad Stankovic's cock in here? While you were meant to be watching Sunny?' They're in the kitchen, where Exley found his wife when he came in from the garage.

Caroline stands by the counter with her back to him, hugging herself so tightly that her fingertips are bloodless. Exley sees her face reflected in the window; her eyes are closed and she is smiling. She hums tunelessly, just audible over the buzzing fluorescents. Despite the heat she wears the shapeless sweater, sleeves dangling to her fingertips, hem brushing her naked thighs.

'Jesus, talk to me, Caroline.'

She doesn't respond, holding herself, droning.

Exley's anger is fuelled by the Scotches he drank on the plane and he takes his wife by the shoulder, trying to turn her to him. She shrugs off his hand, her body rigid.

'Don't. You. Fucking. Touch. Me.'

When he clutches at her again she swivels her head and looks at him over her shoulder and what he sees in her eyes makes him drop his hand and take a step back.

Caroline, still humming, reaches across and pulls the largest, most lethal knife from the block on the counter, and spins, her arm raised, blade gleaming as it points toward his chest, like some deranged King Arthur.

'Put the knife down,' Exley says, seizing her arm. She breaks loose and slashes with the carving knife, cutting him across the back of his left hand. Not a deep cut, but enough to break the skin, and blood wells up.

'You crazy fucking bitch!' he says as she comes at him again. He parries but his fingers are cut now and he knows she is past reason, that he has to get the knife away from her.

He feels the sharpened edge slicing into his left palm as he grips the steel, feels the warmth of the blood, and twists and rips the knife from her grasp, switching it to his right hand.

He shoves Caroline away from him and she hits the fridge with her shoulders, freeing one of Sunny's crayon drawings, which floats to the floor, and the picture of the happy nuclear family (Exley and Caro and Sunny holding hands under a smiley-faced sun) sticks to the sole of his wife's bare foot – a foot tacky with his blood.

Caroline catches hold of the counter, panting, breath smelling of stale tea and cigarettes and wine, cursing him in an unintelligible stream, her body wiry and taut. Then she stretches for the block again and frees another knife, with a smaller, serrated cutting edge.

Exley knows he should retreat, lock himself in his studio, hit the panic button and call for help. But he doesn't. He advances and knocks the small blade from her grasp. She looks at him, quiet now, just the rise and fall of her breath, the buzz of the fluorescent, the hard tick of the wall clock and the hum of the refrigerator.

Then Caroline says, 'I'm glad she's dead,' her voice low and hoarse. 'You were always so smug in your little world of two. Now you know how it feels to be alone.'

She means every word, and Exley hates her for it.

He lifts the carving knife high over his head, seeing the shadow of his arm and the tapering steel lying black across Caroline's face and chest.

'You don't have the balls,' she says.

Exley's read about people who have killed saying that it was all a blur, claiming amnesia, but everything becomes hyperreal, his vision so sharply focused that he can see the pores in Caroline's nose – a pimple incubating just below her left nostril – sees the flecks of foamy spittle at the sides of her mouth, sees her pupils dilated and reddish through the gingery lashes.

Time stretches and he can almost feel the message as it travels from his brain, down his shoulder and right arm, to his hand tightening its grip on the handle of the knife. His arm falls. As the blade arcs toward Caroline's chest he's certain that she is too sinewy and bony – too armored – for the steel to penetrate. It will snap against her chest.

But it doesn't.

There is a moment of resistance as the knife finds flesh and she grunts, then he is right up against her, his weight driving the blade past her breastbone into the chest cavity, into her aorta. She pushes back, almost topples him, fighting for her life, impossibly strong – veins and tendons standing out like a relief map in her neck as she tugs at his arm and struggles with manic energy, her funk rising up at him from beneath her sweater, ribbons of blood slingshot by her flailing limbs.

He loses his grip on the knife handle, his fingers slick with her blood, and he has to hold on to Caroline to keep himself from falling, pulling her toward him in an embrace as warm fluid geysers from her mouth and onto his chest. She looks up at him and her eyes, fixed on his, cloud and he knows he is watching her die and he feels only relief as he releases her and she slips down and lies on the tiled floor in a spreading pool, knife in her chest, their child's drawing still glued to her foot.

Thick, dark blood spews from her mouth and she kicks her feet and pisses and shits herself, and he feels ashamed for her. Then her eyes blink and freeze and something fades from them and he realizes the enormity of what he has done.

Rivers of red follow the grid of the tile grouting and Exley steps back, desperate not to let the blood touch his Reeboks. He retreats farther until he feels his haunches against the counter and he stands still for how long he doesn't know, listening to the fluorescents and the song of the fridge and the measured hammer of the clock until he knows he must do something.

So he finds his BlackBerry in his pocket and scrolls down to Vernon Saul's number and presses the little green button.

chapter 26

BEAUTIFUL. FUCKEN BEAUTIFUL.

When Vernon walks in and sees the mad bitch lying dead, the handle of the knife sticking out of her chest and Nick Exley pacing the kitchen covered in blood, things just kind of slow down, and he goes into the zone and he knows exactly what to do.

Exley is pale as paper, shaking so badly his teeth are doing the flamenco. 'She came at me, Vernon, with the knife. We fought, I dunno what happened, but, Jesus… We better get the cops.'

Vernon holds up a hand. 'Nick, whoa, buddy. Focus. You done right by calling me first.' The white guy stares at him from the far side of hell. 'We can contain this.'

'Contain what? I killed her.'

'You need to chill, Nick. Come.' He leads Exley to the adjoining living room. 'Take a seat. Listen careful now, we don't have much time.'

They sit, Vernon positioning Exley with his back to the mess in the kitchen. 'Nick, what you got to understand is that if this happened out on the Flats, or even in some crap white suburb, nobody gonna give a fuck about it. Just another dead body. But you guys are rich foreigners. It's embarrassing for the authorities when this kind of shit goes down, them so busy bullshitting the world South Africa don't have no crime epidemic.' Talking nice and calmly now, drawing Exley in. 'Believe me, the cops are gonna be all over this. And they gonna ride you hard, my buddy.'

'But it was self-defense.'

Vernon shrugs. 'Hey, Nick, you don't need to convince me of nothing. But you don't want to fuck with the South African legal system. White guy like you, they'll throw your ass into Pollsmoor with a bunch of hardcore darkies and I think we both know how that'll go.'

'Surely I'll make bail?'

'Eventually, maybe. Still, they gonna hold you until you get a bail hearing. Courts are jammed up, so it'll take days, with you stuck in Pollsmoor. Then, being a foreigner and all, prosecutor'll say you're a flight risk, which could delay things, or if the judge is a hardass maybe he denies bail.' He sees the fear in Exley's face and has to bite back a smile. 'Even if you get bail, you gonna have to surrender your passport, then it's gonna be months, maybe even years, with you on trial. And Nick, believe me, I know what I'm talking about, at the end of it there's a good chance you'll be looking at jail time, 'cause they wanna make an example of you. You'll sit for a couple of years at least. Maybe more.' He shakes his head. 'Guy like you, you not gonna make it.'

'So what do I do?'

Vernon pauses, holding Exley's gaze, slowing things down. 'First, you didn't kill your wife, you hearing me?' Exley shakes his head. 'Okay. This is how it goes. You park the Audi, walk in from the garage, see her on the floor bleeding. Then a darkie comes at you with a knife, mad motherfucker with dreadlocks and he wants to stab you too. You fight him and your hand gets cut. Then he runs out onto the deck and away across the rocks. You go to your wife and she's still alive. Just. You hold her – that's how you get all that blood on you – and she dies in your arms. Then you call me.'

Exley slumps, staring down at the tiles. 'It's crazy. Nobody will believe it.'

'Sure they will. Look at me, Nick.' The whitey lifts his gaze. 'There's been reports of some whack-head Rasta running around here. Your wife was alone, freaked out, didn't put on the alarm and left the deck door wide open. He came in to rob the house, she interrupted him and he grabbed the knife and stabbed her. Pocketed her cell phone and then you came in, scared him off. Happens all the time.'

'What about the knife?'

'He took it with him.' He sees the look on Exley's face. 'Don't worry, Nick, I'll sort this. You go find me your wife's phone, okay?'

Exley hesitates and for a moment Vernon fears that he's losing him. 'Nick, this is about the rest of your life, buddy. Be smart.'

At last Exley nods and disappears upstairs. Vernon steps into the kitchen, careful not to track through the blood, and searches the drawers until he finds a plastic bag. He puts the bag around his hand, kneels down beside Caroline Exley as if he's going to check for vital signs, but he draws the blade from her chest – a little suck of air as he uncorks the wound – and drops the knife into the bag. He uses the plastic to smudge any prints on the handle.

He stands as Exley returns, holding out a new Nokia. Vernon opens the mouth of the bag. 'Drop it inside.' The phone clatters in beside the knife. 'Now I bet you're thinking about the surveillance cameras?'

When Exley stares at him blankly, Vernon leads the way across the living room toward the sliding door, pointing out into the night. 'There's a blind spot right there. Part of the deck and the beach are out of their range. You tell the cops that's where the mad bastard went. I've already recommended to the technicians that they install another camera but they're slack fuckers. Lucky for us, hey?'

Exley nods, running a bloody hand through his hair, barely holding on to himself. The furniture of this poor bastard's life has been seriously rearranged over the last few days.

'Okay, I'm gonna stash this in my truck.' Vernon lifts the plastic bag. 'Then I'm gonna call the cops and the ambulance. So you got your story straight?'

'Yes, I think so.'

'Run it by me.'

Exley tries, but he loses his way and ends up shaking his head again. 'The cops will never buy this.'

'Try again, Nick.'

When Exley just stands there, staring, Vernon steps in close, speaking real soft. 'You don't get this right you're fucked, my buddy. Now try it again.'

Exley stutters and stumbles, but he manages to get through the fiction Vernon has created.

'Good, Nick. Just one more thing, this Rasta, he don't say not even one word to you. Like he's dumb. You understand?'

Exley nods and Vernon heads for the door. 'Vernon?'

'Ja?'

'Why are you helping me?'

Turning to face him, Vernon says, 'Because, Nick, you don't deserve this shit. Simple as that. You one of the good guys.'

Exley crumples at last, like he's made of bits of straw that the wind's got hold of, and sinks down onto the sofa, holding his head in his hands.

As Vernon goes out to lock the bag in his truck he has to stop himself from whistling a happy tune. The perfection of the moment almost makes him believe that there is a God up there somewhere.

'I could have stopped it,' Exley says, sitting forward on the sofa.

The very black police captain, his skin shining with sweat, leans in close and says, 'Stopped what, sir?'

Exley stares at him, shaking his head. Good question. Could have stopped his daughter drowning if only he'd paid attention? Could have stopped the fall of the blade and spared Caroline's life?

Exley understands that he's experiencing a form of psychic bleed-through, that his memories of Sunny drowning are cross-talking to the events of tonight. As the procession of uniformed men move around him, as they did three nights before, the deaths of his child and his wife blur and merge and rip the boundaries of his increasingly fragile sense of reality.

It is only when he looks past the black man and sees the cops in the kitchen standing over Caroline's body that he knows hers is the death *du jour.*

'The stabbing,' Exley says, remembering that endless moment when he had the time to lower the blade, walk away and leave his unfaithful wife alive. 'I could have stopped the stabbing.'

'How, sir?'

Exley, catching the eye of Vernon Saul lumbering toward the deck, realizes that he has stepped out of character. That he is about to damn himself, so he lurches back into the role of the innocent man and tells the cop that if he'd come home five minutes earlier he could have stopped it. Tells him how he walked into the kitchen, his wife's lifeblood leaking onto the tiled floor. How he confronted the intruder and sent him fleeing, but too late to save Caroline.

Just as he was too late to save his daughter. The gospel according to Vernon Saul lending these two tragedies the elegance of symmetry.

Leaving Exley a victim.

Free of blame.

Free of guilt.

The captain's tired eyes grant Exley absolution and then the black man is gone and time ramps: the house goes from empty to full in a nanosecond. More cops. More medics.

A sallow man with a shaven head, standing alone on the deck, his outline warped by the glass door, turns to stare in at Exley. Then he too is gone, the medic who pronounced Sunny dead, and as a camera flash detonates, Exley sees him in the kitchen, hovering over Caroline, rolling off a pair of bloodstained latex gloves, the fingers stretching and snapping as he lets the gloves fall into his emergency bag.

Exley holds up his left hand. It is bandaged, his palm strapped tight, and he has a vague memory of this man attending to him, the smell of ammonia rising from his white coat.

A sound like frenzied bees startles Exley. The zipper of a body bag. He sees Sunny's white face swallowed by shiny black plastic, but the bag carried out past him is too big to hold a child, so it must be Caroline, bloody and cold, who lies inside.

Exley's gaze is drawn to the darkness of the beach where his wife, sodden, hugging herself, circles Sunny's body, and then she is in an embrace with Exley, a gush of blood spewing from her mouth, soaking his linen shirt, warm on the skin of his chest.

Exley shuts down, the sofa enveloping him like an Oldenburg soft sculpture, sensory overload tripping his circuits, leaving him close to comatose, oblivious to the men observing the post-death rituals around him.

He goes so far away, so deep into himself, that he doesn't hear the gunfire or the screams of the startled seagulls.

chapter 27

IT HAS BEEN VERNON SAUL'S NIGHT. IF HE'D WRITTEN A SCRIPT IT COULDN'T have gone better. The darkie captain – dressed in casual clothes like he's come straight from home – is calling the shots, assembling his men on the deck. A bureaucrat not a cop, all he's interested in is making himself look good, and a high-profile murder going unsolved will slow this monkey's climb up the ladder, so he'll be focused on closing this case fast as possible. It's not about justice, it's about statistics.

A numbers game.

Vernon, losing himself among the crime techs, listened as the darkie questioned Exley, who, with his bandaged hand and bloody shirt, seemed close to breaking. Fumbling for words. Rambling. Talking one minute about his dead daughter, the next about his dead wife.

But he gave the version they agreed on. Garbled, yes, but that made him all the more believable. A man in shock. A man living through a week of hell. But not a killer.

The captain instructs the uniformed cops to search the rocks on the right side of the beach, where Exley said the attacker fled, and Vernon watches as they slide and curse, battling over the slick rocks, flashlights bobbing. One man goes down, his holstered sidearm clanking against the stone.

Vernon walks out into the street, past the knot of cop vans and emergency vehicles, some of the medics sharing a smoke, one of them laughing softly. He starts his truck and drives down into the dead end, into the darkness. He cuts his headlights and checks that he isn't being observed. Before leaving the truck he kills the dome light and steps out into the lace of mist that floats in off the ocean, feeling it damp on the skin of his face, making him even more alert.

He carries the plastic bag and finds the pathway down to the ocean by the faint light of the moon. It doesn't enter his head for a moment that the mad Rasta may not be in his hideaway down by the sea. Just knows he'll be there.

And he is.

Vernon smells the weed, ripe and rich, overlaying the odor of kelp. He reaches the bottom of the path, his boots hammering on rock, and he sees the glow of the spliff. He unclips his flashlight and sends the beam at the Rasta, who squats in the bush, shielding his eyes, bobbing his dreadlocks.

'It's me, my friend,' Vernon says, and the man shows his teeth in recognition.

Vernon stands over the lunatic and opens the plastic bag, tipping it so that Caroline Exley's cell phone falls at the Rasta's feet. The man stares at the phone and then up at Vernon.

Vernon mimes making a call. 'Pick it up.'

Obediently, the Rasta picks up the phone and holds it out to Vernon, who ignores it, using the bag to grip the bloodstained blade of the knife, offering the handle to the crazy man.

The idiot is confused now. He puts the phone down on the rock, very carefully, protecting it from the lapping waves, and gazes up at Vernon, who stands holding the knife out to him.

'Take it,' Vernon says.

The Rasta jiggles and hops, comes halfway to his feet, but he grabs the handle firmly, pulling the knife from the bag, leaving a nice set of prints. Vernon wraps the plastic bag around his right hand and takes the knife back from the Rasta, holding it by the blade.

He lifts the flashlight to his mouth and grips it with his teeth, directing the beam toward his bare left forearm, his shirtsleeve rolled up to his bicep. Gripping the knife low on the handle so he doesn't disturb the prints, the plastic rustling beneath his fingers, Vernon holds the tip of the blade above his left arm. He shakes the arm, loosening it, relaxing the muscles and the tendons, inhales deeply, exhales, then he brings the steel down hard and feels it bite into his flesh just below his elbow, dragging the knife toward his wrist, opening up a deep gash.

Blood spurts and runs down his fingers and spatters onto the rock.

The Rasta watches Vernon, agitated, hair dancing. Vernon drops the knife at the man's feet and the lunatic jumps back and comes into a low crouch. Vernon takes the flashlight from his mouth, holding it in the bloody fingers of his left hand, directing the beam toward the agitated man, unclipping his Glock with his right hand. The Rasta cowers, covering his face, shaking his matted hair.

Vernon shoots him twice. Head and heart. Dead before he slumps to the rock.

Vernon turns and walks back up to the road, his left arm throbbing, dripping blood. But he feels no pain, only elation, as he limps toward the shouting cops, their flashlight beams raking the night.

chapter 28

UNIFORMED MAN SHAKES EXLEY AWAKE AND HE SITS UP ON THE SOFA, looking around the living room that is now empty of police and medics. He has no idea how long he slept.

'You have to come with me, sir,' the cop says,

So, Exley thinks, this is it. Already offering his wrists for cuffing.

But the cop is solicitous, apologizing in his brutal accent for waking Exley as he walks him outside and through the gate, down to where the road runs dead into the rocks. The area is crammed with police vehicles.

Exley's escort leads him down a narrow path that carves through the dense bush, showing the way with a flashlight. Something scratches at Exley's face, dislodging his glasses, and he holds out an arm to fend off the undergrowth.

He sees a glow through the foliage and then he steps into a scene straight out of a movie: searingly bright arc lights illuminate the flat rocks that rise from the ocean. A cold breeze blows off the water and ribbons of mist swirl in the beams.

A group of cops is gathered around a form that lies on a rock. Exley searches for Vernon Saul, but can't find him.

The captain steps forward. 'Mr Exley, we believe we have the man who attacked you and your wife. Please come this way.'

He ushers Exley through the cops and Exley looks down at the body of a black man, shirtless, emaciated, dressed only in a pair of torn sweatpants, feet bare, toenails curling like talons. The dead man lies on his side, his arms flung out, the ocean tugging at his dreadlocks, setting them afloat and then releasing them back onto the rock.

Where the man's left eye should be is a messy crater and something soft and pulpy oozes from the back of his skull, matting his hair, trails of pinkish blood mixing with the spume from the ocean. There is another wound in his chest, over his heart. Small and neat, just one dark trickle weeping from it.

Exley looks at the man's face, lips drawn back from crooked, rotten teeth, the fringe of beard around his mouth matted with blood. Exley has never seen him before.

'Is this him, sir? The man who came into your house?' the captain asks.

Vernon Saul's face swims out of the dark. He has a cigarette in his hand, exhaling a plume of smoke that hangs in the lights. Staring at Exley. Unblinking.

As Exley understands what Vernon has done, he feels his knees going and he wobbles. The captain grabs his arm and the cop who escorted him steps in and they lower Exley to the rock, setting him down beside the dead man. He stares up at the ring of faceless figures silhouetted by the arc lights.

The captain crouches. 'Are you okay, Mr Exley? Do you need medical attention?'

He shakes his head. 'No, I'm fine. Sorry. Just a shock, seeing this man. Realizing what has happened.'

The captain says, 'So, sir, you're positively identifying him as the attacker?'

Exley looks past the cop, into Vernon's eyes, and says, 'Yes. Yes, it's him,' knowing he is damned now, as surely as if he put the bullets into this man himself.

DAWN GETS AS FAR AS STARTING TO PACK FOR HER AND BRITTANY, GRABBING their clothes from the closet and throwing them into a suitcase. She's not gonna let them take her child away again. No ways.

Then she stops and it's like all her strength – her fucken *spirit* – just drains out the soles of her bare feet and she sits her ass on the carpet, resting her elbows on her knees, staring down at the burn marks and the years of filth spotlit by the morning sun, the room already overheating.

She sits there crying, listening to the growl of the traffic and the horns of the taxis, one of the co-drivers yelling 'Caaaaaape Toooownnnnn' as he passes by beneath.

Dawn wipes snot on the back of her hand and muffles her sobs, not wanting to wake Brittany, who lies sleeping on the bed, clutching the Barbie doll Vernon Saul gave her. Fucken Vernon, she blew all her airtime on him, leaving messages all through the night, each one more frantic than the last. Heard nothing from him.

Dawn dries her eyes on her T-shirt and lights a smoke, the match nearly dying on her she's shaking so bad, sucks in nicotine – wishing, just for a moment, that it was *tik* – and sits and looks at her daughter, sees how totally and completely gorgeous she is with her tangled blonde hair and light skin.

Dawn pulls the clothes from the suitcase and packs them back in the closet. What the fuck was she thinking, anyway? She's got no money. Even if she did have the cash, where the hell did she think she and Brittany were going to go? Her family is poison, no ways she's letting her kid near none of them. Got no friends to speak of – never learned to trust people enough to let them in close. They always want something from you, sometime, and that's the God's honest truth.

Her only lifeline was that psycho Vernon and it looks like she can forget about him. So, fucked is what she is. She don't even have a job no more. Just took her kid and split last night after the thing with the social worker, still hours of her shift left. Got a voice message from Costa saying he's had enough of her crap and she shouldn't bother coming back and he means it this time.

As Dawn shuts the closet door one of its hinges screams and wakes Brittany, who sits up and rubs her eyes. 'Am I going to work with you again, Mommy? Tonight?'

'No, my baby.' Faking a smile, getting her mother shit together. 'Come, go pee, we need to get you to playschool.'

The child slides off the bed in her yellow PJs, and walks like a drunkard toward the bathroom, still clutching her doll. Dawn hears the clang of the toilet seat and soft dribbles as her daughter pisses.

She imagines her life without her baby and fear nearly overwhelms her and suddenly she can't breathe. She flings open the balcony doors, getting a lungful of the traffic fumes. Voortrekker Road lies exposed under the hot sun: take-out joints and used car lots and tired buildings flanking the long, straight road into Cape Town, the flat-topped mountain with its tablecloth of cloud a distant dream through the smog.

Dawn sucks the last life from her cigarette and flicks it away, watching it tumble down to the sidewalk, where black and brown vendors sell sweets and fruit and cheap clothes.

She knows that she's going to have to go out there and sell something too. Her ass. Get on the street now that even the backrooms of Lips aren't an option no more, dodge the Nigerian pimps and the fists and feet and teeth of the territorial whores, and get some money together. Needs money to get a lawyer to fight for her daughter.

As Dawn walks back inside her phone, lying on the TV, starts to ring. She lifts it and sees Vernon's name on caller ID. 'Jesus, Vernon, I been trying you all night!'

'Ja, I got ten thousand voicemails. What the fuck's going on?'

'They gonna take Brittany away, the social workers.' She tells him about last night, gabbling, breathless, desperate to finish before he hangs up on her.

'Dawnie?'

'Ja?'

'Chill.'

'Vernon, fuck, I can't lose her.'

'You relax now, okay? I'm on it.'

'You mean it? Please, Vernon—'

'I'll make this all go away. I promise.' He hangs up.

Dawn lets the cell phone droop to her side and stands staring at her daughter walking from the bathroom, smiling up at her, wondering how something so beautiful could come out of such a fucked-up world.

chapter 30

YVONNE SAUL SLIPS HER FEET INTO CARPET SLIPPERS AND SHUFFLES INTO the kitchen. Vernon is already at the table, dressed in jeans and a neatly pressed shirt, drinking a Coke. Likes his Coke with his breakfast. When he lifts the can to his mouth she sees that his left arm is heavily bandaged.

'What happened to you?' she asks, turning on the stove, getting eggs and bacon out the fridge. Her eyes find the dwindling supply of insulin and she knows she'll have to beg him again.

'Darkie came at me with a knife last night,' he says, burping.

She breaks eggs into a bowl, looking across at him. 'Is it bad?'

He shrugs. 'Could have been my throat.' He smiles – one of those cold smiles he's been using on her since he was eleven – then tips his chair back on two legs, riding it, hands behind his head, all full of himself. 'You look like shit.'

'I couldn't sleep. That next-door baby.'

He shrugs, lets the chair fall forward with a clatter and empties the Coke down his throat, burping even louder. 'Don't worry with breakfast for me. I gotta be somewhere.' He stands and shoves his chair back.

Yvonne is already beating the eggs in the bowl. She stops, the yellow yolk dripping from the egg beater. They'll go to waste now.

'Boy, I need my insulin,' she says. 'It's getting really low.'

She waits for him to lose his temper but he doesn't. Just nods, tucking his shirt into his jeans. 'Okay, I buy you some today.'

He walks out whistling 'Tie A Yellow Ribbon Round The Old Oak Tree.' She hates that song. It was her husband's favorite, they even played it at their wedding, and she can't hear it without seeing his brains smeared all over their bed, positive that Vernon whistles it to torment her. Yvonne feels sick, the smell of the eggs enough to make her puke.

She hardly shut her eyes in the night. The screaming from the next-door shack was the worst it's ever been. She tried to put the pillow over her head, to block her ears, but it didn't help. Whatever sympathy Yvonne had for the little one inside that shack is gone, she's worried about herself now. She can't go without sleep night after blessed night, not with her hypertension and diabetes.

This morning she barely had the strength to drag herself from the bed, and as she pulled her robe over her nightdress she saw bruises on both her arms. Not from Vernon, he hasn't hurt her for a while, and she didn't remember bumping herself. She lifted the hem of her nightdress and saw more bruises on her legs. Not bruises, she realized, but burst blood vessels. From the blood-thinners she's on to control her blood pressure. The stress from living with what her son has become, coupled with not sleeping, is just too much for her.

Yvonne walks away from the stove and opens the back door to get some air. The screams are even louder now. Before she can stop herself she hurries through to the phone in the living room and dials the cops. Speaks to some girl who sounds like a child herself. Tells her about the screams. Gives the address but refuses to leave her name. She hangs up, knowing that she's wasted her time. The cops will do nothing.

Yvonne goes through to the airless bathroom, still stinking from Vernon's morning visit to the lavatory, and soaps under her arms and between her legs, doesn't have the strength for a shower. She dries herself and pads barefoot into the bedroom and pulls on a T-shirt and sweatpants, knows she looks a sight, but who's going to see her?

She slumps down on the bed, arms dangling, staring at dust dancing in a shaft of sunlight that pokes through a tear in the curtain. She sits like that until she's covered in sweat and the room is like an oven.

She opens the curtains, letting some air in, and the first thing she sees is two cops, a man and a woman, in their gray-blue uniforms and bullet-proof vests, walking up to the next-door shack. Yvonne jumps away from the window in case they spot her.

She hears banging on the shack door, the woman cop ordering them to open up. Nothing happens, so she bangs again. Yvonne edges forward, peeping between the curtains, more confident now the cops have their backs to her. The woman leans down and tries to look in the only window of the shack but it's blocked off with cardboard.

The man cop hammers on the door and the thin whine of the child starts up, growing louder and louder, like a siren. The woman draws her gun, a big thing in her hand, and the man takes a step back and kicks at the door, planting the sole of his boot high on the rotten wood. It splinters but holds. He steps back and kicks again and the door tears free of the loops of wire that keep it in place and falls inward.

Now, Yvonne is no stranger to human cruelty, not after what she's lived through in this very house. But nothing, as true as God in all his heavens, has prepared her for what she sees as that door flies open and the bright sun floods the room, hitting the thing writhing on a mattress, and the thing becomes the jailbird and the baby, their shadows flung against the torn walls of the shack.

Terror gnawing at Exley's entrails rips him screaming from his sleep. He is assaulted by consciousness, literally experiences it as a blow to the solar plexus, curling himself into a fetal position, trying to grab onto the coat-tails of oblivion and drag it back. Too late.

Catapulted by panic from Sunny's bed, he stands in the litter of her toys, gasping for breath, his heart a wrecking ball in his chest, his mind full of knife blades and shit and blood and death.

He's dripping with sweat, and even though he wears a clean T-shirt and boxers – he has no recall of shedding the clothes in which he committed murder – his nostrils are full of the old-iron stink of blood. He flexes his left hand, the wrapping of bandage and surgical tape tight on his flesh, a reminder of those moments before he killed Caroline.

When he still had a choice.

Exley goes to the window and stares out into the cauterizing brightness and has no idea how to begin to process the last day, wishing he could retreat into the convenient Hindu trope that there is no reality, that all is *maya*, all is illusion. Newsflash: this is your life, Nicholas Exley, and it is fucking real, okay?

And then the big question tries to batter its way into his consciousness: who the fuck *are* you? Not ready for that. Not now. So, okay, let's ease into this, he tells himself. Let's rather try and figure out who you are *not*.

Not a father.

Not a husband.

Not an innocent.

Which leads to the inevitable answer to the first question: he's a killer three times over. Killed his child through negligence. Killed his wife in a moment of conscious fury. Killed that homeless Rasta by allowing Vernon Saul's dark gospel to prevail.

The doorbell startles Exley and he finds his glasses beside the bed and stumbles into the corridor toward the intercom phone and manages to say, 'Yes?'

'Hey, Nick. Open up.' Vernon Saul, sounding full of spunk and vigor. A real fucking piece of work, as Exley's late father would have said.

Exley wants to slink away and hide, curl up somewhere and let the world continue hurtling forward without his participation, but he hits the button to open the gate and walks down the stairs. He's in his socks and the big toe of his left foot emerges through a hole, naked and pink. He reaches the bottom step and stops, his motor nerves seizing at the sight that awaits him: the cheerful morning light illuminating the horror that is his kitchen.

Exley is astonished by the volume of blood. The tiled floor is awash with it, the plasma drying brown and viscous. There are wild Jackson Pollock splatters across the kitchen cabinets and the counters. The second hand of the wall clock ticks away gamely beneath glass made semi-opaque by blood. The refrigerator sports a red handprint. Exley resists the temptation to walk over and match a palm to it, to see if it is his or Caroline's.

A loud banging on the front door jolts Exley into motion and he follows the spoor of dark blood that the cops and crime techs tracked onto the Labrador-colored carpet. He opens the door to find Vernon flanked by two brown men in blue jumpsuits, each with a kitbag slung over his shoulder.

'Nick, meet Dougie and Oscar. They do trauma clean-ups. Brought them to sort out your kitchen.' The two men nod, regarding Exley with eyes empty of curiosity.

Exley steps back and Vernon heaves his way into the house. 'Nick,' he says, 'why don't you chill in your computer room? I'll get these guys going then we can have a talk, okay?' Without waiting for an answer he heads off toward the kitchen, the brown men at his heels.

Exley doesn't have a better idea so he walks down to the studio and slides open the door, the murk drawing him in, the room silent but for the hum of his workstation. Shutting the door, Exley settles back in the Aeron chair, letting it enfold him. He closes his eyes, trying to breathe through the horrific images his memory keeps serving him, trying to remain detached.

The door bumps open and Vernon, stinking of cheap aftershave and hair gel, loud gusts of air escaping his nostrils, clatters his way inside and falls into a chair that protests at his weight.

Exley sits upright, attempting to present himself with some authority, even though he's in his underwear. 'What do you want, Vernon?'

The big man shakes his head. 'Come again?'

'Do you want money? For what you did?'

Vernon forces a laugh, strangely high pitched and girlish. 'You're kidding me, right?'

'No, Vernon, I'm not kidding.'

'Jesus, Nick, now you've offended me.'

'Then explain to me what you want.'

'I don't want nothing from you.'

'Nothing?'

Vernon shrugs. 'I just want to help, is all.'

'By shooting that homeless man?'

'Come, Nick, where you going with this? You're off the hook. What's the bloody problem?'

'The problem is you went and killed him.'

'Just like you killed your wife.'

'That's different.'

'Ja? How?'

'What you did was cold-blooded murder.'

Vernon laughs. 'You reckon a court of law gonna think what you done is any better than what I done?'

When Exley says nothing, Vernon reaches forward and lays a hand on his bare knee and Exley flinches and wheels himself away from the big man's clammy touch.

'Nick, just take it easy now. You saw the guy. He was starving, living like an animal. Half out of his mind and probably rotten with AIDS.

How long do you think he would've lasted? I did him a favor by putting him out of his misery.' Exley shakes his head. 'Nick, why not just go with the version we told the cops?'

'Because I know the truth.'

'The truth, Nick? What the fuck's the truth? Back when I was a detective I'd interview ten witnesses who seen the same shit go down and each and every one got his own version, swears it's true. Hear me, man, it's not a lie if you believe it, buddy. So, believe the guy killed your wife. Simple.'

In that moment Exley understands that it really is that simple for Vernon Saul. He has the sociopath's gift of wholly believing his own fabrications. Exley shakes his head again, staring at a pilot light winking beneath the console of his computer, like an airplane at night. He feels the urge to phone the police captain and confess. Unburden himself.

'Nick, we not gonna have a problem, are we?' Vernon asks, as if he's reading Exley's mind.

'What do you mean?' Exley says, looking into those lifeless eyes.

'Just understand something here, my friend. Right now the cops are happy as pigs in shit. A high-profile case is closed. They gonna be very pissed off if they have to open it again. Not gonna like you very much. And I can tell you how it'll play out: you'll be the rich whitey who murders his wife then hires some poor colored fucker – that would be me – to waste a homeless darkie and pin it on him. No fucken wriggle room there, Nick. No self-defense. No sympathy from the court. We're talking first-degree murder, on not one, but two counts. You'll die in prison, my friend. That what you want?'

Exley stares at Vernon. 'And you'd support that version of events?'

'Hey, if you drop the ball I gotta look out for number one, Nick. Plea-bargain for all my ass is worth. Nothing personal, understand?'

'Yes, I understand.' And Exley does understand. Understands that his fear has trumped his morality. He manages a hollow laugh. 'Okay, Vernon's version it is, then.'

The big man laughs, too. 'Vernon's version. Hey, I like that! So, we okay, you and me?'

'Yes, we're okay.'

'Good. You just need a couple of days, Nick, to get over the shock. Then things will calm down and you'll be thinking clearer. Ready for your new life. You know what I mean?'

Exley shrugs. They sit in silence, Vernon jiggling his good leg, shaking some change in his pocket, his loud breath washing the room.

A trilling sound announces a Skype call and Exley, relieved at the interruption, wheels himself to his computer and sees the name 'Alberto' displayed in the little orange and white window. Normally he'd ignore this – Alberto Pereira is a dilettante, a Brazilian playboy who bought Life in a Box on a whim – but right now any voice from outside this madness is welcome.

Exley clicks the red key to accept the call and Pereira's tanned face appears on the monitor, all white teeth and dark hair, like a South American racing driver.

'Al,' Exley says, keeping his webcam disabled, unwilling to let the eyes of the world in.

'Nick, where the hell you been? I been trying you on your cell and sending you emails, man.' Pereira's Americanized drawl booms from the speakers.

'I've been busy.'

'Listen, dude, you gotta help me. I'm doing this music video and I need to capture a girl dancing but your system, man, it's giving me hassles.'

'It's not the system,' Exley says, 'it's you.'

'Whatever. I'm emailing you the music right now, kinda of an updated Astrid Gilberto, samba thing. Just get some girl out there in Cape Town to shake her ass nicely and send me the motion stream. I'll make it worth your while.'

'Can't do it, Alberto. Sorry.'

'Nick, I'm not taking no for an answer,' the Brazilian says, smiling irresistibly, shaking his curly locks. 'Just listen to it, okay?'

Alberto ends the call and disappears. In a moment a ping announces the arrival of an email.

'That the music coming through?' Vernon asks.

'Yeah.'

'So play it.'

'No. Not now.'

'Come on, Nick. For me, buddy. I'm a music lover.'

It's the last thing Exley's in the mood for, but he clicks on the MP3 and brassy salsa fills the studio. Staccato drumbeats and absurd Brazilian love calls. Vernon gets a little groove going in his seat, moving his massive shoulders, clicking his fingers. Disturbing to witness. Exley mutes the music.

'I'm feeling it, Nick,' Vernon says, drumming fingers on his knee. 'Where's he, this guy?'

'Rio.'

'So you gonna do it for him?'

'No way.'

'Why not?'

'Jesus, Vernon, at a time like this?'

'Do you good, get your mind off all this crazy shit.'

Exley shakes his head. 'No. And where the hell would I find a dancer, anyway?'

Vernon taps himself on the chest. 'Me.'

Exley stares him, shaking his head. 'He wants a girl, Vernon.'

'No, man, don't be an asshole. I can get you the perfect girl. Professional. Even looks Brazilian.'

Exley waves his hands, killing this at source. 'No ways. Forget it, Vernon. You hearing me?'

Vernon says, 'Ja, ja' but what he's hearing is his cell phone bleating in his pocket. He clicks it open and says, 'Vernon Saul.' Gets to his feet, grimacing, shaking blood into his withered leg. 'Okay, gimme fifteen minutes.' He closes the phone and pockets it. 'That's the cops, down in Hout Bay. They wanna go over a few things with me. Don't worry, Nick, just routine shit.'

'Okay,' Exley says, uneasy in the knowledge that his fate rests in this lunatic's hands.

Vernon looms over him. 'So, I'll speak to you later, buddy, maybe pop in for a beer,' he says, and jolts his way out the door and down the passageway, shouting something in Afrikaans to the guys in the kitchen, leaving Exley to wonder exactly what karmic wind blew Vernon Saul into his once neat little world.

chapter 32

ERNON WALKS INTO HOUT BAY COP SHOP LIKE HE OWNS THE PLACE, STILL high on what happened the night before – that black captain almost ready to kiss his ass he was so pleased at closing the case. Vernon gives the door to the captain's office a half-knock and enters without waiting for a reply, expecting the darkie to be behind his desk, ready to treat him like he's God's gift.

The captain's behind his nice wooden desk, okay, but there's somebody else in the room: Dino Erasmus stands by the window. Erasmus turns and gives Vernon a smile that stretches his nostrils even wider. 'Vernon.'

'This is a surprise, Dino.'

'No, the Boogie thing was a surprise. This one I asked for.'

'Ja? Why?'

'Because it stinks worse than those cunts at that club of yours.'

Vernon keeps himself cool, gives the captain a glance. The black man looks troubled. He outranks Erasmus, but there's no doubt who's driving this session. Still, Vernon plays to the darkie. 'Mind if I sit, Captain?'

The cop shakes his head. 'No, no, Mr Saul.'

Vernon sits, consciously relaxing, his body language talking chilled and in control. 'Okay, Captain, so what's up?'

'What's *up*, Vernon,' Erasmus says, 'is the shit you pulled last night in Llandudno is all too familiar, man. Dead body. Murder weapon. No witnesses. How many times you done it out on the Flats when you a cop? Plant *tik* and a weapon on some fucker who crossed you, say he drew on you?'

Vernon, not looking at Erasmus, says, 'Captain, if the detective has any proof of these allegations I'd like to hear it.'

'Fuck proof,' Erasmus says, leaning on the desk, getting in Vernon's face, snot hanging like tree bananas from the hairs in his gaping nostrils. 'Maybe you got away with that bullshit when you wasted *tik* dealers and gangsters. Who the fuck cared? But now we got a foreigner dead and you're covering up for her murderer.'

Vernon tries to make eye contact with the darkie, who watches a meat fly banging up against the closed window. 'Captain, you got my statement. If you got any questions, please put them to me.'

The captain skids his heavy-lidded eyes across to Vernon and shrugs. 'This is in the hands of Special Investigations now.'

Vernon stands. 'I got things to do.'

'Sit the fuck down, Saul,' Erasmus says.

Vernon looks at him. 'Dino, you want me to stay, arrest me. Otherwise I'm out of here.' He heads for the door, tension making his left leg even heavier.

'I'm going to check forensics with a fine-tooth comb,' Erasmus says. 'And I'm going to talk to your little friend, Nicholas Exley.'

Vernon closes the door – making an effort not to slam it – already scrolling his phone for Exley's number as he walks through the charge office, past a blonde housewife moaning about a break-in and a drunk Xhosa wrapped in a tribal blanket passed out on a bench. By the time he's outside in the sun he's hearing Exley's voicemail.

'Call me,' Vernon says, pocketing the phone.

He lights a smoke as he stares up at the darkie shacks of Mandela Park tumbling down the mountainside like a landslide of shit, spoiling this nice white suburb.

The toxic smell of the solvents used by the two clean-up men drives Exley upstairs. He is operating on the vague understanding that there are people who need to know about Caroline's death and that it is important to behave as normally as possible. So he should search her laptop and send out a bulk email to all her contacts, and call her loathsome sister, Kate.

Exley enters the marital bedroom for the first time since he left for Johannesburg the previous morning. The bed is unmade and discarded clothes litter the room. When she was well Caroline was anally neat. During her episodes her slovenly twin took over and it wasn't uncommon for Exley to find used tampons, the blood gone black and hard, among the cigarette butts in overflowing ashtrays beside the bed.

The curtains are closed, evidence of Caroline's oversensitivity to light, a by-product of her condition. Exley pulls them open, letting the sun in. He'd once joked that he'd have to drive a stake through her heart to get rid of her.

A knife had done the trick.

And just like that he's back in the kitchen, the blade sliding into her, blood welling from her mouth. Exley feels dizzy and has to sit down on the roiled sheets. His mouth is full of hot, acid puke and he is up again, dashing for the bathroom. Something cuts into the soles of his stockinged feet but he has no time to investigate, reaching the basin in time to spew.

It goes on for a long time, this expiation, Exley gripping the ornate chrome taps, gasping, sweat dripping from his forehead, his abdominal muscles in agony from the heaving. At last he spits and rinses his mouth and splashes his face. He sinks down on the toilet and sits with his eyes closed until he feels stronger.

As he crosses back into the bedroom, he checks the carpet and sees a sprawl of electronic components and a shattered casing and realizes that he's looking at the carcass of Caroline's Mac. Deep gouges in the wall vouch for how the laptop met its end.

She was always her own sternest critic, he says aloud, as if he's delivering a eulogy. This makes him laugh, in a way that sounds unhinged and manic.

He gathers up the wreckage and dumps it in the wicker trash basket that sits beside the bed, letting the computer parts join a pile of Kleenex.

The pathetic man-in-his-underwear thing is getting tired, so he finds a pair of Diesels in the closet and pulls them on under his T-shirt. Removes the socks and replaces them with a pair of Havaianas. He takes the garbage down to the kitchen.

The trauma cleaners are finishing up, wadding bloody cloths and paper towels into black bags. Except for the carbolic fumes in the air, there is no sign of what happened last night. Even the carpet is restored to its original color.

One of the men takes the basket from Exley and empties it. 'There you go, sir,' he says, tying off the top of the bag.

'Thank you,' Exley says. 'This looks great.'

'What we do, sir,' the man says, lifting the bulging garbage bag and following his colleague out the door.

'What do I owe you?' asks Exley.

'Nothing. You're a friend of Vernon's.' The guy is trying a smile but it's not quite taking and Exley wonders what Vernon has over these men.

'Well, I appreciate it,' he says.

They're gone and he's alone with the rest of his life, clueless as to what he's going to do with it.

The gate buzzer jams his thoughts and he heads for the intercom, sure that it's Vernon Saul, ready to invade again, but it's Gladys the maid, and Exley lets her in. She wears a beret, dark skirt, blouse and formal shoes with gold buckles, despite the molten heat.

She stands in the doorway and stares at him, her eyes wet with grief. 'Mr Nick, I have heard what is happening.'

'Yes,' he says.

'This man, he is coming in here and doing this thing? To Miss Caroline?'

'Yes. I returned from the airport and I disturbed him.' Exley unconsciously mirroring her formal speech patterns.

'Ay, my gawd, it is too terrible, this.'

She comes up to him and embraces him and again he loses himself in the warmth of this ample ocean of flesh. She releases him and walks through to the kitchen, her heels smacking the tiles, still clucking softly to herself.

Gladys stops exactly where Caroline fell and died. Stands with her hands hanging at her sides and looks around the room. She closes her eyes and stays unmoving for what seems like hours. When she opens her eyes and looks at Exley her expression has hardened. She crosses herself quickly and kisses her fingertips, never taking her eyes from Exley's, her sadness replaced by something else. Something accusatory.

'Mr Nick, Mr Nick, Mr Nick,' she says, shaking her head. 'No, no, no.'

'What?' he asks, wilting under her gaze.

'I can't work here no more,' she says and brushes past him, moving with surprising speed for such a large woman.

'Gladys?' he says, but he doesn't try to stop her as she flees the house. Relieved that she has gone, this woman who can see the mark of corruption on him.

chapter 33

VERNON'S MOOD DARKENS AS HE DRIVES HIS HONDA ACROSS PARADISE PARK. Being needed – the way Dawn and Nick Exley need him – gives him something, sure, something that goes some way toward filling that big hole that eats away at his innards. But it comes with a price tag. Means that demands and pressures and responsibilities burden him. Stress him. Depress him.

He feels it all the more out here, deep in the Cape Flats with its cramped houses and rust-bucket cars and no-hope people blown every which way by the hot wind crashing in off the faraway ocean like a curse. If he didn't have so much to do, so many things to manage, he'd set course for Doc's place and have a shot of his magic juice and just disappear into blankness for the rest of the day, where all his strife and the image of Dino Erasmus's nostrils sniffing after him will just fade to zero.

But no. He has his tasks.

He tries Exley's cell again. That same not-quite-American voice saying he's not available. Vernon leaves no message. He went by the house and rang the bell, knowing he was making himself conspicuous by doing it. Sure that Exley was home. The fucker is hiding from him, and that's a worry. A loose end.

In an attempt to lighten his mood he gets a bit of Motown going on the sound system, Ike and Tina doing 'River Deep, Mountain High.' Always been a sucker for duets. The music helps, him joining in the chorus, fingers tapping on the steering, and by the time he gets to the social worker's office he is ready to do what must be done. He takes the little gift-wrapped parcel from the seat beside him and walks down the pathway, even finding a joke and a cigarette, just like the last time, for the broken old ex-con who works the garden.

The man's eyes, bled of all hope, scare Vernon and he hustles on, making quick despite his dragging leg. He shoulders his way through the mob of sad and useless people and finds the receptionist with her nose deep in a gossip magazine.

'Vernon Saul for Merinda Appolis.'

The receptionist sighs and lowers her magazine and speaks into the phone, then dumps it in its cradle. Her eyes are already back in her magazine as she says, 'She's busy. You'll have to wait.'

Vernon works hard at self-control. Knows he's being punished by being made to wait among this smear of useless humanity. He pushes his way outside, standing in the doorway, and lights a Lucky, consciously calming himself as he inhales, feeling the warm smoke in his lungs. He's nearly done with the cigarette when the receptionist calls him and tells him he can go through.

Merinda Appolis doesn't meet him at the door this time. Remains seated behind her desk, her knees held primly together.

She launches her attack before he even has a chance to greet her. 'If you've come to soft-soap me, Vernon, just forget it, okay? My report will go in tomorrow and I'll have Dawn Cupido in court by Friday. So if you're going to try and change my mind, you're wasting both our time.' She fixes her painted lips into a hard little gash and crosses her arms.

'That's not why I'm here, Merinda,' he says, all serious.

'Well, what do you want, then?'

'Okay if I sit?'

She frees a hand and wags it at the chair opposite her. He makes a production of lowering himself, arranging his leg, resting his bandaged arm on the desk. Sees her look at it, but she says nothing.

'I'm here to thank you, actually.'

'Thank me? For what?'

'For doing what I didn't have the guts to do. I was worried about that child, but I should have reported Dawn long ago. Got you in there sooner. Anyway, you did what needed to be done and it's all in the child's best interests.' She's staring at him skeptically. He puts the parcel on the desk. 'For you.'

'What's this?'

'Open it.' She hesitates a moment, but then her curiosity gets the better of her and she tears at the pink wrapping paper with her long red fingernails. She lifts out a transparent plastic container of Ferrero Rocher chocolates, looking like little hand grenades in their foil wrappers. Cost him a fortune at the Waterfront.

She can't hold back the smile. 'Vernon! My favorite!'

'I'm glad you like them. Just to say thanks.'

'I love them. Not good for my figure, though!' The flirtiness is back and she squirms in her chair.

'Oh, you got nothing to worry about there.' Forcing himself to give her the eye as he stands. 'Well, I know you're busy.'

'No. Sit.'

He shakes his head. 'I really should go.'

'What happened to your arm?'

He shrugs. 'There was an incident last night. All under control.' He edges toward the door. Then pauses, looking awkward and embarrassed. 'Merinda?'

'Ja?'

'I dunno if I'm out of line here…'

'What, Vernon?'

'Will you have dinner with me tonight?'

A blush touches her cheeks. 'Well—'

'If you have other plans?'

'No, no.'

'Do you like Chinese?'

'Oh, I *love* Chinese!'

'Good, there's a nice place at Canal Walk. Why don't you give me your address and I'll pick you up around eight, okay?'

She scribbles on a little pink Post-it which he pockets. He gives her his best smile and leaves her looking happily flustered.

Vernon laughs himself back to the Civic, his good mood restored.

N

Exley wakes for the second time that day. This time it is not terror that ends his sleep, but grief. As he lies on the sofa cushions he dragged into the studio after Gladys left, he mourns his daughter, feeling more loss and less guilt now that he understands that Caroline was at least as culpable as he was, the evening of Sunny's birthday. It is a searing, painful grief, one that will take a very long time (maybe forever) for him to recover from, but it is pure and uncomplicated, almost affirming.

Exley sits up and wipes his tears and walks out of the studio, the late afternoon light washing the front rooms. He is parched but stepping into the kitchen will take him too close to what he became last night, so he goes onto the deck and sits, watching the waves and the seagulls. Sits until thirst finally drives him to his feet and he heads for the kitchen and gets a bottle of Evian from the fridge, trying not to see his wife lying dead on the tiles.

He takes the water back onto the deck. A kayak drifts past, beyond the rocks, carrying a man, a woman and a child, all in lifejackets. The child's giggles drift to Exley on the soft breeze, and he hears the woman shout something and laugh.

Exley tries to remember when he last saw Caroline happy, in more than a transitory, superficial way. It was years ago, before Sunny was born, when her first novel was published. He sees her, radiant and smiling at the book launch in London, posing with him for photographs. Now she's gone. Whatever her life was it is over.

And he ended it.

But Exley can't deny a sense of liberation. Caroline, with her rages and her depressions and the all-consuming selfishness of the psychologically unstable, leached most of the joy from his life. He became a wife whisperer, attuned to the subtlest seismic shifts in her mood, to protect his daughter and himself.

The truth is, he feels little guilt at killing her. Only the fear of being caught and that possibility seems remote. The almost obscene haste with which the cops accepted the sacrifice Vernon Saul threw their way means that it is a done deal. Case closed.

So, sitting out on the deck, watching the last sunlight dance on the waves, Exley thinks, what the hell, maybe Vernon Saul is right: the truth is just the lie you believe the most.

The gate buzzer grinds inside the house and Exley ignores it. But it sounds repeatedly and he goes to the intercom in the living room. The police captain from last night apologizes for intruding and says he has a few questions.

When Exley opens the front door he sees the captain is not alone – he is with a middle-aged brown guy with a snout for a nose.

'Mr Exley, this is my colleague, Detective Erasmus.'

Exley lets the two men enter. Erasmus says nothing, just walks into the house and stops when he reaches the kitchen.

'This where she died?' he asks.

'Yes,' Exley says.

'Already cleaned up, I see?'

'I had the trauma people in.'

'Connections of Vernon Saul's?'

'Yes,' Exley says. 'As a matter of fact they were. Why?'

The cop shrugs and when his gaze settles on Exley, he finds himself looking into the cold eyes of a fanatic. 'Where you from?'

'I'm an American citizen.'

'What, another bloody foreigner come out here to get his wife killed and blame it on our crime epidemic?'

Fragile equilibrium cracking, Exley looks at the black cop. 'Captain, what's going on here?'

'Detective Erasmus is from Special Investigations. He'd like to talk to you.'

'What's Special Investigations?'

Erasmus leans in close to Exley. 'We're an independent unit, reporting directly to the police commissioner. Let's just say we're here to keep the system honest.'

The captain looks pained but says nothing, his eyes out on the horizon. Erasmus focuses his gaze on Exley. 'Tell me what happened last night.'

'I've already given a statement.'

'Tell me again.'

Exley looks across at the captain, who nods, so he runs through Vernon's version.

When Exley's done Erasmus says, 'The first person you called was Vernon Saul?'

'Yes.'

'Why not the police?'

'I was in shock. Mr Saul has been very helpful since my daughter's death.'

'I bet he has.' The cop sniffs and uses a hand to reseat his balls. 'Mr Exley, your wife was having an affair, wasn't she?'

'News to me.'

'There was an incident yesterday. We've spoken to a Mrs Stankovic who tells us your wife and her husband were having a sexual relationship.'

'I don't listen to gossip.'

Erasmus snorts. 'Okay, I'm gonna run something by you. Let's say you come back from Jo'burg and Vernon Saul clues you in about your wife screwing around. You confront her and you kill her.'

'Jesus, Captain?' But the dark cop is far away, somewhere out past the rocks, lost in the honey-colored light.

'So, you get hold of your buddy Vernon and tell him what's up. You offer him money to sort out this mess for you. And Vernon does what he's good at: finds some innocent bugger, plants the knife and your wife's phone on him, cuts himself to make things look convincing, and blows the guy away.'

Exley is rocked on his feet, hearing an almost perfect account of last night's events spewing from this ugly man's mouth. 'I'm not going to listen to any more of this. Get the hell out of my house.'

Erasmus crowds Exley, washing him with his stale breath. 'I would advise you to give all this some thought, Mr Exley. If you come to us and admit what you and Saul did, the courts may be lenient. Continue lying and you're going to spend a very long time in prison.' He hands Exley a card. 'You phone me when you're ready.'

They go, Erasmus striding ahead, the captain giving Exley a helpless shrug.

Exley locks the front door and calls Vernon Saul, getting his voicemail.

'Call me,' he says, dropping the phone as he sinks down onto the cushionless sofa, staring at the sun bleeding into the ocean, wondering how long it would take him to drown if he waded out and started swimming into the gathering darkness.

chapter 34

THE HOT WIND MUTTERS AND CURSES ITS WAY BETWEEN THE MEAN BUILDINGS on Voortrekker, getting tin cans rolling in the gutters, poking the signs on the sidewalk till they swing and creak, rocking the taxis as they gobble up passengers.

Dawn, stranded in the middle of the road – trying to find a gap in the evening traffic to cross over to Lips – takes a blast of grit in the eyes like she's been maced. She curses, rubbing at her eyes, feeling them fill with tears. She's ready to say fuck it and throw a U-turn and go fetch Brittany from Mrs de Pontes and eat marshmallows and watch crap on TV.

Instead she dodges an oncoming Golden Arrow bus, getting a lungful of its diesel fumes, and makes it to the other side. Even though the neon fizzes above her, the club is still closed and she has to bang on the door. Eventually Dennis opens up.

He smiles at her, then swallows the grin. 'Ja?'

'I wanna see Costa.'

'You not welcome here no more.'

'Come on Dennis, for fuck sake.'

He shakes his head but lets her in. The place is empty, not even Cliffie behind the bar, the fluorescent lights turned up, revealing it for the tacky pit that it is, like an old slut without her teeth in. She heads to Costa's office, says a little prayer to some god somewhere and knocks.

She hears his smoker's hack. 'Ja?'

'It's Dawn.'

'Go home, Dawn.'

'Costa, *pleeeeze*.' Knocking again.

Mutters and mumbles and the door unlocks and he opens up just far enough to give her the view of one baggy eye and half of his bandito mustache. 'Dawn, I think I have enough of your nonsense now.'

'Costa, I'm asking for another chance.'

'No, Dawn. Chance is over. You make for me too much trouble. You just go, last night. Leave for me one girl short.'

'I'm sorry, man. It was an emergency.'

'No, Dawn. No, no, no. I found already replacement.'

'I've got a kid. Jesus.'

He digs in his pocket and finds a fifty-rand note. Holds it out to her. 'I owe you nothing, but this I give you from kindness of my heart.'

She doesn't take it. 'Don't fucken insult me, Costa. I deserve better.'

'Goodbye, Dawn. Now you go or I get Dennis throw you out.' He drops the note, which floats down to Dawn's feet, and he closes the door and locks it.

'Fuck you,' she says without conviction. She picks up the money and walks back into the club. The Ugly Sisters stagger in on their high heels, parading their sad flesh in short dresses, the stink of chemicals and cheap perfume sailing in with them like an ill wind.

They're talking at her, laughing, but she doesn't hear, deafened by the roar of the blood in her ears, raw, naked panic got hold of her now, riding her like a jockey. She makes it into the street, gasping down dust and fumes.

'Hey, Dawnie.'

She turns and there's Fidel, her one-time meth merchant, sent by the devil himself.

Fidel, straightened hair dangling like a comma over his one eye, rubber lips smacking as he chews on something, puts a hand on her elbow, his fingers hot and greasy with chicken fat, pulling her close. So easy it would be for the fifty bucks to end up in his pocket and Dawn to slide down an alley with a straw of *tik*, that magic smoke filling her, leaving no room for fear and sadness.

No.

She hits Fidel, a nice short-arm jab with the fist to his belly, and he goes limp as a shirt on a washing line and she gets her ass across the road and out of the path of temptation.

But the devil isn't done with her. Not yet.

A Beemer, newish, cruises slowly toward her, the driver looking to get lucky, even though it's too early for the whores. The white guy at the wheel sees her and stops, checking her out. By reflex her middle finger is already in position to flip him the bird but she holsters it and thinks what the fuck?

The passenger door of the Beamer swings open and in the dome light she sees the guy's wearing a shirt and tie, some salesman maybe, got a few drinks in him and now wants the kind of fun he can't get at home.

Dawn slides in and closes the door. Smells the booze on the john, who is fat, in his forties, breathing heavy as a dirty phone caller.

'How much?' he asks.

'Blow job, two-fifty. Full house, five hundred.'

Crazy prices for the street and he laughs at her. 'You out of your fucken mind!'

She grabs at the door handle, wanting to be gone.

'Wait,' he says. 'I'll give you one hundred for a blow.'

'Two-fifty.'

He mutters something but there's a cop car cruising toward them and traffic's backing up behind the Beemer. 'Okay. Fuck. Where do we go?' he asks, clicking the car into gear.

She tells him to drive up Voortrekker. She'll take him to an old spot of hers, a parking lot behind a strip mall that'll be deserted this time of night. He's fumbling near her knees and she thinks he's trying to feel her up but he's just pushing in the cigarette lighter. He lifts a pack of Camel from his shirt pocket and draws a cigarette out with his lips. When the lighter pops he sets fire to the smoke and sucks away. He's nervous, she realizes. The courage the booze gave him starting to thin in his blood.

Dawn's shitting herself, too. Never in her life has she hooked without being *tikked* out of her brain, so fried she couldn't feel nothing. They stop at a light and she hears the breath of the white man as he exhales smoke and sees his pale hand on the wheel, wedding band glinting.

No ways can she do it. Not while she's straight. She throws open the door and she's out of there. As she slams the door she sees the guy's face staring up at her, then the light is green and the Beemer slides away into the traffic.

Dawn crosses Voortrekker and jumps a taxi. She's breathing hard, not used to this shit no more. She watches the bars and junk food joints ooze past, her head aching from the rap that booms out in the taxi, the bass rattling the fillings in her teeth. The minibus stops near her apartment and she follows other passengers out as the co-driver yanks open the sliding door, telling them to get a fucken move on, he don't have all night.

The driver, a long tall thing with pimples like strawberries, guns the engine, playing the gas and brake pedals, making the taxi rock in time to the music. Rude bastards, these. But you don't say a word – they think nothing of smacking you. Or worse if you're a woman alone.

Dawn stops in at the store and buys chips and marshmallows and then she goes up and gets Brittany from Mrs de Pontes, pays her what's left of the fifty Costa gave her, even though she's getting the kid early.

She takes Brittany home and makes them hot chocolate and French toast and they pig out on the junk food and, as they fall asleep together on the sofa watching some cheesy old movie with Meg Ryan and Tom Hanks, Dawn wonders if there really are guys like that in the world, and if there are why she's never met even one of them.

chapter 35

VERNON, LEAVING HIS CIVIC PARKED SAFELY AT HOME, STEALS AN OLD TOYOTA Corolla near the Paradise Park station. Boosting the rusted piece of shit takes him less than two minutes, a matter of ripping out the ignition wires and joining them in the right sequence.

The car is a mess; empty beer cans, junk food wrappers and newspapers clutter the floor and the seats. He drives a few blocks, pulls up to the curb, opens the passenger door and tips a pile of crap into the gutter, making the car a little more presentable. Then he goes across to collect Merinda Appolis for their date.

She lives in a room behind a house in the smart part of Paradise Park, near his mother's church. Told him not to ring the buzzer, her landlord doesn't like it. He's a lawyer, she said, breathless, as if this was meant to impress the hell out of Vernon.

He pulls up at exactly eight and sees her standing behind the high driveway gate, all dollied up in a dress and heels. She peers through the bars, uncertain when she sees the Toyota, so he reaches across and opens the passenger door.

'Hi, Merinda.'

'Hi, Vernon. Where's your car?' Walking toward him.

'Man, sorry about this wreck, but my Civic's giving me hassles – transmission – so I had to take it in today. Mechanics gave me this as a loan car.'

'Oh, okay.' But he sees she's offended at being seen in this car, snobby little bitch.

She wipes off the front seat with her hand before folding her dress under her broad ass and sitting herself down. He waits for her to get settled then he drives away.

'How come you not working tonight?' she asks.

'Remember that promotion I told you about?'

'Of course, yes.'

'Well, it's come through. I'm up at head office from tomorrow. Only nine to five for me now.'

'Congratulations!'

'Thanks. So we can celebrate tonight.'

She notices the route he's taking. 'Where we going, Vernon?'

'Sorry, I should have said something. I want to ask your advice, Merinda. This new job comes with a nice pay check, so I'm thinking of buying me a house. I'm a bit old to still be living with my mom.' She laughs, all her attention on him. 'Ja, time I think about settling down. So there's a new housing development, over in Extension Three, land for sale. I know it's dark, but you can still get a bit of an idea. I'd like a woman's opinion.'

She laps this up, getting all comfortable in her seat, even resting her hand on his leg. 'Oh, I'd love that, Vernon.' He wants to smack her hand away but he controls himself, leaving Paradise Park behind now, driving into the open land out past the cemetery, a few roads and a sprinkling of street lights hinting at the coming suburb.

He stops the Toyota and climbs out and opens her door, even taking her hand to help her. The wind comes in and she holds onto her blow-dried hair.

'I can choose between a plot here, or that side, closer to the main road,' he says, pointing. She blinks away dust, shields her eyes with her hand, squinting into the darkness at the faraway car headlamps.

He gets himself behind her so she doesn't see him slide on the surgical gloves he slips from the pocket of his jeans. He flexes his fingers. 'So, what do you think?'

She turns to face him but before she can speak he grabs her by the throat, throttling her. She tries to fight Vernon as he lifts her on tiptoe, holding her so that her cat-claw nails and kicking feet can't get nowhere near him. It takes no time at all. He smells her piss and shit, feels her body sag and jerk, and then she's still, her tongue hanging out like she's trying to lick her chin.

Vernon lets her fall to the ground, getting his breath back.

He empties her purse of its money and throws it in the veld. Then he does the thing that makes him squeamish – he comes close to puking – but he knows he has to do it. He forces her legs apart and fishes between them, grabbing hold of her soiled panties and pulling them off her.

The touch of her woman flesh sickens him and he hauls himself to his feet, throwing the panties into the bush. He should do more, he knows, to make this look like a sex crime, but he doesn't have the stomach.

He gets back into the Toyota and drives away, whistling that old Supremes thing, 'Baby I Love You.' He's killed so many people it mostly means nothing to him now. But this was personal and there is a sense of satisfaction, of a job well done.

Sorting out Dawn's problem, getting her deeper into his debt, is a happy by-product of killing this bitch. But really he did it for himself. To restore his confidence. His sense of certainty.

Since he was shot Vernon has started doubting himself for the first time ever since he took the hammer to his father. So, to act like this, to bend the world to his will, makes him feel like himself again.

Fucken invincible.

He dumps the Toyota and walks home, ignores his bitch mother, who sits hypnotized by the flickering TV, and gets into bed and sleeps like a baby.

chapter 36

EXLEY, SWEATING, PROWLS A HOUSE FULL OF GHOSTS. HE STANDS ON THE deck, a hot wind howling in off the ocean. He can smell a fire somewhere in the mountains above him. Earlier he tracked down an email address for Caroline's sister – chickening out of a phone call – and sent her a brief account of what happened. The Vernon version. He received an almost immediate reply: 'I blame you for dragging my sister and her child out to that crime-ridden hellhole.'

If you only fucking knew.

He calls Vernon's cell. Again. Number unavailable. Again.

Exley wants to run. Throw a few things into a bag, grab his passport and head to the airport. Take the first plane out of South Africa. His feet are already on the stairs leading up to the bedroom, when he stops himself and leans against the wall, trying to slow his heartbeat.

That's what he wants, the pig-faced cop. Wants you to panic. Wants you to admit your guilt.

He walks back down into the living room and, restless, lifts his phone again and scrolls for Shane Porter's number. Maybe he needs company. Getting drunk and baked with the Australian wideboy will distract him. But he gets Port's voicemail, the twangy voice telling him to leave a message, an old INXS anthem banging in the background.

Okay, a drink, then, he decides, and opens the liquor cabinet, the mirror back doubling the booze bottles on the glass shelves. He hears his father's Harvard voice say, what's your poison, old son?

Not Scotch, too much heat. Not vodka, it has a way of kneecapping him and reducing him to a touchy-feely mess. Sure as shit not tequila, things are warped enough without risking the wormy mescal. Gin, he decides. A no-nonsense British drink, perfect for the suffocating night. He pours a stiff jolt of Tanqueray and dilutes it with tonic water from the green bottle he finds at the bottom of the liquor cabinet.

He can't avoid the kitchen – no way he will get this down without ice – so he steps onto the tiles and heads for the refrigerator, dumps in a handful of cubes from the ice maker, the G&T bubbling and fizzing, a cool rain landing on the hairs on his arm.

While he has the door of the fridge open he wonders when he last ate. He can't remember. He puts the tumbler of gin down on the counter and lifts out some cheese, sniffs it to see if it's okay. Picks a few kalamata olives from a plastic tub and dumps them on a plate with the cheese. Adds a scoop of hummus and finds a couple of crackers in the cupboard.

He wanders out onto the deck. The wind has dropped to a whisper. Exley sits down at the table and sips the drink. Goes down fine. He tries a cracker with some cheese and his stomach rebels. He pushes the plate away, resigned to a liquid diet. A cold white moon hangs low and heavy over the ocean, like a searchlight on the water, and Exley feels alone and godless.

Whatever faith he once had was a makeshift thing, received wisdom from his mother and her charlatan master: a patchwork of Eastern philosophy reduced to bumper stickers, stitched together with New Age bullshit. When he quit the ashram he jettisoned his mother's beliefs along with the silly white robes, the turban and the name Narayan that had replaced Nicholas for nearly ten years.

Exley, driven by some indefinable yearning, has the phone in his hand again, speed-dialing, listening to the soft purr somewhere very far away.

An aloof voice, genderless, stateless, swollen with enlightenment, answers. 'Namaste.'

'Joan Exley, please,' Exley says, being willfully perverse.

'There is no one here by that name.'

'Durgananda, then. Let me speak to Durgananda.'

'She is in contemplation class.'

'This is her son. It's urgent.'

'She cannot be disturbed.'

'There has been a tragedy. In the family.'

'Swami Durgananda has renounced all family.'

'Let me speak to her.'

'She does not wish this.'

'Tell my mother that her granddaughter is dead.'

'Swami Durgananda has no granddaughter.'

'That's right. She's dead.'

'There is no death.'

Exley ends the call and stares into the night. Oh, there is death, fucker, and when it comes it doesn't come in a whisper of white with a choir of cooing angels or dancing apsara, it comes with blood and shit and piss and torn flesh, thick with the stench of corruption.

Maybe his mother is lucky, insulated from reality by Alzheimer's and her cult worship. Exley sips his drink and for the first time in years allows himself to remember the compound near Taos, boys and girls sleeping in single-sex dormitories, separated from their parents. Doing chores in the kitchen and the fields. Attending class in a low bunker, chanting Hindu praises like parrots, kissing the gnarled and Gorgonzola-stinky feet of the bearded guru - a one-time Bombay bus driver - when he floated in dispensing wisdom and sly glances, smiling with teeth stained red by betel nut through the thicket of his ZZ-Top beard.

When a series of girls accused the guru of messing with their lower chakras he was banished, the ashram left in chaos, and Exley was able to attend the high school in the nearby town.

Laughed at, at first, because of the robes he wore and his dumb Hindu handle, he quickly switched to jeans and became Nick again and drifted farther from his mother, and nirvana became Nirvana as he lost himself in a world of grunge rock, skateboards and computers.

When he won a scholarship to study digital arts at a California college his mother, an elder now on the ashram - one of the keepers of the flame - seemed relieved to see him go. She never met Caroline. Never saw Sunny. He sent her photographs, but had no idea if they had made it past the battalion of censors who intercepted the mail.

Exley finishes his drink and goes inside and builds himself another.

He needs somewhere to sleep – the marital bedroom is out of the question – and takes his gin upstairs with him, medicating himself while he makes up a bed in the spare room, an impersonal cubicle overlooking the mountain, full of unpacked boxes.

When he's done, his glass is empty and he sets course for the stairs. He can't resist a detour to Sunny's room, sitting in the dark on her bed, inhaling her presence. He clicks on the lamp and finds himself gathering up some of her favorite objects – a soft toy she slept with, a drawing, a piece of her clothing – and he takes them down to his studio.

Surrendering to some primitive impulse – like a Pacific islander with his cargo-cult booty – he places the fetish objects around his workstation, Sunny's face smiling at him from the monitor.

When his hand finds the mouse and he calls up his model of her and watches her dance, it no longer disturbs Exley that he can't see past his recreation of his daughter. He starts to work again, his grief lost in the music of the clicking mouse as he coaxes Sunny ever closer to reality.

chapter 37

Vernon's knock wakes Dawn in the morning and gets her out of bed. She wraps herself in an African cloth patterned with giraffes and lions and Zulu huts before she opens the door. He pushes his way in, thick and heavy in his uniform, and says to her, 'Looks like your problems are over.'

'What you mean?'

He throws a copy of the Cape Flats scandal sheet, *The Voice*, on the bed, next to where Brittany is sleeping, her thumb in her mouth. Dawn sees the front page: SOCIAL WORKER STRANGLED. There's a picture of that mean-faced little bitch, Merinda Appolis. God rest her soul.

Dawn can't help it, the words just pop out. 'Jesus, Vernon, what you done now?'

Vernon laughs. 'Me? You stupid or what? I like you, Dawnie, and I want you to keep your brat but no fucken ways I'm gonna kill for you.'

Dawn scans the article: a homeless man found the woman's body last night in the veld outside Paradise Park. Suspected robbery. Maybe a sex crime.

Dawn says, 'What if some other social worker carries on trying to get Brittany away from me?' Speaking soft, so as not to wake the kid.

Vernon shakes his head. 'With the caseloads those people got? Forget it. Your troubles died with her.'

Dawn is still trying to digest this, wondering how she got so lucky, when he says, 'You feel like making a quick couple of grand?'

'Who do I have to fuck?'

'I said couple of *grand*, Dawnie, not couple of *rand*.'

'Funny, Vernon. Funny.'

'No, serious, I got this friend, does video work—'

'I'm not doing porno. Forget it.'

'Jesus Christ, Dawn, will you just shut your fucken mouth?' Vernon looking like he could smack her. 'Listen, he's a legit guy. Does *Avatar* kinda stuff. Needs somebody to dance for a music video. No stripping, nothing. Just dancing.'

Dawn lights a cigarette, squinting at him through the smoke. 'You fucking with me, Vernon?'

'Ah, man, I don't need this grief.' He heads for the door and she sees the couple of thousand walking out with him.

'Wait,' she says. 'Where's this guy?'

'He's Llandudno side.'

'Okay.' She shrugs, knowing she could live to regret this.

'I'm going down to get me some smokes, so get your ass dressed,' he says, opening the door. 'You got somewhere to leave the kid for the day?'

'The babysitter. But I need cash.'

'I'll lend you the cash. You can pay me back later.' He slams the door and his boots bang away down the corridor.

Dawn dives under the shower, soaps herself quickly – keeping her hair out of the water – then rushes through naked and still dripping and puts on her sexiest outfit: a tight low-cut dress and a push-up bra that makes the most of what she's got. Steps into a pair of peep-toes with heels high enough to break her neck on. She drags a brush through her hair to tame it a bit, then gets busy with the make-up. Never met a guy who didn't like a painted woman.

When Vernon comes back he freaks. 'Fuck it, Dawn, where you think you going? Streetwalking? This is a sophisticated guy, for Chris-sakes. Go wash your face.'

She starts to moan but he holds up his hand like he's stopping traffic. 'Just do what I say.'

So she goes back into the bathroom and scrubs her face clean, puts on the last bit of her moisturizer – has to strangle the tube – to give a glow to her skin.

When she comes out he says, 'Now you wear what you always wear onstage.'

'You serious?'

'Ja, I'm serious. Put it on.'

'Turn your back,' she says.

'What?'

'Turn your back!'

He stares at her like she's smoking *tik*. 'I don't believe it, you show your fucken box to a hundred guys a night, now suddenly you shy?'

'This is my bedroom, not a pussy bar. Turn.'

He turns and she pulls on a fresh white shirt and jeans, finds a pair of flops, and she's everyday Dawn again.

'Okay,' he says, checking her out, nodding. 'At least now you don't look like a whore.'

They dump Britt with Mrs de Pontes and Vernon drives them away from the misery of Goodwood, the air heavy with car fumes and something ripe that blows in from the Maitland abattoir, passing the take-outs and used-car lots and sad little strip malls, out to a world come to life from a movie.

They twist down a road to a house made of glass, looking like the ocean's gonna float it away, some skinny white guy blinking at them by the gate, all surprised and confused, a bit pissed off even, that they've just rocked up. Vernon walking him inside, yakking to him, leaving Dawn out on the deck.

Dawn's never been in a place like this. Seen pictures in the glossy magazines, sure, but the only time women like her come this side is if they're cleaning up after the whities or selling their pussies.

But if there's a gap here she'll take it. No question, because when Dawn saw the white guy she saw an opportunity: youngish foreigner – though not as young as she first thought – alone in this beautiful house on this private beach. Vernon filling her in on the way over about the guy's wife and kid dying a few days apart.

She paces the deck, listening to the waves, watching the sun on the ocean, thinking how much Brittany would like it here. Poor kid hardly ever gets to the beach. Such a drag to travel from Goodwood: they have to take two taxis, crammed in with old aunties and stinky kids and tattooed young bastards with rapists' eyes, hot hands ready to grope.

Dawn's feeling her nerves and wonders if she can sneak a quick smoke. Better not. Vernon's still inside with the guy. Dawn hopes there isn't a hassle, but that's Vernon all over, isn't it? Mr Bull-in-a-fucken-china-shop.

Here he comes, Vernon, limping out of the house like he owns it, big grin on his face, the whitey, Nick, following him.

'So, Dawn,' Vernon says, 'I wish I could stay and watch you dance and all, but I'm going on duty now. I'll come by later, okay?'

Dawn nods and Vernon hauls his ass out and she's left staring at this white guy, so pale and thin like the wind could just lift him and float him away.

She does look Brazilian, Exley thinks. Vernon Saul got that much right. With her light brown skin and wild hair, she could be an Ipanema girl.

But when she opens her mouth, she's pure Cape Town. 'Man, I'm really sorry, Nick, if Vernon's taking a liberty here.' That speedy delivery, one word tailgating the next, with a bray that grabs hold of the *r*'s and stretches them.

'It's okay,' he says, but he hears how unconvincing he sounds.

'I think I should go. I can get me a taxi up by the main road.'

'No, please, Dawn, stay,' he says, and suddenly he means it. She's here and Christ knows he needs some human company. What'll it hurt if he does the thing for Alberto?

He manages a smile. 'I've had a pretty tough week. Sorry if I acted like an asshole.'

There's some softness in her eyes, and that's like a balm to him. 'Vernon told me a bit about what happened,' she says. 'I can't imagine it. I got me a little girl, too.'

'Yeah? How old is she?'

'She's four.' Dawn smiles and Exley sees how beautiful she is.

'Same as Sunny.' He's choking up here. 'Listen, I need to go inside and set up some gear. You okay? Need anything to drink?'

'No, I'm fine. You go do what you gotta do.'

Exley grabs a liter bottle of Evian and two glasses from the kitchen and goes into the studio, has a drink of water, composes himself, wiping his eyes. In the steel cabinet he finds a motion-capture suit that'll fit Dawn and drapes it over a stack of hard drives. Then he boots up the software and cues Alberto's music.

When he walks back out onto the deck the woman is down on the sand, barefoot, smoking. The wind lifts her hair as she stands and looks out over the ocean, unaware of him.

'Dawn.'

She turns, leaking smoke, embarrassed, waving the hand holding the cigarette. 'Sorry, I hope you don't mind?'

'Out here it's fine. But computer gear doesn't like smoke.'

'You ready?'

'Yes.'

'Where can I chuck this?' Waving the cigarette again.

'The sand,' he says. 'God's own ashtray.' Sounding lame.

But she's good enough to laugh as she drops the smoke and uses her foot to cover it with beach sand. She comes up onto the deck and follows him through the living room and into the studio.

'Sit,' he says. He pours two glasses of water and hands one to her. Dawn gulps it down and he refills it.

She wipes her mouth on the back of her hand. He sees her fingernails are bitten. 'Sorry, man. I didn't realize I was so bloody thirsty.'

He drinks, catching her warm woman smell under the fading cigarette smoke. Focus, Nick, he tells himself. 'Okay, Dawn, just to give you some idea of what I do here – did you see the movie *Avatar*?'

'Sure. The blue people?'

'Yeah. Well, it was all done with what's called motion-capture. Human actors creating the movements that are married to computer-generated models. You following me?'

'Hey, we got TVs out in the ghetto, Nick,' and he colors but she laughs and gives him a little nudge in the ribs with her elbow. 'It's cool, treat me like an idiot. Safer that way.' Putting him at ease.

He shows her the motion-capture stream of Sunny and then his work-in-progress of her dancing.

'Is that your daughter?' she asks.

'Yes.'

'And what's it? Like a video you shot of her?'

'No. I built her. Modeled her.'

'You telling me that's not real?'

Exley nods and with a mouse-click strips away the artifice, leaving Sunny as a skinless wireframe. Then he dissolves back through to the photo-realistic rendering.

Dawn's eyes haven't moved from the screen. 'Wow, that's fucken amazing.' She puts a hand to her mouth. 'Sorry, but it is. Please, show me again.' She watches it once more and then stares at him. 'So, you're a seriously talented guy, or what?'

Exley shrugs. 'Believe me, there are way more skilled people out there.' He stands and lifts the mo-cap outfit. 'Okay, this is the suit I want you to wear. The sensors will capture your movements.'

'Mnnnn,' she says. 'Kinda kinky.'

He smiles. 'Are you okay to change in here, or would you like the bathroom?'

'No, this is cool. I've changed in worse.'

'Good. Then call me when you're done.'

He leaves her, closes the door after him and goes out onto the deck, watching a cigarette boat speed by, thumping the water, a kayak getting tossed in its wake.

'Nick.' He turns and she stands in the doorway, the suit molding to her curves, and right there Exley feels something that he hasn't felt in a very long time: a hot rush of desire. He pushes it away.

'Great.' He walks through the living room, stops in the empty area outside the studio, on the expanse of white tiles. 'You got enough space to dance here?'

'Ja, no problem. You don't wire me up?'

'Nah, it's all remote.' He enters the studio, keeps the door open, and triggers the motion-capture, speaking to her from the workstation. 'So, why don't we try one? I'll play the music and you get a feel for it. I'm not going to direct you, just go with what works. We can do it as many times as you need.'

'Sure. I'm good to go.'

Exley hits Play and the lush sound pumps from the speakers. Dawn closes her eyes, rocks a little to the beat, moving only her shoulders and her hips, then she starts to jack into the rhythm and go with it and she loses herself in the music and, Jesus, she can dance, an achingly beautiful blend of sensuality and something else – a sadness and pain that comes from way down deep.

Exley has to turn away, busy himself at his workstation, check on the data capture, to still a yearning that no man who has done what he's done should allow himself to feel.

The silver cremation urn winks at Vernon, catching the sun as it rolls on the passenger seat of the Sniper truck when he speeds through a hairpin on the road plummeting down to Llandudno beach. The cheap little urn was waiting for him at the Sniper offices this morning, delivered by his undertaker buddy, along with an envelope containing five crisp new hundred-rand bills. Vernon's kickback for making the connection.

He looks forward to handing Exley his dead kid's ashes when he goes to the house later, to collect Dawn. Smiles at the thought of the pain in the skinny whitey's eyes.

His little reverie is interrupted by headlights flashing in his rearview. At first he thinks it's some impatient bastard wanting to pass him, so he edges toward the curb, but the car stays glued to his ass, lights making like a disco. Vernon pulls over, outside a triple-level pile of stone and glass. A pale Ford slides in behind him. He waits but nobody emerges from the car. Cursing, he cracks the door and levers his bulk out, pain shooting up his withered leg.

As Vernon limps toward the Ford, ready to give the driver a mouthful, he sees Dino Erasmus's ugly face through the windshield and his nut sack yo-yos upward in his skivvies as a nasty little twist of fear takes him low. Erasmus pushes open the passenger door of the car and Vernon slides inside.

'Dino,' Vernon says.

Erasmus looks down his snout and says, 'Didn't know you was a pimp.' Vernon just checks him out, says nothing. 'So, what, you Mr Delivery now? Bringing dark cunt to rich whities?'

'What you want, Erasmus?' Vernon asks, keeping it cool.

'That little whore, Dawn Cupido, you tight with her, ja?'

Vernon shrugs. 'I know her from the club. Threw a dancing gig her way.'

'Ja, the fucken horizontal mambo.' Erasmus's nostrils do a little dance of their own as he sniggers. 'What she give you to get rid of Merinda Appolis?'

This catches Vernon like a kick to the gut and his voice sounds strangled when he says, 'Dino, either you start making some sense or I'm walking.'

'You want sense? Okay, how's this: Merinda Appolis was the social worker in charge of Dawn's kid. Was busy getting a court order to have the child removed from her. On the day Merinda gets herself killed you show up at her office. So here's what I'm thinking: Dawn knows you killed that piece of shit Boogie, says she'll shut her trap if you sort out Merinda Appolis. You go to Merinda, chat her up, invite her on a date and throttle her. Dump her dead ass near Paradise Park. How am I doing?'

Water drips from Vernon's armpits and ramps the corrugations of his ribs. He lights a smoke to give himself a gap, pleased to see that his hands aren't shaking.

He sucks smoke and exhales at Erasmus, who twitches his nose holes. 'Dino, you're out of your mind, my brother. Merinda Appolis asked me to come by there, to ask me questions about Dawn and the kid. Matter of fact, I told her she was doing the right thing, that it was better for the girly to be taken from Dawn. That's it. End of fucken story.'

Erasmus grins. 'You know your problem, Vernon? You think you're too bloody clever. Got something going with Nick Exley. Got something going with Dawn Cupido. Juggling this. Juggling that. Well, my friend, I think you just juggled your ass right into Pollsmoor.'

Vernon opens the door and stands, leaning down to talk to Erasmus. 'Dino, next time you wanna speak to me, you come with a piece of paper, okay?'

He slams the car door, feeling calm and centered as he walks away from the dead man.

chapter 38

WHEN DAWN SAW THAT VIDEO (OR WHATEVER IT WAS) OF THE DEAD KID dancing, she had this flash: blur your eyes and it could be Brittany. Creeped her out, so she pushed it from her mind and did the samba dance thing, which was kinda fun.

Afterward Nick connected up her moves to a little skeleton in the computer and there it went, shaking its bones just like her. The two of them laughing, Dawn making him play it again and again.

But now, up in the kid's bedroom, she finds a cork board filled with photographs of the little girl – on the beach, hugging her parents, opening Christmas presents, playing in a green field full of yellow flowers – and there's no denying the resemblance. Brittany's skin is a bit darker, her hair a bit wilder, and Dawn's never in her life been able to afford such fancy clothes for her kid, but she can't look at these pics without seeing her daughter and it makes her shiver, like somebody walked on her grave.

She hears voices downstairs, Nick paying the delivery guy who has brought them take-out lunch, so she unpins a picture and slips it into her jeans pocket. Dawn ducks out of the bedroom – came up to use the bathroom, not to spy, but what's wrong with being curious? – and hurries down the stairs. The sea, framed by the huge windows, looks like tinsel, crazy with sunlight, and she wishes she could strip off and dive in there.

Another time, Dawn, if you play your cards right.

Nick's in the kitchen, putting their pizzas onto plates.

'Can I help?' Dawn asks.

'Sure, why don't you grab a couple of beers from the fridge? Or would you rather have Coke?'

'No, a beer's good.'

He takes the plates and walks out onto the deck, leaving her in the kitchen. She opens the fridge, digging for the beers, but it's not the cold air that makes the downy hairs on her arms rise. She hears Vernon, as they drove over earlier, saying, 'Darkie comes into the house and stabs the wife dead in the kitchen. Hell of a fucken mess.'

There's no sign that anything happened here (if anything the place is too clean, the antiseptic sting of industrial solvent still in the air) but her imagination's going apeshit, so she snatches two frosty green bottles, one almost slipping from her hand as she shuts the fridge with her elbow, and gets the hell out of there, joining Nick on the deck.

They eat, Dawn vacuuming down her pizza with all the trimmings – salami, shrimp, meatballs – Nick nibbling at something with olives and asparagus.

'You a vegetarian?' she asks.

'Yeah.'

'For how long?'

'Since I was a kid. My mother is into the whole Eastern religion thing, so meat just disappeared off the menu.'

'Me, I like my meat.'

'Guess I just lost the taste for it. My wife and daughter ate meat, so it doesn't offend me.' Something crosses his face and he sets down the pizza slice, reaching for the beer, and he goes far away, staring out over the ocean, lines like a map of sadness on his face. She leaves him be, until he comes back. 'Sorry,' he says.

'It's okay.'

'So, Dawn,' he says, smiling, making an effort, 'how long have you been a dancer?'

'I always loved dancing, since I was a little kid. Always showing off. But I been doing it professional since last year.'

'Where do you perform?' he asks.

Dawn laughs, she can't help it.

'What's wrong?'

'Nick, I'm a stripper in a shithole on Voortrekker Road. I wouldn't call what I do performing, it's more like going to the gynecologist every night.' Dawn laughs again, but she's embarrassed him. 'Hey, I'm not proud of what I do but a girl's gotta pay the rent, you know what I mean?'

'I understand. It's just you have real talent. I've done some work with choreographers and dancers over the years and you're good.' Saying this with a serious look.

'Thanks. I appreciate it.'

'Dawn, I dunno if this would interest you, but I'm building up a library of motion-capture data and I don't have enough dance stuff. Maybe you could come back again? I'd pay, of course.'

Dawn lays her best smile on him. 'Sure. Anytime. In fact, I just lost my job, so it would be a blessing. Serious.'

'What happened?'

She takes a sip of the beer and gives him a fantasy version of what went down at Lips, no social workers, no Brittany, just cartoon versions of the Ugly Sisters and Costa. She plays it for laughs, and he smiles and shakes his head at the craziness of it all. Even eats some of his food.

They finish their drinks and he goes inside the house and brings back a six-pack of the imported beer that tastes a bit like piss to her, but hey, who the hell is she to complain?

Vernon, carrying the cremation urn in a pink plastic bag, clambers over the boulders that flank Exley's house. He'd parked the Civic outside the front gate and was about to buzz, when something said, no, go in the other way. Surprise them.

And there they are, Nick Exley and Dawn, sitting out on the deck, a pair of laughing shadows against the burning ocean, some kind of tuneless electro beat pumping from inside the house.

They don't know he's there and he stands a moment, on the rock where it all began, watching them. Dawn, barefoot, sits with her feet up on the wooden chair, one hand hanging down, resting on the neck of a beer bottle, the other up behind her head, playing with her hair, making little ringlets. Nick leans forward, elbows on the table, telling her something, and she laughs again – a loose laugh, like she's a bit drunk – and juts her titties toward Exley, who looks too bloody relaxed for a guy in his situation.

Vernon skids down the rocks and advances on them, dragging his bad leg, boot scuffing a trail in the white sand, and when they turn toward him the atmosphere changes. Dawn lowers her feet and crosses her arms over her breasts, staring out at the water.

Exley stands, looking uneasy. 'Hey, man, how about a beer?'

Vernon knows that they don't want him here and he feels something old and dark twitch inside him. He turns on a smile to cover his rage as he crosses the deck, his boots like gunshots on the wood.

'No, Nick, thanks.' He sits, putting the bag down beside him, the urn clinking. 'So, how'd it go?'

'Oh, excellent,' the whitey says. 'Dawn's a great dancer.'

'Ja, you should see her show sometime,' Vernon says, giving Dawn a look.

But she comes right back at him. 'I already told Nick what I do, Vernon.' She shrugs her shoulders like she's fucken shrugging him off and he knows he needs to exert some control here.

'No secrets between friends, hey?' he says, and Dawn stays quiet. He turns to Exley. 'And you, Nick, you tell her *your* darkest secrets?'

That gets the skinny fuck's attention and he coughs around the mouth of his beer bottle, staring at Vernon with an attempt at a smile. 'No, I wouldn't want to bore her.'

'Oh, she wouldn't be bored.' Bantering, then getting serious. 'Dawnie, I gotta have a talk with Nick. Go wait in the car.' Chucking the Civic keys at her.

Dawn knows better than to argue and says her goodbyes sharpish, but still giving Exley cow eyes. He walks her to the door, and they whisper a few words, Exley touching her on the elbow. She leaves and he comes back and sits.

'What's on your mind?'

Vernon raises the plastic bag and holds it out to Exley, who takes it, opens it and looks like somebody's kidney-punched him when he sees the silver container.

'Jesus,' he says.

Vernon gets a warm and fuzzy voice going. 'Sorry, buddy.'

Exley, fighting back tears, lifts the urn from the bag and places it on the table, all gentle, like it can feel what he's doing.

'Nick, I know you wanna be alone,' Vernon says, and Exley nods, eyes on the urn, 'but we got us a problem that won't keep.'

Exley looks up and says, 'Erasmus?'

'Ja.' Vernon nods. 'The fucker's like a pitbull. I been putting out feelers with my connections and it's not looking good. He's got a senior prosecutor on his side, seems like they're gonna take this thing the distance.' Bullshitting, of course, but it sounds believable, and he's scaring the little weakling stupid.

'He was fucking aggressive when he was here yesterday. Do I need a lawyer?' Exley asks, nice and stressed.

'No, not yet. That'll just send out the wrong signals. But we're going to have to contain this.'

'Contain it how?' Vernon shrugs and Exley says, 'Erasmus is making all these accusations, but what's he got? What proof?'

'Nick, strong enough circumstantial cases get convictions in court. Especially if the prosecution has the judge in their pocket. Remember there's no jury system in this country, just a judge. And him and the prosecution's born from the same hole, if you get my meaning.'

'So what do we do?'

'What I want you to get nice and clear, Nick, is that I done what I done to save your ass.' Exley's ready to mouth off, so Vernon holds up a hand. 'Whoa, buddy. My balls are on the line here. If things get too hot I'm gonna have to make a deal with Erasmus. Plea-bargain.'

Exley stares at him. 'Jesus, Vernon.'

'I was a cop, Nick. Put a lot of nasty motherfuckers behind bars. How you think it's gonna go for me if I get locked away with them in Pollsmoor?' He shakes his head. 'Not an option. But if I make a deal, I'll get sent to some medium-security prison in another province. Get my own cell. Probably serve no more than six, seven years. I'll be out by the time I'm forty.' He lights a cigarette, draws on it, never taking his eyes off Exley, speaking around a mouthful of smoke. 'Means I'll have to give you up, Nick. And for you, my friend, things won't go so well. In a recent case a foreign guy who hired hit-men to kill his wife ended up pulling a double life sentence.'

'But I didn't hire you!'

'Who's to say?'

'Okay, Vernon, what do you want? Money?'

'You come at me with that crap again, Nick? At a time like this?'

'Then what? Tell me what you want from me.' Desperate, his fingers clenched on the arms of the chair.

Vernon leans forward, crowding Exley. 'I want you to make this whole bloody nightmare go away.'

'How?'

'Simple, Nick.' Vernon, working his mouth like a goldfish, blows a perfect smoke ring and watches it float on the breeze and disperse. Then he looks deep into Exley's panicked eyes. 'You gonna kill Dino Erasmus.'

VERNON SPEEDS ALONG THE COAST TOWARD THE CITY, THE MOUNTAIN looming above, feeling the earth pulling at him as he takes the car through the curves. He hates this stretch of road, with its twists and turns imposed by the chunk of rock. Vernon's a straight-ahead guy. Plain and simple. Grew up out on the Flats, a man-made grid thrown down on the windswept badlands. A place all about forward movement. Something gets in your way, you take it down. End of story. You look back and you're fucked.

But now he feels just a whisper of self-doubt as he fights this road that chases its own tail. Is he getting in too deep, pressuring Exley to do this thing? Will the soft white man crack and take them both down?

Vernon lights a Lucky and breathes out his doubts and fears with the smoke, knowing that even if he wanted to, he couldn't sort this Erasmus business himself. He'd be suspect number one. No, he has to have an unshakeable alibi when Exley does what he has to do. And that is fucken that.

Vernon looks across at Dawn, who rests her head against the side window, watching the sunset. Remembers that night when he first got her into his car on Voortrekker. Changed her life for her. Is she grateful? Not a fuck. She'll drop him in a heartbeat.

'He pay you?' Vernon asks.

'Huh?' She sits up, squinting at him.

'Nick. He pay you?'

'Ja.'

'How much?' She hesitates. 'You don't have to lie, Dawn, I don't want any of your money. I'm not your fucken pimp.'

'Two grand,' she says.

'So, you going back?'

'Ja. Day after tomorrow.'

'I'll bring you through.'

'I can find my own way.' Looking out over the sea again.

He grabs her thigh and squeezes until it hurts. 'Now let's not get too full of ourselves, Dawnie.'

He puts on Percy Sledge – 'When A Man Loves A Woman.' One of her favorites. But Dawn just stares at the light dying over the ocean, not even responding to the music, and Vernon knows he's losing her.

From where Exley sits on the low rocks – right where the water took Sunny – the swell obscures the beach, and the house looks like a lightship adrift on the Atlantic. How he got out here Exley can't recall, but alcohol must have been involved because he holds an empty cut-glass tumbler in his hand. He stands, fighting for balance on the kelp-slick rocks, and has to sacrifice the glass to the deep when he needs both hands to keep from plunging into the water.

Exley makes it back to the beach, the legs of his jeans sodden, his bare feet cut by barnacles sharp as razors, and he leaves a trail of sand and a little blood as he heads for the liquor cabinet to refuel. The level of the gin bottle tells a story. He has been steadily anesthetizing himself since Vernon and Dawn left.

Vernon Saul and his threats destroyed the illusion of normality that spending the day with Dawn – chilling, even flirting in his clumsy way – had brought, sending him right back into a piece of absurdist theater, the hulking, gammy-legged thug a creature straight out of Beckett, Exley terrified by the light of self-belief that animated the maniac's dead eyes as he laid out his plan. A plan so crazy that all Exley can do is use alcohol to purge it from his mind.

On the ice run into the kitchen he stops at the little silver cremation urn standing on the counter, seeing his distorted reflection in the polished surface, ashamed of the man he has become.

Exley sets down the glass of booze and places the fingertips of his right hand against the cool metal of the urn. 'God, my baby, I miss you,' he says, closing his eyes, convinced for a crazy instant that when he opens them he'll see his daughter.

But, of course, the kitchen is empty, the white tiles bouncing cold light back up at him. He stands staring into the funhouse mirror of the urn, listening to the fluorescents buzz and the clock tick and the refrigerator whisper until the rasp of the gate buzzer startles him.

Crossing to the intercom, Exley is sure he'll hear the adenoidal tones of Dino Erasmus, but instead it's Shane Porter requesting permission to come aboard. The Australian strolls in holding a bottle of tequila by the neck, brandishing a fistful of fastidiously rolled blunts, like silkworms jutting between his fingers.

'X-man,' he says, embracing Exley. 'I just heard about Caroline. Jesus.'

Port smells of booze, reefer and an aftershave that could clear backed-up plumbing. When the Australian relaxes his embrace Exley staggers, the alcohol taking him out at the knees.

Porter laughs. 'You're totally shitfaced, aren't you, mate? Well, who the fuck can blame you?'

He heads out onto the deck and sets the tequila bottle down beside the remains of the pizza lunch. Fishing out a lighter he applies the flame to one of the joints, talking in strangled tones as he sucks in the smoke. 'Here, Ex, catch up on this. Durban Poison.'

Exley has a hit, and feels it immediately, this mildly hallucinogenic weed harvested in the faraway Zululand hills. The effect is not unpleasant but he has to sit down. Port joins him, and they bounce the reefer, soft grunts and the smacking of lips the only conversation until the joint is a stub of ash that the Aussie flicks out into the night, the men watching it weave and die like a firefly.

'Ex, I'm out of here tomorrow. Probably for keeps,' Porter says, firing up another doob.

'Yeah? Where're you going?' Exley's voice sounds as if it's coming from deep inside a barrel.

'Sharjah, up in the land of the camel shaggers. They've got a pretty serious cricket stadium up there and they're hosting a tournament next week. Good news is, I've landed a commentary gig. My stint in purgatory is over, old son.'

'Congratulations, Port.' Exley finds the joint in his hand and takes a lung-scalding hit.

'This tournament is small but it's a way back in. And there I was thinking you only found happy endings in massage parlors, mate.' The Aussie laughs, then he gets serious, leans in close. 'Now, Ex, I just had a visit from a fucking nightmare of a copper. Looks like this.' Port jams two fingers in his nostrils and pulls them up toward his eyes in a decent impersonation of the snout-faced cop.

'Dino Erasmus,' Exley says, coughing fumes.

'Yeah, Jesus. That's how I found out what happened to Caroline. Anyway, this cop was asking all sorts of nasty questions about you. Insinuating things about your wife and Vlad Stankovic. I played dumb, of course.'

Exley battles to keep up. 'You knew about them?'

'Mate, the whole of bloody Llandudno knew.'

'I didn't.'

'Yeah, well, you're the husband. Now listen, Ex, I know you didn't kill your missus, you're not that kind of bloke. And to be absolutely honest, I don't care if you did. Sorry to speak ill of the dead but she seemed like a gold-plated cunt to me.' He takes the joint from Exley and vacuums it up before tossing it. 'But this fucking copper is bad news, he's a walking hard-on and he's got you in his sights. Only bloody thing that'll stop that bastard is a silver bullet. You be careful, mate.'

'I will, Port. Thanks.'

'Sorry,' Porter says, delicately picking a shred of weed from his tongue. 'I shouldn't have said that about Caroline. In poor taste.'

'No, you're right about her,' Exley says, feeling a stoner's urge to spill the truth. To unload on Port, tell him how he killed Caroline and about the nightmare Vernon Saul's trapped him in. But he stays silent.

'Well, look on the bright side, you're a free man,' Porter says. 'And my advice is, don't be in a hurry to change that. A wiser bloke than me once said that when a man gets to a certain age there are two things he's better off renting by the hour: boats and women.'

Laughing, Port dips a hand into his jeans pocket and holds up a tiny glass vial. A single blue-white capsule, like a chip of ice, lies at the bottom of the container.

'Medication time!' He shakes the vial and the pill makes a sound like a rattlesnake as it clatters against the glass. 'My farewell gift to you, mate.'

'What is it?'

'I'm no bloody chemist but I reckon there's some Bromo-DragonFLY to bliss you out, a hint of PCPr to keep you chilled and just a twist of 4-FMC to keep you perky.' He places the container before Exley. 'What I do know is this little beauty will put you on speaking terms with the big guy in the sky.'

Exley stares at the pill and nods. The weed has softened the edges of his vision, the flame of Port's lighter multiplying as he brings it to yet another joint.

As the Australian blows out a pungent stream, his fleshy face shining with sweat in the yellow light from the living room, he says, 'Drop that little baby when things get too freaky, mate, and when you reach nirvana send your Uncle Shane a postcard.'

If there's more conversation, Exley doesn't remember it. There's a jump cut and Port's gone and Exley knows he'll never see him again. He wanders into the house and finds he has the empty bottle of tequila in his hand.

Exley approaches the urn again, the air around it boiling and blurring from the booze and the weed. He tucks all that remains of his daughter under his arm and shambles into the studio, slumping into his seat at the workstation.

He sets the urn beside the monitor and gropes for the mouse, the slick plastic skidding away from his fingers like a greased pig. At last Exley corrals it, and sets to work, the shiny urn alive with the reflections of his dancing daughter.

chapter 40

DAWN JUST LOVES THE WATERFRONT. TO HER IT'S EVERYTHING THAT IS magical about Cape Town: a giant shopping mall built around the harbor, with sun-drenched Table Mountain as a backdrop. The place is full of rich white people with tans and foreign accents. All the designer stores are here – from Jimmy C to Louis V – and she feels connected to a big, wide, glamorous world just walking past the brightly lit window displays, holding Brittany's hand.

She bought Britt a cone and the kid is skipping along, a smear of ice cream on her nose. Dawn stops and bends down, wiping her child's face with a tissue.

'Come, get done with that thing now. I wanna take you shopping.'

The cone disappears, Brittany cramming it into her mouth – little pig – and Dawn neatens her up a bit and they walk into Egg, the kid's store where Nick Exley's dead daughter got her clothes.

Young as she is, Brittany knows this place is something special. Britt looks cute, sure, in her outsized T-shirt and Chinese blue jeans, but Egg is designer wear for the under-tens.

'Mommy gonna buy me one like so?' Brittany asks, feeling up an outfit on a kid-sized dummy like she's a fashion buyer.

'Ja. It's your lucky day, girlfriend.'

They find the rails for four-year-olds and Brittany's hands are everywhere, grabbing and tugging, and some snotty brown sales bitch comes over and gives them a frosty smile.

'May I help?' she asks in an accent she stole from the TV.

'Nah, we okay. I need you I call you,' Dawn says.

A hefty blonde woman with two fat kids comes in and the shop girl is across to them, all smiles. Dawn has a tug of war with Britt, until they agree on some outfits to try on, then Brittany drags her toward the changing cubicles. Dawn's got Nick's two grand in her pocket, but the prices of these clothes are sick. Fucked if she's going to blow her cash on this stuff.

When she gets Brittany into the curtained cubicle, she strips her down to her panties, and they quickly select an outfit they both like. It's so adorable Dawn could just pee herself. A loose, sleeveless top with flowers and butterflies embroidered on it over tight little pink hipsters in something soft and floppy. Perfect.

The pants and top are security tagged with plastic sensors the size of brooches that'll get the alarm at the doorway screaming if she tries to smuggle the clothes out. Not a problem. Dawn digs a pair of nail scissors out of her bag and she cuts into the fabric around the tags, removing them. She pulls at a few loose threads. Can't hardly see no damage.

Dawn dresses her daughter, covering the Egg clothes with Brittany's cheap and nasties. Nobody would know. She hides the tags under the shelf in the changing cubicle, grabs the armful of rejected clothes, and takes Brittany's hand.

She dumps the clothes on the sales assistant saying, 'I think maybe your clothes are better for fat-assed kids.'

Marches Brittany out past the heavy whities and speed-walks her through the mall to the road, where the taxis gather like roaches, ready to take the workers back to the Flats. They squeeze in among aunties in cashier outfits and shop girls painted to the nines, lost in a world of mindless chick-talk all the way to Voortrekker.

Back home Dawn makes them toasted cheese, then she washes Brittany's hair and blow-dries it, smoothing out her blonde curls, taking peeks at the stolen picture of Nick's kid, making sure Britt's laser eyes don't catch her in the mirror. When she dresses her daughter in the new outfit – doing a little rehearsal for tomorrow – she's astonished at what she sees.

'Well, Britt, what you think?'

Brittany, pirouetting in front of the mirror, in love with her reflection, says, 'Now I really look like a white kid, hey, Mommy?'

Oh you do, my baby, you do. And not just any white kid.

N

Exley has lost all sense of time in the eternal twilight of his studio. Terrified of coming down, he carries on drinking and takes steady hits on the joints Shane Porter left behind. When monitor blindness and carpel tunnel finally drive him from the room, the seagulls bicker against a hot orange sky.

His cell phone, lying on the sofa, rings and blinks. He picks it up as the ringing ends and sees that he has fifteen missed calls. He doesn't check his voicemail, knows they'll all be from Vernon Saul. Hounding him. Demanding to know if Exley has been down to Hout Bay to buy an anonymous pay-as-you-go SIM card for his cell phone. If he's used it to call Dino Erasmus. If he is executing The Plan.

The phone vibrates in his hand, blaring out its ring tone, and he almost drops it in fright. Unknown Caller comes up on the display but he knows who it is. Takes the call, wanting to stop all this.

'Yes,' he says, his voice a parched whisper.

But it is not Vernon Saul. It's the snout-nosed cop. 'Mr Exley?'

'Yes.'

'Detective Erasmus here.'

'Yes,' Exley says again. Perhaps his vocabulary is limited to this single word? But when the cop asks if he can come around to the house to ask him a few more questions, Exley discovers that his range extends to 'no'. Not wanting this ugly man with his denuding eyes anywhere near the house.

'Why not?' Erasmus asks, pissed off.

'My wife's parents are here from England,' Exley says, 'for the funeral, and they're traumatized enough.' Realizes immediately how dumb this lie is.

'Not my problem. I need to see you.'

'Okay, but not here,' and just like that Exley borrows a line from The Plan: 'Do you know the old Scout Hall in Llandudno?'

'Ja. I know it.'

'Meet me there.'

'I'm in my car, coming up from Hout Bay. See you in ten minutes.'

Exley is committed now and he has to haul ass. He finds his Havaianas out on deck and takes off across the beach, clambering over the hump-backed rocks – just like Vernon showed him – so he can avoid the eyes of the surveillance cameras positioned around the house.

Suddenly he realizes that it doesn't matter if he's seen. He's had enough. It's over. He's going to meet Erasmus to tell him everything. End this thing.

The setting sun throws a gaudy light on the narrow footpath that carves its way through the dense green bush, up the steep slope toward the Scout Hall. To Exley's monitor-fried eyes the overheated landscape is a swirl of acid colors, throbbing and shifting as he forces his starved and exhausted body up the path.

There's no one about. All the walkers are down on the beach with their dogs, enjoying sundowners. Exley comes across the old bench, right where Vernon said it would be. Just a rusted metal skeleton, the wooden slats rotted through and split, lying like matchwood beside the path.

Exley tells himself that there will be nothing under the pile of wood. But there it is: a bile-green plastic bag, the top tied in a knot. Exley opens it, revealing an automatic pistol and a pair of surgical gloves.

Vernon demonstrated on his own pistol the day before, showing Exley how to cock the gun and fire it. Telling him to get in close before he pulls the trigger. Telling him to wear the gloves, so if forensics test his hands they will find no trace of gunshot residue.

Feeling the wind of karma at his back, Exley picks up the bag and takes it with him. To show the cop. Evidence against Vernon Saul.

Wheezing, sweating booze, Exley emerges on the dirt road that leads toward the disused Scout Hall. He can see the building in the distance, silhouetted against the lurid sunset: a shell of brick, with empty window frames and doorways, the roof bare to its trusses, all but picked clean by scavengers.

A light-colored Ford sedan is parked outside the hall and Erasmus stands leaning against the hood, smoking, surveying the palatial homes that follow the sweep of the coastline far below, the sky behind the mountain a strip of dirty red torn from the black sky.

'Must be nice to have money,' the cop says, not looking at him. 'You bloody foreigners come here buying up everything, living in the lap of luxury. But let me tell you, no amount of money is gonna save your ass now.' Exley doesn't reply, fighting for air. Erasmus turns to him, pointing that snout like a shotgun. 'You going down, Mr Exley.'

Exley nods. It's all got out of control and he's got to bring it back. Tell the truth. Tell how he killed Caroline in self-defense and rage. How Vernon manipulated him.

He's about to confess to this creep with his unfinished face when Erasmus says, 'So what really happened with your daughter?'

Exley's confession gets stuck in his throat and he says, 'What do you mean?'

'That drowning. Your wife off screwing Stankovic somewhere, I suppose? And you and that Australian doing what? Getting fucked up on drugs and just letting it happen? You bloody people are degenerate.'

Exley shakes his head, tries to say, no, that's not what happened. Even though it is.

But the cop isn't done. Exley can feel the heat of this brown man's rage and race hatred rising from his body. 'Still and all I'm sure it's a relief now. Daughter dead and gone. Killed your wife. Now your way is free and clear to get yourself some dark meat, way you people always do.' To Exley the man's words have the weight of blows. 'Oh, I know she was by your house yesterday, that little street whore. No time for feeling guilty about your dead family, is there, when you got a bushman mouth sucking on your white dick?'

A surge of fury collides with the substances Exley's been ingesting, and the toxic mix takes out his nervous system for a few seconds, as if he's suffered an aneurism. Dizzy, he falls back against the car, shaking, fighting for control. He has none and his fingers unclench and the plastic bag slips from his grasp and falls to the ground, the weapon inside gonging dully against a rock.

The cop stares at him and then sticks out a worn Hush Puppy and toes the bag open, the gunmetal gleaming salmon pink in the last light. Erasmus laughs when he sees what's inside.

'Oh, sweet Jesus, this is just great,' he says, sniffing the air in delight, his flaring nostrils holding their own little celebration. 'You know, this was my final throw of the dice, meeting you here? I couldn't find fuck all on you and your buddy Saul. My boss told me to drop it. Let's not piss off the foreigners, he said. We need their money, he said. I was looking at being kicked out of Special Investigations. A fucken embarrassment they were calling me. And now? Now, I see a promotion coming my way.'

The cop unholsters his own weapon and points it at Exley. 'Pick up the gun.'

Exley doesn't move. Tries to say something, explain, but his tongue is set in cement. Erasmus jabs him in the ribs with the gun barrel. 'Pick it up now.'

Exley obeys, lightheaded as he bends down and lifts the bag. 'No. Pick up the gun by the fucken butt.' Exley does as he's told, the weapon leaden in his grip.

'So,' the cop says. 'You come here to shoot me? Do it, then.'

Exley feels the trigger cool and slick beneath his finger, but his hand shakes like he's piggybacking a steam hammer, the barrel wagging wildly.

Erasmus laughs at him. 'Can't do it, can you?' He reaches forward and grabs the barrel. Exley's fingers slacken and the cop takes the gun and sets it down on the hood of the car.

Erasmus grins at Exley, gives him a little shove in the chest. 'You bring a gun, sonny, you better have the balls to use it.'

Then he punches Exley in the gut, smiling all the while. Exley falls to his knees, his hands tearing on the rocky road. He knows this is it. His fate is sealed. That karmic wind is howling now, blowing him into as bad a future as he can imagine.

'Take a nice good look at the view,' Erasmus says, 'because all you gonna see from now on is high walls, barbed wire and the smiles of the

AIDS-rotten fuckers coming to rape your tight white asshole.'

Without thinking Exley scoops up a fist-sized rock and draws on some last reserve of desperate strength to spring to his feet and smack the cop on his snout, hearing bone and cartilage go snap, crackle, pop. Erasmus makes an animal sound and sags, blood geysering from his nose, his weapon spinning from his hand. Exley hits him again. And keeps on hitting him until things go soft and wet and Exley is too spent to continue, on his hands and knees, drooling, gasping for breath.

It is fully dark now and Exley is grateful that he can't see what he has done, the cop a dark shadow beneath him. There is no movement. No breath coursing through what remains of that crude nose.

Some instinct for self-preservation drives Exley to throw the rock as far as he can into the thick undergrowth. Then he takes the dead cop's gun and puts it in the plastic bag with the unused surgical gloves. He forces himself to frisk Erasmus, finding his wallet with his ID. He takes that too. Making it look like a robbery.

Maybe.

Finally he grabs the pistol, lying on the hood of the car like it's waiting for a game of Russian Roulette, and dumps it in the bag. He flees the corpse, down into the bush, fighting his way toward the sniggering ocean, his breath coming in torn rasps. He emerges close to where Vernon Saul executed the Rasta, the rocks lying slick and black under the night sky.

Exley throws the guns into the water. Follows them with Erasmus's wallet. Then he strips off his bloodstained clothes and finds two stones the size of footballs. He ties his shirt around one and sinks it. Does the same with his jeans and underwear. Frisbees his Havaianas out into the swell.

He squats down, his dangling foreskin scraping the surface of the rock, and edges himself into the freezing water, feeling his balls shrivel, forcing himself on until he is submerged, kelp tugging at his legs. There is a moment when he is ready to surrender, to give himself to the ocean, ready for some *Finding Nemo* reunion with Sunny.

But the moment passes and he knows he is too pathetic and useless to kill himself. So he washes off the cop's blood and brains and drags his body from the water. Naked and dripping, he scurries over the rocks toward his house, feeling more beast than man, and retraces his steps into the sanctuary of the living room.

He grabs a handful of dishtowels from the kitchen and dries himself, wielding a mop to get rid of his wet footprints on the tiles. Teeth chattering from adrenaline and the freezing water, he stumbles upstairs into the bright bathroom that bears evidence of another, more civilized, Nicholas Exley: a red and white striped toothbrush, shaving cream and razor, an uncapped deodorant stick with a coiled armpit hair caught on the sticky ball. Property of a man he'll never be again.

He gets under the hot shower and scrubs at his skin until it hurts. The bandage on his left hand lifts free of the adhesive tape, slipping down toward his fingers, and he sees the fabric is stained with blood. His or the cop's, he doesn't know. He pulls the bandage free and inspects his palm. His flesh has knitted.

Exley leaves the shower and wraps himself in a towel. He drops the bandage into the toilet and flushes. The fabric swirls and dives like an eel but floats back to the surface. He flushes again and this time the bandage is sucked away.

Exley walks through to the bedroom to dress. As he pulls on his clothes he hears a cat's choir of sirens. He crosses to the window and sees spinning lights high up in the bush, turning the night sky red as blood.

chapter 41

WITHIN AN HOUR A PERFECT LITTLE NEW SOUTH AFRICAN TRIO IS AT Exley's door: the black captain, a power-dressed brown woman who looks like a lawyer, and a geeky white guy in jeans and a short-sleeved shirt with *Sniper Security* embroidered on the pocket in red cotton, a laptop slung from his shoulder.

'Mr Exley, this is Captain Demas from Special Investigations, and Don,' the black man searches for a surname and can't find it, 'uh, Don, from Sniper.'

'Yes?' Exley says.

'From Detective Erasmus's cell phone records we've established that he called you around seven thirty this evening.'

'Yeah, he called and said he was coming over, but he never showed up.'

The woman says, 'Did he say why he wanted to see you?'

'No. Just that he had some questions.'

'And he never arrived?'

'That's right,' Exley says, trying to discipline his facial muscles that seem intent on betraying him. 'Is there a problem here?'

The two cops exchange a look.

'Would you mind, Mr Exley, if uh, Don, checks the surveillance camera footage on the, the...' The black cop looks to the geek for help.

Don points toward the small metal door recessed in the exterior wall, near the front gate. 'It's stored on a hard drive right over there. I can pull the data off onto my laptop in a minute.'

'Go ahead,' Exley says. 'But he wasn't here.'

'Of course,' the black man says.

Exley turns and walks inside. He wants a drink and a hit on a joint. Remembers there are still a few of the little bastards lying out on the deck, like loose ammunition. Enough to get him arrested, if one of these cops sees them. What the fuck, that's the least of his problems. He flops down on the sofa and stares at a tennis match on TV. Two Amazonian women grunting like wild boars.

The geek goes off to do his duty and the cops stand in the hallway, whispering.

'You can sit down if you like,' Exley says.

'No, we won't impose,' the female cop says.

'Impose away,' Exley says, but they ignore him and the woman's cell phone rings and she speaks rapidly in Afrikaans, a low, guttural tongue, words dragged up from deep in her throat like phlegm.

On the TV one of the Amazons hammers the ground with her racket and curses in some hill dialect. The other woman hides tennis balls in her underwear. The whole thing takes on the quality of a primitive ritual, freshly minted, and Exley is transfixed.

A noise behind him turns his head. The geek places his laptop on the kitchen counter and the two captains flank him. Exley can hear snatches of their mumbled conversation over the tennis.

The geek: 'Nothing. No visitors. The detective wasn't here.'

The brown captain: 'Any sign that Exley left?'

The geek: 'No. He didn't leave.'

The black captain: 'You're sure?'

The geek: 'The cameras don't lie.'

Exley has to cough to mask his hysteria-induced hilarity. The technician is dismissed and the two cops come and stand over Exley like attending angels.

'So, Captains,' he says, 'is there some problem with the detective?'

The black captain says, 'His head was beaten in with a rock.'

The brown captain says, 'Up near the Scout Hall.'

Exley says, 'Good God, by whom?'

'We have no idea,' the woman says, her eyes holding Exley's as intently as a lover's.

'Did he have a family?' Exley asks.

'A wife and two children,' she says.

'They have my sympathy. How are they taking this?'

'Well,' the black cop says, 'I imagine they are praying for a miracle. As we all are.'

Exley stares at him stupidly.

'Detective Erasmus is still alive,' the woman says. 'Unconscious. But alive.'

Exley sees them out and closes the door and returns to the sofa. The tennis match has lost its allure, so he gets up and goes out onto the deck and sets one of Port's little joints ablaze.

What next? he asks of the smoke. What the hell next?

Stupid. Fucking. Cunt.

The words run over and over in Vernon's mind like a loop. Two uniformed cops have just left Lips – guys he knows from the force – here to check on his alibi. Telling him what happened to Dino Erasmus: head pulped to mincemeat with a blunt instrument. Probably a rock.

Vernon, suddenly blind to the naked slut on the stage and deaf to the pounding music, is back in a place long ago and far away, hammering his father's brains out.

What the hell got into Exley and made him use a rock, for Chrissakes? Leaving Erasmus alive? He'll wake up and talk. Panic seizes Vernon and he hurries to the men's room.

A drunk Boer is in there, staring at himself in the cracked mirror, but seeing some woman as he says, 'A bitch is a fucken bitch. And you, you're a fucken bitch.'

Vernon grabs him by the shoulders, throws him out and bolts the door. The small room is airless and filled with the white man's stink and Vernon thinks he's going to hurl, his belly clenching up tight, but he breathes it away and the spasm passes, and he splashes water onto his face.

He'll end up in Pollsmoor Prison with all the bastards he sent there. Tattooed mutants, rancid with AIDS, who will rape him year in and year out to get their revenge. He has already been warned.

The mouths of those men shouting at Vernon from barred cells and police vehicles and courtrooms become his father's mouth, calling him a fucken little rabbit and burning him with matches and shoving himself inside from behind, saying this is what I do to little rabbits, leaving him bleeding and crying and all alone, his mommy giving his daddy eggs and beans for breakfast like there was nothing wrong.

Vernon flees the bathroom, his father's sick whispers hanging in the air like old smoke. He tells Cliffie to keep an eye on things and pushes out onto the sidewalk, into the stifling heat and fumes and dust, walking into the night. He doesn't know where he's going, trying to shake those whispers like sandpaper on his skin.

But they follow Vernon and he stops at an intersection and stands under a street lamp that flickers like a strobe light, raining orange flashes down on him, his head dizzy with his father's voice. He grabs hold of the light pole, gasping, his eyes shut.

He hears sub-woofers blasting out rap and when he opens his eyes he sees an old Datsun stopped near him, two brown guys checking him out like he's totally fucken lost it. One guy laughs before the car rattles away, taking its music with it.

Get your head straight, Vernon tells himself, walking again, only now he knows where he's going: to his Civic, to get his spare phone with the anonymous SIM card so he can call that stupid fucken cunt Nick Exley. He sinks down into the seat and dials. Gets voicemail, Exley sounding like somebody from no place at all. Vernon doesn't leave a message.

He sits a while, trying to contain his agitation. Knowing he's miscalculated. Again. Pushed Exley into doing something that was beyond him, something that'll bring them both down. He starts the car, ready to speed across to Llandudno and confront Nick Exley.

Then he kills the engine and calms himself. He has an alibi. If he fucks off across town now and gets seen at Exley's – on his night off from Sniper – he'll draw suspicion. He has to let this play itself out.

Vernon goes back into the club. An old Rolling Stones number bangs away, Mick Jagger singing about *ti-yi-yi-yime* being on his side.

Dawn's replacement – a flabby white thing with dyed hair, sallow skin and bruises – is onstage, naked, and seeing her spread her flesh is like watching open heart surgery.

The studio is blue with smoke, empty booze bottles ring the workstation and stubs of joints lie like broken teeth around the keyboard. Exley lifts the biggest of the ends and gets busy with his lighter, burning his fingers without noticing, sucking at the weed, drawing in smoke and releasing it again, head spinning, but needing more – much more – to keep the horror at bay.

Then his ragged mind feeds him a snapshot of a smiling Shane Porter holding up little bottle between thumb and forefinger, a white pill rattling inside. Exley leaves the studio and navigates his way out onto the deck, the black ocean hissing and snarling beyond. The glass vial isn't on the table and Exley wonders if he imagined it. He crouches down, resisting the urge to slump to the tiles and fold himself into a fetal ball, searching until he sees a shiny meniscus winking at him from under one of the chairs.

Exley opens the container – it takes all his concentration to still his shaking hands – and drops the pill onto his tongue. Chewing the pellet will speed absorption, so he crunches down on it and releases a noxious brew of sulfur and bile, a taste so hideous that he almost throws up. He conjures saliva from somewhere and swills it around his mouth, collecting the grim residue that coats his teeth and tongue, swallowing it.

The effect of the drug is immediate, and as he stands a surge of energy ignites deep in his gut and blasts its way up his spine and out the top of his head. What his mother would call the crown chakra. The *sushumna*. A kundalini awakening, she would say.

But this is no moment of enlightenment. Just chaos and confusion and chemical overload. The world speeds past Exley, motion-blur streaking his peripheral vision in blasts of raw light. When he puts up his hands to steady himself against the sliding door, his fingers pass through the glass, and the rest of his body – a vague arrangement of particles and dust – follows.

Without knowing how he got here he's in Sunny's room, hugging her pillow. Inhaling her smell. Sucking whatever is left of her into himself.

Then the edges of time soften and run like egg yolk and he's back at the workstation and whether it is day or night or now or later is impossible for him to say, and all he can do is lift the mouse and carry on working. Patching together some new reality, mouse-click by mouse-click, reaching for the impossible, going beyond what he has ever done before by attempting to capture the light radiating from within Sunny's face. The light of consciousness. The light of his daughter's soul.

How it happens he will never be able to recall, but he finds himself shirtless, barefoot, squatting on the seat of his ergonomic chair, ripping the lid off the silver urn and digging into all that is left of Sunny, smearing her powdery ashes over his head and torso, like the *Aghoris* – the death-obsessed ascetics, naked and dreadlocked, moving like wraiths in Varanasi's cremation grounds – who so terrified him as a ten-year-old when his mother dragged him along on an Indian pilgrimage.

All the bulwarks Exley erected against faith when he fled the ashram, bricks of cold empirical logic and the sneering jokes about his mother's woo-woo idiocies, crumble around him and gods rise from the dust. Vengeful, interventionist gods. And when these deities arrive they bring with them their dark playmates.

So Exley, covered in Sunny's mortal remains, lays off his bets and directs his pleas and prayers and bribes and promises at gods and devils alike: give my daughter back to me and you can have the tattered remnants of my soul.

chapter 42

DAWN'S HAVING SECOND THOUGHTS, IN THE HARD LIGHT OF MORNING, AS she dresses Brittany in the stolen clothes. Even though she drank nothing but Coke the night before, her head feels thick, and her eyes look yellow in the mirror.

Brittany, though, is full of life. 'Where we going, Mommy?'

'To the beach, my baby,' Dawn says, distracted. She sits down on the unmade bed and lights up a smoke. Coughs.

Her plan, to somehow worm herself and Britt into wealthy Nick Exley's life, seems crude and ugly now. Desperate. There was a vibe between him and her the other day, for sure, but that doesn't mean nothing. The guy's not seeing straight from grief. Taking Brittany there today could backfire, big time. Maybe the last thing he wants is to be with a kid, especially one that looks like his dead daughter. Instead of cementing the attraction, hooking him deeper, he could pull back and she could lose him.

Her phone rings. Vernon. 'Ja?'

'I'm downstairs,' he says.

'We're coming.'

She scoops up the basket with towels and sunblock and a bathing suit for Britt, and grabs her by the hand.

'Come.'

They walk past Mrs de Pontes' door and just for a moment Dawn pauses, ready to knock and lay fifty bucks on the old bitch and leave Brittany with her. But the kid is skipping ahead, singing to herself, happier than Dawn has seen her in ages, and she can't just break her heart like that.

So they go down the stairs – some homeless fucker left a puddle of stinking piss in the lobby – and out to where Vernon sits at the wheel of the Civic. He slides his eyes across to Brittany when they reach the car, Dawn tipping forward the passenger seat so the kid can get in the back. Dumping the beach bag next to her.

'What's this?' Vernon asks. He looks like hell, his skin gray and sweaty.

'Can't get me a babysitter today.'

Vernon cranes his neck and stares at Brittany, then he laughs one of his empty laughs. 'Jesus, Dawn, you're a nasty piece of work.'

'What you mean?' she says settling in beside him, clicking her seat belt closed.

'Don't play Miss Innocent here. I know what you're up to.' She says nothing and he starts the car. 'I got to give it to you, you're fucken cold blooded.'

He slides the Civic into the traffic that streams toward Cape Town, Brittany singing some invented song about the sun and the beach and the fishies.

'Shut the brat up,' Vernon says.

Dawn turns and puts her fingers to her lips. 'Ssshhh, baby, Uncle Vernon's got a headache.'

Brittany goes quiet and nobody says another word all the way to where the rich people live.

Exley works until his eyes are torn and bleeding, his liver and blood thick and sluggish with sour chemicals, his right hand in seizure as it guides the mouse through the final business of creation.

All the alchemy that he could conjure – low magic and prayers and promises to gods and devils alike – is spent. Now is the time to know if he has captured his daughter out there where the dead go and brought her home.

Muttering to himself, his heartbeat rapid and thin, he clicks the render tab, hears the little sighs and grunts of his hard drive and watches the indicator bar, a sluggish green centipede, crawl from empty to full. A sharp ping tells Exley that his daughter is waiting.

All he has to do is trigger playback.

It takes a lifetime for the instruction to navigate its way through the tangle of his cauterized nervous system to the forefinger that hovers, shaking, over the space bar on his keyboard. Exley's finger falls and skin meets plastic and the bar sinks with an almost inaudible click.

For a moment nothing happens. The monitor remains blank. Then Sunny blooms out of the darkness, smiling, staring right into Exley's eyes. He sits forward in his chair and watches her dancing and twirling and dancing and twirling. Exley mutters a last incoherent prayer, waiting for something transcendent, waiting for the miracle to come.

But, when he calls her name and reaches for her, his fingers find glass and she stays trapped behind the screen, forever lost in two dimensions.

He has failed.

Of course he has. This whole absurd quest just an indication of how messed up he is. The little dancing chimera that is Sunny blurs and Exley sees his own reflection in the monitor.

Haggard.

Wild eyed.

A madman smeared with his daughter's ashes.

He closes his eyes and slumps forward, letting his head sag into his hands, feeling the stubble on his face and the grease in his hair. Smelling the ripeness of his body. An image comes to him of a skyscraper losing power, going dark floor by floor, and he feels his life force ebbing.

Then he hears Sunny laugh.

Exley rouses himself and stares at the monitor. She's still trapped there, dancing in an endless loop, and he knows he's hallucinating. But he hears it again, his daughter's laughter. Frantic, he rolls his chair forward and searches his computer's audio mixer for any faders that are open, allowing a recording of Sunny to leak through.

When Exley hears the laugh once more he realizes that it is coming from the beach and he pushes the chair back, sending it crashing into a stack of hard drives. He stands unsteadily, the after-image of Sunny imprinted on his retinas. He lurches forward, rips open the studio door and staggers out onto the deck, the blinding sun hammering down on him in an avalanche of light.

And there she is, Sunny, running toward him from the water, her arms outstretched, laughing, her hair a blazing halo.

Exley sprints across the deck, tripping on the stairs and landing on his knees in the sand. He finds his feet again, shouting Sunny's name, and he rushes at her, lifts and whirls her, the sun streaking and flaring, the world a place of madness and miracles.

chapter 43

BRITTANY SCREAMS IN TERROR AS THIS HALF-NAKED WHITE STRANGER TACKLES her and spins her, her hair flying out from her head like a maypole. She beats her little fists against Nick Exley, shouting for her mommy, begging to be put down.

Dawn, planted in the sand by the sheer weirdness of the moment and some sick dread, frees herself and rushes at Nick and pulls Brittany from him. Nick loses his balance and falls backward into the low waves, his mouth hanging open like a retard's. He's covered in dust, sweat and old booze and weed and general fucked-upness oozing from his body.

On his hands and knees, Nick crawls from the water, saying 'Sunny, Sunny' over and over again, spit and snot dangling from his mouth like bread mold.

Dawn holds Brittany close, feels the kid wrap her arms and legs tight around her, like a monkey, making little 'hah, hah, hah' sounds in her ear. Dawn pats her back, whispering, 'It's okay, Britt. It's okay, baby.'

Nick pulls himself up to standing and the sun is behind him now, so he gets a clear look at Brittany, who stares at him, terrified. Dawn sees the truth hit him and his knees buckle and he weaves, and it looks like he's going to go down again, but he stays on his feet somehow like a boxer hearing the bell.

Dawn knows she should say something, should be begging this poor man's forgiveness, but she can't find words and it's him who says, 'I'm so sorry,' begging hers instead, his face as tragic a thing as Dawn's ever seen and she's seen plenty.

'I thought – I'm sorry,' Nick says in a torn voice. 'So sorry.'

He staggers toward the house and Vernon Saul, who's stood still as wood through all of this, steps forward and puts an arm around Nick and half-carries him up the stairs to the deck, saying, 'Take it easy, buddy. Take it easy now.'

As they go into the house, Nick looks back at Brittany, who holds onto Dawn for dear life. The man's face is so haunted and Dawn is so sick with guilt she could puke.

Vernon gets Exley inside and drops him on the sofa.

'Nick, what the fuck you do last night, man? To Erasmus?' The stupid bastard is still gazing out at Dawn and the kid. Vernon leans down and gives him a little smack on the cheek. 'Focus, for Chrissakes. What happened to the plan?'

Exley stares up at him and he looks so lost for a moment Vernon almost finds it in himself to feel pity. 'Nick, that's just Dawn's kid, okay?' Exley nods. 'Now what went down last night?'

'I did what I had to do,' Exley says. His voice is a flat, dead whisper.

'You know you left him alive?'

Exley nods. 'They said that. The cops.'

'What did you tell them?'

'Nothing. Nothing.'

'What if he comes out of his coma and talks? What then?'

'Maybe he died. In the night.'

'No. I know a nursie over there by the hospital. The cunt is still alive. In ICU. Unconscious, but still alive. You better pray he fucken dies.'

Exley stands, staring into Vernon Saul's pitbull eyes, too far gone now to be afraid of the darkness there. 'Vernon, do me a favor: fuck off.'

He walks into his studio, Sunny still dancing her endless dance. No, not Sunny. Not his daughter. Just a thing on a computer. Cold, digital, man-made. A travesty. He smacks the keyboard, killing the playback.

Exley feels lost, as if he'll fragment and disappear entirely into some godless black hole of pain and guilt. He sacrificed everything at this digital altar and came up empty. Life, whatever it may be, is not his to manufacture.

But it goes on. Twisted and misshapen and tormented, yes, but his trip is not over. And the hell he has wreaked in the past few days will have to be answered for. But, just maybe, he can take one faltering step toward redemption.

He finds his filthy T-shirt lying on the floor of the studio and pulls it on, kills the monitor and grabs a soft toy – a little brown bear – from the litter around the keyboard, blowing on its fur to get rid of a fall of ash, then walks back out through the living room, each step an act of will. Vernon Saul stands watching, a squared-off silhouette in his body armor. Exley ignores him and goes down to the beach to where Dawn sits on a rock in the shade, holding her white child, stroking her blonde hair, soothing her.

Exley feels his heart pound as he gets closer. Not Sunny. Of course not. But the resemblance is uncanny.

The girl tenses when Exley approaches and grabs at her mother, burying her face in Dawn's thick hair. Exley stops a safe distance away and kneels down in the sand, as if he's about to propose marriage.

'Brittany, I'm really sorry I frightened you.' One eye peeps at him and he holds out the little bear, trying to control the tremors in his hand. 'This is Mr Brown. He is very angry with me for making you scared. He wants to be your friend.'

Both eyes looking at him now, blinking away tears, but staring at the soft toy. The child, moving slowly as a sea anemone unfurling, frees one of her hands and reaches out and takes the bear by the arm, and there is the hint of a smile on her face as she brings it to her chest and hugs it close.

'What do you say, Brittany?' Dawn asks.

'Hullo, Mr Brown.'

Dawn has to fight back a grin. 'No, what you say to Uncle Nick?'

'Thank you, Uncle Nick.' The child looks white, but she has her mother's guttural accent.

'It's a pleasure,' he says, and he sits down on the rock beside Dawn.

The child hums something and whispers into the bear's furry ear.

'I'm truly sorry, Dawn,' Exley says.

'Please, it's okay. Really. I understand. You must feel terrible.' Dawn puts her hand on his. 'I think maybe we should go.'

'No,' he says, and he can hear the desperation in his voice. 'Please don't go. I'd really like the two of you to stay.' He looks at the girl. 'What do you say, Brittany? We can swim and build sandcastles and get McD's for lunch?'

The child thinks for a moment, deciding whether he is to be trusted, consults the bear, whispering in his ear again, and then she nods. 'Mr Brown say it's okay.'

'Good. Excellent.' He stands. 'Dawn, I need a shower in the worst way. Why don't you and Brittany make yourself at home. Okay?'

She looks uncertain, but she nods. Exley walks through the living room and sees that Vernon Saul is gone. He climbs the stairs, has a moment of lightheadedness halfway up, then he composes himself and moves on. He stops in the doorway to Sunny's room, but he doesn't go in. He closes the door for the first time since she died and walks through to the shower.

He strips and turns the shower to cold, letting the icy water pummel him into alertness, watching Sunny's ashes drain from him and swirl down the plughole. Then he gets the water as hot as he can stand, before he cranks it back to cold. Repeats the process a few more times, gasping for breath.

Exley feels something happening in his chest, the muscles spasming, and for a moment he's sure he's having a heart attack, then the tension is released and with it comes a flood of tears, hot and salty on his face, merging with the shower water.

He sits down, with his back to the tiles, his arms dangling loose, and lets the pain and grief well up. When he can cry no more he stands and shuts off the shower. Dries himself. Finds some drops for the eyes that stare back at him from the mirror, a contour map of burst veins. He brushes his teeth and his tongue, shaves and combs his hair and dresses in a fresh T-shirt and baggy swimming shorts.

Exley walks down the stairs, sure that Dawn has taken her kid and fled, but he sees her standing at the water's edge, watching over the child who splashes in the surf, wearing a pink swimsuit. His phone, lying on the living-room table, flashes and rings. Unknown caller.

When he answers it he hears Vernon Saul's voice. 'You're lucky. He's gone. It's over.'

Exley ends the call. He thinks of the cop's family. Then he puts that thought in a box with all the other things that fill him with terror and guilt and drops that box into the toxic waste dump that he stores deep inside himself. Stuff that'll have to be dealt with, he knows.

But not now.

He walks into the studio and sees the room through fresh eyes. It is sordid. Despite the A/C the room stinks of days of madness and weed and booze and old sweat. The cremation urn stands open, its lid upturned beside the keyboard. Exley, filled with self-loathing, stares down into the urn and sees the dregs of his daughter's ashes at the bottom. He replaces the lid and carries the container across to the steel cabinet and locks it away.

The mouse is tacky to the touch when he clicks open the Sunny folder and deletes all the information in it. The motion-capture data. The reference photographs and the texture maps. The model that has obsessed him. As the hard drive churns, wiping all trace of his daughter's digital doppelgänger from its memory, Exley closes his eyes, an aurora of after-images swirling then fading to nothing. He powers down the work station and hears it sigh itself into silence.

Dousing the lights, he leaves the studio and slides the door closed. He crosses the living room and goes out into the sun, still dizzy, still torn around the edges, still an approximation of a man. But lighter, now.

Exley walks across the sand toward the woman and the child at the water's edge. Not his wife. Not his daughter. But they're alive. And they're real. And they're here.

chapter 44

YOU DON'T FALL IN LOVE, NOT IF YOU'RE DAWN CUPIDO. YOU LOVE YOUR KID, okay, and you love *things* – shoes, nice clothes and stupidly expensive face lotions – and maybe, just maybe, you have a bit of a kitschy soft spot for puppy dogs. But men? Never. Men are the enemy, to be preyed upon before they prey on you.

Just how it works.

But sitting here on the beach, in the shade of the rocks, Brittany splashing happily in the shallows, Dawn looks down at the sleeping face of Nick Exley and she can imagine somebody falling for him. Not her, of course. Never. His face, as he lies sprawled on the sand, snoring softly, has relaxed, those stress creases have smoothed out, and he looks gentle and sweet. She hates herself for what she did this morning.

Hates herself for sticking around here, too. Much as she tries to con herself into believing it's because she feels sorry for him, she knows the truth: she's desperate for a new life for her and Britt, and Nick Exley, screwed up and vulnerable as he is, could be their ticket out.

He's worked hard through the day to win Brittany's trust. Doing it in a cool way, not pushing. Just bringing a few toys out of the house – a beach ball, a bucket and spade – leaving them for her on the sand. Making sure she has a supply of fizzy drinks. Handling her the way only a parent of a small girl could. Heartbreaking to watch.

A fly buzzes in and lands on Nick's cheek and he twitches. Dawn waves the fly away, her hand still hovering over him when his eyes open and he looks startled, blinking. Dawn pulls her hand back and he sits up.

'I wasn't trying to smack you,' she says. 'There was a fly.'

'Thanks. Okay. Shit, how long was I out for?'

'Maybe an hour. It's fine. You needed it.'

He reaches for a bottle of beer and takes a drink; it's warm and he pulls a face. Runs a hand through his hair, his eyes on Brittany. 'Looks like she's having fun.'

'Man, you'll never know what a treat this is for her.'

'She's beautiful,' he says.

'Ja, she is.' Dawn catches his eye and laughs. 'Come on, Nick, ask the question.'

'What question?'

'The one about how a brown chickie like me gets to have a white kid like that.'

'That was the last thing on my mind,' he says.

'You're lying.'

He smiles. 'Okay. So, how?'

Dawn lights a smoke, speaking softly, even though Brittany is playing in the water, singing. 'The father was white, so there's a lot of milk in the coffee.'

'Where is he? The father?'

'Out the picture. He was just a sperm donor.' She shrugs. 'Truth be told, he was never in the flipping picture.'

'Then he's an idiot.'

'He never even knew, Nick.' She should shut her trap but she doesn't. Something in his eyes, the pain and hurt that live there – and how she added more – make her want to confess. 'I was hooking. He was a john. I was doing a lot of drugs back then. I don't even remember him, but looking at Britt I know he had to be a whitey.'

There's no shock on Nick's face. Not even surprise. He just nods. 'Well, she's a gift.'

'Ja, she is. Almost makes me believe in God again.' She laughs and grinds her cigarette dead in the sand. Then she's serious. 'I don't do it no more, Nick, the hooking. Or the drugs. Okay, shit, maybe a bit of weed now and then, but that don't count, hey?'

'No,' Nick says. 'It doesn't. Dawn, we've all screwed up. Christ knows I have.' He looks away over the ocean, then he shrugs and smiles at her. 'Don't you want to swim?'

'I forgot to bring my swimming things, I was so busy getting madam's stuff together.'

'I could get you one of my wife's swimsuits. Or is that kind of creepy?'

'No. It's cool. I'd like that, thanks.'

He disappears into the house and returns carrying a dark blue one-piece Speedo. It's unused, still has a price tag dangling from the fabric. 'Caroline wasn't much of a swimmer,' he says.

Dawn stands and takes the Speedo. 'I'll go change.' She calls across to Britt, who doesn't hear, busy dumping sand from the bucket, laughing as a low wave collapses the mound.

'I'll watch her,' Nick says.

Dawn squints at him. 'You sure?'

'I'm sure.'

She nods and crosses the sand and walks up onto the deck, looking back to see Nick standing over Brittany.

Dawn takes the stairs to the bathroom and cuts the price tag off the swimsuit with a pair of nail scissors lying on the basin. Wonders if they were the dead wife's, too. Trying not to look at the few cleansers and cosmetics lined up on the tiled surface, because they'll drain away the happy feeling that's crept up on her.

Dawn strips and pulls on the Speedo, checking herself in the mirror. It's crazy, her laying her goods out for sleazy bastards to view every night, but she feels exposed. Thank God the suit, even though it's a size too small, is as modest as can be, like something a girl swimmer would wear at the Olympics.

She walks down the stairs and pauses on the deck. Nick's in the ocean. He's kind of skinny, with the flat, unmuscled body of a teenage boy, the waves gently lapping at his belly. What amazes Dawn is that Brittany is in with him, and he's holding her, cradling her in his arms, keeping her afloat, both of them laughing.

Dawn goes to the water, tugging the swimsuit out of her ass-crack. Nick sees her coming and he looks at her – really *looks* at her – and she feels stupid and shy and is relieved to let the sea swallow her up, even though it's cold enough to freeze her tits off.

⚡

Exley, standing at the open refrigerator, the cool air soothing his sunburned skin, can't bear the thought of Dawn and Brittany leaving. The day, even though it started as a waking nightmare, has been an unexpected boon.

He takes out a couple of beers, opens one and stands at the kitchen window, watching mother and daughter down on the beach. Dawn, unaware of his gaze, walks out of the water, adjusting the Speedo where it cuts into her groin. Brittany, looking for sea shells, says something that makes Dawn laugh as she lifts a red towel and dries her hair, then bends forward at the waist with her legs spread wide apart – he can see the swell of her breasts against the wet Lycra – and shakes the last moisture from her curls. She straightens, her hair falling across her face, and she drops her head back and sweeps her hair behind her neck, shouting something to Brittany, her voice lost in the chatter of the seagulls.

Exley rests the cold bottle against his forehead and shuts his eyes. He's not drunk, but he's been drinking beer steadily all day. A kind of mildly alcoholic infusion to keep him calm and offset the hallucinogenic that's still messing with his serotonin receptors, feeding him little flashbacks that fry his synapses. Afraid if he sobers up completely his nervous system will rebel and the weight of his actions over the last days will plunge him into a state of frenzy and terror.

A sharp knock on the kitchen door startles him and he sees the pallid Sniper technician – Dave? Don? – standing out on the deck with a lightweight aluminum stepladder on his shoulder, a bag of tools hanging from a belt at his waist.

'I'm finished, Mr Exby.'

Exley nods, doesn't bother to correct him.

The guy arrived earlier, announcing that he wanted to mount another surveillance camera to cover the deck and the beach, removing the blind spot. Exley, reluctant to have his time with Dawn and her child interrupted, had almost told him to get lost, but he'd shrugged and let the man do his drilling and his cabling.

Exley walks the technician to the front door and buzzes him out. He grabs the beers in the kitchen and steps down onto the sand. Dawn, standing with the late sun golden on her face, her skin still dripping water, smiles at him and takes one of the bottles.

'Thanks, Nick,' she says.

He says, 'Cheers,' and drinks.

Brittany holds up a shell and calls to her mother and Dawn walks over, drinking from the bottle. She bends to look at what the child shows her, presenting a view of her ass that takes Exley's breath away. He feels a rush of desire, his cock stirring in his shorts, and he crouches to hide this sudden tumescence.

His child is dead. His wife – dead by his hand – is barely cold. He's a cop killer. But here he is in the grip of lust, made all the more intense by how inappropriate it is.

Dawn is back beside him, and he can smell her, a hot saltiness, and her arm touches his as she sits and he feels like a high school kid getting a boner in class.

'We haven't done any work,' she says.

'On a day like this, who the hell can think of work?' She smiles but he knows he's being a thoughtless asshole. She's an unemployed single mother, for Christ's sake. 'Dawn, we can do some capturing tomorrow, okay?'

She nods and says, 'Sure,' as if he's fobbing her off.

'I mean it. Why don't you and Brittany stay and we'll do some work in the morning?'

She looks at him. 'Sleep over, you mean?'

'Yes. Britt can sleep in Sunny's room. You can take the guest bedroom.'

'No, Nick, I couldn't put you out like that.'

'You wouldn't be putting me out.'

'Anyways, Vernon's going to be here soon. To take us back.'

Exley sees this opportunity slipping away. 'Dawn, I've really enjoyed having you and Britt here.'

'Us too.' She rests her fingertips on his arm for a moment.

'Please stay,' he says. Something in his voice makes her stare at him and her eyes narrow and she blinks and looks away, maybe spooked by the weight of his need. 'Please,' he says again.

She plants her beer bottle in the sand and gets to her feet and he knows he's blown it. But she shouts, 'Hey, Britt, you wanna have a sleepover?'

The child, kneeling on the wet sand, nods. 'Only if I can sleep with Mr Brown.'

'Ja, I'm sure he'll be okay with that.' She turns back to Exley and smiles down at him. 'Nick, looks like you got yourself some lady guests.'

Exley realizes he's been holding his breath and he releases it, in time to hear Vernon Saul's ridiculous car burping to a halt in the street. By the time Exley stands the buzzer sounds inside the house.

Dawn's smile evaporates. 'That's Vernon. I don't think he's gonna be too thrilled.'

'I'll handle him,' Exley says, with a confidence he doesn't feel.

The skinny whitey, all pink in the face, barefoot, dressed in shorts and a T-shirt, comes out to the front gate, instead of buzzing Vernon in.

'Somebody upstairs is looking out for you, buddy,' Vernon says, jerking a thumb up at the sky.

Exley shoots him a blank look. 'Meaning?'

'Darky down in Mandela Park tried to sell Erasmus's cell phone. Cops arrested him a few hours back and the stupid bastard was wearing Dino's watch, all nicely engraved by his wife.' Exley is still looking blank. 'Jesus, Nick, join the dots, my brother. You took Erasmus's service pistol and wallet. Then this darky comes along and swipes his phone and watch. Cops are going after this guy for murder and robbery. Seems he's already done time for assault.'

Exley's nodding now. 'Shit. Okay.'

'Cops want this thing to go away as quick as possible.'

'What about the prosecutor Erasmus was working with?'

'Already moved on, believe me. They'll give Dino a nice funeral and his widow'll get death compensation and a pension and that'll be that.'

Exley shrugs. 'A lucky break, I guess.'

'For fucken sure.' Vernon looks toward the house. 'So, Nick, where's the girls?'

'Inside.' Battling to hold eye contact. 'We need to finish the motion-capture in the morning, so they're staying the night.'

'Ja?'

'Yes.'

'Let me speak to Dawn,' pushing past Exley but the little shrimp blocks him and puts a hand on his body armor. Vernon laughs. 'And now? You gonna stop me from going inside?'

'I'd rather you didn't.'

'Nick, fuck it, man, I just wanna talk to Dawn, now get out my way.'

'Don't make me call Sniper, Vernon.'

'So that's how it is?' Vernon staring down at him, ready to snap him like a twig.

'Yes, that's how it is.'

Vernon pulls himself away from the edge, putting a lid on his rage. Even forces a smile that hurts his face as he steps back and holds up his hands in surrender. 'Whoa, Nick. Chill, my man. Things are getting to you.'

Exley shrugs and Vernon feels the poison inside loop up through his innards, seeping into his bloodstream. 'Okay, you have a good night. But I'm warning you, that's rough trade you got inside your house. Don't be fooled by the nice packaging.'

'Thanks for that insight,' Exley says, and Vernon can feel his knuckles connecting with that mouth, ungrateful little fucker's teeth flying like popcorn.

Vernon turns and gets into the car. He watches Exley enter the house and close the door, then he starts the Civic and takes off at speed, roars

EXLEY LIES IN THE DARK ON THE SOFA IN THE LIVING ROOM, COVERED BY THE sheet he brought down from the linen closet, his head on a new foam pillow still thick with the smell of the plastic it was wrapped in. The house is quiet but not empty, the ghosts of his wife and daughter diluted by the presence of Dawn and her child.

Exley catches a trace of Dawn's scent, a mix of cinnamon, woman sweat and tobacco. As he sees her splashing in the waves, laughing, her hair dripping water, he feels his cock harden.

Lifting his head from the pillow, Exley sits up, the sheet sliding from his body. He stares down at the erection tent-poling his shorts, willing it to wilt, but it doesn't obey. He can't remember the last time he was this turned on. Maybe back in New Mexico, as a teenager, when he lost his cherry? Definitely not when he and Caroline first slept together, which was arousing more on a cerebral than a physical level.

Exley flicks a finger against his swollen dick. You, my friend, are an unwelcome visitor.

In an effort to distract himself, he thinks of the child asleep in Sunny's room. He remembers the evening – pizzas and Disney DVDs – Brittany rattling off her own commentary in that garbled, staccato accent. He thinks of Vernon Saul telling him that yet another black man is being sacrificed to protect Exley's privileged white ass. Thinks of anything but Dawn lying up in the spare room.

It doesn't help.

So he allows the images of horror that he has kept behind an emotional firewall to seep through: Sunny dead on the beach, Caroline spewing blood, the cop's skull turning to pulp.

But still his desire is not dimmed. If anything, his cock is even harder now, painfully engorged, throbbing against his belly, the brew of grief, guilt, terror and bloodshed working as a potent aphrodisiac. Perverse, of course, but there it is.

Jesus Christ, you sick bastard, he says out loud, lie down and go to sleep.

But the words slide away into the darkness and Exley finds himself standing and walking to the stairs, his hard-on like a dowsing rod leading him upward.

The door opening wakes Dawn and she thinks it's Brittany, but there's enough moonlight coming through the curtains for her to see Nick Exley, standing in the doorway, wearing only a pair of shorts.

'Nick, what's wrong?' she whispers, sitting up, holding the sheet against her chest even though she's sleeping in a T-shirt and panties.

'I'm sorry,' he says. 'This is crazy.' Turning to go.

Dawn knows, right then, that it is her call. Does her life stay as it is? Or does it change? She says, 'Nick, come here.'

He does, with his almost hairless boy's body and his surprisingly big cock, and when what happens happens, it feels shockingly intimate. It's the first time Dawn has ever slept with a man sober, and it's the first time since she was raped as a child that she's let a penis into her without a condom. Even the messed-up night that Brittany was conceived she knows a rubber was used. It must have torn (cheap shit she got free from the sex clinic) but there was no barebacking, ever.

So, this is terrifyingly intense, this broken man with all his pain, deep inside her, carrying her with him, making her feel things that are better left forgotten.

Exley, lost in this woman's heat, her hair flung dark against the white linen, is visited by his dead wife, her memory coded into his skin. He feels the hard bones of her blue-white, freckled body, her inverted nipples fleeing his hands and mouth. Caroline always holding back, unyielding, fighting him, even now.

He pushes through her and into Dawn, her dark body fuller, warmer, more welcoming, her nipples hard against his chest, her breath hot on his face.

Nick's cock thickens and hardens and she can feel the small spasms low in his stomach, his breath coming in gasps, sweat from his face dripping onto hers, and that's okay – Dawn's no stranger to guys getting their jollies – but now there are no chemicals to keep her dead and detached and safe and she tries to stop herself but she can't and she feels the orgasm welling up in her, bringing with it all the self-loathing and shame from so long ago.

She fights it, her mind filled with the same hot disgust she felt then. Tries to push it down and away. But it explodes inside her and she hears the filth on her mommy's bed say, 'You like it, you little whore, you like it, don't you? You. Fucken. Like. It.'

Nick falls asleep almost immediately – lying on her with his arms and legs spread like he's in freefall – and Dawn slips out from under him and leaves the room without waking him.

She walks naked into the bathroom and has to pass through the main bedroom, its king-size bed a tangle of sheets. Dawn flashes on him in that bed with a faceless woman who is now dead. She pees and wraps herself in a towel and goes downstairs to where her cigarettes lie on the table in the living room, in the mess of pizza boxes and McD's kiddy food and DVDs. A pillow and a blanket lie on the sofa, where Nick slept. Or lay awake.

Smoking, standing at the glass doors staring out at the moonlight on the water, Dawn feels the presence of the dead woman and child, not like ghosts, but how they live on in the man sleeping upstairs, and always will.

Dawn goes back up and pauses at the door to the spare room. She can hear Nick's soft snores. She walks down the passageway to the child's room. A nightlight is on and Brittany sleeps clutching the little bear, her face hidden and, surrounded by the clothes and toys and photographs of Sunny, she could almost be the dead girl.

Dawn is gripped by a crazy panic and turns her sleeping daughter's head to see that it is still her, that she hasn't been stolen away, her soul bartered in exchange for the return of this rich white kid.

Stupid thoughts. Of course it's Brittany, mumbling, her little hand reaching out and grabbing at Dawn, who curls up on the narrow bed with her daughter. But she can't sleep. Terrified for herself and for her child.

This isn't their world. She sees how easily Brittany could slide into it, how happy she could become, here in this house with its beach and its endless supply of junk food and kid's movies.

And what happens when it's all taken away? Because it will be. That's how it is, for sure. People give you things but just as quick they take them back, and want more from you than they ever gave.

At first light Dawn packs Brittany's things, and creeps into the spare room to get her clothes. Nick sleeps on. She feels guilt, for an instant, but knows she mustn't weaken. That she has to protect them.

She goes back to the child's room and dresses Brittany and lifts her from the bed. Her sleeping daughter is a deadweight, and Dawn feels like a donkey carrying the bags and the kid down the stairs, trying to make no noise.

Dawn heads for the front door and sees one of those keypads beside it, suddenly terrified that Exley set the alarm and when she opens the door it'll scream and wake him. But the door opens without a sound and she closes it and breathes the fresh, cool air of morning.

She stresses again when she comes to the high, barred front gate. Locked. No handle. Then she sees a little button to the side and she jabs it and the gate clicks opens and they are free.

She takes off in the direction of the main road, far away, high above the sleeping suburb. Brittany wakes and wants to pee. Dawn lets her do it at the side of the road, the child trickling her piss into some rich person's gutter. Then the kid won't walk, so Dawn has to carry her, wondering how the hell she's going to get all the way up that mountain.

She hears the whine of an engine and a little truck battles it way up toward her, two surfboards in silver covers tilted in the back catching the sun like mirrors. Dawn waves the truck down.

A couple of young white guys with long blond hair and fluff on their chins, dressed in wetsuits, look up at her.

'Hey,' the driver says.

'Give us a lift, man,' Dawn says.

'Where you going?'

'To the taxis.'

'We going down to Hout Bay. We can drop you there, okay?'

'Cool,' Dawn says, and the passenger gets out and lets her sit between him and the driver. They smell of seawater and weed. Brittany sleeps on, Dawn hugging her close.

The truck takes off, old-school reggae buzzing through the speakers. Bob Marley telling her: *no woman, no cry.* The guys don't speak, which is fine with Dawn. She thanks them when they drop her at the circle near Mandela Park, black workers already piling into the taxis on their way to the city.

Dawn gets her and Brittany into a minibus, letting the Xhosa chatter calm her, watching the mountains and trees of the rich give way to the low, ugly suburbs of the poor. Going back to where she belongs.

chapter 46

VERNON IS WOKEN BY THE WHINE OF A POWER TOOL. HE SITS UP ON DOC'S rancid sofa, sun blasting through the broken window, all manner of stench welcoming him back to the world. He checks out his watch. After ten. He doesn't have to work, but he still needs to get his ass into gear.

He feels rested. His mind calmer, focused now. His rage wrapped up nice and tight, ready for when he needs it. He knows all he has to do is keep chilled and a plan will come about how to deal with Exley and Dawn, forming piece by piece in his mind, like his plans always do.

He needs to take a piss and walks deeper into the house than he has ever been, toward the noise. The short corridor leading from the living room to the kitchen is crammed with old newspapers and magazines and bits of broken furniture and junk food boxes. The linoleum, cracked and buckled, is sticky with something that grips at Vernon's shoes, making kissing sounds as he walks.

He stops in the kitchen doorway and sees Doc, wearing a pair of old swimming goggles, at work at the kitchen table, cutting into something with a small power saw. The room is a mess. The sink is filled with dirty dishes that spread across onto the tabletop smeared with something dark and greasy and hundreds of flies buzz around, eating. A big box freezer rattles and moans and more flies hang over it in a thick cloud.

Doc looks up at him and nods, then carries on with his work, the saw screaming, its blade black with blood. Vernon steps closer to the table and sees that Doc is busy sawing the toes off a human leg, amputated just beneath the knee. The leg belonged to a whitey. A woman. The toes are painted with chipped red nail varnish.

Fucken Doc. Selling body parts from the police morgue to the darkies for muti. Witchcraft. Juju.

Vernon is ready to reverse his ass out the room and find the piss-house when he is struck by an idea. He waves his hand and Doc shuts down the saw, the blade rattling as it slows.

The old boozer looks at Vernon through goggles peppered with bone chips and flesh. 'Ja, Detective?' he says, using the opportunity to suck on the bottle of brandy that rests beside the amputated leg.

'Doc, what can I use to keep a kid quiet?'

'Permanent?'

'No, man. Just for a couple of hours.'

'How old's this kid?

'Four or five.'

Doc nods, then he rummages in a kitchen drawer and comes out with a small bottle with a rubber stopper.

'Put ten or so of these drops in Coke or milk or whatever. Should sort it out.'

Vernon takes the dusty bottle, the label long gone, and stashes it in his pocket. Not sure yet if he'll need it. But it soothes him to know he has this, as insurance. Doc fires up the saw and starts his work again, detaching the big toe and placing it in a small ziplock baggie. Gets busy on the next toe.

Vernon leaves the kitchen and goes looking for the toilet. The passage runs dead at a bathroom so stinking that he almost hurls. There's no light, but enough of a glow comes in from the passageway for him to see that the pot overflows with shit. The little room is heaven for the flies, singing like a church choir.

Vernon doesn't go near that filthy pot, just unzips and drills his stream of piss onto the floor, and who is ever going to know? He finishes and leaves the house and goes out to his car.

He can't face going home now, with his mother hovering around like a lost shadow, so he sets course for Voortrekker Road and Lips, knowing this is the time he'll find Costa alone in the empty club, counting his money.

He's going to sit himself down in Costa's office and tell him to give Dawn another chance and if the bastard tries to argue Vernon'll lean back in his chair, nice and relaxed, and say, 'Costa, buddy, remember I know where the fucken bodies are buried.'

And the Greek will look at him and feed a cigarette in beneath his mustache and nod and do exactly what he's told.

chapter 47

XLEY'S EYES FLICKER ONCE AND THEN OPEN. WIDE. THERE IS NO GENTLE transition from sleep to wakefulness, with dreams dispersing like mist. He's pitched straight into a roll-call of the dead: Sunny wet and lifeless on the beach. The bloody Rastafarian. Caroline prone on the kitchen floor as life leaves her. The cop's smashed skull.

Exley sits, fighting for breath, alone in the bed in the spare room. Then he remembers last night, remembers Dawn, and even if that memory isn't enough to temper the hell of the others, it does get him standing, pulling on his shorts over his chafed dick, knowing that at least he won't begin this day alone.

Exley goes into Sunny's room. The bed is empty and he hears no voices. They're out on the beach, he tells himself.

He pads downstairs and across to the deck, slides open the door onto the beach. It's deserted but for a mob of seagulls fighting over the pizza crusts that Brittany dumped on the sand last night, Exley promising that she could watch the birds feed in the morning.

'Dawn?' he shouts. No reply.

He goes into the deserted kitchen, then runs upstairs again and sees their bags are gone, feeling a tightness in his chest and the grip of panic at his throat.

What did he do? Or what didn't he do? He has no idea.

Trying to reach Dawn through Vernon Saul is not an option, and he has no phone number for her. He doesn't know her last name, or even if Dawn is just her stripper's handle.

What he does know, as he walks unsteadily back down the stairs, is that the little oasis of comfort that Dawn and her daughter brought is gone. It was just an illusion. Like his belief that yesterday's crying jag in the shower had straightened out his head.

Standing near the kitchen, all alone and sober, the events of the last days hit him and take him down. Exley starts to shake and even though he staggers out onto the deck into the blazing sun, the tremors continue. He sinks into a squat with his back to the wall, clenching his jaw to stop his teeth rattling, and feels madness coming in to claim him.

He has no skin. No muscle and sinew and bone. Nothing to contain him, to stop what he is leaking away, disintegrating and dispersing into a future of infinite pain.

Exley has come, he understands, to the place where the debts are paid.

chapter 48

L IKE FUCKEN CLOCKWORK, IS HOW IT WENT. JUST LIKE VERNON KNEW IT WOULD.
He stands on the sidewalk outside Lips, in the familiar sun-
bleached ugliness, lighting a smoke, hearing the rat's-claw scratches as
Costa locks up after him from the inside. The Greek has agreed to take
Dawn back. From tonight.

Vernon didn't even have to bring out the threats. The fat white bitch
Costa got in as Dawn's replacement went and OD'd, so the Greek's
desperate.

Vernon, inhaling nicotine, finds himself standing across from
Dawn's apartment block, staring up at her place. On the sidewalk beside
him a homeless darkie woman with white blotches on her face curses
out a one-legged brown guy on a crutch, his remaining foot bare and
cracked as elephant hide.

'Go to her, go to your whore!' she shouts.

The cripple says in Afrikaans, 'But it's you that I love. To her I'm
just a sex toy.'

Vernon laughs at the ways of the world, wondering how the next
part of his plan is going to come together, how he's going to get Dawn
away from Nick Exley. But he's not hassled, knows he's in the flow. That
things will just come together for him now he's at his creative best.

And he'll be fucked if he doesn't see a flare of sunlight as Dawn's
balcony door swings opens, like a welcome mat telling him to come on
up.

The cramped apartment has never seemed so ugly. Or so hot. Dawn
forces open the kitchen window in the hope of a breeze but all she gets
is the stink of the plumbing so she slams it again. Nothing for it but to

unlock the balcony doors, letting in the stale KFC and taxi fumes.

Brittany sits on the bed, eating a bowl of ice cream, talking to Mr Brown, and it is Uncle Nick this and Uncle Nick that. Long and elaborate tales of how she swam with Uncle Nick, and how he bought her pizza and how he's got a whole pile of Disney movies.

'Hey, Britt,' Dawn says, switching on the TV, giving it a smack to settle the picture that wobbles and floats and then locks on some South African kid's show with crude talking puppets. 'Come watch.'

But Brittany isn't interested. She's been given a taste, now, of another life, of a world beyond her dreams.

Dawn stares at the stupid puppets, their voices scratching at her nerves. She kills the tube and just parks there on the sofa, lights a cigarette wishing it was a joint, trying to tune out her daughter's ramblings, but can't help hearing Brittany telling the bear how her mommy's gonna marry Uncle Nick and they gonna all go live there by the sea, Mr Brown too.

Jesus. Enough.

She's about to lose it with the kid, shout her to silence, when the all-too-familiar Vernon-knock sounds at the door. She puts a finger to her lips and Brittany, God bless her, shuts up. The two of them sit like statues, staring at each other. The knock comes again.

Vernon shouts, 'Hey, Dawnie, I know you in there. Open up. I'm not pissed off, I promise. I got good news for you.'

It's pointless to try and avoid him so Dawn unlocks the door and he comes banging in, looking like he's slept in his rent-a-cop gear.

Dawn doesn't meet his eyes, turns her back on him and goes and stands on the balcony, smoking. She hears him grunt as he sits, and the thump of his boot as he adjusts his gammy leg.

'So, Britt,' Vernon says, 'you have a nice time there by the sea?'

The sick bastard knowing just how to get at Dawn.

Of course, this starts the kid up again, with her tales of the wonderful world of Uncle Nick.

Dawn turns. 'Britt?' The child ignores her, pouring out tales of yesterday. 'Brittany!'

This gets her attention and she looks up at Dawn. 'Ja?'

'Go wash your face, it's full of ice cream.'

'But I wanna tell Uncle Vermin 'bout swimming in the sea.'

'Brittany, I'm not talking again,' Dawn says in her serious voice, and the kid sighs and humps herself off the bed, carrying the bear, moaning and grumbling to him as she goes into the bathroom.

'Close the door,' Dawn says, and the door slams. Then she looks at Vernon, who sits with his hands locked behind his head, a cheesy grin spread across his face.

'So, Dawnie,' he says, 'Llandudno not up to scratch, you back here so soon?'

Dawn tries to keep her expression neutral, to give nothing away, but his pebble eyes miss nothing. He's got that thing abused kids grow up with, of being able to read signals in the air. See things. Make connections others can't. Comes from watching people very carefully, sensing their moods, trying to protect yourself from them.

'Trouble in paradise?' he says, and again she doesn't reply. Doesn't have to. He knows that something is wrong, the smile relaxing, becoming more genuine. 'Well, then my news is gonna be even more welcome.'

'Ja? What?' she asks.

'I just been over by Costa. He says you can come back. Immediate.'

'Serious?'

'Ja, dead serious. What you reckon?'

'It's okay, I suppose.' She shrugs, keeping cool. But, Jesus, she needs this lifeline now.

'There's a condition, though, Dawn. From Costa.'

She knows what it is but still she says, 'What?' He just shrugs. 'The rooms?' Dawn asks.

'Ja. You gonna have to work them. From tonight.' She nods. 'You understand, Dawnie? No excuses?'

'Ja,' she says, 'I understand,' and feels a circle closing around her with a solid little click and she's back where she was and where she always will be, and that, as they say, is fucken that.

chapter 49

WHAT RESCUES EXLEY FROM HIMSELF IS A MATCHBOOK. HOW LONG HE SAT there shivering in the sun he doesn't know, but later, when he takes off his T-shirt, his face, neck and arms are thermometer-red.

His spell of catatonia ends when the wind, a hot little zephyr that hang-glides down from the mountain, ruffling the waves and stirring the beach sand, sends something scuttling into Exley's naked foot. That contact, that merest of brushes, is enough to break the spell, to switch his attention from the blank screen within himself to a close-up of his right big toe with its yellowish nail, grains of sea sand sprinkled like talcum powder on the cuticle.

He pans left from the toe and registers the object that has re-engaged his nervous system: the matchbook that the wind sent skidding like a hockey puck across the wood of the deck, the cover flapping in the breeze, the crudely rendered silhouette of a nude woman dancing and beckoning. Exley reaches down and lifts it.

The word *Lips* is printed in a flowery font, the letters a blur of red ink from a poorly registered offset print job. Below it is a line of copy that he has to squint to read: *For Gentlemen of Distinction*. There is an address out on Voortrekker Road, a place he has never been.

Exley understands that this is a portent. An omen. He has been sent Dawn's matchbook, from the bar where she used to dance. They'll know her there. Know where he can find her.

Exley stands, animated by a sense of purpose: he has the power to transform the lives of Dawn and her daughter. Lately he has been all about death and destruction, but now he can do some good. He knows this is some crazy shot at redemption, a way of cooking the karmic books, which is laughable of course.

But so be it.

The day is almost gone, the sun sagging toward the choppy sea, the shadows lying black and heavy across the beach. Soon it will be dark and this bar, Lips, will be open for business.

Exley showers, his sunburned skin stinging under the hot water. He dries himself and rubs aloe vera cream onto his arms and face to soothe the throbbing, and dresses in dark jeans and a black T-shirt, imagining this will make him look anonymous.

Reversing the Audi from the garage, he punches the address on the matchbook into the GPS and lets the schoolmarmish English voice – he dubbed her 'Caroline' the first time he heard her – guide him out to Voortrekker, a long, flat road that drains the city of its broken dreams and traps them in an endless smear of short-time hotels, escort agencies and pussy bars.

chapter 50

DAWN STANDS IN THE MIDDLE OF VOORTREKKER, STRADDLING THE WHITE LINE like a tightrope walker, the wind from the passing traffic buffeting her.

She's seen plenty of pedestrians killed, right here on this strip. Dragged under the wheels of buses, their insides bursting out onto the tar. Or smacked by the cowboy taxis and thrown, heads exploding like watermelons when they hit the curb.

So when she runs toward Lips, a car and a minibus growling down on her, she must be begging for this to happen to her, too.

Horns blare and she hears the tearing sound of brakes and smells rubber, a furious voice – *you mad cunt!* – chasing her into the club, but she makes it.

No easy way out. Not tonight.

She ignores the woman with the mustache, who welcomes her back with a look and a sniff. Cliffie is too cool to say a word, just checks her out from behind the bar, wiping at a glass with a cloth. The club is still empty but the house lights are dimmed, just a single red follow-spot stroking the ramp, and Dawn lets the shadows pull her through the curtain and backstage.

The walk down to the dressing room takes forever, past the peeling beige paint like bad skin on the walls, under the bare yellow light bulb, along the wine-colored carpet tiles (some of them missing, crop-circles of old glue on the bare concrete beneath), the passageway a funnel pouring her down toward the pink door at the end, a door that stands open, leaking blue-green fluorescent light and *tik* smoke that curls out like when the darkie ice-cream man came round when she was a kid, ringing his bell, lifting the lid off the box on the front of his bike and the dry ice drifted into those nightmare summer days, her uncle sending her for a lolly that stained her mouth, standing in shadow inside the house watching her, waiting to get something in return from those cold purple lips.

Dawn pushes open the door and the fat Ugly Sister turns to her and blows out a stream of *tik* fumes, her eyes like rips in her bloated face, her meth-branded mouth gaping on rotten teeth. The skinny one slumps at the mirror, staring at Dawn in the dirty glass, and says, 'Her Highness come back to us.'

The fat whore cackles and passes the *tik* pipe to her partner in this relay race to oblivion and the skinny bitch's head disappears in a cloud of toxic smoke that smells to Dawn, right then, like heaven.

'Lady Di, Lady Di, *Laaaaay-deeee Diiiiiii,*' the fat one says, standing, doing a little curtsey that gets her breasts swaying, one of her dark teats brushing Dawn's arm. 'What's this we hear that there gonna be visitors to the royal box tonight?' She grabs Dawn's goods, through her sweatpants.

Any other time Dawn would punch her into yesterday but now she just laughs like you do when you don't wanna cry and slumps down on a stool. The Ugly Sisters are carping and crowing and all Dawn can think when she looks at them is, this is me, couple of years, this is me.

Then she stops thinking and reaches out and takes the little glass pipe from the skinny one, that familiar heat on the palm of her hand as she closes her fingers around it, brings the pipe to her mouth and feeds the glass between her lips already nice and puckered up, and sucks, her eyes closing, her lungs swelling as the smoke fills them and fills her brain – her skull feels like it's going to crack open – no room for the image of Brittany looking at her, crying, and she's seized by a coughing spasm and smoke and snot explode from her.

Dawn bends double, fighting for breath, forehead touching the make-up counter. She sits up, eyes and nose streaming, a bungee of drool dangling from her lip. She flails at her face with the back of her hand. 'Jesus.'

But she has another hit and it goes down smoother, and by the time she passes the pipe back the angels are singing nice and sweet and there's a glow to the light bulbs and whatever trouble there is in this big wide world, baby, none of it is hers.

Exley, drawn along by the hissing traffic, sees the pink neon lips smooching the night. He slows the car, searching for a parking spot in this street lined with old rust-buckets and pick-up trucks and minibus taxis, the Audi a visitor from another tax bracket.

He's startled by a banging on the side window and turns to see a feral brown whore, anywhere between fifteen and death, lifting her dress above her navel, showing him a liverish cesarean scar, shoving her thicket of pubic hair up against the glass. He accelerates away, car horns braying, until he finds a spot farther up, guided in by a black man in a day-glo green bib.

Exley locks the Audi and waves at the car guard, who says something in a foreign language. Exley stands on the sidewalk a moment, composing himself, before he allows an old Police song to draw him into the club. A creature of indeterminate gender squats behind a table and demands fifty rand from him. He pays up and gets a pair of red lips rubberstamped on the underside of his right wrist.

He pushes through a throng of men, all white, all big, catching a glimpse of naked flesh up on a ramp, flashes of dismembered limbs through gaps in the crowd. A hand grabs him and spins him and he's looking up into the face of Vernon Saul.

'The fuck you doing here, Nick?' Vernon says, dressed in a crisp striped shirt and an ironed pair of jeans.

'I want to see Dawn.' Shouting over the music.

'She don't wanna see you.'

'I want her to tell me that. Where can I find her?'

Vernon laughs and shrugs. 'Okay, Nick, you wanna see Dawn, then come see her.'

Vernon pushes into the mass of bodies like an icebreaker, clearing a path through the shouting, sweating men, Exley carried in his wake.

They arrive at the edge of the ramp and Vernon shoves aside an old man in shorts and knee-socks, his glasses in danger of being smeared by the naked vulva that gapes at him. When the dancer lifts herself up from a back-bend, Exley, his knees pressed into the walls of the ramp by the men behind him, sees that she's Dawn, her eyes closed, her mouth sagging, her movements as slow as if she's submerged in oil, lagging behind the beat. Not that these men care, their eyes feeding on her, mouths grunting and cursing and promising and begging.

Dawn is oblivious, her wet hair falling like seaweed onto her breasts, one hand rubbing her erect nipples – Exley remembers their texture on his tongue – the other opening herself. There is a surge of lust and Exley is pushed even farther forward, his breath squeezed from him, close enough to Dawn for bullets of sweat to land on his face when she shakes her hair.

'Dawn!' he shouts, but she doesn't hear him. So he stretches out and grabs her hand. He feels a paralyzing pain in his arm. Vernon has him by the elbow, his fingers digging into the nerves, and Exley's arm falls, useless.

'We don't touch the girls while they onstage, Nick,' Vernon shouts, his spittle wet on Exley's ear. 'That's what the rooms is for.'

The music fades and Exley watches as Dawn stumbles through a curtain, the T-shirt and jeans she wore to his house left discarded on the ramp.

Dawn, naked flesh shining with toxic sweat, goes into the dressing room and the Ugly Sisters welcome her like she's one of them, holding out another *tik* pipe, and Dawn takes her fill as Costa comes in through the haze saying, 'The rooms, Dawn. Now.'

Sylvia the cleaner brings the clothes she left onstage and Dawn stands, steadying herself with a hand to the wall, wondering how the hell she's going to get into those denims. But the Ugly Sisters, like her ladies in waiting, are there to help, and the two of them fight her into the shirt and jeans – why worry with the panties? – and she floats down the corridor and out into the club, scanning the hazy pack of men, all of them wanting to do her.

She doesn't care. Let them all line up and fuck her, like that porn star she read about, who did it with a thousand and something men in Las Vegas.

Dawn grabs a big Boer at random – looks like he's straight off a tractor – hot waves of booze coming from his body; if you put a match to him he'd burn like a Christmas pudding. Somebody touches her arm and in the smear of *tik* she's looking into the face of a man who could be Nick Exley's double. Jesus, she realizes, beyond surprise out here in methland, it *is* him.

So she takes his hand and walks him away from the bar, through the curtain toward one of the rooms, smiling over her shoulder, saying, 'This is going to cost you, Mister Nick.'

Exley lets Dawn lead him into a narrow cubicle, barely big enough to contain the skinny foam mattress that lies on the floor, covered by a gray sheet. A foil pack of condoms and a roll of toilet paper lie beside the mattress.

A fluorescent strip gives the hutch the feel of an autopsy room, the chipboard walls unpainted and unadorned. The place stinks of sweat and come and piss and desperation.

Dawn closes the door and leans her back against it, smiling at him, and he can see how blown she is, her pupils like pinpricks.

'Nicky, Nicky, Nick,' she says, leering at him, unbuttoning her shirt, the muscles of her face as slack as if she's hitting g-force.

He steps up to her, frees her hands from the buttons. 'Dawn, no. Stop.'

'Sa'madder, Nick? You couldn't get enough of it last night.' Her fingers fumbling for his zipper, grabbing at his penis.

He puts his arms around her and holds her to him. 'Dawn, listen to me. I want you to leave here with me, now. You understand?'

She looks at him, trying to focus. 'And then?'

'We'll get Brittany and go to my house and straighten you out.'

'And then?'

'Then we'll see, Dawn. Okay?'

She shakes her head, pushes at him until he releases her. 'Uh-uh. You'll dump us, won't you, when you had your fun? Like they all do.'

'I promise you, Dawn. I won't. Leave with me. Please.'

She stares at him and then she starts to cry and she pounds on his chest with her fists and says, 'Why did you have to make me come, you bastard? Why did you have to do that to me?'

She cries harder and her fists loosen and he holds her as she shudders, slumping against him, and he feels her tears falling like a warm rain on the skin of his neck. He takes her face and tilts it up to him, wiping away snot and tears with his fingers, and he kisses her on the mouth.

'I won't leave you, Dawn, I promise.'

Exley takes her hand and walks her out of the room and back into the club. At the curtain through to the bar Vernon stands beside a swarthy man with a creased face and a bandito mustache, something of the old, sad Charles Bronson about him.

The man says to Exley, 'Money. You give the money.'

Exley pulls out a roll of bills – he has no idea how many – and throws them at Chuck Bronson and pushes a way through the men. Vernon blocks them, but the older guy says, 'Leave her go, Vernon, leave her go. But she not coming back, never, to cry to me. Never.'

Vernon's hand falls from Exley's shoulder and the crowd parts and lets them through and they're out of the sweat and the noise, into the street.

'Where's Brittany?' he asks.

Dawn doesn't answer, just points across the road. Exley half-carries her through the hot stream of traffic into the foul lobby of a squat apartment building. They stagger like alkies up a flight of chipped stairs, and spring the child from behind a door barred by countless locks, from the clutches of a bloodless crone dressed in black widow's weeds.

Brittany climbs up Exley and wraps him with her arms and legs. 'I tole Mr Brown you coming. I tole him.'

Exley, carrying the child and somehow keeping Dawn on her feet, leads them to the Audi and drives them back toward Cape Town and its floodlit mountain. In the yellow slashes of street light Exley sees that Dawn is asleep beside him, the child dozing in the rear, strapped into Sunny's car seat, and he can't understand, for a moment, how these people have come into his life, and what he is meant to do with them now that they have.

But he drives on thinking that maybe, just maybe, something can be saved.

chapter 51

VERNON SITS IN THE DARK, AN INVISIBLE PRESENCE OUT ON THE ROCKS, watching the house. Sitting in the same place it began, only eight days ago, his destroyed leg laid out straight, his left hand massaging blood into the wasted muscle above the knee. His good leg is bent, propping up his right arm that moves like a metronome bringing a Lucky back and forth to his mouth, the cigarette cupped in the palm of his hand like he's in a prison yard. His Glock lies on the rock beside him, oily in the dim light of the skinny moon.

The house is in darkness and he imagines the three of them inside, Exley, Dawn and the child. Exley and Dawn in the marriage bed, fucking away the ghost of the mad wife, and the brat in the dead girl's room, wearing her PJs, sleeping with her toys. Becoming her, just like Dawn planned.

Vernon grinds the butt of his smoke to nothing on the rock and slips Doc's little bottle from his pocket. It takes all his strength to unscrew the teat-shaped rubber cap, the grooves gummed fast from years of disuse, and free the glass dropper. He takes a whiff at the open neck and grunts and pulls his head away. His eyes water and his nostrils burn from something sharp and chemical, like gasoline mixed with nail-varnish remover.

He replaces the cap and stows the bottle in his jeans. Relaxing himself. Playing the waiting game. He knows there'll be no sleep tonight, not with the fury raging hot in his blood. No sleep until this thing is over and he's done what he's got to do.

Dawn wakes, lost. Takes her a few seconds to understand she's in the spare room at Nick's house. A hundred Zulus are doing a war dance in her head and her mouth tastes bitter, her tongue thick with slime. Her lips are gummed and burnt and she remembers smoking the *tik*, the glass hot as a tailpipe. Remembers breaking every promise she made to herself.

Fuck.

She sits up and the room tilts and falls away from her and she puts her hands to her face, closing her eyes until things stop moving. When she opens them the sun blasts through the white curtains like a hammer to her eyeballs.

Dawn's wearing a T-shirt with something written on the front over her tits. She twists the fabric and reads *Burning Man 2001*. Big enough to be Nick's. If she knew it was the dead wife's she have to tear it off, way her nerves feel this morning, sticking up through her skin like little feelers.

She lifts the hem of the T-shirt and sees she's bare naked underneath. Flashes back to the Ugly Sisters rolling her jeans onto her, pulling them up tight into her gash, no panties in the way. Remembers the ugly little room at Lips, when she was all over Nick like a *tik* monster from the gutter.

How is she going to face him?

But the thought of Brittany gets her standing and wobbling out the door and into the bathroom. She pees, humming something, eyes closed, trying to chill herself. Hold it together for the kid, Dawn. Hold it together, bitch.

She washes her face with the soap in the basin and squeezes some toothpaste onto her finger and cleans her teeth. Not up to using one of the pair of toothbrushes that dangle from little hooks under the mirror.

Dawn finds a huge towel, fluffy and white as a polar bear, hanging behind the bathroom door and wraps it around her waist, under the T-shirt. Checks herself out in the mirror. Pure street whore. But what can she do? What's done is done.

She peeps into the child's room and sees that the bed is empty. Hears voices from below and walks down the stairs, taking it nice and slow, making no noise on the carpet.

The sound of Britt's laughter leads Dawn toward the kitchen and she stands in the doorway, watching Nick and her daughter, their backs to her, making breakfast. Brittany is up on a chair by the table, stirring egg yolks in a glass bowl and Nick dips in a finger and then paints the tip of the kid's nose with the yolk. Brittany laughs, furiously wiping her nose on a kitchen towel.

Nick walks over to the stove where something splutters in a pan. As he flips burgers he sees Dawn. 'Hey,' he says. 'You sleep okay?' Smiling at her like fuck-all went down last night.

Dawn nods. Doesn't trust her voice yet.

Brittany jumps from the chair and comes over and hugs Dawn tight around the knees even though she doesn't deserve it. Dawn strokes her daughter's hair, hating herself. Then Britt's off again, back up on the chair, clanging a spoon against the bowl.

'Is this okay, Uncle Nick?'

'Perfect,' Exley says, and he pours the yolks into a pan. 'Burgers and scrambled eggs okay?' he asks Dawn.

'Thought you're a vegetarian?' Finding her voice.

'Soya patties,' he says with a shrug.

Dawn has to laugh at this rich guy cooking the meat substitute her family ate when she was a kid because they were too poor to afford the real thing.

Nick plates up and the three of them take their places at the table, Brittany at the head, Dawn and Nick facing one another. Britt takes each of their hands and closes her eyes. There's an awkward moment, then Nick reaches over with his free hand and takes Dawn's and looks at her and she can't meet his eyes, so she closes hers and listens to her daughter saying a little prayer in a voice so sweet and pure it's enough to break her heart.

Tears come. Tears of shame and self-loathing and she has to leave the table, hurrying out into the living room.

She hears Nick say, 'Eat up, Britt, your mommy isn't feeling good.' He comes after Dawn and finds her standing by the door open out onto the deck, watching Cape Town putting on one of its shows: all shiny sea and creamy sunlight and a sky so blue it looks like a movie effect.

He lays his hand on her back. 'Hey,' he says.

'Jesus, Nick, I fucked up big time.'

He turns her to him and holds her. At first she resists then she softens against him. 'Dawn, it's done. Let it go.'

She wipes her eyes, fetching a smile from somewhere. 'So what is this, Nick, some *Pretty Woman* fantasy you got going here? Like you're Richard Gere and I'm Julia Roberts and you're gonna save me?'

'Believe me, Dawn, if anybody is being saved, it's me.'

'Ja?'

'Yes.' He's staring at her, and then through her, going somewhere deep inside himself. 'Dawn, I've done some things in the last week—'

She doesn't want to hear this. Not now. So she puts a finger to his lips. 'Ssshhh. Leave it go, Nick. This is too nice to spoil.'

She takes his hand and they walk back into the kitchen and they eat their breakfast, Brittany bubbling away and Nick joking with her as if his dark moment never happened and Dawn wonders if anything could ever be this bloody good again.

After breakfast Exley and Dawn sit on the deck, Brittany and Mr Brown down on the beach. Dawn wears a pair of Exley's shorts, belted at the waist, her bare feet on the chair, wrapping her legs with her arms, chin on her knees. She looks calmer; the ashen layer under her copper skin has faded.

'So what happens now?' Dawn says, turning her head to look at him.

'Do you have a passport?' he asks.

'Ja, I do, actually. That guy from Lips, Costa, took some of us to dance at club up in Mozambique a few months back. A total fucken disaster. But why you asking?'

Exley tries to keep the tension from his voice. Knows he's gambling now. 'I went online, found out I can book the three of us on a flight to Bali, leaving tomorrow afternoon.'

'Bali?'

'Yeah.'

'Why Bali?'

'Because we don't need visas and it's the other side of the fucking earth.'

'You serious, Nick?'

'Yes. I want to get away from this,' sweeping his hand from the beach to the house. 'From everything that's happened. And I want you and Brittany to come with me.'

'And after Bali?' Dawn asks, unfolding her legs, sitting upright.

He shrugs. 'We'll see. There are plenty of options.'

She shakes her head. 'So this isn't just, like, some holiday thing?'

'No.'

'Talk to me, Nick. Tell me what you're thinking.'

Exley stares out over the ocean. 'I guess I'd like to make a life with you and Brittany. In the States, maybe, or Australia.' He finds the courage to look at her. 'What do you say?'

She's staring at him. 'We can't replace them, Nick. Your wife and kid.'

'Jesus, don't you think I know that?' His voice is harsher than he intended and she jerks like she's been slapped. 'Sorry,' he says. Too late.

'No, I'm sorry,' she says, standing and walking over to the railing, turning her back on him, and he knows he's lost her.

But after a while she faces Exley and says, 'Fuck, Nick, this is big stuff. Too big.'

'Okay, I understand,' he says, standing, talking fast, selling this. 'But what about taking it a step at a time? Bali for two weeks? We chill out, have some fun. Then we talk about the future?'

She walks into the living room. 'What about your stuff?'

Exley follows her. 'All of this came with the house,' he says gesturing at the furniture. 'I have a buyer for my computer gear. Sunny and Caroline's things I want to pack up and give to charity, or whatever.'

'And your wife? Her funeral?'

He shakes his head. 'Her body is going to be flown to England. To her sister. She'll be buried in some graveyard alongside her parents. It was her wish.' A flash of guilt makes him turn away for a moment, until he's ready to continue. 'There's nothing for me here, Dawn.'

She's nodding. 'Britt don't have a passport.'

He hesitates. 'She can use Sunny's. Nobody will ever know.'

Her eyes skid away and he can't read her expression.

'It's just paper, Dawn.'

She nods. 'I know.' Watching him. 'You got it all figured out, haven't you?'

'No,' he says. 'No way.'

'Okay, Mister Nick,' she says. 'Let's do the Bali thing. Reckon I'll look cute in a sarong.' Smiling at him. 'Then we see, okay?'

And that's good enough for Exley. For now.

Dawn's head is spinning from more than the meth hangover. Feels like she's on one of those Japanese bullet trains she's seen on the TV, and it's speeding off, taking her farther and farther away from her life.

Trying to ground herself, gather her thoughts, she steps back out onto the deck, staring into space, but something catches her eye, something in the water where the low waves lick at the beach. At first she thinks its just a piece of driftwood, then she sees it's the little bear, Mr Brown, and it's kinda creepy because he lies on his back with his legs and arms spread, floating in the surf, the water washing him onto the beach, then pulling him back, just like he's a dead body. Dawn flashes on Nick's little blonde girl lying dead in that selfsame water. The image freaks her out and she looks around for Brittany.

No sign of her.

'Britt?' she calls, walking down onto the sand. Does a three-sixty – a pirouette – the rocks and the sea and the sky blurring. 'Brittany!'

Exley, coming down a little from the tension of laying out his proposition to Dawn, feeling looser now that she's agreed to some of it, wanders into the kitchen and gets himself a bottle of Evian from the fridge. Walks into a Caroline flashback, catching her last violent shudders on the tiled floor. Wills her away.

Jesus, it'll be good to leave this house.

As he drinks from the bottle he crosses to the window and sees Dawn on the beach, agitated, calling her daughter's name. Then she's shouting for him, her voice thick with fear. Exley drops the water and bolts out of the kitchen and across the deck.

Dawn stands near the surf, one hand raking her hair. 'I can't find her, Nick. And she didn't go into the house.'

Exley sees the bear in the water and he sees Sunny floating, those last bubbles of breath leaving her and rising to the surface where they vanish.

He sprints across the sand and up onto the rocks to get a vantage point, to see if Brittany is in the ocean, being pulled away from land by the current, his breath louder then the surf, and just for a moment – in a near-subliminal flash-cut – he glimpses Vernon Saul squatting on those rocks and fears for Dawn's girl.

Exley blinks and there's nothing there but the play of sunlight and shadow, and he scans the empty water and the beach until his eyes find a pale flare inside the wooden rowboat.

The child peeps up at him, the sun torching her hair, laughing as he hurtles from the rocks, swoops down on her and lifts her from boat, the girl saying, 'I were hiding, Uncle Nick, I were hiding away.'

He has to fend off Dawn's flailing hands as she sprints across the sand, wanting to hug the child and hit her, shouting, 'Don't you ever do that again!'

Brittany starts to sob and Exley hands the wailing girl to her mother, who grabs her and envelops her and rushes her up the steps into the house.

Exley rescues the drenched bear from the waves, its body dripping water, and carries it across the beach and into the living room, where Dawn hugs Brittany, soothing her, saying, 'Oh, my baby, my baby, you made me so scared.'

FOLLOWING THEM IS PISS EASY. THE AUDI'S GOT MUSCLE UNDER THE HOOD but Exley drives slow, with the top down, Mr Richie Rich giving his new girls a treat. Vernon, his Civic tucked in three cars back, sees Dawn's hair blowing in the wind as the Audi takes a wide curve on the ocean side of the coast road, sees her laughing when she turns to the kid strapped in the back.

When they get to Camps Bay, making like the French Riviera with its beach and sidewalk cafés and blonde cunts in tea-bag bikinis, Vernon has to sharpen up. Here the Audi is just another car in the stream of Ferraris and Porsches and SUVs with jukebox grilles.

But when the Audi snakes up toward Table Mountain and then down to the city and the foreshore, a cloud of pollution hanging like mustard gas over the office towers, Vernon knows where they are headed, and once they're on the freeway he puts foot and leaves them behind, takes the Monte Vista off ramp, shoots down to Voortrekker and finds himself a parking spot across from Dawn's place.

Vernon lights a smoke and waits, Tony Orlando warbling 'Tie A Yellow Ribbon' over and over in his brain, till he punches in a Temptations CD – 'Papa Was A Rollin' Stone' – to shut the fucker up.

When Dawn unlocks the scuffed and pitted door and leads Exley into the tiny apartment it's difficult for him to hide his distaste. The place is squalid. Not dirty but about as ugly a room as he has ever been in.

Dawn takes Brittany's hand, saying, 'Nick, hang in here, I'm just gonna drop Madam over with Mrs de Pontes.'

'Are you sure you want to leave Britt there?'

'Ja, I'm just gonna stress about her and the sea. Better this way.'

He nods and their voices echo away down the corridor, Brittany complaining, Dawn telling her it's just for tonight, she has to help Uncle Nick pack up some stuff, and there'll be a treat tomorrow. A big one, she promises.

Exley crosses the stained and mangy carpet – it may have been beige, long ago – and stands looking out through the padlocked balcony doors. The doors are barred and rusted razor wire spirals around the railing of the small balcony, even though the apartment's on the second floor. The traffic on Voortrekker rumbles and throbs, the bleats of the minibus taxis and their yelling drivers rising up to him.

He turns and scans the place, feeling somehow disloyal as he does it. A molting sofa. A small TV set, one side of the plastic casing held together by duct tape. A double bed, neatly made, covered by an off-white comforter that's frayed at the edges. A troop of soft toys arranged across the pillows.

Unframed postcard-sized photographs of Brittany – as an infant, a toddler, dressed as an angel in a nativity play – are stuck to the brown walls, edges curling away from the damp plaster. A closet is squeezed in beside the bed, one door dangling from a broken hinge. Next to the bathroom is a kitchen sink under a frosted-glass window, a microwave oven and a hotplate on the counter.

The lack of beauty, the lack of grace, scares Exley. No matter how poor he and his mother were (or he and Caroline in the early days) the places they lived in were always cluttered with books, fresh flowers and framed prints rescued from junk shops, old furniture hidden beneath bright cloths and cushions.

This place is imagination's graveyard.

Jesus, what the fuck are you doing? he asks himself. What are you thinking? And there's a moment there when he's ready to get the hell out and not look back.

Too late.

Dawn walks in and closes the door and locks it, turns to him and scans his face. 'What were you expecting, Nick? A penthouse?'

'No, no. It's fine.'

She smiles at him. 'Don't bullshit me. It's a fucken hole and I know it.' She crooks a finger at him. 'Come here.' Walking across to the kitchen window, forcing it open.

Nick follows her and his nostrils twitch at the gassy plumbing stench that wafts in. The narrow window offers a slice of a railroad line, a bridge, a strip of low-rent stores and then an endless expanse of small cramped houses and faceless ghetto apartment blocks.

'You know what that is?' she asks.

'The Cape Flats?'

'Ja. Ever been there?'

'No.'

'Okay, that's where I grew up. For most people living out there, a place like this is their idea of heaven. When I was a kid I lived in a house smaller than this room but there were sometimes ten of us in it. I never wanted that for Britt, so I shat off and did whatever I had to do, to get us here and keep us here.'

'I understand, Dawn,' he says.

'No, Nick, you don't bloody understand. By the time I was Brittany's age my uncle and his three sons, and sometimes their buddies, had been raping me for years.' She sees his face but continues, relentless. 'It went on until I was ten and the social services finally got it together to take me away from my fuck-up mother and put me in an orphanage. I ran away when I was sixteen and started hooking.'

'I'm sorry.' His words hollow to his ears.

'Don't be. It's a long time ago. Believe me, it goes on out there every day, kids raped and murdered like some epidemic.' She lights a cigarette, inhales and looks him dead in the eye. 'So me, I'm damaged goods, okay?' Exhales. 'But Britt, now, she's my jewel. I won't let that shit happen to her. Ever. And yes, I fucked up last night and I'm grateful to you for saving me. Saving us. Honest to God, I am. But let me tell you one thing straight: I won't never let Britt get hurt. Not only in that way, the way I was, but in any way. You hearing me?'

'Yes.'

'Like I won't let her get used to things and then lose them. I know you're on some crazy grief trip and you see me and her and you think, okay, this could work, and maybe you even mean well, but what if down the road you wake up and go: hang on, I'm Nick Exley, what the fuck am I doing with that colored whore and her bastard kid?' He tries to protest but she wields the cigarette like a weapon, shutting him up. 'Wait. I want you to know what that would do to Brittany. I want you to really think now. I've told you what I am. I've told you what I won't let happen. So, you got second thoughts just walk out that door, no hard feelings.'

'I'm not going anywhere,' he says, ashamed she can read him so well.

'Okay, then.' She exhales smoke, left breathless by this outpouring. 'But, Nick, you ever hurt Britt and I'll kill you. I'm not kidding. I will.'

'I know.'

'Good.' Dawn crosses to the closet, opens the hanging door and starts throwing clothes and underwear onto the bed. She points to a cheap suitcase leaning against the wall. 'Don't just stand there looking cute, get packing.'

Exley lays the suitcase on the bed and unzips it and starts to cram in a jumble of female clothing, some large, some small. Almost as if he has a family again.

Vernon, slumped behind the wheel of the Civic, blows a succession of smoke rings, each one more perfect than the last. He sits up when he sees Dawn and Exley leave the building, the whitey wheeling a suitcase. Exley collapses the handle of the case and stows it in the trunk of the Audi and opens the passenger door for Dawn. Vernon has to catch a cackle at that, Exley treating this street whore like she's a lady. Then Exley's behind the wheel and the Audi's floating its pretty German ass down Voortrekker and gone.

No kid. Beautiful. Upstairs with the old Porra babysitter.

Vernon feels a surge of adrenaline that gets his fingers drumming on the steering wheel. He has to force himself to wait ten minutes, making sure Exley and Dawn don't return. He locks the Civic, ducks across the road and drags himself – leg paining and stiff from the time in the car – up two flights of stairs. He bangs loudly on the old woman's door, knows she's deaf or maybe just pretends to be when it suits her. Bangs again and hears shuffles and scuffs but the door stays closed.

'Eh?' A muffled voice from inside.

'Mrs de Pontes, my name's Vernon Saul. I'm a friend of Dawn's.'

'Eh?'

'Please open, she wants me to bring Brittany to her.'

'I not know you. I not open.'

Vernon's about to give the door a kick when he chills himself and reaches for his wallet and pulls out a fifty-rand note. He moves his withered leg aside and kneels down, grunting, and slides the banknote halfway under the door. It disappears in a flash.

'She tole me to give you one more, when I get the kid,' he says, using the doorknob to haul himself to his feet, panting as if he's just run a city block.

There is a clanking of chains and the turning of locks and the door opens far enough for him to see a little face wrinkled as a tortoise staring up at him. 'Dawn she send?'

'Ja, I tole you. There's been a change of plan with her and Nick. They want me to drop Britt off with them.'

'Why she not phone?'

'Her airtime's finish. Come, please, I'm late.'

The old woman opens the door and Brittany stands beside her, holding a little brown bear. 'You know him?' the old bitch asks, pointing a claw at Vernon.

'Ja, it's Uncle Vermin.'

'I phone Dawn,' the old woman says, digging into her dress pocket and fishing out a huge black Nokia as ancient as she is.

If the kid wasn't there Vernon would put the old bitch's lights out, permanent, but he can't freak out the girly, needs her docile and cooperative.

So he switches on a smile and says, 'You won't get Dawn now. They gone to the movies.'

'Movie?'

'Ja. I'm meeting them when they done. At the Waterfront.'

The old Porra looks suspicious, then Vernon gives her a glimpse of his wallet and greed wins the day.

She lowers the phone. 'Okay, give money.'

Vernon lays another note on her, and the woman gets Brittany's bag and Vernon takes the kid's hand and walks her down the stairs.

'We going to the Waterfront, Uncle Vermin?'

'Ja,' he says.

'To Mommy and Uncle Nick?'

'Ja.'

Once they're on the sidewalk he points to a take-out joint. 'You wanna juice?'

She nods. 'Guava.'

Vernon stands by the hatch and orders the drink. The zit-faced boy behind the counter fills a plastic cup from a glass container of bright pink slush, and gives Vernon the drink with a corrugated straw sticking out the top.

Vernon gets the kid into the back seat of the Civic, tells her to buckle up, and while she battles with the seatbelt he stands by the driver's door, balances the drink on the roof of the car and finds Doc's little bottle in his pocket. He loosens the cap, squeezes ten drops into the juice and stirs it with the straw. He screws the cap back on the bottle and stows it, then slides in behind the wheel, the kid still fighting the seatbelt, her tongue sticking out in concentration.

'Here,' he says, giving her the juice, clicking the seatbelt home for her. Watches as she takes a good, strong hit of the spiked drink.

Vernon starts the car, forcing his way into the traffic, checking the kid out in the rearview. By the time they've driven two blocks her eyes are starting to droop. He stops at a light and frees the plastic cup from her fingers and tosses it out into the gutter. The light turns green and he drives on, watching her in the mirror. She's gone, chin on her chest, head rocking with each bump.

'Doc,' he says, 'you fucken beauty.'

GOD ONLY KNOWS HOW YVONNE SAUL'S GOING TO GET THROUGH THE DAY. The sun is high and fierce, pumping in through the living-room window, sweat running between her breasts and down her thighs as she sits on the sofa. She forces her eyes to focus on the blinking green display of the DVD player, sees that it's past four in the afternoon and she doesn't know how long she's sat herself here, not moving.

Yvonne feels weak. Disconnected. Her body craving insulin. Her supply is finished and she hasn't injected herself in nearly twenty-four hours. She's been phoning Vernon since yesterday, leaving messages on his voicemail, begging him to stop by the chemist. He never called her back and now she's out of airtime and doesn't have a cent to her name.

When she stands to go get herself some water, she feels dizzy and has to put a hand on top of the TV, knocking a teacup to the floor, where it shatters. She shuffles her carpet slippers through the mess and into the kitchen. At the sink she opens the faucet, the water warm as blood when she puts her hand under it. She lets it run, feels it cooling slightly, but never going to get cold.

She wets a dish towel and puts it to her face, covering her forehead and her eyes, sees bright lights like falling stars. Yvonne breathes deep and lets the cloth drop, looking out the kitchen window. Knows she's really seeing things when that sick little jailbird from next door comes walking up, carrying a plastic bag, and pushes open the broken door of the shack and goes inside. No sign of the woman and the child, but he's back. Bailed already.

Yvonne gets herself away from the window, battling for breath, terrified that he'll see her and know it's her that called the cops. She walks slowly back to the living room, supporting herself on the wall, barely making it to the sofa.

She feels her heart beating too fast, and her head feels too light on her shoulders. The armpits of her dress are wet with sweat and she can feel the salt itch between her thighs. She closes her eyes, the banging of the blood in her ears almost drowning the rumble of Vernon's car.

She says a little prayer of thanks, listening to his footsteps on the pathway and his key in the door. Please God, let him have the blue chemist packet in his hand. But when he pushes open the door with his foot he's not carrying no packet, he's carrying a child. A white child with blonde hair, flopping like a dead thing in his arms.

He kicks the door closed and dumps the child next to Yvonne on the sofa, taking a fluffy toy from his pocket and throwing it down beside the girl. Yvonne stands and backs away, feeling the wall against her shoulders.

'Boy,' she says, her voice a whisper torn from deep inside her. 'What you done now?'

He stares at her with his dead father's mad eyes. 'Relax. It's just sleeping.'

'No, Vernon. You can't do this. Not with a white child.'

'Take it easy,' he says, wiping sweat from his face with his palm, his hair hanging down like a noose over his eye. 'She's as colored as us. I just need you to watch her for an hour or so, okay?'

Yvonne shakes her head. 'No, Vernon. Please.'

Her son moves fast, grabs her by the front of her dress and slams her back against the wall, her head hitting the bricks. He slaps her and she slides down to the floor, weeping.

'Get up,' he says, nudging her with his shoe. She doesn't move and he kicks her in the ribs. 'I said get up!'

She obeys, using the back of the sofa to pull herself upright. He leans his face so close to hers she feels his spit on her skin. 'Now you fucken do as I say. You hear me?'

'Ja.' She nods.

'Good. I'm showering and going. I'm back here in two hours.'

He leaves her and she stares down at the child, sees that its little chest is moving as it breathes. She hears him in the shower and thumping around in his room and then he's back, in his uniform, with that big gun holstered at his hip.

'Vernon,' Yvonne says. 'My insulin.'

'Stop bitching at me. I'll bring it when I come back.'

He slams out, leaving her alone with this pale girl child, and Yvonne wishes she'd taken a coat hanger to her womb thirty-three years ago and saved herself all this heartache.

Dawn dumps the belongings of Nick's dead kid into black garbage bags, feeling creeped out and sad. This only child of rich parents was given everything she wanted but she's gone now, the closet crammed with clothes and toys a heartbreaking reminder of who she no longer is. As the bags swallow her things – tiny red rain boots, a one-eyed doll, little-girl panties – the kid fades more and more into nothingness.

Dawn can't get Britt's face out of her mind, feeling again that panic on the beach when her child went missing. Wonders how Nick hasn't gone mad with the loss of his daughter. She looks up and sees him in the doorway, checking out the stripped room.

Dawn stands. 'You okay?'

'Yeah. Thanks for doing this. I don't think I would have been strong enough.'

'It's cool, Nick.' She drags one of the bags toward the door. 'You done? With your wife's stuff?'

He nods. 'It was weird, going through her things.'

'You must be freaked out.'

He shakes his head. 'No, it's not that. They were just things. The person I married left a long time ago.' She's staring at him and he shakes his head. 'I guess I'm not making sense.'

He sits down on the bare mattress and tells her how his wife went cuckoo after the kid was born, about her rages and her depressions. How their marriage was over years ago. His words coming in a tumble, like some cap has been popped and everything just spills out.

'I'm sorry,' she says when he's done.

'The reason I'm talking like this is so you don't think I'm some cold bastard, my wife just dead and I'm already moving on.'

'Thanks.' She means it. It does reassure her and Christ knows she needs reassurance. She takes his hand. 'Come, let's have a break, okay?'

He nods and they go downstairs and she knows it's forward of her but she heads for the fridge and snags the bottle of white wine she's seen chilling in there.

She holds it up. 'You mind if I open this?'

'No. Go for it.'

Dawn finds a corkscrew in the kitchen drawer and carries the bottle and two glasses through to the living room, where Nick has slumped down on the sofa. She pours the wine, hands him a glass and raises hers. 'To Bali.'

He smiles and she sips her drink and it tastes so damn good that she immediately has another slug. She takes her smokes and slides open the door to the deck, wanders across to the railing and fires up.

Nick follows her. 'You can smoke inside.'

'Nah, I'm gonna kick it. I'm gonna smoke my last one before we get on that plane tomorrow.' She looks at the cigarette and then flicks it out onto the sand. 'In fact, that's it. I'm done. I'm an ex-smoker.' He's looking at her, really staring. 'What? Don't you believe me?'

'No. I believe you.'

'What, then? You having second thoughts about Bali and all?'

He shakes his head and smiles away whatever's hassling him. 'No. No second thoughts.' He moves in and starts to kiss her. She tenses, then relaxes and kisses him back, telling herself she can do this. Chill. Go with it. He's one of the good guys.

There's tongue action and they're right up close, his hands everywhere, and she can feel him getting hard and she knows what's gonna happen now, so better that she gets in the driving seat and controls things and she walks him backward into the living room, pushing him onto the sofa, his glasses sliding from his face, landing on the carpet, reflecting two hot little suns.

Dawn pulls his T-shirt off and strips him of his shorts and underwear and gets a handful of his veiny cock. Tries not to see the untold others over the years, shoved in her face and forced inside her, tearing her front and back, stinking things she learned to hate as much as the men they grew out of.

She shoves her curls away from her face and goes down on him, his blondish pubic hair surprisingly silky as it rubs her cheek. She runs her tongue from his balls up the shaft of his dick, the skin so soft, getting his salty, sweet taste in her mouth, feeling him clench his butt muscles as he says, 'Jesus, Jesus, Jesus.'

Keeping him in her mouth, she frees her hands and loses her shirt and jeans, straddling him, gripping his cock in her hand, feeling it pulse, a drop of moisture like a teardrop rolling from the slit. She pushes herself up on her knees and works the head of his penis through her trimmed pussy hair and around her lips that are hot and heavy and sodden.

She breathes, loosens the pelvic muscles that have clenched with old fear, and takes him into her millimeter by millimeter, experiencing this like she never has before, trying to erase the past when all sensation was locked deep behind a barrier of hatred.

Really concentrating now. Feeling the walls of her vagina expanding as he fills her, feeling her swollen clit sliding down the length of him. When he's inside there's a moment's fear, all the bad shit welling up, and she has to force herself to keep moving her hips, riding him and riding on through the darkness.

This is now, Dawn, this is now, she tells herself. She can feel his ass pumping and hear him sucking air and she has a choice, in that moment, to pull back and take herself into the safe place she lived in all those years, to protect herself, but she doesn't and as she lets it happen, the past is gone, falling away and left behind.

It's different to the other night, when this thing ambushed her. This time she wants it. Rushes toward it. That feeling rips through her and blows its way up her spine and she hears herself scream and laugh, and she's sweating, slumped forward, her mouth eating his.

They lie there for she doesn't know how long and then he sits up and pours wine and gives her a glass.

'That was nice,' she says.

'Just nice?'

'Listen, stud, don't you start getting ideas, now. We'll stick with nice.' But she smiles at him and puts her arm around his skinny ribs. He holds her tight and she falls asleep on his chest, feeling his heartbeat.

Brittany wakes up and her head is sore, and her tummy. To open her eyes is hard and when she does she sees a place she doesn't know. She feels Mr Brown fluffy by her hand and she picks him up and holds him to her chest.

'Mommy?' she says. '*Mommy!*'

Nobody says nothing to her, so she looks round and sees a room and a TV and the room is getting dark. She climbs down off the sofa, holding tight on Mr Brown, and then she sees a old auntie lying on the floor, sleeping. So she goes to the auntie and pulls at her dress.

'Auntie. *Auntie!*' she says but the old lady don't wanna wake up.

Brittany feels big tears on her face and she is very, very scared now. She goes to the door but the handle is too far away. She sees another door, open, and walks through and she's in a kitchen and she has to chase away flies that buzz on her. Hates flies. They carry germs, her mommy says.

There's another door, with a key inside it. Brittany sits Mr Brown nicely down on the ground and she takes a kitchen chair and pulls and pulls and pulls, making a squeaky noise until the chair is by the door. She climbs up and gets her hand to the key and it won't turn but then it does and she opens the door till it bumps the chair, so she gets down and moves it so she can go outside with Mr Brown and she's in a small yard with sand and no grass.

The sun is going to sleep now, but Brittany sees an uncle standing by a shack, over a little fence. The uncle has got lots of pictures on him and he calls her, 'Girly, girly, come here.'

So her and Mr Brown go to the fence. 'You want nice sweeties?' the uncle says.

She shakes her head. 'No. I want my mommy.'

The uncle picks her up and flies her over the fence. 'Come. We gonna phone your mommy.'

He carries her toward the shack door and she doesn't want to go in there and tries to get loose and drops Mr Brown in the sand and the uncle takes her through the door and closes it shut tight.

chapter 54

EXLEY IS ROUSED FROM THE DEEPEST SLEEP HE'S HAD IN DAYS BY THE SOUND of Vernon Saul's drumming boots. He opens his eyes and sees Vernon heaving his uniformed bulk up from the beach and across the deck, walking straight toward the open door where he and Dawn lie naked on the sofa.

Exley sits up and gently lifts Dawn's head, her hair spread out across his chest. 'Dawn?'

'Mnnnn?' she says, her eyes closed, voice thick with sleep.

'Wake up. Vernon's here.'

'Don't let him in.'

'Too late, Dawnie, I'm already in,' Vernon says, removing his sunglasses, grinning at them.

'Jesus Christ, how about ringing the fucking bell?' Exley says, standing, stepping into his shorts, aware of Vernon's eyes on his groin. Dawn sits up, reaching for her T-shirt, fighting her way into it, her hair a bramble patch.

'Sorry, buddy. I was just checking out the other side of the rocks, thought I'd drop in and see you're okay.' Uninvited Vernon sits and throws his bad leg out to the side, digging into the flesh of his thigh with his fingers, grimacing. 'Bloody thing's giving me grief today.' He sniffs the air as if he can catch the scent of sex. 'So, what's this, then? The Love Boat?' Winking at Dawn, who stands, her T-shirt reaching halfway to her knees, her arms folded across her chest.

Vernon sees the suitcases and bags parked at the foot of the stairs. 'Hey, you guys going somewhere?'

'No,' Exley says. 'That's Dawn's stuff. She's moving in.'

Vernon wags a finger at him. 'Nick, I was a cop for too long not to recognize pure bullshit when I hear it. You're ducking, aren't you?'

What the hell, Vernon Saul can't do a thing, Exley tells himself with a certainty he doesn't feel. If he reveals any of it, he'll be sending his own ass to prison.

'Yeah,' Exley says, shrugging. 'There's nothing for me here.'

'And you, Dawnie? Just fading away too?'

'Ja, Vernon. Leaving behind all the glamor.' She tries for throwaway, but Exley hears the tension in her voice.

'Hell,' Vernon says, 'after all the good times we had.'

Exley steps between them. 'I'd offer you a drink, but we've got a lot to do.'

'Sure, of course. I understand.' Vernon makes no move to go, settles deeper into the chair, his arms thrown out across its back. He looks from Dawn to Exley. 'But there's a couple of things I need to tell the both of youse. Updates, you know? You first, Nick.'

'What?' Exley asks.

'That night when your kid drowned out there,' jerking his head toward the beach, 'you know I was up on the rocks?'

'Of course. So?' Exley says.

'Well, I was up there a whole long time. Saw your missus in the kitchen with that old guy she was shagging. Saw you and that Aussie getting your heads fucked up on weed. Saw your kid come to you and you send her away.'

'Vernon—' Exley says, dread uncoiling low in his gut.

Vernon holds up a hand. 'Let me finish, Nick. You gonna want to hear this. I saw her go up on those rocks, your kid, after you ignored her. Saw her trying to reach out to that little boat. Knew what was gonna happen. I coulda shouted to youse. Coulda stopped it. But I thought, fuck it. Fuck these rich white cunts. They bringing this shit on themselves, so fuck them. And I just sat there. Watching.'

Exley's face is bled of color as he stands over Vernon, feeling his throat constricting, like he's going to pass out.

Vernon smiles up at him, relaxed, enjoying himself. 'Then I saw her go into the water, your girl. Again, I coulda called. Or come down quick. But I just sat my ass there and waited. Saw her go under once, twice, three times. Saw your whore of a wife come screaming out and you going into the water, bringing the kid out dead. Then I came down and made like the hero. Funny story, huh, Nick?'

'Jesus, Vernon,' Exley says in somebody else's voice. 'Why?'

'Because I could.' Shrugging. 'That's why.'

The same rage he felt when he killed Caroline takes hold of Exley and he lunges at Vernon Saul, grabbing for his throat. The big man swats him aside and Exley hits his head on the tiles, stunned for a moment.

Vernon stands, unclips his pistol from the holster at his hip and points it at Exley. He cocks the gun and Exley looks past the black snout over at Dawn, who stands, frozen, a hand to her mouth, staring at him.

Exley closes his eyes and thinks of Sunny and sees her now: the flesh-and-blood Sunny, not the digital counterfeit. Sees her and waits to die.

Dawn knows Vernon's going to shoot Nick. Can see it in his face that he's tipped over some edge. Then he'll shoot her, and Brittany will be left all alone.

When he works the slide on the Glock – a sound like a man coughing – Dawn looks for a weapon and there's only the half-empty bottle on the table, so she grabs it by the neck and swings it, wine pouring down her arm, hammering it onto Vernon's head.

The bottle shatters and she's left holding the jagged neck. Vernon, bits of glass like highlights in his hair, wine and a trickle of blood zigzagging down his forehead onto his cheek, hardly even looks her way, his eyes and the pistol still on Nick.

Dawn sees the flesh of his neck rising from his body armor, sweat and wine and blood flowing into the creases in his skin. Knows she has just one chance. She jumps at him and slashes the broken bottle across his Adam's apple, feels the glass bite deep and knows she's done good when blood honest-to-God geysers out of him, spraying onto the white wall above Nick, and the Glock falls from Vernon's hand and hits the tiles.

Nick is frozen, eyes still closed, so Dawn gets a foot in like a soccer player, kicking the gun, sending it clattering toward the kitchen, where Vernon, sagging to his knees, can't reach it.

When Vernon hears Tony Orlando warbling 'Tie A Yellow Ribbon' he knows he's fucked. He's on his knees, blood pumping in thick jets from his throat, fumbling for the Glock that's not there no more. Vernon's vision softens and blurs like he's drunk and his mouth is full of something warm and salty.

When he tries to speak his tongue swims and the words won't come. But this is important, what he has to say to Dawn. Wants her to know this thing.

'Dawnie!' he shouts, but all he hears is a wet whisper. 'Dawnie, I took your girly.'

He smiles blood up at her and she's shaking him and screaming and hitting him but it's not her he's seeing, as he hears that song. He's seeing his father, with his tattoos and his tongue and his fists and his fingers and his fat thing.

His father beckoning him, saying, 'Come. Come, you little rabbit. I'm waiting. I'm fucken *waiiiii*-ting!'

And Vernon smells him and tastes him and feels him and then he's there.

Jesus, more blood.

A lot of it. Vernon Saul going to his final reward in lurid, pulsing Technicolor. Exley, now that he understands that he's not dead, convinces his limbs to move and gains his feet and crosses to where Dawn, a blood-soaked banshee from a slasher flick, straddles the dead man, shaking him, slapping his face, yelling, 'Where is she? Where's my baby?'

Exley grabs her from behind, his arms looping her chest, and tries to drag her off Vernon, saying, 'Dawn, he's dead. Dawn!'

She fights him and the tiles are slick with blood and Exley loses his footing and both of them end up sprawled across Vernon's body like mud wrestlers. Dawn slips from Exley's grasp and is back on Vernon, banging his head against the floor, the gash in his throat like a second mouth, gaping and grinning as she pounds away.

'Where is she, you fucken bastard? What you done with her?' She's panting, spit dangling from her lips.

Exley lifts Dawn's cell phone from the table and holds it out to her. 'Dawn, call the babysitter. Maybe Vernon was lying.'

Dawn stares at the phone like it's an alien artifact, then her breathing slows and she blinks and nods and comes back into herself. She takes the phone and stands, speed-dialing with a shaking red finger.

Dawn paces the tiles as she waits for the call to be answered, pushing her hair from her face with a bloody hand. Exley hears one side of the conversation, Dawn's voice rising and sobbing, and he goes to her as she lets the phone slip from her grasp and clatter onto the table.

'When?' he asks.

'About two hours ago. He gave her money. Said I sent him. Jesus, Nick, this is my fault.'

'Dawn, listen to me. We'll find her, okay?' She looks through him into her worst nightmare. 'But first we have to do a few things here. I need you to help me to move him out of sight.'

She nods and they each grab a leg and drag Vernon into the passageway where he'll be invisible from the windows, his body leaving a wash of blood in its wake. Exley pats him down and finds a set of keys in his pocket and puts them on the table near the front door. He kills the lights in the living room, to hide the carnage.

'Okay,' Exley says. 'Now we're going to have to shower before we leave. Strip off your clothes down here and get a fresh set from your suitcase.'

Dawn obeys, on autopilot. When they are both naked Exley gets her to sit on the bottom step of the staircase and lifts each of her bare feet, using his T-shirt to wipe them free of blood.

She starts to shake, hugging herself. 'How we gonna find her, Nick?

What if that sick fuck killed her?' She sobs, a high keening sound.

Exley embraces her. 'Dawn, no, he was using her as a lever. He wouldn't kill her, because then she'd be useless. Believe me.'

She pushes herself away from him and looks into his eyes. 'You promise?'

'I promise,' he says, muting his own doubts. 'Do you know where he lives? Lived?'

'In Paradise Park, with his mother, I think. I dunno exactly where, but I can make some calls.'

'Okay. We'll find her.'

He cleans his own feet and he takes her arm and they go upstairs into the shower, forensic in its brightness, and wash Vernon's gore from their bodies. Exley soaps Dawn's hair, a mass of blood-caked dreadlocks. Then he turns her body under the jets of water, inspecting her. She's clean.

Dawn leaves the shower and dries herself. 'Jesus, Nick, I done a lot of bad shit in my time but I never killed nobody.' She starts to shake again.

Sheer adrenaline-fed hysteria almost makes Exley say, 'Relax. It gets easier after the first one,' but he bites his tongue and holds her until the shakes subside.

They dress and go downstairs. Avoiding the blood, Exley pockets Vernon's keys. When he sees Dawn retrieve the gun from near the kitchen door and tuck it into the waistband of her jeans, he asks no questions. They enter the garage from the house.

Exley raises the garage door, opens the street gate with the remote button and reverses the Audi out. The door death-rattles down and the gate slides closed. Vernon's white Civic skulks under a street light.

'Can you drive, Dawn?' Exley asks.

'Ja, I can drive.'

'I'm going to take Vernon's car. Follow me, okay?'

She nods and scoots behind the wheel of the Audi when he exits. Exley finds the button that releases the central locking of the Civic and seats himself. The car stinks of smoke and cloying aftershave. His feet are too far from the pedals, but he doesn't adjust the seat, just edges farther forward, hunching over the steering wheel.

Exley turns the key and some old Motown number blares out into the night, something about the tears of a clown. Startled, he bumps his head against the plastic skeleton that dangles from the rearview mirror, fumbling around the dashboard until he finds the button that mutes the CD.

He slams the Civic into first gear and as he touches a foot to the accelerator the engine howls and the car spurts forward like a premature ejaculator. Exley turns the car, wary of its unwieldy power, and heads up the hill, trailing exhaust fumes, watching for the cool blue head-lights of the Audi in the rearview.

When he gets to the turn off to the Scout Hall he flags Dawn down and tells her to pull over to the side and douse the headlamps. The road is empty of cars and pedestrians but he has no way of knowing if they are being observed from one of the houses that rise like watchtowers from behind their high walls.

Exley parks the Civic outside the Scout Hall, just about where he pulped Dino Erasmus's head to hamburger, and uses the hem of his T-shirt to wipe away his prints from any surface he remembers touching. He pockets Vernon's keys, leaves the car unlocked and jogs down to where Dawn waits in the idling Audi.

Dawn, allowing Nick Exley to drive her back into her past, rests her face against the car's side window as they cross the bridge from Voortrekker Road to Paradise Park, watching a long train snake beneath them, its windows a yellow stream of light.

Soon as they're off the bridge the hot wind that haunts the Flats hits them, rocking the Audi on its springs. Blowing in her mother's shrill, drunken laugh and the sound of her high heels tap-tapping on the cement floor of the house as she leaves Dawn behind. Blowing in the wheeze of her uncle's breath and the sniggers of her pimply cousins as they come into the bedroom, and even though Dawn hides her head under her pillow there's no escape.

Never.

But it's not her head she sees under the pillow, it's Brittany's, and the terror Dawn feels jolts her upright and she grips Nick's leg, her fingers digging deep enough to bruise. He doesn't flinch, just places his left hand over hers.

'You okay?' he asks.

She nods, but she's not okay. Can't get it out of her head that while she was riding Nick's cock – thinking of nothing but her own pleasure – her child was kidnapped by Vernon Saul.

Dawn, willing Nick to drive faster even though she knows he can't, watches the cramped ugliness fly past, night turned to day by the orange light towers. Garbage litters the streets and blows up against the razor wire and chain-link fences surrounding the box houses. Washing flies from the windows and balconies of the low-rise apartment buildings, concrete bunkers hunkered down on the shifting sand.

She made calls and got an address for Vernon, deep in Paradise Park, Dark City side. The territory of the 28s gang, in this violence-torn hellhole. She understands how visible they are in the Audi – could be targeted by the gangs or pulled over by the cops – but they speed on, Dawn telling Nick where to go, no GPS gonna guide him through this maze.

Silently praying that she'll find her child at Vernon Saul's house. Alive.

She keeps telling herself that Vernon took Britt to get Dawn away from Nick, get her back under his control. Took her child to show her that he could do it, and he'd do it again – or worse – if she didn't obey him.

Must be the truth.

Nick passes a taxi and somebody shouts something that gets stuck in the throat of the wind. They come to an intersection, a bunch of young bastards leaning on a gang-tagged junction box, checking them out, their T-shirts billowing like spinnakers.

Dawn rests her fingers on the Glock lying in her lap. Let them fucken try. But they do nothing except stare and Exley drives on.

'Turn here,' Dawn tells him, and they're in another narrow street, identical houses jammed up tight like uneven teeth. 'Go slow, now,' she says, searching for numbers. 'Okay, stop.'

They're at a house with a concrete wall, some of the panels missing, the uprights leaning like drunkards. Dawn's out of the car, the Glock held close to her body. She's no marksman but she's been around enough pimps and dealers to pick up basic gun skills. Anyway, what's there to know? Point and shoot.

She steps through the broken wall and jogs up to the front door and turns the handle that gleams silver in the street light. Locked. She knocks. No sound from inside the darkened house. She knocks again and Nick is at her side. She hears the sound of Vernon's keys jangling as he tries one then another and unlocks the door. They step into the room, a yellow streak of street light following them in.

Dawn sees something – someone – lying on the floor and her heart pounds.

'Britt?' she says. 'Brittany!' She kneels down and the room is washed by dirty green fluorescent as Nick finds the switch.

A woman, maybe sixty, lies on her side, her eyes half open and her mouth gaping, false teeth slipped off her gums. Dawn's seen enough dead people in her time to know this woman's gone, but she places her fingertips just below the jaw to check for a pulse.

Nothing.

Dawn shakes her head, panicking now, on her feet, rushing into the two small bedrooms. One smelling of sick old lady, the other – sparc as a prison cell – heavy with Vernon's hair gel.

No sign of her child. Maybe he took her somewhere else. Maybe she's lying dead, under the shifting white sand of the Flats. As she checks the bathroom and kitchen, Dawn hears herself praying, old Catholic stuff from so far back she doesn't know how she remembers it.

The kitchen door stands open onto the night and Dawn runs out. Just a cramped backyard, a sagging clothes line, a bare yellow bulb dangling from a cord, light kicking off a low wire fence that separates the house from the shack next door.

Dawn, gun in hand, spins, shouting her daughter's name. Searching the shadows.

'Dawn!'

She turns to Exley, who points over the fence, and Dawn sees the little bear, Mr Brown, lying in the dirt outside the shack. She vaults the rusted wire in one leap, letting the Glock lead her to the door, yelling her child's name. Hears a soft cry.

Dawn grabs the handle and shoves. The door gives but doesn't open. She steps back and kicks it up near the lock and it flies inward and she's in the shack, where a paraffin lamp throws shadows into air thick with *tik* fumes.

She glimpses a torso covered in prison tattoos lying on a torn mattress and then she sees Brittany, naked, on the floor reaching up to her, and she keeps the gun on the thing on the bed and scoops her child up with her free arm, holding her tight, saying, 'Baby, baby, baby.'

STRADDLING VERNON, CAREFUL TO STAY CLEAR OF HIS HALO OF BLOOD, EXLEY frames a head-shot in the viewfinder of the digital SLR, searching for some understanding of why this man was chosen to decide Sunny's fate.

All he gets by way of an answer is his own reflection in the milky pupil of one half-open eye. He presses the shutter release and hears the guillotine clang of the camera's mirror, the flash bleaching Vernon's gore-smeared face, his lips twisted into a sneer.

Kneeling, lining up a profile view – the zoom lens probing the craters of old acne scars – grabbing reference shots of the dead man's Kevlar vest and the soiled bandage on his arm, Exley knows that he'll only drive himself mad with these questions. And with questions about why his daughter is dead, but the child upstairs, her not-quite-doppel-gänger, is alive.

Trying to follow some karmic thread linking the two girls, Exley is back in that shack out on the Cape Flats, air thick with meth smoke, the emaciated man – all ribs and tattoos and dangling purple dick – passed out on the shredded mattress, his mouth a wet sag of rotten teeth.

Dawn grabbed the naked child and fled, Exley left to gather up Brittany's clothes and the little bear, rushing after mother and daughter, asking if the child was okay, Dawn shouting at him, 'Go! Just get us the fuck out of here!'

Driving through the endless sprawl of poverty, the car slowing to a crawl behind a horse-drawn cart loaded with junk, a Dickensian flashback in the swirling gauze of dust, the animal's flanks covered in fly-encrusted sores, the horse unloading a stream of yellow dung as it staggered along.

Exley overtook the cart on a blind corner, a minibus taxi bearing down on them, fog lights frying the Audi, horn screaming, but passing somehow with a thud of wind and gangsta rap, and then they had free passage to the unspooling black ribbon of Voortrekker Road. Dawn was silent all the way to Llandudno, holding her child so close they seemed like a single organism.

Exley arrived at the house expecting cop cars and flashing lights but was met with darkness and quiet as he stowed the Audi in the garage. Even before the roller door had closed, Dawn rushed the child into the house and up the stairs to the bathroom. Exley heard the lock turn and water drumming into the tub.

They are still up there and Exley knows to leave them be and concentrate on what he needs to do, which is to empty his mind of unanswerable questions and flip Vernon onto his belly and photograph him from the rear.

Exley sets the camera down and grabs the straps of the Kevlar vest, straining to move the corpse. There's a sucking sound as the body armor pulls free of the drying blood and Vernon's head lolls, the jagged wound in his throat gaping on a pasta of torn blood vessels and the building-block stack of his neck vertebra. A prolonged moan emerges from the dead man and Exley falls onto his ass, his breath coming in gasps.

Exley has to laugh as he lifts himself and grabs at Vernon again. At last he gets the corpse rotated, sweat dripping from his forehead. He pushes damp hair away from his face and reaches for the camera, trying to frame up a back view, but his hands shake so badly the lens won't settle. Exley inhales deeply and locks his abdominal muscles, an old yoga trick from his youth. This steadies him enough to fire off a series of shots, the flashbulb exploding like sheet lightning.

He exhales, stands and walks into the soothing gloom of his studio, the flash barrage still dancing in his vision. He lets the chair embrace him as he scrolls though the images on the camera to see that he has what he needs to build a convincing model of Vernon Saul.

N

No. No. No. No. No. No. No. No. No. No. No. No. No. No. No.

That one word like a jammed CD in Dawn's brain, all the way from Paradise Park to Llandudno, gripping Brittany too tight, her damage and her child's damage one and the same, Dawn seeing her daughter's life becoming the same living hell as hers.

But now, as Dawn bathes Britt in the huge oval bathtub the color of sunburn, she battles to understand that everything is okay.

That her prayers were answered.

'I had me a bad dream, Mommy.' The child is half asleep, whatever shit Vernon gave her still in her blood, and her voice is a woozy whisper. 'About Uncle Vermin and a other uncle.'

Dawn, who has inspected every inch of her daughter's body and discovered that by some miracle she has not been touched, violated, raped – had done to her what was done to Dawn – soaps her down and says, 'That's all it is my baby. Just a bad dream.'

She lifts her from the tub and dries her, the child drooping, eyes closed. Dawn carries her through to the spare room and puts her to bed. Brittany clutches the dusty Mr Brown close and falls asleep.

Dawn isn't normally on speaking terms with God but she does her best now to thank him. Then she slips from the room and walks back into the nightmare downstairs.

The studio door slides open and Exley swivels in his chair as Dawn enters. Her T-shirt is dark with water and her hair hangs in lank tendrils.

'She's okay,' Dawn says. 'That piece of filth must have passed out before he could do anything.'

'You're sure?' Exley says.

'Believe me, I know about this stuff, Nick.' She shakes her head. 'Fuck, when I think of what could have happened.'

He stands and takes her in his arms and she rests her head on his shoulder.

'Is she sleeping?'

'Out like a light.'

'Jesus.'

'Ja.'

The gate buzzer rips the silence and Dawn jerks away from him. 'Who's that now?'

'Wait here,' Exley says, heading for the stairs, checking his watch. Ten-thirty.

The buzzer sounds again as Exley reaches the darkened passageway outside the bedrooms, stopping at a window that frames the street. A red Sniper truck is parked under the street lamp by the gate, and a brown man in body armor – a Vernon-clone – rings the buzzer.

Exley lifts the intercom phone from its cradle. 'Yes?' he says, feigning sleepiness.

'Sorry to disturb you, sir. I was wondering if you've maybe seen Patrolman Saul?'

This is the moment where Exley could risk everything and lie. Say he hadn't seen Vernon. Gamble that nobody spotted the pimped Honda outside the house.

But he says, 'Yes, he was here earlier. For a short while.'

'Ja, another patrolman saw his car,' the man says, and Exley closes his eyes, breathes. 'Any idea, maybe, where he went afterward?'

'No. Look, it's late. You woke me.'

'I'm sorry, sir. My apologies.'

The rent-a-cop steps away from the gate and crosses to his truck. He reaches in through the open driver's window and brings a microphone to his face, the spiraling black cord catching the street light. After a short conversation he holsters the mike and fires up a cigarette, leaning against the vehicle, his eyes on the house.

Exley watches from the shadows, waiting for a cavalcade of cops to roar down from Hout Bay. But the man finishes his smoke, grinds the butt dead under his boot, lowers himself into the truck and drives away, his red taillights swallowed by the bush.

Exley goes downstairs to where Dawn hovers near Vernon's body, the pistol in her hand.

'It's okay. It was a Sniper guy, asking if we'd seen Vernon. He's gone,' Exley says. 'What were you going to do, shoot it out?'

Dawn drags the side of her mouth down in a smile, uses her T-shirt to wipe the weapon clean of prints and clips it into Vernon's holster. She stands and takes in the carnage. 'Okay. So, where do we start?'

Exley puts his hand on her arm. 'Dawn, let me take you and Brittany back to your place. There's no need for you to get caught up in this.'

She shakes her head. 'No. This is as much my mess as yours. What are we gonna do with him?'

'Get him to the boat. I'll row out to sea and dump him.'

She nods. 'Let's do it.'

Exley grabs hold of one boot and Dawn grabs the other and they drag the body through the living room and onto the deck – Vernon's partly severed head beating a jaunty little tattoo on the wooden slats.

Halfway across, the motion detectors kick in and hard white light floods the deck and the sand. Exley knows the surveillance cameras will have woken with the lights, capturing the clumsy dance he and Dawn do with the dead man, sending the information to the hard drive near the gate. They tumble Vernon's thick frame down onto the beach and both stand gulping air.

'Jesus, he's heavy,' Dawn says, resting her hands on her knees like a sprinter after a race. A storm is blowing in and the wind whips her hair. She pushes it away from her eyes. 'Come, we better hurry.'

Getting Vernon to the boat is hard work, their feet sinking to the ankles in the soft sand. Heaving him into the rowboat is beyond them. After three failed attempts – Vernon thudding back down onto the beach before they can get him over the lip of the wooden hull – Exley tips the boat so that one brass oarlock touches the ground. He uses rocks to wedge the rowboat in position and he and Dawn roll Vernon aboard.

Exley removes the rocks and the boat rights itself, Vernon's withered leg dangling over the gunwale like shark chum. Exley is nearly out on his feet and the thought of still having to row out beyond the breakers, into the teeth of the wind, seems inconceivable.

While Exley finds the oars stowed between the rocks and places them beside Vernon in the rowboat, Dawn gathers fist-sized stones and fills the pockets of the dead man's uniform, wedging some between his body and the Kevlar vest.

They free the boat from the sand, pushing it out into the waves, sinking to their waists in the icy water. Exley hauls himself aboard and sits with his feet on either side of the corpse, hooking the oars in the locks, bracing his legs against the thwart, every muscle straining, battling to gain enough momentum to fight the swell and the wind. Eventually the boat moves and he finds a rhythm with the oars, pulling farther and farther away from the beach, Dawn lost in the darkness.

Exley, teeth chattering, drenched by waves that smash the rowboat, passes the guano-covered rocks, the seagulls like a scatter of shrapnel against the night sky. Then he is beyond the breakers and the ocean is calmer and he makes better progress, the glitter of Llandudno's lights softened by the spray hurled toward the land by the gale.

When he is far enough out, Exley ships the oars and sits for a minute, gathering his strength, staring down at the dead man, the boat rocking and creaking.

Does he feel any satisfaction, knowing this man who allowed his daughter to die is dead himself? Not enough to salve the pain of Sunny's death or to erase his own guilt. And there is little solace in the knowledge that all the people who can speak of Exley's guilt are now gone.

Rousing himself, he checks for the lights of any nearby craft. When he sees none he grabs hold of Vernon's legs and pitches them over the side. Then Exley gets behind the corpse and, bracing himself against the gunwale, uses his feet to drive the rest of Vernon's body into the water.

Slack mouthed, gasping, drinking salty air, he drags himself to the side of the boat. In the moonlight Exley sees Vernon Saul floating face down, arms spread, before he sinks into the ocean, and then there's nothing but the expanse of black water stretching down to Antarctica.

chapter 56

THANK CHRIST THIS IS A RICH PERSON'S HOUSE. DAWN SCRUBS THE BLOOD-splattered living-room walls, and the white paint – thick and velvety – washes easily. If this was out on the Flats she'd be down to raw brick before she got the blood off. Still, she's covered in sweat by the time the walls are free of Vernon's mess.

And waiting for her is the expanse of gore-encrusted white tiles. Looks like an ice rink after a very nasty hockey game.

She dumps the bloody rags and paper towels into a garbage bag, rolls off the orange gloves she found by the kitchen sink – making a rubbery snap as she frees her hands – and walks up the stairs.

Dawn goes into the spare room and kneels beside the bed. She panics for a moment when she can't hear Brittany breathing over the raucous howl of the wind and lays her palm lightly on her daughter's chest, feeling her lungs expand.

The child moans and her little hand scuttles across the bedding like a crab and grabs hold of Dawn's thumb, gripping hard. Dawn kisses Brittany on the forehead, smelling soap and shampoo, and waits until her fingers loosen before she withdraws her hand and stands, wiping away a couple of tears that have sneaked their way down her cheeks.

No time for this now, Dawn.

She heads downstairs and opens the sliding door onto the deck, the wind pulling at her hair like she's in a girl fight. She thuds the door closed after her and crosses to the railing, drifts of wet foam coming in on the squall, checking if her smokes and lighter are still where she left them earlier. There they are, snug against the wooden upright, where the gale can't get to them.

She turns her back on the blast, shields the lighter and gets a cigarette going. Sucks nicotine and lets out a mouthful, all thoughts of her earlier resolution to quit gone with the smoke. She's halfway through the cigarette when she sees the little rowboat coming in out of the dark, the storm driving it toward the beach. Nick jumps into the water and pulls the boat onto the sand and comes across to her panting, wet, teeth chattering, the spotlights hammering him.

Dawn flicks the butt of the cigarette out into the wind and follows him into the living room, sliding the door shut. Nick takes a liter of Scotch from the drinks cabinet and has a hit straight from the bottle. He holds the Scotch out to her and she shakes her head.

'You okay?' she asks.

'Yes. He's gone,' he says, taking another drink.

'What now?'

'Now I've got to bring the bastard back.'

Trying to avoid Vernon Saul's dead eyes staring at him from the computer monitor, Exley knows to a bone certainty that his days as some bargain-basement God, breathing faux-life into tangles of inanimate polygons, are over. If he pulls this off, uses this digital deceit to allow him and Dawn to fly to freedom, he has no idea what he will do with the rest of his days. But it will not be this.

He tries to detach himself from the process and work on autopilot like he's done so many times before, but he can't – Vernon Saul is with him, his presence filling the cramped room.

Exley Photoshops a close-up of Vernon's face, eliminates the telltale flashbulb glare in the pupils, paints away the dried blood that stains the mouth cranberry red and invisibly mends the raw gash in the neck.

He exports the retouched portrait into an el cheapo face-modeling application, the kind of thing he would never normally bring himself to use. The gizmo was sent to him in the hope of an endorsement (that he never gave) by a cabal of code bandits and hackers who chopped and stole from other programs and threw together a mess called, with megalomanic lack of irony, SixthDay, using the creation myth as their inspiration: on day six God created man in his own image.

Moving quickly, with none of the attention to detail that is the hallmark of his work, he wraps Vernon's face around a ready-made mesh of a male head, a crude thing, poorly built and riddled with imperfections. This is down and dirty and on the fly. All that time allows.

After he returned from the burial at sea Exley grabbed his laptop and Vernon's keys and went out to the little door recessed in the wall beside his front gate. He used the stubby, tubular key on Vernon's chain to open the tumbler lock and jacked his laptop into the hard drive of the recorder that stored the data from the security cameras dotted around his house.

Feeling like a target in the glare of streetlight, shivering in the wind, Exley pulled a multiple-viewpoint display up onto his laptop and saw all eight cameras. Three on the ocean side of the house captured Vernon arriving that evening, crossing the beach and humping up onto the deck, disappearing into the living room. Speeded up, his gimpy walk was manically comical.

Exley shuttled through the footage, saw him and Dawn reversing out of the garage in the Audi, Vernon's Civic beyond camera range. Shuttled deeper and saw them coming home, the garage door closing after them. They next appeared dragging Vernon's body across the beach, the high-speed video lending a Keystone Kops quality to their movements, Dawn's hair flapping like a lunatic bird roosting on her head. Exley saw himself coming back up onto the deck after the burial at sea, a wild and disjointed marionette.

Fingers flying on the keyboard and touchpad, Exley erased the incriminating footage from the Sniper hard drive's memory. Instant, seamless amnesia.

Then came the crucial moment. He'd seen that the recess housing the recording unit was hidden from the lenses, a small blind spot in the view of the surveillance cameras. Reckoned that if he headed away in a straight line – walking an imaginary tightrope – he would avoid the cameras and be able to hang a right, get beyond their reach and cross to the open ground beside his garage and clamber through the window he left open. Crucial to him being able to return later and feed his created images of Vernon into the hard drive, undetected.

Exley moved, waiting for the spotlights to kick in, exposing him and exposing the flaw in his plan. But they remained inert and he made it around the side of the house, skinny enough to wriggle through the narrow garage window.

The software chimes like a microwave oven, signaling that the render is done and a bald-headed Vernon smirks at Exley from the screen. Rotating the head, viewing it from all angles, Exley tweaks a slider that thickens the jaw and squares the face, alphas Vernon up. Using another slider, he brings the eyes closer to the nose and works on the brow-to-chin ratio to compress the face and add even more heft to the lantern jaw.

Delving into the cheesy accessories Exley finds a hairstyle that's a close enough match to Vernon's gelled spiky do and drops it onto the bald head. Looks like it's made of shellac – none of the shine and bounce and believability of the one he created for Sunny's model – but it's all he can bring himself to do.

However misguided and obsessive, his modeling of his daughter was an act of love, using his artistry as a way of expressing his grief, but by evoking Vernon Saul, Exley knows he's messing with something occult to save his own skin and he wants to be done with it. Wants to be free of this room and the memory of the mad thing crouched on this chair, smearing himself with his child's ashes, gabbling incoherent prayers.

Dawn, on her hands and knees, takes a small white scrubbing brush to the cement between the tiles. The expanse of floor is clean. The leather furniture is spotless. But, Jesus, this tacky blood sticks stubbornly to the grid of grouting.

There is nothing for it but to move from one tile to the next, getting in with the hairs of the brush. Knee- and backbreaking work and she's getting a contact high from the ammonia in the cleaning solvents.

Nick comes through from his studio, stretching, rubbing his eyes behind his glasses. He blinks, taking in the room. 'Christ, Dawn, you must be exhausted.'

She shrugs and stands, her back cramping. 'How you doing?'

'Okay. But still a long way to go.'

Nick puts his arms around Dawn, her gloved hands hanging limp at her sides. She steps out of the embrace, staring at him.

'What?' he asks.

'I'm thinking that some bad shit went down involving you and Vernon? That he had something over you?'

He hesitates, looks away, out at the storm. 'Yes.'

'Something that you did?'

'Yes.' Eyes back on her now.

'Okay, Nick, I want you to make me a promise.'

'What?' he asks, and she can see him tensing up.

'I want you to promise that you'll never tell me a word about it. Ever.'

He releases his breath and finds a tired smile. 'I promise, Dawn. I promise.'

Exley's running out of time and his body is failing. His vision is blurred and some fucker has injected pool acid into the rods and cones of his eyes. His nerves are a fester of barbed wire spiking beneath his skin. Tension pumps out as sour sweat, filling his nostrils with his own stink.

The carpal pain in his thumb spasms to his right elbow as he grips the mouse, the little curve of plastic all that anchors him to the work station and reality, rotating the evolving model in three dimensions, creating texture maps from his blood-rich reference photographs, teasing, finessing, tugging this rough beast into some approximation of Vernon Saul.

Exley is fighting the clock, yes, but he's fighting something else too: a fear that if he does this too well, makes the sick bastard too lifelike, he'll somehow reach across to the dark side and bring him back, with his killer eyes and his withered leg, trailing blood and salt water.

Exley modifies a freebie mesh of an American Marine he found in a public domain library online – couldn't risk using his credit card to buy a more sophisticated model from one of the Hollywood effects houses. The thing he's working with lacks detail and the hands are crude mitts, but (after he tears off the helmeted head and replaces it with Vernon's) he's left with a chunky, brown uniformed man in boots and a Kevlar vest.

Exley grabs the left leg and with a few mouse clicks shrinks it on the horizontal axis, until it resembles Vernon's withered limb. When the figure moves there will be no flapping of the cloth of the trousers around the scrawny leg the way it would in real life. Slave to time, Exley can't afford this luxury.

He finds the motion-capture data of Vernon from the session after Sunny's funeral and loops a stream of him walking, that thump and drag perfectly duplicated. Exley marries the mo-cap data to the 3D model, positions the virtual camera so it looks down at Vernon from the angle of the surveillance cams and sets the figure in motion. And there he is, Vernon Saul, with his bouncer's shoulders and his lurching walk.

Suddenly the room is thick with the odor of cheap hair gel and sweat, and Exley sees the dead man deep underwater, hovering near the seabed, arms floating away from his body, hair waving as the current strokes it, the stained bandage swimming away from his arm. Then Vernon's body jerks as if his heart has been hit by the paddles of a defibrillator and his eyes flicker and his fingers flex and his legs start to kick, the strong one moving powerfully, the runt flailing at it its side, and he churns upward through the water, breaking the surface, drinking air, looking for land.

'My God,' Dawn says, 'it's him.'

Exley didn't hear the door slide open and he drops the mouse in fright before he sees that Vernon is still safely trapped on the monitor.

Dawn, her face drawn and shrunken – all huge eyes and cheeks hollow with exhaustion – looks from the screen to Exley. 'Hey, you okay, Nick?'

'Yeah, I'm fine,' he says.

Dawn leaves a Coke beside his keyboard and backs out of the room, saying, 'Fucken scary, Nick. Wow,' and he's not sure if she's talking about him or the animated Vernon, limping on a treadmill.

Exley hits the pause bar and levers himself from the chair, takes the Coke and walks out of the studio and sees the first faint blue light of morning bruising the sky out over the ocean. The wind is still whipping, hurling spray and spume at the house.

The living room is blindingly clean, the tiles kicking back the hard halogen spots. Dawn's near the kitchen, filling a garbage bag with paper towels and dirty cloth.

'Have you slept?' Exley asks.

'I'm going to now.'

'I'll come up when I'm done.' He steps toward her, awkward and disconnected as he embraces her, feeling the cords of tension in her neck and shoulders. He brushes his dry lips against her forehead – her hair ripe with the smell of cleaning fluids – and dives back into the studio.

Exley takes the rendered model into his compositing software. Matches the camera angles. Bleeds the color on the digital Vernon to resemble the near-monochrome of the surveillance footage. Applies an effect to the model that creates the staccato, jerky movement of the video. Shrinks Vernon as he walks, to duplicate the perspective of the cameras.

Finally he lays a mist of noise over the whole thing, digital drop-out, swirls, banding, leaves it looking like a *Nine Inch Nails* video. Lots of distortion behind which to hide the imperfections.

He does a test render. It works. Exley needs to do some frame painting and clean up the motion when Vernon opens and exits the street gate, but what he has achieved in the last hours is near miraculous.

Exley finds a type font that matches the time-code window and sets the beginning of each camera view at fifteen minutes before they left for the Cape Flats. He does a final render and has to accept that he is done. Has manufactured evidence that before Exley and Dawn drove away in the Audi, Vernon Saul exited the house.

Alive.

Exley dumps the data onto his laptop and clambers out of the garage window, the sky beyond the mountain a blue velvet backdrop. The wind has died, leaving an eerie silence. Exley checks to see that the road is empty – no pre-dawn joggers or dog walkers taking a short cut to the beach – and retraces his route back to the Sniper box.

He gains access to the hard drive and connects his laptop, starts to dump his revised history of the night onto its memory, knowing that if his work is found wanting, he and Dawn are done for.

As he watches the progress bar crawl from left to right he sees head-lights flare high on the road twisting down the mountain. A yellow roof light glows like melting butter and he knows he's watching a Sniper truck switchbacking down to him.

He checks the progress bar: sixty-five seconds to go.

Exley watches the truck, tries to guess how long it'll take to reach him. Knows he should rip out the USB cable, interrupt the transfer of information, lock the little door and run for cover.

His fingers are already on the cable, ready to uncouple it, when nervous exhaustion, terror and the residue of Port's designer drug still sloshing around his synapses feed him a premonition so pungent it is impossible to ignore: that the Sniper tech – the somnambulistic Don – is in the passenger seat of that truck, being ferried down to plunder this hard drive of its secrets.

Fifty seconds to go.

You're fucken crazy man. You're tripping. Get the fuck out of here.

But Exley stays his hand, lets the transfer continue, knowing if he aborts it he'll leave evidence of his tampering, leaving him as exposed as if he's been caught red handed.

Forty seconds to go.

The truck is closer now, and he can hear the whine of its transmission as the driver shifts down.

Thirty seconds.

The roof light disappears behind the dense bush and Exley has no way to measure the speed of the truck.

Fifteen seconds.

Exley stares at the progress bar, willing it on, and suddenly it accelerates and flies to its finish, like a track athlete whose anabolics have kicked in. He can hear the engine of the truck getting louder.

He rips the laptop free and slams the metal door shut, battling to hold the computer under his arm while he finds the keyhole and locks it.

Then he runs, praying that in his haste he's holding the line that'll keep him free of the motion detectors. He plunges to his right, then races across the open ground – surely to Christ he's levitating – and dives through the garage window, hitting the cement hard, chipping his tooth on the metal of the laptop. Looks up and sees the bloom of headlights on the window that still swings and squeaks on its hinges.

The truck growls its way along the road. Exley can hear the mutter of the radio and the moan of brakes as it stops outside his house. He flips open the laptop, selects the fake Vernon data and hits delete, slides the computer along the cement, hiding it under the Audi as the hard drive starts to whine and crunch.

Exley sprints up the stairs and peers out at the street. His sixth sense was on the money: Don, a halo of sunshine outlining him as the first rays creep over the mountain, unlocks the door to the Sniper box and slides his laptop from its pouch. A starburst flare drags Exley's eyes up the slope. Another car on its way down and it doesn't take a psychic to divine that this will be the cops.

Exley heads into the bedroom and tears off his blood- and seawater-stained clothes, and finds a pair of boardshorts and a T-shirt. As he pulls the T-shirt over his head, he sends his glasses flying, and, nearly blind, has to drop to the carpet and crawl and fumble until he finds them.

He runs down the stairs, almost falling, and gets himself into the studio. Hauls up all the incriminating evidence of his deception on the workstation monitor and block-selects. Knows this purge will not stand up to forensic investigation, but it's the best he can do for now.

As he hits 'delete' the buzzer sounds and Exley closes his eyes and breathes, fighting dizziness, before he pads along the pitching and yawing corridor to the intercom phone mounted near the front door and croaks, 'Yes?'

THE BLACK POLICE CAPTAIN STEPS THROUGH THE GATE. HIS FACE IS SO HAUNTED and sleep-deprived that Exley, standing in the doorway of the house, feels as if he's looking into a dark mirror. The Sniper technician is a motionless silhouette out on the sidewalk, still jacked into the surveillance camera hard drive.

Exley opens his mouth to speak but no words emerge. He swallows and tries again. The voice he hears is unconvincing. 'Captain, you're up early.'

'I'm sorry, Mr Exley,' the cop says around a yawn. 'I just need to ask you a few questions.' Exley steps back and lets the man into the house. The captain surveys the sitting room, the sky already a hot blue rectangle framed by the glass doors. 'Are you alone here?'

'No. A friend and her child are sleeping upstairs.'

'Was she in the house overnight? Your friend?'

'Yes. Why?'

'Then I wonder if I could have a word with her also, please?'

Exley is tempted to refuse but he sees lies like a ring of dominoes encircling him and knows what'll happen if one topples, so he climbs the stairs and enters the spare room, where Dawn sleeps with her arms around the child, clutching her close. Exley kneels and strokes Dawn's hair, whispering her awake.

Her eyes flicker open, clouded with fear and disorientation as she stares up at him.

'Dawn,' he says. 'There's a cop here. He wants to talk to us both.'

'Shit. What they found?'

'Relax. Just stick to our story, okay?'

She nods, clutching at his hand. 'I'm scared, Nick.'

'It'll be fine.'

Exley strokes her hair and fakes a smile, leaving the room as she slides from the bed trying not to wake the child. He goes back downstairs, to where the cop roams the tiled living room. The technician is inside now, setting up his laptop on the kitchen counter.

The captain says, 'Vernon Saul came by here last night?'

'Yeah, he did,' Exley says. 'Like I told the Sniper guy. It was in the evening, must have been around eight-thirty. Why?'

'How long did he stay?'

'Maybe a half-hour. My friend and I went out and he left before we did.'

Rubbing her face, her hair a mess of curls, Dawn comes down the stairs, barefoot, in a pair of sweatpants and a T-shirt, and Exley feels doubly at a loss. He doesn't know the captain's name and doesn't know Dawn's surname. So he says nothing.

The cop nods at Dawn. 'Good morning.' He introduces himself, giving a name so clotted with clicks that it remains a mystery to Exley.

Dawn says, 'I'm Dawn Cupido.'

And the black cop gives her *that* look. The one that says: what you doing in this rich whitey's bed, you colored slut, his wife not even cold?

The captain wanders across the tiles into the living room, stands by the sofa with his hands in his pockets, eyeballing her the whole time. Forces her to walk over to him. Little power game he's playing. Fucker.

'Do you mind me asking where the two of you went last night, Ms Cupido?' Just enough weight on the *Ms* to diss her.

'To fetch my daughter from the babysitter,' Dawn says, keeping cool.

'And where would she be? The babysitter?'

'Goodwood.'

'Goodwood?' He raises his eyebrows and his mouth turns down at the corners like he ate something bad. 'Long way from here.' Putting her in her place nicely.

She doesn't reply and the cop just nods, hands in the pockets of his brand-name jeans. Too expensive for a captain's pay scale, just like his shoes: little tasseled Gucci loafers, color of red wine. The real thing, not some Chinese knock-offs. Dawn wonders if he's on the take, this cop, and if that makes him more dangerous.

Dawn watches him take a step backward, his heel landing with a sharp clack on a white tile next to something dark that oozes out from under the sofa, a smear the size of a tongue. Blood. Vernon Saul's blood, gone thick as syrup. Somehow she must have missed it, in her frantic clean-up. How big is the puddle under the sofa?

She drags her gaze away from the cop's feet up to his eyes. He's giving her a flat, empty stare, like he can see right into her head, and Dawn knows all the luck she had was used up on Brittany and she's going down, down, down, for what she did last night with that broken bottle.

'Dawn,' the cop says, getting all familiar now, giving her a little smile. 'Vernon Saul was a bouncer at your strip club, right?'

'Ja,' she says, forcing herself to stare into his eyes, which are yellowish and bloodshot. Don't look down, Dawn. Don't look at that fucken blood.

'Did he introduce you to Mr Exley?'

'Ja, he did. Why?'

The cop shrugs and rocks a little on his heels, shaking some change in his pocket, swallowing a yawn, sinking his chin to his chest, eyes – honest to God – on the floor.

Okay, Dawn, here it comes. She sneaks a look at Nick, who stands the other side of the sofa, expressionless. Dawn's eyes are back on the cop, who's head is still lowered, and she can't stop herself from looking down at his left shoe, which jiggles a bit, the toe of the loafer lifting, leaving the tile, sliding to the side, hovering over Vernon's blood, which has dried almost brown at the edges, but is still thick and red and tacky in the middle of the stain.

'Captain?' It's the nerdy white guy, in the kitchen with his laptop.

'Yes?' the cop says, swiveling to his right, planting his foot millimeters from the wet lick.

'I have the surveillance camera data on screen.'

The cop nods and walks toward the kitchen, his shoes tick-ticking on the tiles. Dawn gets behind the sofa, rests her ass on the back and gives it a little shove and it rolls easily on its metal castors. Far enough to cover that blood.

Dawn's heart is climbing its way out of her chest and into her mouth and she's hanging for a smoke. But she doesn't move, trying to chill, forcing her hands to stop throttling the cool, creased leather of the sofa, looking over at Nick, who stares at the cop and the technician standing by the computer. He's pale under his tan and she knows this isn't over yet.

The cop joins the technician at the laptop. Exley edges forward and watches over their shoulders as Vernon hobbles his way across the beach and into the house.

'He arrived at 20:25,' Don says.

The captain holds up a hand and the geek pauses the playback. Turning to Exley, the cop says, 'Was it common for Vernon Saul to enter your property this way?'

Exley shrugs. 'He told us he was doing a routine patrol on the other side of the rocks and decided to drop in.'

The captain nods and waves the technician on and Don finds the footage of the fake Vernon leaving the house. This is it. The money shot.

The cop observes, expressionless, as Vernon jerks his way across the driveway and out the gate.

'He left at 20:55,' Don says.

The men watch Exley and Dawn reversing out in the Audi. The time code jumps forward by two hours as they return home with the child. Then the screen goes to black.

'That's it,' Don says, shuttling back to Vernon's departure from the house. The tech-head freezes the sequence as Exley's counterfeit Vernon walks out the front door. He zooms in, advancing the video frame by frame, his index finger punching the space-bar.

'Something wrong?' the captain says.

'No, just an interesting moiré pattern over here,' Don says, wagging a finger at the animated Vernon. 'Banding and artifacting.'

Exley feels a single bead of cold sweat detach itself from the hair at the nape of his neck and run down his spine, tracing the contours of his vertebra.

'In English,' the captain says.

'Uh, well, it's just to do with the way the lenses of the cameras deal with light. There's an element of distortion. I think we can enhance the quality of our surveillance footage by recalibrating the cameras.'

'But there is nothing suspicious here?'

'No, no. I was just making a technical note.'

'So this is of no relevance to this investigation?'

'Uh, no.'

The cop exhales. 'Then you can leave.'

The technician reluctantly stops his analysis, shuts down the laptop and scuffs out of the house without a word.

The captain wanders back out into the living room and Exley tails him. 'Okay, the video footage seems to agree with you.'

'What's going on, Captain?' Exley asks again. More forcefully, now that part of the battle seems won.

'Vernon Saul has disappeared. His car was found abandoned up near the Scout Hall. Where Detective Erasmus was murdered.' The man stares at Exley, who waits for an accusation. But the cop just clears his throat and carries on, 'Seems you and your friend were the last people to see him. A bit of a mystery, you could say.'

'Well, I hope he's okay.'

'Yes. To make things worse, when we sent officers to check on his house out on the Cape Flats they found his mother had passed away. Apparently a diabetes-related heart attack.'

'That's horrible,' Dawn says.

'Yes, yes.' Nodding at Dawn, then his eyes are back on Exley. 'Why was he here last night?'

'Vernon has become a friend, Captain,' Exley says. 'He drops in quite regularly.'

'He didn't say anything about where he was heading?'

'No, nothing. We assumed he was on duty.'

'Well, he never clocked in for his shift down at Sniper.' The cop looks at the suitcases. 'You're leaving?'

'Yes. Later today.'

'Well, I imagine you won't be taking many happy memories with you.' He wanders across to the glass doors and stares out at the morning. The wind has died but the beach is littered with debris: kelp, driftwood and ocean-bleached trash from container ships.

'Quite a storm last night,' the captain says. Exley stays mute, willing the man to go. 'Ms Cupido, are you leaving with Mr Exley?'

Dawn looks at Exley, who answers for her. 'Dawn and her daughter are joining me on a short vacation.'

'Nice.' The cop nods, looking out the window, hands in pockets. Something attracts his attention. 'Now what the hell is that?' he asks, freeing a hand and pointing out at the beach.

Exley comes up beside him and follows his finger to where the waves fizz against the low rocks near the beached rowboat. Something dark juts out from behind the rocks. A brown uniform leg ending in a boot.

chapter 58

THE POLICEMAN UNLOCKS THE DOOR, SLIDES IT OPEN AND STEPS OUT ONTO THE deck. Exley, staring at Dawn, feels that all his blood has drained into his shoes. Fighting the urge to flee, he joins the cop outside.

The captain walks down the steps and onto the sand, making his way toward the rocks. 'Well, will you look at that?'

Exley follows, each step taking him closer to the boot and the brown leg. Knows that when he reaches the rocks he'll see Vernon Saul with his torn throat gaping at the sky. Hears the shrieking laughter of the seagulls circling above him, as if they're in on this nasty little cosmic joke.

The cop stops, his hands on his hips. 'Looks like you've got yourself a problem here, Mr Exley.'

Exley knows that he is damned. That karmic balance will be restored and there's nothing to be done about it. This understanding brings a fatalistic acceptance and his anxiety evaporates. The time has come to tell the truth. To unburden himself. He's about to invite this dark man inside to hear his confession when the captain kicks his loafer against the sand-encrusted boot.

'Hell, but this big boy stinks.'

The air is thick with a foul odor of decomposition, but Exley, even in his disassociated state, is taken aback by the lawman's cavalier attitude.

'Never mind,' the cop says, 'I'll call the trash removal people. They can deal with this.' The captain has his cell phone in his hand, dialing, stepping away from the rocks.

When Exley gets closer he understands that what he believed to be Vernon Saul's boot is really a muck-encrusted flipper, and as he steps around the boulder he sees the bloated carcass of huge brown bull seal washed up by last night's storm.

Exley has to turn his back on the policeman as hysterical laughter spills from him, mirth that he just can't contain. Mirth of such magnitude that when he staggers into the house, incapable of speech, Dawn is certain that he is crying.

chapter 59

FLYING INTO NIGHT, LEAVING THE BODIES AND THE BLOOD FAR BEHIND, EXLEY feels a sense of stillness for the first time in weeks, even though the screen in front of him says he's traveling at 935 kilometers per hour.

He spent the day looking over his shoulder waiting for the cops to arrest him, and at Cape Town International passport control there was a moment's anxiety as a uniformed Xhosa woman looked repeatedly from Sunny's photograph to Brittany, before she stamped the document.

Now, sitting on the plane, feeling the thrum of the jet engines beneath his stockinged feet, Exley's starting to relax, but the horrors of the last week still run like his own in-flight movie when he tries to sleep. So he sits with his eyes open, watching the little airplane inching eastward on the monitor.

The day was taken up with unloading his dead family's belongings at a homeless shelter, returning the Audi to the rental company and signing the last papers authorizing the shipping of Caroline's body. By some quirk of synchronicity she's in the air now, too, on her way to England.

Exley and Dawn barely had time to speak after the cop left, and she fell asleep as soon as the plane took off. The child, covered by a blanket, dozes in the seat between them. She's restless and her fingers twitch and grab at her mother's shirt. Without waking, Dawn puts an arm around her, muttering something. Exley reaches out and touches the girl's hand. Her skin is soft but somehow thicker, more durable, than Sunny's.

At sunset Exley went into what had been his studio, the room empty except for an orphaned ADSL cable snaking across the dented carpet, and the silver urn standing in the corner. His work station now lived in the Waterfront loft of a rich young geek, the memory scoured of any evidence of chaos and mayhem.

Exley lifted the urn and went through the living room, toward the deck. Dawn and Brittany sat on the sofa eating chips and drinking Coke, surrounded by suitcases and child-sized Hello Kitty backpacks, evidence of a shopping spree earlier that day.

'What's that, Uncle Nick?' Brittany asked, her eyes drawn to the shiny object in Exley's hand.

'Come, baby, let's go up and make ourselves pretty,' Dawn said, standing. As Exley passed her she touched him on the elbow, mouthing, 'You gonna be okay?'

He nodded and waited until they were on the stairs, the child jabbering about Bali and airplanes, then he crossed the deck and went out onto the beach, the sand warm beneath his bare feet. The evening was still and the ocean barely moved, reflecting the oranges and purples of the sky.

Exley waded into the water, the skin of his legs beneath his shorts stinging from the cold. He lifted the urn and stared at it, trying to see Sunny, but seeing only his reflection. Searching for something profound to say, Exley came up empty, so he kissed the urn and twisted off the lid and upended it, the last of his daughter's ashes floating downward, lying like a veil of dust on the gently rolling surface of the ocean that killed her. Exley closed his eyes, saying goodbye, feeling the soft current tugging at his legs.

'Uncle Nick. Uncle Nick!' Brittany twists in her seat and has hold of the fine blond hairs on his arm.

'Yes?' he says

'I wanna pee-pee.'

Trying not to wake Dawn, he unbuckles Brittany's seatbelt and walks her down the darkened tube of the Airbus, holding her hand. The lavatories are occupied and a middle-aged woman, joining them in line, reaches down and strokes the girl's hair, saying, 'You have a beautiful daughter.'

'Thank you,' Exley says.

Back in his seat, mother and child asleep at his side, Exley slips a creased photograph of Sunny from the inner pocket of his jacket, holding it under the beam of the reading light. A picture he took a few weeks before she died as she stood in the living room showing off a new outfit, smiling at him.

Yesterday in Dawn's apartment, when this photo came tumbling out of the pile of clothes she threw at Exley to pack, he'd been about to hand it to her, thinking it was a snapshot of Brittany, before he realized it was his daughter and pocketed it.

He's been unable to confront Dawn with the photograph and knows he never will. He accepts there was calculation in all of this. Knows it was by design that her child appeared that morning dressed just as Sunny used to dress, her hair worn the way Sunny wore hers.

Exley, understanding there are no accidents, remembers the night in his studio, when, covered in his daughter's remains, bent out of shape by chemicals and madness, he gabbled those incoherent prayers, and he wonders if those prayers have been answered, after all.

Not exactly in the manner he begged for, of course, but that is the way of these things. And if they have been answered, then the inescapable truth is that he has entered into a covenant with something, somewhere.

But he has no idea who to thank.

Or who to fear.

26 MAR 2013